THE BLOOD WITCH

THE BROKEN BLADE
BOOK TWO

EVELYN WARD

CONTENT WARNING

The book you are about to read is book two in the Broken Blade trilogy. If you haven't yet, we urge you to read The Queen's Blade to start Fey's story.

Before you begin, please know this book contains strong adult content, including graphic sex scenes, violence, murder, and so much fucking swearing.
It also contains violence against a child (prologue only), a scene in which consent is dubious (dub-con), and references to drug use/overdose, domestic abuse and suicide.

You were warned in the beginning that this series will include queer romance and on-page sex (MF, MM and FF), as well as polyamory (why choose). If that's not something you're comfortable with, turn back now.
If you've been waiting for it, well... this one is for you.

PROLOGUE
FIVE YEARS PREVIOUSLY

Death comes in many forms.

Death can be the creeping cold of a winter's night when you have no home to keep you warm. Death can be slow starvation, each day leaving you weaker and weaker until you're simply too hollow to go on. Death can be a violent monster, a familiar face you once loved that masked something truly evil.

And death can come from a single mistake.

Feet pounding against the pavement, running as fast as she could, Vee knew she was going to die. Her breaths came in ragged gasps as she pushed herself to go even faster, praying to any deity who might be listening for an extra burst of speed. It didn't matter that her heart felt like it might explode, didn't matter that her leg muscles burned so much she thought they might give out at any second; they had no choice but to run.

Run or die.

Jayce was slowing down already. Barely nine years old, he was even younger than Vee, and his short legs couldn't keep up. Maybe if he hadn't spent so many years surviving off scraps and stolen food, he wouldn't have been so stunted. Maybe then he could have kept up with her. But there wasn't ever enough to go around. Even with Vee sharing what she could, it was never enough. It wasn't his fault...

Even if he was the reason that they got caught.

"Come on, Jayce!" Vee shrieked at him, looking back over her shoulder to see him struggling. The men were coming, closing in behind them. She could hear their shouts, hear their feet heavy on the gravel. They were so close now. Too close. "Hurry up!"

The extra two years she had on him were enough. Still a kid, sure, but Vee's legs were long and built for running. If she were alone, she could have escaped them easily. If she were alone, they never would have gotten caught stealing.

Behind her, Jayce's foot hit a rock at the wrong angle, and he stumbled, his ankle twisting as he fell forward with a pained howl.

No, no, no, Vee thought, panicked, skidding to a stop, eyes locked on the entrance of the alley behind them. She rushed back, grabbing Jayce's arm and hauling him upright, but it was too late.

Three men rounded the corner, looking nowhere near as winded as Vee and Jayce were. Of course not. They were plump, pampered with food and excess while she and Jayce were barely keeping themselves alive. Vee pulled on Jayce's arm, trying to pull him to his feet, but his ankle twisted again, and he fell back to the ground with a grunt.

"There you are, you little thieves," one of the men shouted, advancing. Males from the Witch faction weren't nearly as scary as real Witches, but you didn't need to have power over the elements to hurt someone. You didn't need to control Earth or Air or Fire or Water to break someone's neck.

Her mouth dry with fear, Vee tried one last time to get Jayce to stand, but already knew it was a lost cause. It was too late now, anyway. The men were already here, surrounding them. They'd lost their chance to escape.

She could still run. *Should* run. She knew the streets of the Eternal City like the back of her hand. She could easily lose them if she ran now. Jayce was the one who'd gotten them caught, Jayce was the one who'd messed up picking a Witch's pocket, whose hands hadn't been quick or skilled enough to stop him from getting noticed. She could leave him here to deal with the consequences on his own.

That was the first rule in their little gang of strays: Don't get caught. But Jayce swore he'd been practicing, swore he was ready. And everything had been going so well until...

Too late. Too late to run now, even if she were to abandon him. Still gasping for air, Vee realized she had waited too long to decide. She and Jayce would take the fall for his mistake together.

One man reached out and grabbed Vee by her hair, pulling her away from Jayce hard enough to hurt. She shrieked, kicking out at them, but he just laughed. Laughed like she was nothing. Laughed as she swung her arms and kicked, her fists and feet hitting nothing but air. Laughed at how small she was, how weak she was.

She was nothing to them. They were nothing. Just two kids no one cared about. And now no one was going to stop these men from exacting whatever punishment they saw fit.

Jayce didn't look at them as they approached. He looked at Vee, terror in his eyes. Young. He was so young. He knew what would come next. He knew they would hurt him.

Help, his eyes pleaded. *Help me, please.*

Vee fought and struggled, spitting and cursing as she thrashed, but the man holding her just shook her by the hair, and it hurt so badly she screamed. She was too small and too skinny to do anything to them. Jayce needed her help, needed her to protect him, but she was just as malnourished and helpless as he was.

"Where's my coin purse, you little shit?" the man asked, advancing toward where Jayce lay on the ground. Jayce tried to scramble away but was quickly pushed back down to the pavement.

They wouldn't find the coin purse, not on Jayce anyway. Vee had dropped everything they'd managed to pickpocket that day as soon as they'd been caught. She'd abandoned it all in an alley trashcan where another one of their gang could find it. Jayce's brother had taught them that little trick. That way, if you ever get caught, you don't have the evidence on you. But more importantly, the gang still gets the money. Even if you don't come back alive, at least they'll get to eat.

Jayce's brother had been clever like that. But clever wasn't enough to keep you alive in their world. Clever didn't stop Jayce's brother from getting caught one too many times. Didn't stop him from being beaten to death in an alley just like this one after he broke their first, most important rule.

Don't get caught.

"He doesn't have it!" Vee shouted at them, knowing it was futile. They wouldn't listen, not to her.

Jayce screamed when the first kick landed. It caught him in the chest, right against his ribs. He screamed again when the next kick hit the small of his back.

These men would kill him, just like the men who killed Jayce's brother, Vee knew. Kill him and get away with it because no one cared about kids like them. No one cared about poor scavengers just trying to steal enough to stay alive in this city. No one cared about the forgotten strays. These men were rich. They wore high-quality clothes of the upper-class, of the Witch nobility. The Queen didn't care what men like them did, so long as they kept paying their tithes to the crown.

It wasn't fair. The few silver coins they'd get from all their work today meant nothing to men like this. But that money could keep their whole gang of strays alive for a few more weeks. It wasn't fair that they wouldn't share it.

Jayce tried to block the third kick, his arms coming up to defend himself, and there was a sickening crack as a bone broke. Jayce screamed so loud it sounded like his throat might break.

The entire world came to a stop when Vee heard that sound.

Jayce was like a little brother to her. She'd promised to protect him and keep him safe. She snuck him extra food for years. She'd held him when he cried over his brother's death. He looked to her for protection, and she was failing him. Vee was letting these men beat him to death right in front of her.

Something was roiling inside her, something bright and hot, like a fever. It pulsed and grew, and grew, and grew, until Vee couldn't feel anything but this glowing energy inside herself.

"*STOP!*" she yelled, as loud as she could, louder even than Jayce's screaming. Loud enough that it echoed all around her.

And they did. All three men stopped in an instant. Frozen in place, like statues.

Ba bump.

Ba bump.

Ba bump.

How strange. Vee noticed a new sound all around her. A sound inside of her. No... not just one sound. Four sounds, four distinct heartbeats, entangled with her own. She cocked her head to the side and listened to it, marveling at how interweaved it was with that light suddenly burning inside her.

Ba bump.

Ba bump.

The hand that held her hair was limp now and Vee scrambled out of that grip, looking at the surrounding men in shock. Her scalp throbbed where he'd held her.

They were all completely still, as though stuck in that singular moment of time. Only their eyes moved, wide and full of terror.

Terrified... of her.

Ba bump.

Ba bump.

"Jayce," Vee whispered, scared that if she were too loud, she might break this spell, might shatter whatever magic was causing this. "Jayce, come here."

He did, scrambling to his feet and retreating behind her, away from the men. She could feel him, too, could feel the beat of his heart, the pulse of his blood in his veins. She could feel his thoughts, distant and foreign. Fear, yes, but now something else. Relief. Hope.

I wonder...

Vee reached her hand out, closer to that pulse, the energy coming from these men. Reached and *pulled*, drawing that energy to her.

"It's okay, Jayce," she told him as the men screamed. "It's okay. They can't hurt you anymore."

Bones cracked and shattered as the men contorted, and Vee watched in fascination as their bodies twisted and bent. That pulse inside them responded to her whims, as pliable as a hot wire.

"We're safe, Jayce," she said, a smile twisting across her face as power surged inside of her. "No one can hurt us anymore."

PART ONE

CHAPTER I

FEY

Within the quiet confines of her coven's temple, Fey let the tight grip she held on her power slip, just a little. In the two years since her new powers had awakened—the two years since she'd taken the antidote that purged the Allium from her blood—only here did she allow herself that luxury.

Only here did it feel safe.

It was a little like untensing a muscle. Slowly, incrementally, Fey let the leash slip, and let all that dark, delicious power fill her. Raw and unfiltered, her elemental power thrummed beneath her skin as it rose to her call. And as it did, the world around her sharpened.

The temple smelled like rain. Never mind that the outside dawn rose crisp and cold without a single cloud in the sky. Day or night, snow or shine, the earthy smell of petrichor permeated the interior of the Water Coven temple, as though the Goddess herself were making her presence known to all the Witches in attendance. With her power filling her, Fey could smell every element in the air around her, every speck of moisture, every dust mote, could feel every blade of grass trying to push its way through the thick stone walls.

Fey loved this smell. It was nothing like the light citrus that perfumed the Air Coven temple, or the slight spice she often smelled on

High Priestess Leandra and associated with the Fire Coven. No. This smell was different. It reached inside of her and tugged at something ancient, something that defined her very essence.

Fey breathed in deeply through her nose, filling herself with the smell of rain. Her power stirred in response. Not just Water, but all four elements, humming to life under her skin.

The smell was stronger deeper in the temple, but Fey rarely ventured past the first few pews. She preferred her spot here, seated as far as possible from Sana's podium, tucked into a forgotten corner, close to the stone walls. Here, she could sit unnoticed, unbothered, and just be. She would have stood if she could have—would have leaned against the oak doors that led outside if it wouldn't have brought undue attention to her. But the only Witch standing here was Sana. All the other Witches sat, backs straight in their pews, rapt with attention.

They came here to listen to their High Priestess speak.

Fey came to smell the rain, to feel the comforting presence of the Goddess. She came to let her magic off the leash, if only for a few hours. Here, where it felt safe. Here, where her magic felt more contained.

Where she couldn't hurt anyone.

In the months following the night of the Blood Moon, the night Queen Edelin had fallen, Fey had tried to keep it together. But her new powers were unpredictable and messy. Anger came easily to Fey, especially then, with the deaths of Willow and Lilith so fresh and raw. And with that anger came Fire.

Fey learned to swallow it down, best she could. She learned to force those new powers down inside herself and leash them tight.

But *Goddess*, it felt so good to let that power out.

"Welcome, my children, on this beautiful day," Sana spoke, hands resting gently on the wooden podium in front of her. She greeted them all with a matronly smile, and the congregation listened eagerly, all eyes on her.

All eyes but Fey's. Sana's words washed over her as she let her eyes close, her body attuned to the rhythms of the temple.

"Today, I invite you all to meditate with me on the virtue of balance. A virtue our Goddess holds most dear."

For over a year now, Fey had attended Sana's sermons but had listened to maybe a handful of them. She preferred the sounds of the temple itself, the gentle conversation of water on stone, the soft flow of breath. She let her attention drift, let her powers swell, and Sana's voice became nothing but a gentle hum in the distance.

"Balance is all around us, my children. The balance of life and death. The balance of joy and pain. Remember that there can be no light without dark, no dawn without night. Even in the Goddess herself there is balance. Creator and destroyer. Compassion and vengeance."

There was so much power in this room. So much strength. Her own gifts pulsed under her skin in recognition as she breathed it all in.

Here was sacred. Here was right. Here, Fey could unleash her power —just a little, but enough—to feel in control, to let it stretch before she pushed it deep down inside herself again.

What a tragedy to be given the gift of all four elements but have to keep them hidden inside.

"Consider the seedling. To grow, it needs both the rain and the sun, a balance of cloudy skies and nourishing light."

The old queen had taken so much from them by cutting off entire generations of Witches from their full range of power, all to keep herself on the throne. In the end, her betrayal of her own Faction had cost the Queen everything, including her life. And though those Witches who had their powers taken away were free now, were learning to harness their newfound gifts, Queen Edelin's greed had cost Witches the throne.

The council still held that fragile peace Fey and her sisters had sacrificed so much for, but the realm was a powder keg ready to erupt. And every day that passed without another Witch who could command all four elements—without another Witch like Fey—was another spark with the potential to set the realm ablaze.

The council might continue to rule the realm, but so many Witches were waiting, hungry for a new queen to emerge and set their world right once again.

Don't think about that, Fey thought, scolding herself for the dark turn in her thoughts. *Not here. Not now.* This was her time to be close to the Goddess. This was her time to be herself.

And all too soon, it was over.

Sana's melodious voice disappeared, replaced by a rising chatter as the congregation began to rise and converse among themselves. Through the rhythm of their conversations, Fey could make out sharp words and phrases directed at her.

She's here, a voice said.

The Broken Blade.

The true queen.

Rage, hot and sudden, flashed through her. Fey opened her eyes, focusing on the pew in front of her, avoiding the stares of the congregation. Willfully ignoring their words.

Time to go.

It hurt to rein it in, to pull that power back inside of herself and lock it away once more. But she did it, just as she had done countless times over the last two years. She locked that power away, deep inside of herself, and rose to leave.

On the wooden pew she left behind, a charred imprint of her hands remained, burned into the wood.

CHAPTER 2
AMALIA

The world does not stop to mourn the death of a single Witch.

The morning after Willow died, the sun still rose in the east and set in the west. Birds announced the morning with song, just as they did every day, and just as they would until the end of time.

The morning after Lilith took her last icy breath, the world continued to spin as though nothing had changed. Dawn came and went. People loved one another. People hated one another. Often the two groups were one and the same.

Even the death of Queen Edelin didn't stop the world from moving forward.

The world does not stop to mourn the death of a single Witch, even when it feels like it should.

But for Amalia, former princess of the realm, one of only two Witches alive blessed with all four natural elements, the world stopped the day her mother died. Even now, two years later, it showed no signs of starting again.

Sunlight...

Amalia blinked against the bright light bleeding into her room. She groaned, raising her hand to cover her eyes.

Sunlight.

What time was it? Morning? Afternoon?

She didn't know. Didn't care.

Someone had come in and opened the curtains to let the light into her room. Maybe they had meant it as a kindness. But it was so bright. So bright it hurt to look at.

She could close them. Get out of bed, close the curtains, and return that blissful dark to her room.

She could...

The effort would be too much. An overwhelming amount of work to even get up out of bed. Even imagining it exhausted her.

Eyes closed tight against the light, Amalia fumbled with her blankets, pulling them back up and over her head. Darkness returned.

She went back to sleep.

CHAPTER 3
FEY

It took Fey nearly three hours of strength training before she felt in control of herself again. Three hours to burn through the rage that threatened to consume her, bringing her body to the point of exhaustion. And only then did she stop. Only then did she trust herself to come back to her body and her own mind.

That white hot rage had finally dimmed, and though Fire still pulsed beneath her skin, it felt more like a dull ache, numbed by the pain in her muscles.

It was getting worse, she realized. The leash she used to hold her new powers in check was slipping more and more each day, and the tighter she gripped it, the harder it fought against her.

Day after day, Fey pushed that rage and pain down inside herself, using every ounce of restraint and power to keep it at bay. And day after day, it fought her, refusing to be tamed, refusing to be caged.

Let me out.

With a groan, Fey forced herself across the gym to where she'd stashed her bottle of water. She drank deep, desperate to quench her thirst.

She hadn't bothered warming up. Hadn't bothered easing into her workout, or even stopping by her sisters' apartment to let Joy and Alice know she was here. She had just thrown herself into it, venting her frustrations and her anger on the heavy punching bag Alice had installed. That was a mistake, and her muscles would pay for it for over the next few days, but for now Fey felt blissfully drained.

For now, at least, she felt in control.

Somewhere in the building, her two remaining sisters were awake, preparing their midday meal. Drinking coffee and planning their day. Somewhere they were living their lives, each day taking them further from their past, blissfully in love. Happy.

Fey could join them now that she was more in control of her thoughts. She could stumble up the stairs to the home Joy and Alice shared and let herself be soothed by their company. By their love.

She wouldn't, though. Not today. They were happy. They were moving on and moving forward.

Fey was the one still stuck in the past. She was the one trying to contain the monster inside of herself, the one still trapped in the memory of poor Willow's death. And she didn't want to bring them down with her. They were healing. And they deserved their happiness. They deserved to move on.

She didn't want to see them. Didn't want to remind them of their past and their sacrifices. Swallowing down her memories, Fey finished the last of her water and changed out of her exercise clothes. She had another idea. A better one.

She needed chocolate.

REGINA'S BAKERY was a staple of the Shifter neighborhood Fey now called home. For over twenty years, through feast and famine, it had endured. There had been times all too recently when food had been so scarce that Shifters were dying of starvation by the hundreds in the Eternal City. Times when Regina had only enough staples to sell basics like bread. But she had come into her shop every morning, making what she could and selling it at cost, trying to keep her people alive.

And now? Now Regina's Bakery flourished.

The warm scent of oven-fresh bread hit Fey the moment she opened the door. A quick glance around revealed the store was empty, not a single other patron in sight.

Good, Fey thought. She preferred to do her shopping in peace, alone. And with her rage tugging on that leash, the fewer people she saw today, the better.

"One moment!" came a gruff voice from the back. Regina, taking advantage of the momentary lull in customers to get some more work done.

Fey didn't waste time looking around at the general goods for sale in all corners of the shop. She went straight to the bakery case, peering through the glass at the pastries and sweets housed there. Fewer than usual, she noticed. In fact, the case had been steadily looking emptier and emptier in the last few months.

"Ah, it's the Witch!" Regina said in greeting, emerging from the back of the shop and wiping her hands on the stained white apron she wore. Regina was an intimidating woman, in both stature and personality. She had the sand-colored eyes of all Lion Shifters, and though her hair was going silver with age, the white strands that peppered her golden blonde curls added a lovely shimmer that sparkled in the sunlight that drifted in through the windows.

"Morning, Regina," Fey said, glancing up. When they'd moved into the neighborhood, Fey and her sisters had been the only Witches who'd shopped here. But times were changing—the *city* was changing—and Regina's shop was quickly becoming one of the most popular bakeries in the district.

Still, Fey liked to think Regina still took special care of her and her sisters. A reward for being among the first of her Witch clients.

"This is morning to you, eh?" Regina scoffed, glancing pointedly at the clock on the wall. "Your Vampire is a bad influence on you. Up all night, sleeping during the day..." She shook her head disapprovingly, clicking her tongue.

"Well, it's not like he has a choice, does he?" Fey answered with a smirk. Sun couldn't kill a Vampire as powerful as Alastair, but it would probably hurt like hell. And even if it didn't, with Alastair spending nights managing his nightclub and his days in bed with her, Fey wasn't sure he'd change his hours even if he could.

"How're your sisters, dear?" Regina asked, leaning on the glass counter. She towered above Fey, nearly six and a half feet of Lion trapped in a human body.

"They're good," Fey answered. "I just came from their place, actually. Alice converted one of the spare apartments to a gym."

"And the little one? Joy?"

A grin twitched at the corners of Fey's lips. Of course, to Regina, Joy would be the "little one." She was half the Shifter's size, though Fey would bet a fair amount of gold that Joy was twice as deadly, even considering Regina's Lion form. Joy had been an unstoppable force before, but now that she could control three elements? Well, now she held an overwhelming amount of power in her small, delicate hands.

Would Regina still think of Joy as the *little one* if she knew it had been her hand that had brought down the old queen? Her blade of air that had taken Edelin's head?

"Joy is... Joy." Fey shrugged. "She's happy. They're happy."

"Good," Regina nodded. "So... what brings you in, hm? I'm running low on bread, so what's in the case is all we have today. But I have some brownies in the oven right now if you're looking for something sweet."

Fey's mouth watered. That's exactly what she was looking for. "*Yes.* Some brownies, please. And some of your famous pork buns, if you have any left." Jasper had mentioned them in passing the last time she'd stopped by the club. *Better than sex*, he'd told her. And then with a wink and a wicked grin, he'd added, *well, not the sort of sex I could give you.*

Regina chuckled. "I have a few I don't mind parting with, for you, Witch. Goddess knows my brother doesn't need to eat so many."

Regina gave her a rough grin before ducking into the back.

"I've been meaning to ask you, love," she called, her voice easily carrying across the small shop. "My last two shipments of flour were light—your sister on the council, Alice, maybe she could bring it up with them, yeah? Find out what's going on with—"

The bell above the door chimed, interrupting Regina and announcing another customer. Fey turned from the bakery case to watch them enter—a young couple with their child, maybe three years old. Witches, even. It warmed something in Fey's chest to see it. With the establishment of the council, Alice insisted the city was slowly but surely becoming less segregated. And here was proof.

Fey tried to offer the couple a smile. But when the woman caught sight of her, she stopped in her tracks, gripping her child tight to her chest.

"The Queen…" she whispered, sounding dazed. The smile slipped from Fey's face, and her lips curled into a sneer.

"No," Fey said in a dark voice. That warmth in her chest didn't die, but instead morphed into something hotter and more dangerous. "You're mistaken."

"It is you," the Witch's partner insisted, eyes going wide as he stepped forward. "You're the Broken Blade. Our true queen." He stared at her in awe, gaze roaming over her from the top of her blood-red hair all the way to her boots. And it didn't matter that Fey wasn't wearing her Queen's Blades uniform—hadn't worn it since that bloody night she'd overthrown her own queen—that's what he was picturing when he looked at her.

It's how they all pictured her.

"No," Fey repeated, voice hardening. The heat in her chest grew a little more, threatening to become an inferno. She took a step away from them, wanting more space to find a semblance of calm, only to find the glass of the bakery counter against her back, trapping her there. "I'm not—"

The man stepped forward. And with horror, Fey watched as he knelt, coming to one knee before her on the spotless floor of Regina's shop.

"Your Grace," he murmured in deference. At his side, his partner lowered her head and repeated the words, bowing slightly at her waist.

In an instance, that heat in Fey's chest roared to life, threatening to overtake her.

LET ME OUT.

Fire. It feasted on her rage, happily licking against her skin from the inside. Fire danced at her fingers, Fire burned behind her eyes, and in her mind she no longer saw the family in front of her, she saw every Witch who had looked at her like that for the last two years all at once.

Everyone who had called her *queen*, who called her "Your Grace," and the Fire wanted *out, wanted to destroy them all.*

She could do it, Fey knew, feeling the flames lick over her skin and dance up her arm. She could take the whole shop down, and everyone in it. She could take down the whole damn block...

"That's enough of all that!" Regina said, coming out from behind the counter, waving a flour-speckled dishcloth at the couple. Fey hadn't noticed her return. She was lost in the flames, consumed by her rage.

Rising from his knees, the man frowned, confused, unaware of the offense he may have caused. Unaware of how close he was to death.

Let me out, the fire screamed inside of her, burning hotter and hotter and hotter.

And she wanted to. She wanted to let it out, wanted to let it take over her and give in to it.

This is why she held it so tight, why she pushed it down inside herself and leashed it. This is why she did everything she could to swallow this power down.

Because it felt so *good* to burn.

"We're closed!" Regina snapped, shooing the couple out the door. "Closed for the day, out, out, out!"

The couple put up a minor protest but were no match for Regina's sheer size and determination. She had them out the door in seconds, slamming it shut behind them and flipping the sign from *open* to *closed*.

"Take a deep breath," Regina ordered, glancing back at Fey. She engaged the lock as well and pulled the blinds closed, hiding them from the busy street. "They're gone, Witch. Take a breath and control yourself, damn you."

But Fey couldn't breathe. Rage swirled inside of her, hot and deadly as an inferno. It didn't want to go back inside, didn't want to be held back anymore.

Fey could take down the whole city with power like this, couldn't she? Burn the whole damn realm to ashes, and there was nothing that could stop her. No *one* who could stop her.

Regina turned back to her, her eyes showing just a flash of fear before she swallowed it down and spoke. "Your bag, Fey. Look at your bag."

Through the haze of rage and pleasure, Fey glanced down, Fire flickering in her vision as it danced in her eyes, over her arms. The long-handled canvas bag she used to hold her shopping was gone. Only a scrap of fabric remained, still smoldering and charred at her feet. She opened her hand, where she had been clutching the handle, and found nothing there but ash.

Fire coated her hands. Bright blue and white flames danced over the skin of her palms, over her fingers.

It was beautiful.

"Breathe," Regina snarled. Not the voice of the friendly shopkeeper Fey knew, but that of a Lioness. An apex predator accustomed to being obeyed.

Fey took a deep, shuddering breath and released it. The flames pulled back closer to her skin. She called Water, called Air, called Earth, she called everything inside of herself to push it down, down, down. Another deep, intentional breath and the flames were gone, pulled back inside her where her other powers lay.

Dormant, and waiting for her call.

Let me out, it purred, the demand barely more than a whisper under her skin. Suddenly the shop felt too cold, too still, and her heart pounded painfully in her chest.

"Are you alright?" Regina asked.

"No," Fey said. She was exhausted from fighting herself, exhausted from the effort of holding back. "No, I'm not alright."

She glanced around the shop, worried about the damage she may have done. But aside from the burnt wreckage of her bag, there was nothing.

Fey took a breath and counted to ten. Then, just to be sure, she did it again. Her muscles relaxed slightly, the tension in her shoulders easing. That blaze inside of her still waited, still wanted out, but it was manageable now. Contained.

"I'll get a broom, and you can sweep that up," Regina said, looking pointedly at the ash on her floor. Fey almost laughed. She'd had many reactions to her powers before—fear, distrust, even envy. But only Regina made her feel like a misbehaving child. "I'm sure I have another bag in the back you can have, no extra charge."

"I'm sorry," Fey said, shaking her head. "I haven't lost control like that for a while. It's just..."

"I know," Regina said. And maybe the Lioness was telling the truth. Maybe she knew a thing or two about losing control. About leashing a monster inside.

Regina ducked into the backroom and returned with a long-handled broom, handing it to Fey. Fey took a deep breath and started to sweep.

Regina watched her for a moment, the store silent but for the rhythmic sound of the broom against the shop floor, and then asked, sadly, "You've seen the posters?"

Fey's jaw clenched. Two years ago, when the Queen had revealed Fey's identity to the realm, she had blanketed the city with posters with Fey's name and face, hoping to draw her out from wherever she was hiding.

But now, with the Queen dead, the posters that were being put up had a different message. They used the same image as before, but rather than listing her fabricated crimes, the posters said only three words, in big bold letters.

OUR TRUE QUEEN.

"Yeah," Fey answered through clenched teeth, keeping her eyes on her sweeping and not looking up at Regina as she spoke. "I've seen the posters."

In the beginning, Fey had paid little attention to the calls for her to take the throne. It was just a matter of time before another Witch with all four powers was discovered, she reasoned. If not in the city itself, then in one of the surrounding octants, surely. And then everyone would realize she wasn't special, wasn't chosen by the Goddess to rule.

But years passed. Thousands of young Witches came into their powers. Thousands more received the same antidote to Allium that had revealed Fey's gifts.

And still Fey remained the only Witch in the realm besides the former princess who could control all four natural elements.

Over time, the whispers from her Faction grew. There was no need for a council when they had a queen who could lead them, people started to say. Wasn't her existence enough to prove that the Goddess had blessed her to be queen? Hadn't the Goddess herself sent Fey to put a stop to Queen Edelin's horrors?

By the time the whispers grew to shouts and members of her Faction started to demand the council be dissolved and Fey be crowned queen, a fundamental shift had occurred in the Eternal City. A few weeks later, someone on the street knelt to her for the first time.

Fey had been forced to pay attention after that.

Fey knew she was no queen. She was a killer, raised on hate and violence and blood. She spent years honing her skills, years turning herself into a perfect monster. And no matter how much time she spent trying to cage that monster inside of herself, trying to be like every other Witch, it still fought to escape.

Goddess help her, she was trying. Trying to be the savior, trying to be the hero the realm saw in her. But no amount of twisting herself to fit the mold others made for her was going to change who she was. What she was.

By the time Fey finished cleaning the ash from the floor, Regina had packed her shopping into a new bag. She'd even slipped in an extra brownie, still warm from the oven.

Fey kept her head down when she left the shop, avoiding eye contact with the people she passed.

She tried to ignore the eyes that lingered on her, tried to ignore the murmurs, just as she tried to ignore the hum of Fire inside her that rose in response.

The Fire that wanted *out*.

CHAPTER 4
ALICE

The council hadn't even assembled yet and already Alice could feel a tension headache brewing behind her eyes.

Why did I ever agree to this? she asked herself, for the hundredth time.

When the High Priestesses first offered her a seat on the council as their Faction's representative, Alice had slammed the door in their faces. The idea of a former Blade, the very Witch responsible for the fall of their old regime, taking up the mantel of leader was borderline psychotic. But they'd been persistent, and bit by bit they'd managed to wear her down and convince her she really was their best choice.

Their only choice, really, after Princess Amalia had abdicated her role. The Priestesses had bickered amongst themselves for weeks over whether one of them could be the singular representative, before deciding it simply wasn't possible. As leaders of their own covens, loyal to their members above all else, they couldn't be trusted to remain impartial.

No, the representative of the Witch Faction had to be someone who could uphold not just the well-being of every Witch in the realm, but the well-being of members of all four Factions. It had to be someone with no loyalty to the old leaders, someone with a history of putting the common good above their own needs.

Someone like Alice, the dead Queen's Blade. The Witch who had taken down an empire.

That had been the impassioned plea Sana had made to her, at least. And, finally, Alice had agreed on the condition the High Priestesses continued their role as advisors.

It was a condition that—less than two years later—they were consistently failing to meet.

Alice pinched the corners of her eyes, trying to ignore the pulsing pain in her head. Ten minutes past the time they were meant to begin, and she, the Water Coven High Priestess Sana, and the Vampire Faction representative Cassiel Salvatore deSanguine were the only members of the council who had bothered to show up.

It really shouldn't have surprised her. Leandra was busy helping Fey with her classes nearly every morning, and Linh, the High Priestess of the Air Coven, had been very clear in her distaste for the council and everything it stood for. She barely bothered to show up anymore, and when she did, she did nothing but scowl and complain. And Claudia...

Claudia was simply gone.

Something had changed in her, after the Queen's death. The High Priestess of the Earth Coven had grown weaker and more wane with each passing day. She'd lost weight, disappearing into herself so suddenly that her skin was hanging off her frail body. Then one day she'd taken to her bed and simply not gotten back up. She had finally passed away, just a few weeks ago, plagued by an extended illness that no healers seemed capable of treating. From what Sana had told her, it would be a long time before the Earth temple picked a new High Priestess. They were in mourning, and of all the temples, they were perhaps the slowest in enacting change.

It could take years for them to elect another Coven leader. Years before another Earth High Priestess sat at this table with them.

Shifting in his seat, Cassiel Salvatore deSanguine sniffed loudly and looked pointedly at the clock on the wall, then to the empty chair at his side. As always, he immaculately dressed himself in a rich black suit with a dark red lining—the colors of his Faction's house. "I see our council woman from the Demon Faction has once again not deigned to attend."

"Oh, she's here," Alice said, gesturing at the room around them with one hand while continuing to pinch the bridge of her nose with the other. It hadn't taken long for Alice to recognize the telltale signs of the Demon's presence. The shadows along the walls were a darker shade than usual, stretching far beyond where they should, given the light of the room. And they flickered, ever so slightly, when you weren't looking directly at them. "She's just not... *here*, here."

Cassiel rolled his eyes and sat straighter in his seat. "Kallista," he called into the room, amusement echoing in his dark voice. "If you could be a dear?"

There was a pulse from the shadows, barely noticeable, before they withdrew. A moment later, the rear door of the throne room opened, and Kallista entered, head held high.

"So nice of you to join us," Cassiel said with just the barest hint of a sneer in his voice. "I do hope we are not inconveniencing you terribly by asking that you attend in person."

Kallista shot him a disdainful look as she took her seat. The Demon was devastatingly beautiful, even as her blood-red lips curled with distaste.

"I was not aware my physical presence was a necessity," she said. She and the Vampire glared at each other for a long moment. He was the first to look away. "After all, Kellos hasn't been present for the last... what is it now? Three meetings?"

"Two," Alice corrected. "And he will send a proxy representative today, apparently."

"Oh?" Kallista asked. She looked around the room, pointedly. "And where, pray tell, is this proxy now? Did he send us a little mouse to hide in the corners? A bat, for the rafters?"

"Not a mouse, no," came a breathless voice from the main entrance, farthest from the council table. "I'm here! Sorry for the wait!"

The Shifter who entered, hurrying across the long room to where the rest of them sat, was nothing at all like the Lion Shifter Kellos who usually represented their Faction. He was young and fit, pale-skinned to

Kellos's golden-brown hues, and wore his long brown hair tied up away from his face. His eyes were a metallic grey, and they darted over each council member in turn, as though he couldn't quite settle on where to look.

"A Hawk?" the deSanguine said, dismissively. His dark eyes raked down the Shifter's body, sizing him up and clearly unimpressed. "The Shifters have sent us a *Hawkling* to replace Kellos?"

"Not a replacement," the Shifter said, seating himself in Kellos's chair and scooting it closer to the table. It dragged across the floor noisily. He ignored the hostile tone in Cassiel's voice, which Alice suspected either made him very brave or incredibly stupid. "And not a Hawk, either. A Falcon."

He gave them a wild smile in greeting. "I'm Silas. Kellos is, regrettably, still detained. I'm just here for this meeting, maybe two, to make sure our Faction is suitably represented in his absence."

"Kellos has been regrettably detained for quite a few meetings now," Kallista mused. "Should we be worried?"

"Is the old cat finally ready to croak?" the deSanguine added.

Alice couldn't help but think of Claudia, stuck in bed and slowly fading away until death finally took her in her sleep. It felt like the whole city was growing weaker by the day.

Absently, her fingers drifted over the scar that marred her Blades mark.

"No, no." Silas flashed them an easy smile. "Nothing at all to worry about. He is just recovering from a bad cold and needs his rest. Nothing serious. He sends his regrets and hopes he'll be back on his feet in time for the next meeting."

"With all the continued buzz from Prey for the Crown lately, I'm shocked Kellos didn't send a Deer, or..." Cassiel waved his hand, searching for the words. "Or a Rat, or some such beast."

Silas's smile was a touch more dangerous as he answered. "Rats *are* predators, I assure you. Something to keep in mind when dealing with them," he told the deSanguine. "And the PFTC has no problem with Kellos or me. We are happy to work with our nonpredator brethren, so long as they remember their place in the food chain. They understand the necessity of a predator representing them. And... we're all predators here, aren't we?"

His eyes flashed as he spoke.

"I imagine we are," Alice conceded. Her headache had receded somewhat, and she was eager to get started so she could get home. To her Joy. She peeled her fingers from her scar reluctantly. "Now that we are all here, perhaps we should start the meeting, then? What is on our agenda for today?"

"Bread," Sana said, shuffling her notes. She sat straight-backed in her chair, acting more secretary than High Priestess at these meetings. "Or, rather, wheat. The price of wheat has risen substantially over the previous year, and it is becoming a problem for many of the Fallen."

"We don't use that term anymore, Witch," Kallista said, leaning her delicate chin on her hand and turning to glare at Sana. "We do not see ourselves as having Fallen from the Goddess's grace, you know. That was always your Faction's term, not ours."

Sana winced. "Right. Of course, my apologies. The price of wheat is presenting a problem for many citizens," she amended.

"Well, why has the price been rising?" Cassiel asked in a bored tone.

"A few reasons," Sana demurred, eyes skimming over her notes. "But I think we should focus more on the solutions than on the cause, and I do believe—"

"The farmers are dead," Alice interrupted, and when the rest of the council looked at her, a little shocked, she continued. "Most of the realm's wheat comes from the fourth octant and was farmed by three families from the Witch Faction. Two of those families were killed in the aftermath of the Blood Moon. One had close ties to the Queen's Temples, and the other..." Alice shrugged. "The other family, very likely, were killed out of sheer spite against the Crown. Or because they were rich and unprotected, take your pick."

Cassiel winced, but Kallista and Silas at least didn't seem bothered by the news.

"Yes," Sana said in a heavy voice. "Thank you, Alice. Those deaths have left the farms untended, and the wheat unharvested. We offered the farms to the remaining family in that octant, but..." She paused and pursed her lips. "They are stretched thin enough with their own work and their own farm. They don't have the manpower necessary to maintain another one, let alone two."

"I think we can help with that," Silas said, tilting his head sharply to the side. It was an unmistakably predatory motion and made Alice itch to touch the small knife she still kept on her, hidden at her side.

They are not your enemies, she reminded herself. *Not anymore.* She forced herself to keep her hands still on the table in front of her.

"The fourth octant is mostly Shifters, after all," Silas continued, eyes darting to each of them and finally settling on Sana. "I know of a rather substantial herd of Elk who live there. I'm sure I can speak to some of them about taking over the farms and getting our wheat supply back up and running."

Sana blinked. "But these are Witch farms," she said, stressing the word Witch. "If they are taken by some Shifters, other Witches could see it as an act of aggression."

"Do you want the wheat or not?" Alice snapped and instantly regretted it when Sana flinched. Goddess above, diplomacy would be the death of her. Taking a breath to calm herself, she continued in a softer tone. "The farms are empty, correct, Sana?"

"Correct," Sana replied, quickly recovering from Alice's temper.

"Then they are abandoned. And something that has been abandoned by definition cannot be taken. Let the Shifters have them. There's no use wasting good food to appease the dead." Alice turned to Silas. "How quickly can you have those farms occupied?"

"Within the month," he assured her with a smile. "I'll fly there myself to oversee the transfer and find out if they can salvage any of this year's harvest. With any luck, we could have more wheat heading to the city within the quarter."

"Good," Alice replied. "Let's have a vote on it, then."

"I worry about the precedent this might set," Sana insisted, her eyes on Alice. "If, in the event of a family's total annihilation their belongings become a free for all..." She dropped her voice, likely thinking the other council members could not hear her, and directed the rest of her statement toward Alice, and Alice alone. "Then what is to stop the full slaughter of members of our Faction?"

"Why are you always so convinced the rest of us are always mere seconds away from murder?" Kallista asked, sounding exasperated. "If you recall, it was *your* Faction that racked up the highest body count in the War of the Fallen. Given your history, shouldn't it be the rest of us worrying about our potential annihilation?"

Alice fought not to roll her eyes. There was no doubt at all from those at this table who the strongest person in the room was, and it wasn't either of the Witches by any stretch of the imagination. From the moment she'd shown up, Kallista had made it clear in a thousand different ways that her power was above and beyond anything the rest of them could even hope to reach. And if the stories were to be believed, the eighth octant was full of Demons just like her. It was almost laughable that she would find herself concerned about their Faction at all.

"The dead can't own land," Alice insisted, bringing them back to the matter at hand. "And whatever precedent this sets, we'll deal with it when it comes up. I won't hold back food from our citizens over someone's unfounded fears, Sana."

To her credit, Sana relented. It was one of the few things Alice had found she liked about the Water Witch. Sure, Sana came with her own prejudices and fears about the other Factions, but she was learning to overcome them. She knew when she was beaten and never seemed to hold a grudge about it.

"We should vote, then," Sana said, setting her notes aside and grabbing the ledger where they recorded official council votes. "Factions in favor of transferring ownership of the two wheat farms and their holdings in the fourth octant to Shifters of Silas's choosing at a later date, please raise your hands."

Alice was the first to raise her hand, and after that, it was unanimous. Sana recorded it as such.

"What can be done in the meantime?" Kallista asked. "Harvesting and grinding wheat is time-consuming, I imagine, and that's assuming anything in the fields can be salvaged for immediate use. The city needs flour now."

"Not just the city," Sana clarified. "The entire realm is experiencing this shortage. And, unfortunately, it is going to get much worse before it gets better. Each shipment from the fourth octant has been less than the last, and we are approaching winter in a few months. What we have, and what can still be harvested this season, will have to last until the next year."

"Did the Queen have any emergency stores?" Cassiel asked, not bothering to look at any of them. He was like this every meeting, only half appearing to pay any attention. Yet, every time Alice thought he wasn't listening, he'd jump in with some brilliant suggestion.

It annoyed the hell out of her.

Sana shuffled through her papers, searching through their records.

"Uh, yes, here it is," she said, finally, eyes skimming the page. "Yes, she did! I have the inventory here. And there are..." Her eyes widened. "Goddess bless us, there are several tons of flour stored here in the palace storerooms."

Alice nodded. Finally, something going right for a change. "Good. Have it all removed and dispersed to the stores in the city. Wait..." She stopped, drumming her fingers on the table and thinking. "No. No, have half of it dispersed to stores in the city. Then have the palace accountants divide and distribute the rest to the other octants. And make sure they distribute it based on population, not evenly to all eight," Alice insisted. Sana's pen skittered across the paper as she made notes. "There's no need to give the same amount of wheat to the second octant as the fifth, when they have four times the population. All in favor?"

The vote was again unanimous, and they moved on to other business. And other business after that. And even more, after that.

The meeting lasted until well after midnight, and by the time they all agreed to call it a night, Alice was mentally and physically spent. Silas, to her surprise, had been a remarkably effective stand-in for Kellos. Despite his youth, he was smart, and his solutions had been clever without being too self-serving. Alice hoped that if Kellos's absence continued, he at least kept sending Silas as their representative.

"You did well today," came a soft, feminine voice at her side.

Alice glanced up to find Kallista leaning on the table at her shoulder, staring down at her. She tried to swallow the fear that leapt into her throat.

Even now, after all this time working with her, the Demon made her uncomfortable. There was something dangerous about her, something that still set her on edge. One of the first things she learned during her training in the Queen's army was how to assess a potential threat and recognize when she was outmatched.

Alice had no illusions that in every way possible, Kallista had her outmatched. She genuinely hoped that there would never come a day when they stood on opposing sides of a battle.

"Thanks," Alice replied simply, straightening and hoping the Demon would take the hint and leave.

"You're good at this, you know," Kallista continued, those dangerous blue eyes boring into her.

Alice shrugged. "It's not hard," she demurred. "It's just like solving a puzzle." Sure, it had been difficult at first, but now Alice found it suited her. *Leading* suited her.

Who would have thought the big bad Queen's Blade, a monster in so many folktales, could be a diplomat?

"I think you aren't used to compliments," Kallista said, raising an eyebrow at her. "You don't need to undervalue yourself. You are good at this. I'm not trying to stroke your ego, Witch, I am simply stating a fact."

Alice snorted, but she didn't argue. Goddess help her, she liked Kallista, almost as much as she feared her. She didn't want to, didn't want to trust the Demon for a myriad of reasons. But she'd definitely grown on her over these last months.

"Will you stay on? After the princess comes of age?" Kallista asked, picking an invisible speck of dirt off her dress with long painted fingernails.

Alice paused.

That had been the agreement when the High Priestesses had appointed her. After her first, and only, council meeting, Amalia had shown no interest in continuing. They had decided a new representative should lead the Witches in her stead until she reached the age of majority.

"I'm not sure," Alice answered, honestly. "The princess is..." *A brat? Incapable of handling her own emotions, let alone assuming responsibility for an entire Faction? A representation of everything Alice had fought to overthrow, of everything that had infected the city when the Witches ruled?*

Alice cleared her throat and said, politely as she could, "The princess is complicated. If she decides to take her seat on the council after her eighteenth birthday, I will respect her choice and step aside."

"And if she doesn't?"

Alice shrugged. "Then my continued presence on the council will be decided by the High Priestesses. They are the closest thing our Faction has to a ruler, after all."

Kallista smiled, admiring her nails. "For now," she said, and Alice didn't miss the ominous tone in her voice.

Alice gave her a long look, straightening to her full height.

Shit like that is what makes it so hard to trust you, Demon, she thought.

"And what do you mean by that?" Alice didn't bother to hide the menace in her voice.

"Don't play dumb with me, Alice," Kallista said, waving the words away. "It insults both of us. You know what I meant."

Alice's eyes hardened. "My sister," she answered darkly.

Kallista nodded. "Yes. Your sister. You've seen the posters, haven't you? It would be hard not to at this point, I imagine."

Alice had. She had heard the rumors, too. Calls for Fey to be crowned queen. Arguments that her very existence was proof of a new, Goddess-chosen royal line.

"Fey isn't interested in ruling," Alice said simply.

Kallista shrugged, somehow making even that simple motion look elegant. "Few good rulers are. Only a sociopath would want the job, if you ask me."

"Believe me, Kallista," Alice insisted. "Fey is more sociopath than queen. She doesn't want it, and between you and me, she would be terrible at it. And you might want to keep those thoughts to yourself when you are on the council. Do you think so little of your role here that you are so happy to throw it away? To give up the throne to a new dictator?"

"Oh please," Kallista laughed. "I know this new leadership won't last, just as much as you do. You have a power vacuum in this city, and

I've lived through enough of those to know that they breed monsters. Someone will make a play for the throne, Alice. Whether you want to believe that or not doesn't change the fact that it will happen."

"Why are you here if you believe that?" Alice asked, stone-faced. Her headache was finally gone, but she was tired. Oh, so tired.

"Because I think the council is a good idea," Kallista said. Alice held her gaze, hoping to see some evidence of a lie in her eyes, but saw nothing there. "I do, Alice. I think it's brilliant. And I think it's the best shot any of us have at keeping the peace in this realm."

"But?"

"Peace is a fool's dream," Kallista insisted. "Life is entropy, Witch. We can spend our whole lives fighting for stability, but eventually everything falls to chaos, no matter how hard you try to stop it. Chaos is the one constant over the course of time."

"Why not you, then?" Alice challenged. "You say a power vacuum breeds monsters—who's a bigger monster in this city than you? Why don't you make a play for the top spot?"

Kallista made a face, scrunching her nose in distaste. "If I didn't know you better, I'd be insulted."

"You know what I mean, Demon." Alice shook her head. "If the strongest beings in the realm will fight to take the throne, then why not you?"

Kallista shrugged. "I don't want it."

"But it's so hard to believe my sister doesn't feel the same?"

Kallista smiled, a wide and wicked thing. "Clever little trap you set for me there, Witch, I'll give you that. Truthfully? I believe you when you say your sister doesn't want it. And Goddess help us if she ever does, with all that power at her pretty little fingertips. She's just as likely to kill us all as she is to rule us. But me? I've never had any interest in ruling. I simply don't need that sort of stress in my life." She examined her fingernails, as though bored. "It ages you terribly, and I don't need the wrinkles."

Alice snorted. "So... you believe the council is doomed to fail? That peace is doomed to fail? But every meeting you're still here, still trying to make the realm a better place. Why?"

Kallista almost smiled. "I suppose... I suppose I'm hoping you'll prove me wrong."

She'd heard enough. Alice gathered her things, piling them up and scooping them into her arms. "I look forward to trying, then," she said, heading toward the exit. "I'll see you at the next meeting, Kallista."

It was late. Later than she'd hoped to stay. But knowing Joy, she'd stayed up to wait for her. As she left, Alice's finger traced the edges of her scar, wishing she could still feel Joy through her mark.

CHAPTER 5

FEY

"You're lying," Jasper accused, a playful smile curving his lips. It wasn't the same smile he gave the other patrons—the flirtatious one full of the promise of sin. Fey liked this smile better, the one he seemed to save just for her.

"Not lying," Fey assured him with an easy shrug. "Hand to the Goddess, I'm telling you the truth."

"Exaggerating, then. Come on, you must be," he pestered.

"Nope. Not exaggerating. Not even a little."

Jasper shook his head in bewilderment, his green eyes sparkling. Fey glanced at him but quickly looked away, a pink blush coloring her cheeks. Just like Alastair, Jasper was so good-looking it was sometimes hard to look directly at him.

"You're saying they *knelt* to you?" he asked with a chuckle, leaning his elbows against the bar. His thick muscles shifted under his shirt with the movement. "They actually got down to their knees and knelt? In the middle of the store?"

"Just one knee," Fey protested, as though that made a difference. She plucked a corner off the brownie in front of her and popped it into her mouth, rolling the treat over her tongue. "But yes. Right in the middle of the store. He just...dropped down and knelt."

Goddess, Regina's brownies had no right being this delicious. Fey let out a soft moan as she swallowed the bite of chocolate goodness. She licked a few errant crumbs from her fingers, finally feeling like herself again.

She was glad she'd stopped by here. These days, when her thoughts became too loud and her rage flared too close to the surface, it was oddly comforting to swing by The Last Drop. Even with the sun still hovering above the horizon, and the club yet to open for the night, at least she could find some company here. A distraction.

For whatever reason, this club was starting to feel like home.

"Well," Jasper said, leaning over the bar to pull the brownie toward himself. "I certainly can't blame a guy for getting on his knees for you. Especially when you make noises like *that*."

Fey laughed and flicked a crumb at him.

"How often does this happen to you?" Jasper asked, face turning serious again. He broke off a piece of brownie for himself, ignoring Fey's scowl. *Greedy fucking Wolf.* He'd devoured the pork buns she brought him in a matter of seconds, and there'd be blood if he ate much more of her dessert. "The, uh, kneeling, I mean?"

Fey shrugged. She plucked a cherry from her drink and rolled the stem between her fingers. "Depends, really... when I'm in our neighborhood? Hardly ever. But anywhere else? At least once a week." She exhaled slowly, letting her head tilt back. "And then there are the posters..."

"Oh, is that why you've become a hermit?" Jasper asked, licking chocolate from his fingertips.

Fey shot him an irritated look and then quickly glanced away. The way he licked and sucked the chocolate from his fingers was borderline pornographic. "I haven't become a hermit," she argued, staring at her drink. "I go places."

"Where?" Jasper asked with a laugh. "And here doesn't count!" he added when she opened her mouth to respond.

"What do you mean here doesn't count?" Fey asked incredulously.

"I mean exactly what I said. It doesn't count. You're here... what? Maybe once every few weeks? If that? And only when we're not busy.

You see me and Alastair, and no one else. And as much as I love to see you, gorgeous, it doesn't count."

Fey scowled. Her rage remained tightly leashed, but it didn't stop her irritation from bleeding through. "I go to work. I go running every morning. And I go see Joy and Alice at least once a month, for family dinner."

"Also doesn't count," he answered smugly.

Fey curled her lip at him, but rather than backing down, Jasper just smiled wider at her, giving her a sharp-toothed grin.

"How do those not count?" she demanded.

"Your sisters live right on the outskirts of our neighborhood," Jasper said, ticking his points off on his fingers. "You run alone, despite knowing every Wolf working here would run with you, in whichever form you wanted. Me included, fuck you for never asking, by the way. And you don't see anyone at work. Do you ever go shopping in the other districts, Fey? Go to the bars or restaurants there?"

No, of course she didn't. Why would she?

"I have everything I need here," Fey insisted with what she hoped was a casual shrug. Jasper snorted a laugh.

"Look, I'm not trying to get on your case," he told her in a kind tone, tearing another piece from her brownie with his fingers. Fey reached out to snatch it back, but he playfully batted her hand away. "But even you have to admit you've put some pretty thick walls around yourself, Fey."

He tossed the piece of brownie into his mouth.

"I'm here spending time with you, aren't I?" Fey argued, her irritation clear in her tone and gripping her drink a little too tight.

Eyes locked on hers, Jasper swallowed, his throat bobbing with the motion. As he leaned across the bar, angling himself closer to her, his smile slipped. "Yeah," he said in a husky voice, eyes drifting to her lips. "You are, aren't you?"

They were close enough now they were nearly touching. Fey froze as he reached up to touch her face gently, his thumb tracing the corner of her mouth.

"You have chocolate on your face," he told her. Fey's breath caught as he drew his thumb over her bottom lip. Then it was gone,

Jasper bringing that finger to his mouth to lazily lick the chocolate off.

"If you eat one more crumb of my brownie," Fey whispered, trying to ignore the quaver in her own voice. Her skin was hot where he'd touched her. "I will skin you and hang your pelt behind the bar."

Jasper laughed and opened his mouth to reply. But then his eye snapped to something behind her, and the laughter died on his lips. He straightened, pulling away from Fey, his eyes narrowing.

"Viv?" Jasper asked, a mix of irritation and concern in his voice. "What are you doing here? Is everything okay?"

Fey turned, following his gaze across the empty club. No, not empty, not quite. There was a teenaged girl there, striding across the vacant dance floor, smiling sheepishly at them as she approached. Her soft brown hair was just long enough to brush over the top of her shoulders as she walked.

She's the spitting image of Jasper, Fey noticed. The golden-brown hair, the green eyes speckled with grey, even his full, pouty lips. Hell, she even had his crooked smile.

"Everything's fine," the girl said with a shrug. The bag on her shoulder shifted with the movement, a strap coming loose and falling down her arm until she tugged it back into place. "I was just bored, so I figured I'd come here and—"

"You're supposed to be with Nan today," Jasper interrupted, eyes narrowing and face darkening. His voice was a soft growl. "Nan in the evenings every night this week—you know that, Vivian. So why are you *here?*"

Vivian rolled her eyes. "Nan is taking a nap," she explained. "She's always taking a nap, Jas. And there's nothing to do at her place, anyway, so I thought—"

"Stop," Jasper interrupted, holding his hand up. "You did not think. Fuck, Viv, you're not old enough to be in here. Who even let you in?"

Vivian pouted, pushing her bottom lip out dramatically as she gestured over her shoulder at the door. "Mara did. She knows me, Jas. And I asked her if you were here before she let me in, by the way. It's not like I just walked into a bar, okay?"

Jasper's growl was low and vicious in his throat. His eyes shot to the door of the club. "She's only sixteen, Mar!" he shouted across the bar. "You can't let a sixteen-year-old in a fucking night club!"

"I'm almost seventeen!" Vivian argued, raising her voice to match Jasper's and stamping her foot. Fey took a sip from her drink to hide her smile. The other Wolves working at The Last Drop treated Jasper with the same wary respect and obedience as they did Ferus, the club's assistant owner. It was a treat seeing this kid go head-to-head with him, completely without fear. "And the club is closed anyway, so it's not like I'm in any danger or—"

"Go home, Vivian," Jasper told her. "Closed or not, this isn't any place for a kid. Go back to Nan's."

The girl just rolled her eyes. "I'm not a kid, Uncle Jas, I just—" She stopped suddenly, spotting Fey. Her eyes widened, and her fingers rose to tug at her hair, almost nervously.

"You're her, aren't you?" Vivian asked, taking a few steps toward her. "The Broken Blade?"

The name twisted in Fey's stomach, mixing unpleasantly with the chocolate and alcohol there.

Jasper rolled his eyes.

"Fey," he said, irritation clouding his voice. "This is my sister's kid, Vivian. Viv, this is Fey. I'm sure she's thrilled to meet you, but she has to go home now. Don't you, Viv?"

"I recognize you from the posters," Vivian said, ignoring Jasper entirely and reaching inside her bag to pull one out. Fey recognized it immediately.

Let me out, that Fire roared inside her. A sneer rose to her lips.

"Oh, no, these aren't mine!" Vivian said, seeing the cold look of rage pass over Fey's face and quickly shoving the poster back into her bag and out of sight. "I... I tear them down when I see them around the neighborhood. These are just from my walk over here." She looked a little sheepish, as though she realized that bringing up the posters was a mistake.

True to her word, all the posters peeking out of Vivian's bag were torn, as though they'd been ripped from their nails.

"Sorry if I shouldn't do that... I just figured, like, if you wanted to be queen, why would you have gone through all of that trouble, you know? Why kill the old queen and...and start the council and everything?"

"I didn't start the council," Fey said, automatically. "I have nothing to do with it." That was Alice's domain, not hers. Fey popped the last bit of brownie in her mouth and chewed, letting the taste dull the flare of anger she'd felt. It was an almost touching gesture that Jasper's niece spent time taking down the posters. She wondered if that was the reason she saw so few of them in the Shifter district.

"But... you did kill the Queen, didn't you?" the girl pressed, taking another step toward her.

Fey hadn't. But it was a lie she was happy to keep living with, so she nodded.

"That was cool, you know?" Vivian continued, giving Fey a small, shy smile. She tucked a strand of hair behind her ear. "Everything you did, I mean. To try to fix what she broke...to try to make it better, for everyone, even... even us."

Fey forced a smile.

"Thanks," she said. "It's nice to meet you, Viv."

"Vivian," the girl said, pulling a face and tugging her bag over her shoulder again. "You can just call me Vivian. Only Uncle Jas ever calls me Viv. Well, him and Alastair. All my friends call me—"

"*Home*, Viv," Jasper interrupted angrily.

"Oh, come on," Vivian whined. "Look, I'm bored, okay? And I could be out there"—she gestured at the exit behind her, toward the neighborhood streets—"getting into trouble and causing mischief, but instead I'm here, aren't I? And I thought... maybe Alastair could give me a job, you know? And then you wouldn't have to worry about where I am, would you?"

Her eyes sparkled hopefully when she said it, and she gave Jasper a crooked grin that was a mirror image of his own.

"You're too young," he insisted. "And you are out there causing mischief all the time, so don't give me that. I only hear about a portion of what you and your friends get up to, and even that is too much. If Nan knew, she'd have a heart attack, I can promise you that."

"Well, maybe I wouldn't be causing so much trouble if I had a job. Did you ever think of that?"

Jasper sighed loudly, and Vivian shot Fey a victorious smile.

Setting her bag down on the bar, Vivian hopped up onto the stool next to Fey. Her feet didn't quite reach the floor.

"What're you drinking?" she asked, looking at the glass in Fey's hand and cocking her head.

"A Shirley Temple," Fey lied, taking a sip and shooting Jasper a glance, daring him to correct her.

Vivian leaned forward and sniffed the air. She scrunched up her nose. "Doesn't smell like a Shirley Temple to me... smells like alcohol... and the stuff Uncle Jas uses to clean the windows."

"It is alcohol, which is why you shouldn't be here, Viv," Jasper started. "Grab your bag. I'm taking you home."

"Please, Jas," Vivian pleaded. "Just let me talk to Alastair. I know he'll understand. I don't have to serve drinks or anything. I can just... clean up, or help Mara at the door. Or maybe even help Ferus beat people up. I know I'd be good at it. I'm so much stronger than the other Wolves my age. Please."

Jasper opened his mouth to argue again, but before he could, another voice cut through the quiet of the bar. A voice that sent a delicious tendril of heat through Fey's body.

"Well, hello Vivian," Alastair said in a voice dark as midnight. He came down the stairs from the upper level of the club slowly, hands in his pockets. Fey turned to watch him. He moved like a predator, full of coiled energy and menace. It was a joy to watch him move. "It's always such a fun surprise when my bouncers let a child into my club."

Alastair wore his usual work attire—a black suit and tie—though the tie hung open and unknotted at his collar, like he'd dressed in a hurry. Fey would have bet all the gold in their bank that the sun had just set seconds ago, and Alastair had used every bit of his preternatural speed to rush to see her.

"I'm not a child," Vivian insisted. "And I'm here for a job, so it's not like I snuck in to get drunk or anything. I just want to help clean up or run security. I promise I'd do a good job."

"I can't hire minors," Alastair explained, reaching the bottom of the stairs and crossing the empty dance floor toward them. "Even if they are just cleaning." He glanced away from her, eyes locking on Fey's. Hunger danced in those golden eyes.

Vivian pouted.

"Come back when you're eighteen, and then we can talk about a job," Alastair told Vivian, a clear dismissal.

He came to a stop next to Fey, standing so close she could feel the heat from his body. Smiling down at her, he reached up to run a finger down her cheek.

It was such a small thing, such a tiny gesture. And it shouldn't provoke such a reaction. Still... Fey's eyes fluttered shut as his finger traced down her skin, leaning into that touch. It was automatic, this reaction to him.

"Hello, Witchling," Alastair greeted her. "Aren't you a sight for sore eyes?"

CHAPTER 6
ALASTAIR

He'd felt her the moment he'd woken up. The instant the sun had gone down and his eyes had opened for the night, he knew she was nearby. It was like waking up in a lightning storm. Like waking up to a tornado in your home.

Fey.

His Witchling was here.

Alastair hadn't bothered with showering. Hell, he hadn't even bothered to dress properly. Her presence pulled him to her like a vortex, and he was oh so happy to be pulled under.

"I'm so glad to see you," he told her, voice husky. He touched her cheek softly, brushing his fingers lightly over her pale skin. He couldn't stop himself from touching her whenever she was around. He was addicted to the feel of her skin.

Goddess, she was beautiful. Fey's eyes slid closed, and when she leaned into his hand, it took all of his admittedly limited self-control not to prop her up on the bar and take her right then. To show her how he really wanted to touch her...

"Why do I have to wait until I'm eighteen? That's a stupid fucking rule," Vivian was saying, crossing her arms and glaring at them.

He'd almost forgotten they were there. Alastair managed to break his attention away from Fey, and look to Jasper instead, raising an eyebrow.

"Language," Jasper scolded Vivian, and she glared at him instead.

"What?" she asked. "You say it all the time, Uncle Jas. Fuck, fuck, fuckity fuck."

"Okay, that's it," Jasper told her, unlatching the section of the bar that opened to let himself out. "Come on. I'm taking you back to Nan's."

Vivian scowled at him and snatched her bag from the bar as he took her by the arm to lead her out. But she turned when they were halfway across the dance floor and shouted over her shoulder.

"Good to see you, Alastair! And nice meeting you, Fey!"

Alastair chuckled, watching them leave and giving her the smallest wave goodbye.

"That girl is a menace," he murmured to Fey as the door shut behind them. "And she'll only get worse once she's actually old enough to work here, mark my words."

"I didn't know Jasper was an uncle," Fey said, absently. "I didn't even know he had a sister. He's never talked about her."

Alastair's smile slipped.

"Her name was Alicia," he told Fey in a low voice. "She used to work here."

Fey's eyes flashed as the memory surfaced. "Wait... Alicia? The bartender who was murdered by her boyfriend?" she asked. "That was Jasper's *sister*?"

Alastair nodded.

Once, years ago, Fey had invoked the memory of that night as evidence that Alastair wasn't the cold-hearted bastard he claimed to be. As though painfully eviscerating the asshole who'd taken Alicia's life and leaving pieces of him around the city somehow made him *a good guy*.

Alastair glanced over at the dark cloud of rage filling Fey's eyes and almost smiled. Maybe in Fey's eyes that's exactly what it made him.

"I'm glad you killed him," Fey said decisively. "The fucker deserved it."

"He did."

He could still picture Alicia, like it was just yesterday. She'd been so happy, so full of life before that dipshit had come along. He'd deserved what Alastair had done to him, and more.

"That's how Jasper started working here, you know," Alastair told her. "I convinced him to step up and take Alicia's job. Vivian's dad had never been in the picture, and Jasper was already helping raise her. They needed the cash. Times were hard for the Shifters, back then."

"Vivian's dad wasn't the one who...?"

"No," Alastair answered, cutting her off. "No, he was just someone Alicia had been seeing on and off for a while, years and years before I knew her. Actually, if I remember correctly, Vivian's father came from your Faction." He grinned at her, eyes twinkling. "You Witches enjoy taking a ride on the wild side, don't you?"

Fey rolled her eyes.

Stepping closer, Alastair brushed her hair from her shoulder. With Fey here, he didn't want to be thinking about the past. He wanted his full attention on her.

"Not that I'm complaining, Witchling, but what brings you here tonight?" he asked, changing the subject. "Is everything alright?"

Fey took a deep breath and leaned into his chest, her body relaxing against him. "I had a bad day. I needed some company."

His arms rose to wrap around her automatically, pulling her closer.

"I can be very good company," he promised. He could feel her smile against his chest.

"I'm sure you can," she answered, a teasing lilt to her voice.

"Come with me, Witchling," Alastair said, pulling her to a stand and smiling down at her. "Why don't we go up to my office, and I can show you just what good company I can be?"

She let him lead the way.

HIS OFFICE HAD CHANGED VERY little in the years since he had first encountered her, digging through his desk. Still, Fey considered the room carefully, as though memorizing it.

"I miss this place," Fey admitted. Her eyes moved around the room, pausing for several breaths on his bookshelves and the armchair he kept next to them.

"Does it bring back memories?" Alastair asked, shutting the door behind them and turning the lock.

Fey glanced over her shoulder at him, smiling wickedly. "Oh yes," she laughed. "It does."

Alastair chuckled low in his throat, moving behind her and wrapping his arms around her midsection, burying his face in her neck. "You should make a habit of visiting me more often at work, Witchling. I miss you when I'm here. Your visits go a long way to dull the monotony."

"Is that so?" she asked, leaning back into him. Goddess, she felt good pressed against him. He groaned, running his hands over the curves of her body.

"You got a new desk," Fey noticed, smiling.

"I did," Alastair answered, brushing her long red hair aside and kissing the back of her neck. "And I made sure this new one was... properly reinforced."

Fey chuckled, and it was such a delicious sound he couldn't help himself from licking her neck where the noise had come from.

"Alastair..." she started, a slight warning in her voice. But she'd wanted a distraction, hadn't she? He could be distracting. He could be very, *very* distracting.

He ignored the warning, licking up her neck again and earning a soft gasp from her.

"I've missed you," he whispered into her neck.

"You saw me just last night," she reminded him, her voice slightly breathless. She writhed against him.

He *had* seen her last night. Had spent the entire evening in bed with her, keeping her up late into the night, worshiping her with his tongue.

"Far too long ago," he murmured, kissing down the back of her neck.

Her answering laugh quickly turned to a moan as he bit down lightly on her throat. His hands moved further down, gripping her hips and pressing her even closer against him. He needed to feel her, every part of her.

"Jasper was flirting with me again, you know," she teased, and Alastair's hands paused.

"Oh?" he asked, moving to the other side of her neck, kissing and biting at the skin there. "What a naughty little puppy." Fey smiled and relaxed back into him, enjoying the attention.

"And did you like it, Witchling?" he asked. The soft pink blush that rose to her cheeks was answer enough. Keeping one hand on her hip, he brought the other to the tie hanging loosely around his neck.

"Maybe you need reminding who you belong to, hm?" he asked in a dark voice, nipping at her ear.

Fey laughed.

"Oh, Alastair," she said, her voice dripping with venom. "I don't belong to anyone."

Oh yes, that's what he'd wanted to hear. As he pulled the tie from around his neck, he slid his fangs over the sensitive skin of her throat and was rewarded with a soft gasp.

"We'll see about that. Hands, Witchling," he ordered.

Fey smirked, glancing over her shoulder at him. But she complied, putting her hands before her and crossing her wrists. She stayed that way as he looped the tie around her wrists, binding them together.

"Alastair," she warned as he tightened the knot, pulling a little harder than necessary.

"You're *mine*, Witchling," he said, lips pressed to her ear, and she moaned softly, arching against him. "Don't forget that."

The top she wore hugged her curves tightly. *So fucking perfect*. He dropped her wrists, hands circling her waist and moving up her curves until he cupped her breasts, squeezing them hard enough to elicit another gasp from her.

Goddess damn him. He loved that sound. Loved that he could make her moan like that, loved how she responded to him. His fingers circled her nipple through the thin fabric of her shirt and pinched until she arched against him again.

He turned her around, so she faced him, and took her face in his hands. She was so beautiful, her eyes alight with desire for him. And just a trace of fear.

So perfect.

"On your knees, Witchling," he commanded, stroking her cheek softly with the pad of his thumb.

Fey smiled at him, something wild and dangerous flashing in her eyes.

"Make me," she challenged.

Alastair grinned. He loved this. Loved that challenge that flashed in her eyes, loved the resistance. He lowered his mouth to hers, his lips hovering right above hers as he repeated the command.

"*On your knees.*" He wrapped the words in persuasion this time. An ancient gift, one few Vampires possessed. Immediately she complied, dropping gracefully to her knees in front of him, without a single thought. He kept his hand on her face, tilting her chin up toward him and smiling down at her in victory.

Fey's expression changed, rage flaring to life behind her eyes.

"Fuck your persuasion," she snapped. "That's cheating." But she made no move to stand or fight off his influence.

He ran his thumb along the curve of her bottom lip. He could spend all day looking at her like this, down on her knees for him. Could spend his whole life just like this, and he would thank the Goddess for every blessed second.

But he had bigger plans.

"*Suck,*" he commanded, pushing the tip of his thumb into her mouth as the persuasion took her. Her lips wrapped around the tip of his finger, and her eyes closed as she sucked greedily on it, her tongue teasing the pad of his thumb.

"Good girl," he told her, pulling the thumb from her mouth and dragging it down her face.

"Fuck you," she spat.

"Tell me to stop," he teased. He let go of her face, his hands moving to his belt instead. Her eyes followed his fingers hungrily. When he undid his belt and paused, her tongue darted out to wet her lips. "Tell me to stop and I will, Witchling. You know I will."

She didn't. She watched him remove his belt, watched him unzip his pants slowly and take his cock out, his fingers trailing down the length.

"Tell me to stop," he said, again, threading his hand in her hair and twisting her face to look up at him.

Eyes blazing, Fey held his gaze and said nothing.

"*Suck*," he commanded again, and Fey moaned as she shifted forward and took his cock in her mouth.

CHAPTER 7

FEY

The noise Alastair made as she swallowed him sent a jolt of heat down her body and straight between her legs. Fey let out a desperate sound of her own as her lips stretched around his length and she took him deep in her throat.

He knew she could fight off his persuasion whenever she wanted. It was even easier now, with all four elements at her command. She could shrug off his influence like it was nothing.

But it was nice to let go like this. To let someone else take control.

As her tongue rolled over him, Fey let herself go, surrendering completely to his command.

"Fuck, Fey." Alastair shuddered, his hand clutching her hair and his head tipping back. "Your mouth feels so good."

Fey's eyes shut, and she moaned around him again. With her hands tied in front of her, she couldn't touch herself, and her body craved his attention. She wanted his hands on her, wanted to feel him in more than just her mouth.

"Such a good Witch," he whispered, and Fey's groan turned to a snarl. Alastair chuckled, Goddess damn him, gripping her hair hard and pulling her even closer, pushing his length further into her throat. Then, just as suddenly, he pulled her away, yanking his cock out of her mouth.

Hand still gripping her hair, he pulled her up and off her knees until she was standing in front of him. He was still smirking at her, that cruel smile, and a part of her wanted to slap it off his face.

"What's wrong, Witchling?" he said, mockingly. "Don't you like being my good girl?"

She did. She loved it, and he knew it. Just hearing him say it made her wet. But she ground her teeth together, staring him down.

"I don't belong to you, Alastair," she taunted him. "And I'm not a *good* anything."

He laughed, stepping closer into her space and forcing her to step backwards. Back, back, until she felt the wood of his desk against the back of her thighs. He lifted her up onto the desk and then pulled her down by her hair until she was laid before him like a sacrifice.

"I think you're lying," he mocked, face so close to hers she felt his breath against her lips. His tongue snaked out, teasing her lips, making her arch and writhe beneath him. When he finally kissed her, she was desperate for it, opening her mouth for him and letting him take what he wanted.

Alastair's teeth scraped against her lips before he pulled back. His hand left her hair and gripped her wrists, still bound, forcing them above her head and pinning her to the desk. When he straightened, Fey felt the loss of him pressed against her like an ache. With a dark chuckle, he dragged his free hand down her body, feeling her over her clothes.

Fey arched off the desk, needing that touch, craving it. His fingers were like fire on her skin, and she was burning from it. He stared hungrily down at her as his fingers paused at the waist of her pants.

"You still want to pretend you don't belong to me, Witchling?" he asked, slipping his fingers under her clothing and sliding them over her center. Fey bowed off the desk, gasping, as his fingertips teased her. "You and I both know that's a lie. Tell me who you belong to, Fey."

Fuck, he knew exactly how to touch her. Fey moaned, head rolling as his fingers worked, bringing her closer and closer to the edge.

"Tell me," he repeated. When she didn't answer, he paused, then pushed his fingers inside her, curling them until she cried out, loud enough to be heard through the thick wooden door of his office.

His fingers worked inside her as the palm of his hand settled against her, rubbing her. Fey's breath was coming in ragged pants, and she locked eyes with Alastair above her.

Dark hunger swirled in his eyes as he focused on her pleasure. *Good.* That meant he was distracted.

Fey summoned a gust of air with barely a flick of her fingers, and though it was nothing compared to what she could do if her hands were free, it caught him off guard. He grunted in shock as a blast of wind hit his shoulder, pushing him off her and away for a moment.

"I don't belong to you or anyone, Alastair," she teased with a grin.

His eyes shuttered, something dark and dangerous rising in his gaze. *Uh oh.*

Fey had no time to react before he was on her, and she found herself flipped over onto her stomach on the desk. Alastair pulled her pants down roughly and brought the palm of his hand down on her ass with a smack.

Fey yelped, half in pain and half in shock.

"Do you like that?" he asked, roughly, his hand rubbing against the mark he'd made on her skin. She groaned, but it turned into another yelp as he slapped her again, the sound ringing across his office.

"Alastair—" she started, but his fingers slipped insider her again and she broke off, all words forgotten.

"Fuck, I love seeing you like this," he told her, voice guttural. "So wet and needy for me. Practically dripping down my hand. You love this don't you, Witchling?"

She was close. Fey's fingernails dug into the wood of the desk as she pushed back against his hand. Her back arched and her hips rolled as she lost herself in the sensation, chasing her climax.

And just like that, it was gone. Alastair pulled his fingers from her without warning. She heard the telltale rustle of fabric as he undressed behind her. Her pussy clenched, mourning the loss of those skilled fingers, but before she could complain, she felt him shift to stand directly behind her. His hands gripped her hips, holding her tight.

"Oh no you don't," he told her. "You don't come until I tell you to."

His cock pushed against her entrance, and she writhed in his grip, wanting to push back, wanting to take him.

"Will you come for me?" he asked, pushing the head of his cock against her, teasing her with it.

Fey whimpered, desperately clawing at the desk.

"Answer me," he snapped. He slapped an open palm against her again and gripped her tighter, his fingers digging into her flesh. "Will you come for me, Fey?"

Fey couldn't push herself closer to him, not while he held her so tight. She groaned, struggling helplessly in his grasp.

"Yes!" she gasped, trying and failing to push against him. She'd say anything, anything he wanted to finish what they'd started. Anything to feel that touch again.

"Such a good girl," he murmured as he thrust inside her.

Fey screamed as he filled her, stretching her. It didn't seem to matter how often they did this, how often or how hard they fucked, it was still a shock to her body to accommodate him.

Stars exploded in her vision as he pulled out and thrust back into her, hard enough the desk jolted forward.

His hand moved up the curve of her ass as he moved inside of her, coming to rest on the small of her back. He pushed, gently, with his palm.

"Arch your back for me, Witchling."

She did unquestioningly, eager to have more of him inside of her. The sensation immediately changed as her body arched, the tip of his cock hitting somewhere new inside of her and making her gasp.

Alastair swore, his hands gripping on her hips. "*Fuck yes*, just like that."

Her legs were shaking, and her body quivered underneath him.

"That's right, Witchling," he groaned, as though reading her mind. "You're so close, aren't you? Come for me. Be a good girl and come on my cock."

He thrust into her again and again, and she couldn't take it anymore. With one last scream she lost herself, body shuddering as she reached her peak and exploded, the world disappearing under a wave of pleasure.

"Fuck, Fey," Alastair groaned behind her, "I can't—"

He moaned and shuddered, burying himself deep inside her as he joined her in his release.

Fey gasped as they finished, her body collapsing fully onto the desk, her muscles exhausted. Her heart was beating so hard she thought she might pass out.

"You okay, Witchling?" Alastair asked, panting as he fought to catch his breath. He leaned over her, planting a kiss gently between her shoulder blades, and reached for the tie around her wrists. His fingers tugged the knots free, pulling the fabric loose.

She nodded, cheek pressed flat against the desk.

"You're sure?" he prodded with a chuckle. She groaned as he pulled out of her, the noise turning to a whimper a second later as she felt something soft and silk between her legs, cleaning her. His tie, she realized.

"I'm sure," she said, her words coming out in gasps. "But... I'm not sure I can move my legs."

Her legs trembled from supporting herself on the tips of her toes against the desk. Alastair laughed, and suddenly she was being lifted into his arms and tucked tight against his body.

Fey breathed in his scent and eagerly nuzzled against him. He carried her to his desk chair, seating himself and settling her on his lap until she rested comfortably against his chest.

"That wasn't too rough, was it?" he asked.

"Goddess no," Fey laughed. "Though... I may have a bruise in the shape of your hand on my ass for a few days."

"Good," Alastair said, peppering her cheek with gentle kisses. "I want you remembering this every time you try to sit down."

Letting out a contented sigh, she cuddled closer to him, wanting to feel as much of his skin against hers as possible. She loved this. Not just the sex, but the aftermath. Alastair could never seem to stop touching her, after. Like he couldn't get enough of her.

His hands caressed her, moving gently over her body. When they reached her wrists, Alastair paused, fingers skimming over the damaged and bloody skin of her knuckles.

"What happened today?" he asked, raising her fingers to his lips and kissing the wounds there.

"It doesn't matter," she said, too exhausted and content to go into it.

Alastair's jaw clenched, and he gripped her hand hard enough to hurt.

"Oh no, Witchling," he told her in a dark voice. "You don't run from me. Not ever. Tell me what happened."

Fey sucked in a breath. He loosened his grip on her but didn't let her go.

"I... lost control," she admitted.

"Lost control?" he repeated in a tactfully neutral voice. "And what does that mean, you 'lost control'?"

"Well," she demurred, running her hands over his bare chest, feeling the hard muscle under his skin. "Today that meant I nearly burned down Regina's Bakery..."

Alastair chuckled. "Oh, I bet she loved that."

"It wasn't her fault," Fey told him. "Wasn't my fault either, not really. But..." Her jaw tightened. "There was a Witch. Two Witches. They called me *queen*, and..." She paused. "I lost control. Only for a moment, but that was enough."

Alastair waited patiently for her to continue.

"I just... I'm trying to control it," Fey explained. She dropped her hands from his chest and stared down at them. Hands that had taken countless lives. "The anger. The rage. I'm trying to hold it back—"

"Why?" Alastair interrupted.

Fey stopped. She glanced up and stared into his eyes. He was serious.

"I'm dangerous, Alastair," she told him.

He quirked an eyebrow at her. "I know that, Fey," he said. "And *you* know that. So why hide it from them?"

"Because..." How was he not understanding this? "Because when they look at me, they don't see someone who's dangerous. They look at me like I'm... like I'm here to save them. Rule them. They don't see what's really inside me, they don't see this... this destruction inside me."

"So let them see it."

Fey rolled her eyes.

"I'm serious, Fey," Alastair insisted. He grabbed her hips tightly and maneuvered her until she was straddling him. "They don't see you. The real you. They don't see what you are. So why are you trying to hold back? Why aren't you letting them see it?"

Why...?

"Because it's dangerous," Fey answered. Her voice sounded so small.

"*You're* dangerous. You said so yourself." Alastair said. He took her face in his hands. "Listen to me, Witchling. This is who you are. Why are you running from it? Why are you trying to make yourself less, for *them*?" He spat the last word out, like it left a bad taste in his mouth. "For the last year, I've watched you try to make yourself smaller and smaller, and I've held my tongue. But I won't, not anymore. You're not a queen, Fey. You're a fucking goddess."

"Don't be blasphemous," Fey warned him, narrowing her eyes.

Alastair grinned. "You're *my* goddess, then. Stop trying to be what they see and be yourself. Let it out, Witchling. All that power, all that *rage*. Stop *trying* to hold it back. Let them see it. Let them see *you*."

Something in Fey's chest roared with approval at that.

Alastair leaned forward, kissing her lips softly before he added. "Let it out, Witchling. If you don't want them to kneel to you, fine. They can cower instead."

Fey smirked. "And if I burn down Regina's store?" she asked, trailing her fingers down his chest.

"We'll buy her another," Alastair said, matching her grin. "We have the money. Hell, we'll buy her two, for the inconvenience."

He leaned forward, pressing a kiss to her chest.

"And if I burn down the entire city?" Fey asked.

Alastair kissed up to her collarbone. "Then you can rule over the ashes, Witchling. And I'll be right there beside you."

Fey moaned as he licked up to her neck.

"Stop holding yourself back. Let it out, Witchling. Let all of it out. If you're angry, be angry. If you want to burn them all, then do it," he spoke into her skin. "But never make yourself less, not for anyone."

Let me out, that pulse beat inside her.

So she did.

Tilting her head back and with Alastair's arms locked around her, Fey let her power out.

Fire filled her, but it wasn't an inferno like she'd feared. White hot power unfurled just under her skin, flowing from her chest all the way to her fingers and toes.

Alastair groaned against her skin. Could he feel it? Feel that power coalescing inside of her? Fey let more of herself go.

Water came next, and she hadn't even realized she'd been holding that part of herself back, using it as a weapon to keep her rage in check.

Fey reveled in the power inside her. Her body relaxed as she let herself go. Maybe Alastair was right. Maybe she didn't need to hold it back. Her Fire stayed under her skin, warming her but releasing no flames.

"Do you feel that?" Alastair asked. "Do you feel all that power you've been neglecting?"

She did. And it felt incredible.

Taking her hand from his chest, Fey stared down at it, twisting her fingers, marveling at the power just under her skin. Electricity cracked, and for a moment lightning arched between her fingertips.

"Well, that's new," Alastair said, staring at her hand in wonder.

It was. And it was lovely. Fey watched the power, watched it arch between her fingertips again, and smiled.

"You're so beautiful," Alastair told her, taking her hand and licking up her palm. A spark jolted over his tongue. "I love you, Witchling."

Fey froze. And all that power rising inside of her evaporated away to nothing.

It wasn't the first time he'd said it. She'd heard him whisper it before when he thought she wouldn't hear. Heard him murmur it as she fell asleep in his arms.

But he had never said it to her face.

Sensing her tension, Alastair leaned back to look at her.

"I—" Fey opened her mouth, her heart suddenly racing.

Alastair pressed his fingers to her lips, cutting her off. "You don't need to say it back to me. Not yet."

"What if I never say it?" Fey asked, lips brushing against his fingers. Her mind was reeling. Had she ever said it to anyone? She loved her sisters, more than anything, but had she ever even said it to them? She couldn't recall.

"Then you never say it," Alastair said, leaning back in his chair like it didn't matter at all. "You never have to." His fingers traced her lower lip. "Besides," he said with a growing smirk. "I don't need to hear you say it. I already know you love me."

Fey snorted. "Is that so?"

"I mean, look at me." He raised an eyebrow, gesturing down at himself. Fey couldn't help but look, running her eyes over his body and biting her lip. "Who wouldn't love this?"

"Goddess, you're arrogant," she said with a laugh.

He smiled, taking her hand to kiss her wounded knuckles again, and Fey realized how quickly he'd managed to calm her, how expertly he handled her rush of fear.

He sees me, Fey thought, watching him run his tongue over her skin. *Truly sees me.*

And, even more, he accepted her. Her rage, her power, her moods. He saw it all. And he cherished it.

"I love you, too," Fey told him, and Alastair stopped, eyes flashing as they jumped up to capture her gaze.

"Witchling," he started, voice husky.

"Don't make a big thing of it," Fey said quickly, pulling her hand back from his grasp.

"How can I not?" Alastair asked, pulling her close. She struggled playfully as he wrapped his arms around her, pulling her hard against his chest and kissing and licking at the bare skin of her arms, her shoulders. Her neck.

Fey groaned as his teeth slid across the sensitive pulse of her neck, grinding against him.

"What did I do to deserve you?" he asked.

"Something wicked, no doubt," she laughed.

"Stay here with me tonight," Alastair murmured against her neck.

Fey shook her head, laughing. "Not tonight. I have work in the morning, and I'm not sleeping on that awful mattress you have up in your room. You know it's impossible to get any sleep in this place."

Alastair pulled a face. "Come now, it's not that bad. I'm sure you could—"

As if on cue, the music from the club started, a deep thumping bass that shook the furniture enough to make the books rattle. Fey laughed.

"You think I could sleep through this, Alastair? That anyone could sleep through this?" she asked mockingly. He frowned, and she leaned forward to plant a soft kiss on his lips. "I'll see you tomorrow evening, right? Ferus is running things then?"

Reluctantly, Alastair nodded. "He is."

"Good." She gave him one more lingering kiss, then hopped off his lap. "We can have dinner together tomorrow, after I get home from work. But I'm getting out of here before it gets too busy."

"Fine," he said, watching her as she gathered her clothes. "But Fey?"

She turned toward him, pulling her pants back up to her waist. "What?"

A smile broke across his face. "I love you," he cooed.

Fey snatched his tie from the ground to chuck it at his face.

CHAPTER 8

JASPER

The floor shook with every bass line from the club's music, the beat so strong you could feel it in your bones. Jasper moved to the rhythm of it, weaving effortlessly around Sid—the other Wolf bartending tonight—to grab another bottle.

He lived for this. Lived for the almost deafening roar of the music, the burn of alcohol in his blood, the tipsy haze that descended on him at this point in the night. He was always careful to never get drunk at work, not *really* drunk, but on nights like this he enjoyed walking that fine line between buzzed and messy.

This was exactly what he needed after that unexpected visit from his niece. She had pulled out every trick in her book to delay him and convince him to let her hang out at the bar with Alastair and Fey. By the time he'd finally managed to get back to work, he was running late for his shift and Ferus had been pissed off enough to make him work at the VIP bar instead of downstairs.

Not that Jasper cared much either way. Slinging drinks up here with Sid wasn't much different from slinging them down there. The patrons were just as drunk, just as horny, and the music was just as good.

Maybe it wasn't such a bad idea for Vivian to work here, actually. Hell, at least he could keep an eye on her if she was here, make sure she wasn't getting into too much trouble. Half the time she was meant to be with her Nan, Jasper suspected she was actually out with her friends, causing mischief.

Her mother had been like that when they were kids.

So had Jasper, come to think of it.

Is this how Nan had felt when she was trying to raise the two of them?

Goddess help her, Jasper and Alicia had likely been even worse. It's any wonder Nan lived long enough to see her granddaughter take up the mantle.

But thoughts of Vivian and Nan all felt distant now that he was here, in his element. Here, where he belonged. On the other side of the VIP bar, Sid popped the cork on a bottle of bubbly for a group of university students, celebrating the end of their exams. Their merriment was contagious.

A Demon with wicked eyes and feathers weaved in his hair ordered a round of shots for his friends, and Jasper filled them to the brim after he'd lined them up, adding an extra one for himself. He flashed Sid a wink as he downed it, and the other Wolf returned it with a laugh. This was the life. Good booze, loud music, and the scent of lust heavy in the air.

The Witch currently trying to catch his eye wore that smell of lust like a heavy perfume. She leaned over the bar far enough that her breasts threatened to spill out of her top, biting her lip when he finally came over to get her order. Jasper gave her a flirty grin as he poured her drink and wasn't surprised when she slipped her number across the bar toward him before she left.

The slip of paper went into the trash the moment her back was turned. The motion was so automatic, Jasper didn't even question it.

Not that the Witch wasn't attractive. She was stunning, and those curves were to die for. A couple of years ago, she wouldn't have had to slip him her number at all. He would have already been leading her to the stockroom, with one hand snaking up her skirt to feel those delicious curves, excited to show her a good time.

But something had changed. And with the music and the booze and the wonderfully numb drunk he had going tonight, he didn't want to think too hard about what it could be. Didn't want to think about why he couldn't seem to bring himself to enjoy his random hookups anymore.

For now, he didn't want to think at all. He wanted to have fun.

He wanted to be a little numb.

When a familiar face appeared in the crowd, coming from the back hallway and making his way toward the bar, Jasper's grin widened and his good mood rose even more. Right on schedule.

"Evening, boss," Jasper shouted over the music as Alastair leaned an elbow against the bar top, his eyes skirting over the crowd. Jasper was already pulling a bottle of whiskey from under the bar—the boss's favorite.

"Good crowd tonight," Alastair remarked, drumming his fingers on the wooden bar. He looked relaxed. Hell, he wasn't even wearing his tie.

Jasper grinned in answer and set a glass in front of him, glancing at the crowd as he poured. It *was* a good crowd tonight. Hell, business had been phenomenal lately. And it wasn't just the recent changes Ferus had started instituting, either. It was also the sudden surge in patrons from the Witch Faction. With any luck, this could be their best year yet. They were on track to make record profits this season, and—

Every cell in Jasper's brain stopped firing.

Mine.

The smell had been lost to the crowd, overpowered by the hundreds of other patrons who smelled like sex and lust and desperation. But when Alastair leaned closer to touch his glass, the scent hit Jasper like a bolt of lightning. A delicious, mouthwatering smell of sex and power.

Fey.

But not just her. He could smell both of them, their scents tangled together. Arousal and strength and heat. He groaned, every nerve in his body firing, every instinct inside him coming to life. That smell reached into his chest and pulled something there, something he'd been trying so desperately to ignore.

Mine.

Had anything ever smelled so amazing in all of creation? Was there anything—

"What the fuck, Jasper!" Alastair snapped, leaping back from the bar and the growing spill of whiskey. Jasper jolted back to life with a start. Liquor cascaded over the brim of the glass in front of him. He'd been so distracted he'd kept pouring into the already full glass until the bottle was nearly empty, and the boss's top shelf liquor was suddenly flooding the bar top.

Alastair flicked drops of whiskey off his fingers with a dark scowl.

"Sorry, boss." Jasper winced, grabbing a towel and trying to mop up the spill. Fuck, he was a mess. "I'll pay for it."

"What you just spilled probably cost more than your monthly salary, puppy," Alastair told him, watching Jasper's desperate attempt to mop it up.

When it was clear one measly bar towel wasn't doing the trick, Jasper gave Alastair an apologetic smile and ducked further behind the bar to grab some more.

Sid came over as he grabbed a handful of bar towels and chuckled sympathetically.

"At least he washed his hands," he grinned.

Jasper barely spared him a glance. "What?"

Nodding toward where Alastair stood, still wiping whiskey off his fingers, Sid's grin widened. "The boss. At least he washed his hands, you know? Trust me, it was worse earlier. He smelled so much like her pussy there wasn't a soft cock in the bar."

A growl started in Jasper's chest, lost to the music.

"You weren't here for it, were you?" Sid asked, laughing and shaking his head. "I forgot you were late for your shift tonight. They were, uh… not quiet about it. It was quite a show."

Jasper straightened, the spill forgotten. His hands flexed.

"You wouldn't believe the sounds that Witch makes," Sid continued. He threw back his head to groan, hand reaching down to grip himself over his pants. "I had to head to the stockroom to relieve some of the tension, if you know what I mean."

"What the fuck did you just say?" Jasper hissed.

Sid's smile slipped. He glanced at Jasper, and whatever he saw there left him pale.

"I didn't mean any disrespect," Sid said quickly, holding his palms up between them. "But you've seen her. You know how hot she is. I mean... fuck, the things I would do to that woman..."

Jasper shot forward to grab Sid by the throat. He slammed his back against the wall hard enough that the liquor bottles above the bar shook.

"You don't get to talk about her like that," Jasper snarled. Sid's eyes went wide with fear. Someone at the bar shouted. Someone else screamed. The music kept going, the heavy beat echoing in Jasper's skull. "You don't get to think about her like that. Do you understand me?"

Terrified, Sid nodded.

"Sorry, Jas, I-I wasn't thinking, I—"

"She's not yours to think about," Jasper continued, canines elongating. He was too close to shifting, too close to losing control. The hand tightening around Sid's throat began to grow razor-sharp claws. "She's not yours to fantasize about. She's—"

Mine.

The word rolled through his head and toward his lips with so much certainty it shocked him back to his senses.

Where had that thought come from?

What the hell was he doing? Jasper loosened his hand from around Sid's throat. The other Wolf immediately twisted to show more neck, submitting fully and whining in apology.

"I..." Jasper started.

"*Drop him,*" a furious voiced commanded.

Alastair. Jasper let go of Sid immediately and took a step back, eyes on the ground and his heart pounding. He couldn't seem to catch his breath. He could feel Alastair there, standing next to him, but he couldn't look at him, couldn't meet his eyes.

Mine. The word still echoed in his mind.

But Fey wasn't his. Wouldn't ever be his. Why had he felt that so strongly in that moment? Sure, they flirted; who wouldn't flirt with her? Like Sid said, she was gorgeous. It was just dumb fun, and that's where it ended.

Wasn't it?

"Sorry Jas," Sid murmured to Jasper. "It won't happen again."

"A free round for everyone," Alastair shouted, voice rising above the din of the crowd. The announcement was met with cheers. In a lower voice, he added, "Sid—get Ferus to pull someone from the lower bar and get enough liquor into this crowd to make them forget what they just saw. And Jasper?"

Licking his lips, Jasper fought through the haze in his head and managed to meet his stare. Alastair's face was tight with rage.

"My office," Alastair said, anger filling his voice. "*Now*."

Fuck.

Alastair didn't wait for a response. He just turned around and walked away, fury coming off him in waves.

Jasper took a deep breath. Then another. He managed to huff an apology to Sid, who graciously accepted it, before he dragged himself out from behind the bar and toward the back hallway. Toward the smell of them.

A large part of him wanted to run into that office, toward those intoxicating scents. Wanted it more than he'd wanted anything in his life.

Jasper forced himself to walk instead. It took him a long, long time to reach the office. And when he finally did, he couldn't bring himself to enter it. He just stood in the doorway, head down, trying to breathe through his mouth.

Alastair sat at his desk, his palms flat on the wooden surface before him. It was a stance Jasper had seen him take many times before. A stance right before he snapped and broke someone's neck.

When he spoke, Alastair's voice was dangerously low. "Close the door."

Jasper swallowed.

"With all due respect, boss," he managed to say, reaching up to rub the back of his neck, "I, uh... I'd rather not do that."

The idea of being trapped in this room, with these smells?

He wasn't sure he'd survive it.

The cold fury in Alastair's eyes only grew.

"I wasn't fucking asking," he said, coming to his feet. "I let you get away with a lot of shit around here, Jasper, and you know it. But assaulting one of my employees isn't one of them. You get one chance to explain to me what the fuck happened out there."

Jasper forced himself to look at him. Fuck, he was really pissed, wasn't he?

Screw it.

Jasper took a deep, shuddering breath through his nose and closed his eyes to savor it. Head back, eyes shut tight, he forced himself to say, "I made a mistake, boss. It won't happen again."

"Not good enough." Alastair's voice was tight with rage. "Try again."

It was so hard to concentrate when it smelled so good in here. Jasper took another deep breath. "Sid said something he shouldn't have. I had a problem with it." He licked his lips. "It won't happen again."

Alastair's eyes narrowed. "What did he say?"

"It doesn't matter—" Jasper started.

"It does fucking matter if I'm asking you. Tell me what he said."

"He said..." Jasper swallowed. "He made a comment about a woman. That he, uh... that he wanted to touch her."

Alastair blinked, slowly.

"That's it? That's all he said to you?" he asked. From the skeptical look in his eyes, he wasn't buying it for a second.

"And he may have jerked off in the stockroom," Jasper murmured.

"Jasper." Alastair tapped the surface of his desk for emphasis. "I, personally, have walked in on you fucking someone in that room on two separate occasions. Scratch that, three. Three separate occasions."

Jasper's lips twitched at the memory.

"I should be making one of you hose down that room once a week, with the amount of fluids that get exchanged in there. Who the fuck cares if Sid jerked off in the stockroom? What does it matter to you that he was talking shit about some woman?"

"It was Fey," Jasper said, so quietly he almost hoped Alastair couldn't hear him.

The Vampire went impossibly still.

"My Fey?" he asked.

Our Fey, something whispered in Jasper's chest. He swallowed it down. Fuck, he needed another drink. It was too quiet here. He wanted the music back.

"He said he heard you tonight. You and Fey. That he, uh... got excited, listening to her," Jasper explained.

A muscled twitched in Alastair's jaw.

"And that's why you lost control, isn't it?" he asked, voice low. "You were, what... protecting her?"

Jasper nodded, slowly.

"He had no right to talk about her like that," Jasper said, his temper rising again. His muscles itched to shift. "It was disrespectful. And... And I just lost it, I—"

"Are you trying to fuck her?" Alastair interrupted.

Jasper's heart stuttered. "What?"

"You heard me, puppy," Alastair said, stepping closer. His face was blank, but a storm raged in those amber eyes. "I've seen the way you look at her. I've seen the little ways you like to touch her. I've put up with the flirting, and kept my fucking mouth shut throughout all of it. But you need to answer the question right now. Do you want to fuck my Witch?"

The look in Alastair's eyes told Jasper he already knew the answer to that question.

Jasper took one last deep breath, closing his eyes to really enjoy it. He could taste her in the air. It was intoxicating.

When he opened his eyes to look at Alastair, he made no effort to hide the hunger in his gaze. Or what that smell was doing to him.

"Yeah," he answered calmly. His lips pulled up into a cocky grin. "Yeah, I want to fuck her. And if she ever asked me? I wouldn't even hesitate." Holding Alastair's gaze for a few moments longer, he added in a husky voice, "And I'd make sure it was a night she'd never forget."

Alastair's eyes glittered dangerously as he assessed the Wolf in front of him.

If those were his last words, at least he was going out honestly, Jasper thought to himself.

"Close the door, Jasper." Alastair said, his voice low. "I think it's time you and I had a little chat..."

CHAPTER 9
FEY

The sun crested the horizon, bringing a touch of warmth to the chilly morning air. Fey looked out at the Witches gathered before her on the palace lawn and smiled.

Time to begin.

"How many of you hold power over Air?" she asked, letting the wind carry her voice over the grounds. Today, she didn't need to enchant the words, to call Air to carry them further. The morning was still and crisp and the group watching her was silent as a grave. They were hanging on her every word.

Hands raised in answer—more than she'd expected.

Fey nodded as she stared at those raised hands, as though considering them, one by one.

"And how many of you can fly?" she asked.

Several of the Witches holding their hands up glanced at one another, confused. One by one they lowered their hands, until only one Witch remained, her hand high in the air and a playful smile on her face.

Fey smiled back at Joy from her spot above the crowd. The wreckage of Solare created a perfect stage on the palace lawn for these demonstrations, the terrain creating a natural platform from which she could instruct the Witches gathered below.

Fey had been teaching these classes for over a year, but this morning drew the largest crowd to date. Most of the Witches who attended these lessons were younger, many having just come into their powers. But others here were old enough to be mothers. Some were even grandmothers. These were Witches still learning to embrace their new powers, the ones taken from them during their Awakening on the old queen's orders. And now that entire crowd watched her, puzzled but excited.

"Joy?" Fey called out to the singular Air Witch still raising her hand. "Why don't you come up here and give us a demonstration?"

There were whispers in the crowd as Joy bounded up the lawn to join her, blonde hair flowing behind her on a gentle breeze. As the final living Queen's Blade, she was nearly as famous as Fey, though less recognizable. To see the last of the Queen's Blades with their own eyes was the sort of thing these Witches would go home and tell their families about. A story they'd pass down to their children.

Joy stepped in front of Fey, smiling at the surrounding crowd. Then, dramatically, she lifted her foot as though ascending a staircase. There was nothing below her as Joy stepped delicately into the air, first with one foot, then the other. But she rose, step by step, into the air above them and stood there, beaming down at everyone, several feet above the ground.

She wasn't flying, not really. She had merely made a solid block of Air to support herself. With a flourish, Joy took another step, and then another, ascending an invisible staircase above the crowd.

"Now most of you won't have the skill and control necessary to do what my sister here can do," Fey said. *And hopefully none of you have her flare for the dramatic*, she thought with a smirk as Joy spun in the air above them and bowed, smooth as a dancer. "But using concentrated air to slow your fall or even help you balance could mean the difference between life and death. That's what we'll be working on today. Air Witches—you're with me today. Everyone else? Leandra will be taking over your lessons on the Eastern lawn."

Joy gave one final twirl, then floated gracefully back to the grassy lawn.

Fey tried not to smile. Tried, and failed, her face breaking into a wide grin as Joy met her eyes and laughed.

It was nice to know that hadn't changed. Sometimes Fey felt like everything in her world was so wildly different now. But this? Her love for her sisters? The happiness they brought her every day? That was still the same.

"I can stay and help for a few hours, if you'd like," Joy told Fey as the students drifted into groups. Some of them moved across the lawn to join Leandra, the High Priestess of the Fire coven, and others stayed, eagerly awaiting their Air training. "Alice is sleeping anyway—the council meeting went late last night, and she came home exhausted."

Fey gave her a grateful nod. "Thanks. We'd really appreciate the help. And the students always love your instructions."

Across the lawn, Leandra had already divided the other Witches into smaller groups, sorting them by their elements and strengths.

Fey had laughed when the High Priestess of the Fire Coven had approached her about this—offering her a salary paid by a tithe from each coven to help instruct Witches in the city on how to use their powers. Fey had known her days of serving the Crown were far behind her, and that chapter of her life was stained with blood.

But Leandra wouldn't be persuaded to give up, and since the first class had only been four young Witches, Fey had figured what the hell. Why not? It would give her something to do. At least, until Leandra realized what a mistake she'd made and found someone better for the job.

But now that class of four was almost two hundred strong. And it was growing every day. Once word got out, Witches had come from all over the city, wanting to learn from her.

From the Queen's fabled Broken Blade.

Fey and Joy worked together for the morning, demonstrating how to concentrate air in one place to make it into something more solid. They took their time, moving amongst the Witches, offering helpful tips and correcting errors. Fey let Joy do most of the encouraging. Many of the Witches were still frightened of Fey, even those who she had worked with from the beginning. She'd figured out over time that while they might be fine learning from her, most weren't entirely comfortable speaking to her one on one.

They only stopped when the bell atop the palace bell tower tolled midday, and the group broke for lunch. Dismissing her students and giving Joy a hug goodbye—and a promise to swing by to see her later that day—Fey turned and made her way across the lawn.

Leandra inclined her head in greeting as Fey approached.

"How were they today?" Fey asked.

"They're doing well," Leandra told her. "Some of them are picking up on their powers remarkably quickly. Better than I'd ever hoped."

Fey nodded. She'd noticed that same thing, too. For many of the older Witches, their control over their new elements came naturally, and surprisingly quickly. It was as though a part of them had always known that a path to those powers existed, and now that the gate was unlocked, it was an easy path for them to follow.

Still, when Leandra looked out at the crowd as they relaxed and ate their lunches, she didn't look proud. She looked worried.

"Something you're not telling me?" Fey asked, eyes narrowing warily.

Leandra released a heavy breath. She looked tired.

"We're missing one," she said simply, with just a hint of sadness coloring her voice.

Fey knew without asking who Leandra meant.

For months after Fey started these lessons, Leandra insisted the princess would come. "Just give her time," Leandra had said, over and over, day after day.

They had. The coven leaders had given Princess Amalia time, and space, and everything else she could have desired.

And, still, she hadn't shown up.

Not once, not even for a single session.

Fey didn't particularly care if the princess ever joined her classes or not. A small part of her was relieved every morning she arrived and didn't see those familiar brown curls in the crowd waiting for her. Didn't see the living reminder of the world she'd turned her back on, the code she betrayed.

And who could blame Amalia for staying away, when the class was taught by the very Witch she blamed for her parents' deaths?

Leandra pursed her lips. "I'm worried about her," she confided in Fey. "She barely eats anymore. Hardly ever leaves her room. She won't talk to me, and now that Linh isn't coming by the palace anymore... I don't know if she talks to anyone."

Fey bit her tongue to keep her own opinions in check. It had been a mistake to put Amalia on the council, in her opinion. And a bigger mistake to keep her in the palace locked away from kids her own age. It was no mystery to her at all why the princess was retreating.

"Maybe if you tried to talk to her—" Leandra began.

"No," Fey said, anger rising in her chest.

Leandra blinked and shut her mouth.

For a moment, Fey pulled back on her rage, ready to leash it once more.

But...

Let them see you.

Fey let it out instead. Let that rage burn against her skin. And when she turned to look Leandra in the eyes, she knew the Priestess could see it burning in her gaze.

"I'm not going to talk to her, Leandra," Fey said, feeling the strength of that power in her voice. "Because I'm the last person she wants to talk to. Don't forget that I killed her parents. I'm the reason she's alone."

Leandra swallowed and opened her mouth as though to speak, but Fey continued. "You want to give her some support? Let her be a kid. Let her meet new people, let her put some distance between herself and all this pain she's been put through. Let her grow up. You have her trapped in the same cage she's been in since she was born, and you're wondering why she doesn't sing for you all like a happy little bird. You need to open the cage and let her out. She doesn't need me, Leandra. What she needs is freedom."

"I just think a little closure—"

"No," Fey insisted. "And I won't have this conversation with you again. My answer is no. There's no such thing as closure, Priestess. There's no putting this behind her and getting over it. There's no healing. There's only surviving it, one day at a time. And I can't help her do that. Only she can."

Leandra didn't stop her when she turned to walk away, and Fey let that rage continue to burn, feeling more herself than she had in years.

CHAPTER 10
VEE

Their clubhouse had rats.

Vee had seen one the other week, chewing on a bag of chips one of the new strays had left out. It had been a massive thing, bigger than her hand, and it had glared at her when it saw her as though daring her to do something about it. Daring her to stop it.

There were Rat Shifters in the middle octants, Vee had heard once. She sometimes wondered if there were any actually living in the city. Even if there were, though, this wasn't one of them, she was sure of that. This was just an ordinary rat, hungry and skinny, like the rest of the strays they'd collected in their clubhouse over the years.

Vee preferred to spend her time on the clubhouse roof, but once she'd seen the rat, she'd wanted to investigate it a little more. So, she had left out little bits of food, like bait, on the main floor of the warehouse they all called home. A cracker here, a piece of cheese there, and then she'd waited and waited, until *skit skit skit*, they had come crawling out of the walls to investigate.

She was good at holding still, at pretending to be nonthreatening. She'd had a lot of practice over the years.

The first rat to investigate her bait was the same one she'd seen before, the first time she'd noticed them. He was missing a part of his ear, but it moved just as well as the other one when he twitched it, listening for predators before venturing out of the wall and scampering to the piece of cheese.

Vee let him have it, let him enjoy his victory before she took control of him.

Rats had remarkably fast heartbeats. Compared to Witches and Shifters, anyway. It beat quickly enough to make her dizzy, and it made controlling them with Blood Magic difficult.

That was a problem. She could command their blood, make them move and obey her, but she had to keep the heart beating. Had to keep that blood flowing through their system, or they ran out of oxygen and just... well... died.

That was the first lesson she'd learned, with those three men who had attacked her and Jayce in that alley all those years ago, when she'd first discovered this power. Hold the blood in place for too long and oops! Dead as the old Witch queen! She could still move them, afterwards, still manipulate their bodies, but what was the point? They were just puppets with broken strings.

Corpses weren't nearly as entertaining as live victims.

After that, Vee learned to keep the hearts beating. They lasted longer that way. And it was way more fun.

The rat had almost finished his piece of cheese when Vee moved, twitching her finger and reaching out with that pulse of power that filled her. She captured it mid-bite, and the rat's body froze—stiff and immobile in her mental grasp.

With rats, you had to be delicate, too. They might seem big, especially when you're not expecting to see one and then... there it is! Eating the chips you were going to eat! But they're smaller than you'd expect. Their bones are tiny, and some of them are so incredibly fragile, almost as thin as eggshells. You needed to remember that when you made them move.

Vee didn't want to hurt them. They were just innocent creatures trying to get by. Just like her. Just like the strays.

Not like the people she did hurt.

With another flick of her finger, the rat dropped the food. His forearms jerked as she made him move, the movement unnatural and stilted.

That was another thing that was difficult with small animals—it was so hard to get the movements to look right. It just didn't seem natural, the way they moved when she controlled them.

The rat walked to her, standing on his hind legs, forearms curled against his chest. She made him stand there, at attention, while she waited for the next one to come out and investigate the bait.

And the next.

And the next.

In a little over two hours, she managed to find seven rats living in their clubhouse. It wasn't a surprise to her that there were so many. They were all lax with food here, now that food was plentiful, and their clubhouse had been an old warehouse before it had been abandoned and the strays had started congregating here. There were probably already rat nests in the walls from years and years ago, and all these guys were doing was taking up new residences in abandoned nests.

Vee hummed aloud as she made them all line up, feeling each of their heartbeats individually. Seven was a lot to control at one time, but she didn't feel like she was overextending herself. Not even close. If there had been more rats, she probably could have handled them easily as well. But seven was all there was, so that was all she had to work with.

Humming louder, Vee tapped her fingers against the floor, marking a beat. One by one, the rats joined her, tapping their hind paws, then their tails.

One by one, they twisted, bending to one side, then the other. Then she added the arms, synchronizing the movements, first one side and then the other.

One, two, bend, bend, three, four, left, right.

By the time she'd mastered it, and had all seven rats dancing before her, their movements a grotesque, jerky, and unsteady mockery of a jig she'd once seen, Vee was laughing so hard her sides felt like they might split open.

CHAPTER II

ALICE

"Your hands are still too low, babe. You need to raise them up higher, like this." Alice raised her own fists in demonstration.

"I know my stances, sister," Fey said, rolling her eyes. But Alice noticed her hands dropped a fraction lower, unintentionally, as she spoke. "And I'm holding my hands exactly where—"

Fey's nose crunched as Alice jolted forward, delivering a quick hit to her face.

A shame. If her hands had been just an inch higher, Fey probably could have stopped it.

But that was how the Witch had always been, wasn't it? She only ever learned a lesson when it was written in blood.

"See?" Alice said smugly, as Fey reared back, swearing. Blood leaked from her broken nose, dripping down her chin. "If your hands were where they were supposed to be, you would have blocked that."

"Fuck," Fey groaned, the words muffled and strained. "You are such a fucking asshole."

"Oh, don't be such a baby," Alice said. It was bleeding an awful lot, though, wasn't it? Fey hinged forward at her waist, letting the blood fall through her fingers and onto the mats that covered their workout room floor. Glancing over for Joy, Alice gestured the other Witch over. "A little help here, love?"

Joy grinned, stepping forward and placing her hands gently on either side of Fey's face.

"Hold still," she said to Fey. "This won't hurt at all, sister."

Alice felt a small pang of jealousy, watching Joy work. She was proud of her, of course. So damned proud that Joy had picked up Med Magic so quickly after discovering her connection to Water. But she felt no stirring of magic at all as she watched Joy call her power, using it to heal the wound. No hint of that pulse of magic she felt whenever another Witch called to Fire.

There was another horrible crunch as the cartilage in Fey's nose reset, and Alice winced involuntarily at the sound.

"All better," Joy declared, taking a step back. Fey reached up to wipe the blood from her face with a scowl.

"Thanks, love," Alice said, stepping forward to give Joy a kiss on the cheek. "I think that's enough for today."

Flicking the blood off her fingers, Fey shot her an angry look.

"Doesn't seem fair that you get to sucker punch me and then say we're done," she grumbled. She reached up once more, touching the sides of her nose as though feeling for signs of the break, and Alice's gaze drifted to Fey's arm. The smile on her face faltered.

The tattooed sigils that covered Fey's arms were unhidden. The spell each of them used to keep their marks undetected, including the scarred and broken Blade's mark on the inside of Fey's forearm, wasn't active.

When had Fey stopped hiding her marks?

Alice wasn't sure why, but it unsettled her.

A little voice inside her head whispered, menacingly, that maybe she'd been a little too quick when reassuring Kallista, after all.

Tearing her eyes away from the sigils, Alice searched Fey's face for... something. Some sign that Kallista was wrong, or maybe even some sign that she was right. She missed the days when she knew exactly what her sisters were feeling. When they were connected.

The scar on her own arm ached.

"How are you, anyway?" Alice asked Fey, gently.

Joy approached with a damp towel, holding it out for Fey, who snorted loudly.

"Well, my nose fucking hurts," she replied.

"I mean it, babe," Alice pressed. "How... have you been doing?"

Fey dabbed at the blood drying on her chin, eyes narrowed at Alice. "Why?" she asked, suspiciously.

Joy let out a bright laugh at the answer, and it echoed around the room. So very Fey.

"Gee, I don't know, babe," Alice said, rolling her eyes. "Maybe because you're our sister, and we care about you? Maybe because we see you so rarely now?"

Fey's green eyes remained narrowed and wary.

Fine.

"There are... rumors," Alice said. She reached up, rubbing a hand over her scalp. She needed a trim, needed to take a razor to it before the hair got much longer and started to curl.

"What rumors?" Fey asked, shoulders pulling back as she stood a little straighter.

"Rumors that you might be seeking the crown after all."

"Alice!" Joy gasped, sounding shocked. Alice couldn't bring herself to look at her, to see the outrage in her lover's face. She held Fey's stare, preferring the cold anger rising in Fey's green eyes to the hurt she knew she would find in Joy's.

"Fuck your crown," Fey hissed. She took a step toward Alice, and this time Alice could feel that pulse of power, that delicious burn of Fire.

"Stop!" Joy stepped between them, putting her hand up to Fey's chest. "Alice, apologize."

"I said nothing that warrants a—"

"Apologize," Joy insisted, face whipping around to scowl at her.

"I..." Alice took a steading breath. "I'm sorry, sister. A little Demon has been putting thoughts in my head. I know... I know how you feel about being queen."

Fey's eyebrow rose.

"Kallista?" she asked, sounding surprised. "The shadow Demon made you think that?"

Alice nodded.

"Ignore her," Fey said. She stepped back, turning away from Joy and Alice, and wiped the wet cloth over her face. That pulse of power dissipated, and Alice let out a shaky breath in relief. "She's just trying to rile you up."

"I think she's scared," Alice confessed.

Fey paused.

"Kallista is scared?" she repeated. "That's a terrifying thought."

"Tell me about it," Alice muttered.

"Mind if I hop in your shower?" Fey asked, gesturing to the dried blood on her chin and chest. Sweat coated her body, most from her training session with Alice, but some from her lessons this morning. "I'd rather not walk home while looking like I got in a fight and lost."

"Knock yourself out," Alice said. "Your old room is empty. The shower is all yours."

Fey gave her an appreciative grin and a wave on her way out, tossing the blood-soaked towel at the clothes bin near the door and missing. The blatant disrespect of it made Alice smile.

She missed this—missed living with Fey. She'd moved in with Alastair so gradually, Alice hadn't really noticed it was happening until it was over. One day, her sister was just gone. She missed the days when they'd been parts of the same whole.

She missed Fey.

And sometimes... sometimes she worried Fey was growing into someone she didn't recognize anymore.

CHAPTER 12

FEY

I love you, Witchling.

Fey replayed Alastair's words over and over in her mind as she made her way home. Even on the thousandth repeat, they made her feel oddly warm inside. Made her walk a little more quickly, eager to see him. She'd stayed long enough at her sisters' place that the sun had already set by the time she made her way down the familiar streets to their home. He'd be there by the time she arrived, awake and waiting for her.

They had the entire night head of them to spend with each other.

She couldn't wait to get started.

Alastair must be feeling just as eager as she was because Fey had barely opened the door and stepped over the threshold when a pair of hands grabbed her, pulling her inside and pinning her against the wall.

A hard male body pressed against hers, and Fey laughed, tilting her face up to gaze up at him.

"Alastair, can't you—"

The rest of the words died before they made it past her lips. She stilled, her smile slipping as she stared up at the male who had her pinned, his forearms braced on the wall on either side of her head, caging her in.

Soft brown hair, not midnight black.

Tan, sun-touched skin. A jaw lightly peppered with stubble.

Green eyes flecked with gray, not warm amber gold.

This wasn't Alastair, it was Jasper. Jasper staring down at her, his face close enough that their noses were touching. Jasper with a crooked smirk on his face.

"Jasper?" Fey tried to ask. But the moment she opened her mouth, lips forming the question, Jasper closed the gap between them and kissed her.

It wasn't anything like kissing Alastair. Alastair kissed her as though it was a matter of life and death, kissed her like he wanted to possess her. It was hot and rough and rushed and took her breath away every time.

This was completely different. Jasper kissed her softly, patiently. When he opened his mouth and ran his tongue over her lips, she couldn't stop herself from opening for him, couldn't stop herself from arching up into him when he groaned in encouragement, leaning further into her, pressing his body into hers.

No.

Fey brought her hands up to Jasper's chest to push him away. But instead of stopping him, she gripped his shirt tighter, her treacherous hands pulling him even closer. Wanting to feel his body against hers.

Her head emptied as Jasper gently cupped her face, his tongue softly caressing hers. Her mind went blank, and there was no world outside of this, of his mouth, his body...

"You could at least let her get through the door," a familiar voice said, breaking the spell cast over the two of them.

Alastair.

Fey jerked her head back a little too quickly. The back of her head hit the wall behind her, and she gasped. Stars danced in her front of her eyes, either from the kiss or the knock to her head, or some terrible combination of the two.

"Are you alright?" Jasper chuckled. "That sounded like it hurt."

Fey swore in answer, twisting to peer over his arms to where Alastair stood, leaning against the kitchen doorway.

"Alastair," she said. She searched his face for some sign of anger, of the betrayal he must be feeling. Of the murderous rage she knew lurked right below the surface.

She found none.

"Happy Birthday, Witchling," Alastair said with a smirk. He looked amused, not angry. No more homicidal or murderous than usual.

"It's not my birthday..." she argued.

"He knows," Jasper told her, moving closer and peppering her neck with soft kisses. His body pressed her hard against the wall, and her mind sputtered again.

"Well, I didn't *know*. I figured it was a long shot." Alastair shrugged. "But considering we've been together two years now, and you still won't tell me when your birthday actually is, I figured today was as good a day as any to celebrate. Looks like you're already thoroughly enjoying your present."

Lips pressed against the bare skin of Fey's neck, Jasper laughed. "Jealous already, boss?" he asked. The soft brush of his lips against her skin as he spoke sent a shiver down her spine.

Alastair's only answer was an angry grunt, and Jasper laughed even harder, nuzzling further up Fey's neck until his mouth was over her ear.

"I don't think he's good at sharing," he told her, and his voice reverberated through her entire body. "But luckily for you both, I'm an expert."

"Jasper," she said. "I need you to give me a little space..."

"Why?" he asked, his words soft and warm against her skin. He licked her, a delicate touch with the tip of his tongue, right below her ear, like he was tasting her.

"Because I've been practicing boiling things alive," Fey answered, happy the words held a bite she didn't quite feel at the moment. "And if you don't give me some room to breathe, you're going to be my next test subject."

Jasper chuckled, but to his credit, he moved back, at least a bit.

"What is this?" Fey asked, eyes narrowing on Alastair as he stalked toward them. He came to a stop next to Jasper, who kept one arm on the wall angled over Fey but shifted a fraction to give him room.

"Consider this a gift," Alastair told her. He reached out to grip her chin and tilted her head back. Fey's breath hitched as his thumb softly caressed her lower lip. "Do you remember me asking if you would enjoy this? Having two men share you?"

"I..." She didn't remember. Hell, she was having trouble remembering her own name right now. And the fog in her brain only got worse when Jasper started inching closer to her neck again.

"Imagine it, Witchling." Alastair was saying, his voice husky. "I'm sure you've thought about it. You can have both of us tonight. In whatever way you want us."

Fey hesitated.

"Is this... is this supposed to be some sort of test?" she asked, searching his face for the answer.

"No," Alastair shook his head. His thumb continued to stroke her, moving across her lips delicately. "No test. No trick."

"A... a reward, then?" she guessed. "For saying I love you?"

Alastair's lips tweaked upward in a smile. "A reward? Maybe it is...a reward for you." His fingers trailed down her skin. "For being such a good girl. And a reward for him." His eyes darted over to Jasper. "For wanting to protect you. To please you."

Before she could ask more, he pulled her away from the wall and toward his chest. "The choice is yours, Witchling. Jasper can join the two of us in bed tonight. But if that's something you don't want? Then he will leave right now and never say a word about this to anyone." His gaze flicked from Fey's to Jasper's, eyes narrowing. "Right?" he asked in a threatening voice.

"Absolutely," Jasper agreed, and Fey jumped at how close his voice was. He was right behind her, close enough that his breath fluttered her hair.

"I—" Fey started to speak, but Jasper chose that moment to brush her hair to the side and bend down to press his lips against the back of her neck. She shut her mouth quickly to swallow a moan and swallowed hard before continuing. "What happens if he stays?"

"If he stays, he and I will give you a very, very good night, Witchling," Alastair told her, his lips poised right above her own. Jasper's hands were on her waist now, and he nipped her at her neck, his sharp teeth gently scraping against her skin. "And when he leaves tomorrow, he will never say a word about this to anyone. Will you, puppy?" Alastair asked.

"Not one word, boss," Jasper answered, and Fey's body arched as he licked her neck and nipped at her again.

"I was just about to start dinner," Alastair said. His hands moved to her waist, and Jasper's moved further down, automatically, to grip her hips instead. "After we eat, you can have a shower and relax. Maybe enjoy a glass of wine. And, when you're ready, we can head to bed together. All three of us."

"No," Fey said, breathless. Both males stilled. Behind her, Jasper shifted away from her, his hands leaving her body with a heartbreaking sigh.

"Bed first," Fey amended. "Then dinner. Please."

"Fuck yes," Jasper growled. He made a small, appreciative noise in the back of his throat, instantly reaching for her again.

"As you wish, Witchling," Alastair said, smiling wickedly down at her. He brought his hands up to cup her face. "Bed it is."

CHAPTER 13

FEY

Could someone die of pleasure?

The world was spinning around her, and it was impossible, absolutely impossible, to keep herself from being pulled into that whirlpool as both Jasper and Alastair touched her.

Her body pressed hard against Alastair's chest as he kissed her, their height difference forcing her to stand on her tiptoes to reach him. Behind her, Jasper pressed into her back, caging her between the two of them.

Someone's hand was on her stomach, moving under her shirt and brushing against her bare skin. She gasped, releasing Alastair's mouth.

Jasper was there in an instant, his fingers tracing her jawline and angling her face toward him as he bent down to claim her mouth for his own.

A low snarl came from Alastair's chest, but Fey was too lost in the kiss to care. Alastair's hands gripped her hips hard enough to bruise, and it was the perfect contrast to the gentle way Jasper kissed her. The hand on her stomach moved higher, brushing against her breasts.

Alastair's snarl grew louder, and Jasper broke their kiss with a laugh.

"A bit possessive, isn't he?" he chided, giving Fey a lopsided smile.

"Fuck you," muttered Alastair. His hands gripped Fey's hair, tugging her head back toward him and leaning down to kiss her again. "Wait your turn."

Fey melted against Alastair's chest and relaxed into the kiss. Jasper's fingers rolled up her body, tugging her top over her shoulder, and he leaned down to lick the skin there. She moaned hungrily, writhing between them, caged by hard muscle.

"Bedroom," she murmured against Alastair's lips. Pressed between the two of them, she felt Alastair's cock twitch in response. "Now."

They stumbled to the room together, Jasper managing to peel off Fey's shirt somewhere along the way. Alastair kept her attention on himself, kissing her lips and face, whispering all the things he wanted to do to her. Wonderfully dirty things. When they finally reached the bed, he lifted her, sitting down on the edge and settling her on his lap so she straddled him.

Behind them, Jasper pulled his own shirt over his head. He tossed it aside but looked to Alastair for confirmation before approaching the bed.

Hands grasped in Fey's hair, his lips pressed to hers, Alastair asked her, "Do you want us both, Witchling?"

Fey moaned, writhing in his lap, and Alastair flashed Jasper a quick smile.

That was all the invitation the Wolf needed. Dropping to his knees at the edge of the bed, he ran his hands gently up Fey's stomach and chest from behind, his fingers teasing her flesh.

Fey gasped as his fingers found her nipples through her bra. Jasper immediately repeated the motion, groaning at her reaction.

"Kiss him," Alastair ordered, leaning back to give them room. Jasper slipped his face next to hers, angling her face toward his to kiss her.

Alastair made no move to stop them this time, just watched as he unbuttoned his own shirt. The way Jasper kissed her was almost chaste, the touch of his tongue gentle and reverent. Fey let out a small whimper of pleasure, grinding herself down onto Alastair's lap.

Alastair's hands came up to grip her hips in response, pulling her down harder, pushing her down against his hard length in encouragement.

One of them managed to unhook her bra, and the straps fell loose, the lace fabric falling from her breasts. Alastair tossed it aside, kissing her exposed neck. Jasper broke their kiss to look down at her, sucking air through his teeth at the sight.

His eyes moved down her body. "You're so beautiful," he said.

Alastair licked at Fey's ear. "Look at him, Witchling. See how much he wants you?"

She did, glancing over her shoulder at where Jasper knelt behind her. His eyes were glazed, pupils blown wide. His cock strained against the fabric of his pants, and as she watched, he gripped himself through his clothes, showing her just how excited he was.

She barely had time to enjoy the sight of him before Alastair lifted her off his lap, flipping her on to her back.

Fey sucked in a breath, but before she could move, Alastair was there next to her, hands threading through her hair and pivoting her face toward his.

Jasper reached for her pants, and Fey arched her back off the bed to help him remove them, staring down at where he knelt between her legs.

Hand flexing in her hair, Alastair yanked her gaze back to his.

"Eyes on me, Witchling," he ordered. "I want to see every reaction, every bit of pleasure he gives you. I want to look in your eyes when you come on his pretty face."

Fey swallowed, nodding.

Jasper slid her pants off with skilled, practiced hands and spread her legs wide. She gasped as his fingers trailed over her panties.

"How do you like it?" he asked, fingertips brushing against her through the fabric. Fey opened her mouth to speak, but... she didn't know.

"Soft and slow to start," Alastair answered for her, his eyes never leaving hers. "And then as rough as you can. She'll let you know when."

Jasper nodded, licking up her thigh and planting a soft kiss on her through the fabric of her panties, before slipping his hands under her and gently pulling them down her legs.

"Fuck, Alastair," Jasper said in a rough voice, staring at her. "She's so perfect."

His breath tickled over her as he spoke, and Fey trembled. Alastair smiled.

"She is, isn't she?" he said.

When Jasper's tongue slid over her, Fey cried out, bucking her hips to chase the sensation. But he followed Alastair's instructions, moving slowly, softly across her flesh, in a gentle caress.

Alastair glanced down the bed at him, and his gaze hardened.

"Fuck," he whispered, licking his lips as he watched.

Hand still tangled in her hair, Alastair angled Fey's head down, lifting her up so she was staring down her own body at Jasper, kneeling between her legs, his hands lifting her thighs.

Jasper looked up at her, eyes burning into hers as he licked, groaning softly in the back of his throat as his lips closed around her clit to suck.

It was too much. Fey collapsed back against the bed, back bowing. Her hands left Alastair's body to grip the sheets, and after a moment she felt him shift away from her, sliding off the bed to remove his own clothing.

Jasper groaned as he feasted on her, his pace picking up. He was listening to all her body's subtle reactions and adjusting his tempo and speed to give her exactly what she needed.

When Alastair returned to the bed, his bare cock pressed into Fey's side as he kissed down her neck and chest. His mouth found her nipple, and he sucked it, teeth nipping at her.

It was too much, too much sensation all at once. When Jasper suddenly slipped a finger into her, his teeth scraping playfully against her as she moved on his hand, Fey knew she couldn't last much longer.

"Alastair," Fey gasped, writhing on the bed.

He looked up at her, her nipple falling from his mouth.

"Are you close, Witchling?" he asked. His hand curled around his cock, stroking himself as he watched her.

"I—" Fey cried out, hips rolling as Jasper slipped another finger into her.

"Don't you dare fucking stop, Jasper," Alastair snapped, never taking his eyes off her face. Jasper groaned in answer, his fingers curling to hit that perfect spot inside of her.

Fey couldn't think. Her body was on fire, her legs shaking. Alastair stared deep into her eyes, his gaze hungry.

"That's right, Witchling, come for us," he ordered, fingers reaching out to twist her nipple. "I want to watch you come undone on his tongue."

With a scream, Fey gave him exactly what he asked for. She threw back her head, her hips bowing from the bed with the strength of her release. Jasper managed to keep her in place, holding her bucking hips down with one hand while he continued to fuck and suck at her, until she collapsed back on the bed, spent.

Alastair didn't give her a second to rest. He grabbed her immediately, pulling her out of Jasper's grasp and rolling her onto him until she was straddling him on the bed.

Setting her dripping pussy down on his cock, Alastair rolled his hips beneath her, dragging his hard length over her too sensitive skin.

"Fuck, you look so good when you come, Witchling," he told her, moving against her.

She heard a sound of agreement from behind her as Jasper hastily removed his clothing. He came up on the bed, chest against her back, his fingers dancing over her bare skin.

"He's right, you know," Jasper murmured against the skin of her neck. "You look so beautiful. So perfect." His fingers trailed down her sides and to her hips. Gently, he pushed her down onto Alastair, sliding her body up his length while she moaned.

Throwing his head back against the pillows, Alastair swore. He twitched underneath her, harder than she'd ever felt him.

Wordlessly, Jasper lifted Fey's hips, giving Alastair the room to maneuver his cock to her entrance, and groaned in time with Alastair as he pressed into her.

Fey released a shuddered gasped as Alastair entered her, arching her back against Jasper's hard body. His cock twitched against the curve of her ass as he helped slide her down until Alastair was fully inside her.

Alastair's hands slid up to her thighs, stroking the soft skin there as he held her against his hips, keeping her still.

"Do you think you can take both of us, Witchling?" Alastair asked, eyes bright. He rolled his hips underneath her, moving his cock deep inside of her until she cried out.

"I—I don't know how to—" She was lost in the sensation, unable to even understand the question. As if in answer, Jasper's fingers snaked down her spine, gently caressing her lower back before dipping lower to circle her asshole.

Startled, she sucked in a breath, pussy clenching tight around Alastair's cock.

"You don't have to say yes," Jasper told her. His fingers teased her, testing her. "Tonight is all about you, gorgeous. About what you need from us."

"I..." Fey's nerves were on fire, and below her, Alastair was moving his hips just enough to drive her to distraction as Jasper played with her ass.

"Yes," Fey gasped, shuddering with need as Jasper nuzzled into her neck. "Do it. I want it. Both of you."

"Lube," Alastair said. He was having trouble staying still, hips twitching with the effort of holding Fey there without fucking her fully. "In the top drawer, next to the bed."

Jasper gave Fey a soft kiss on her cheek before leaning around her and reaching into the drawer.

"Come here, Witchling," Alastair demanded, bending her down so she lay flat against his chest. He pulled her into a kiss, sliding his cock out a few inches before roughly thrusting it back in, earning a stifled moan from her.

"I love hearing you make that noise," Alastair told her, releasing her mouth and rolling his hips again.

Fey lost herself in the feel of him, almost forgetting what was to come until she felt Jasper's fingers teasing her again. This time, they were slick and wet.

"Stay like this," Alastair urged, pressing her close to his chest. "Just like this, Witchling."

She whimpered as Jasper slipped a finger into her, and then another, coating her inside. Just as she was getting used to the sensation, relaxing around him, his fingers withdrew.

Her mouth went dry, and a tendril of fear began to creep in.

As if he knew, Jasper's hands were suddenly there again, running gently over her back and shoulders as he positioned himself behind her, leaning over her to whisper in her other ear.

"I'll go slow, okay?" His voice was soft. "You can stop me if it's too much."

Fey nodded, heart hammering in her chest, as she felt his tip press against her.

"Relax, Witchling," Alastair murmured in her other ear, his voice slightly breathless. "Take a deep breath. You'll have to relax to let him in."

How could she relax? How was it even possible to relax, like this? But she managed to take a breath, letting it out slowly.

"Good girl. Another," Alastair ordered, and as she did, she felt Jasper press harder against her entrance, and slowly, oh so slowly, he began to push himself inside.

Every time Fey tensed, Jasper's soothing touches and gentle words managed to get her to relax again, and on her next deep breath, he pushed in even further.

Inch by inch, Fey fought against her raising panic, feeling like she might break. It was too much. They were too much.

Deep breaths, she told herself, forcing herself to relax until finally, mercifully, Jasper was inside of her.

Jasper let out a shuddering breath as his hips finally hit against her body, his limbs twitching with the effort of moving so slowly.

"How do you feel?" he asked her, his voice deep and guttural.

She tried to answer but could only moan, partially out of pain and partially out of... *want*. She felt like she was on the brink of something she'd never experienced before and, Goddess save her, she wanted *more*. More of whatever this could be. More of whatever they could offer her.

"For fuck's sake," Alastair snapped, cock twitching inside her. "Jasper, hurry up. If I can't fuck her soon, I'm going to go mad."

Jasper chuckled, his breath lightly tickling Fey's ear.

"Is he always this impatient?" he teased. When she let out a strained laugh in response, he asked, "Are you ready, gorgeous?"

At her nod, he began to move, pulling out just a fraction before sliding back in. It was too much, even those small movements. Fey turned her head and bit down on Alastair's shoulder to keep from screaming.

Unable to stop himself from moving inside of her any longer, Alastair swore, his hips bucking.

"Fuck, Jasper," he gasped. "I can feel you moving inside her, and it's
—" He clenched his teeth tight, his breathing ragged. *"Fuck, yes."*

Jasper kept a slow tempo, easing her into it, and before long, she
couldn't bite down on Alastair any longer. Tilting her head back, Fey let
out a sharp cry of pleasure.

It felt incredible. It was so much sensation, almost too much, but
Goddess it felt good to have them both inside of her like this. It felt
right.

"That's it, Witchling," Alastair encouraged her, moving his hips in a
perfect opposing rhythm to Jasper's, pulling his cock out just as Jasper
entered her. "You're doing such a good job, taking both of us."

Fey cried out again, putting her hands on Alastair's chest to rise even
further.

"You look so fucking good right now," Alastair panted, his hands
on her hips, driving himself into her again and again, his tempo
increasing.

"You do." Jasper snaked his arm around her waist and pulled her up
onto her knees until her back pressed to his chest. "Just look how beautiful she is, boss."

Alastair swore, nearly bowing off the bed as Jasper held her tight
against his chest, her body on full display for him to see.

"Such a good girl," Alastair murmured, his hips moving faster.
"Taking two cocks like this." He punctuated his words with deep
thrusts, his eyes glazing over. "My perfect fucking Witchling."

Fey couldn't think. Her entire body was alight with sensation. The
initial pain at having Jasper inside her was gone, and now all she felt as
he thrust deep into her ass was a wave of pleasure, pushing her closer to
the edge.

She looked down at Alastair, meeting his eyes as Jasper's hand
circled her breast and squeezed.

"Alastair," she whimpered, unable to tear her gaze from his face,
unable to look away from the pleasure in his eyes.

At the sound of his name, Alastair came, his back arching off the
bed and his hands digging painfully into her hips. He roared, driving
himself into her hard as he filled her.

Behind her, Jasper murmured her name, his own pace faltering.

With Alastair still pulsing inside her, Fey reached back, running her fingers over Jasper's cheek.

"Come with me," she said, and he nodded, his cock twitching as he thrust deeper inside of her. "Please, Jasper."

Eyes locked on hers, his hand trailed down her body to touch her. It took barely a brush of his fingers over her sensitive clit to send her over that edge.

The force of her orgasm was enough to make Fey scream louder than she ever had before. Arching back against Jasper's body, she lost herself in the sensation, shuddering as his fingers expertly touched her, driving her higher and higher. With a final groan, he bit down on the nape of her neck, and she felt him pulse inside of her as he joined her.

CHAPTER 14
JASPER

He must be dead. That was the only explanation.

Because this? This was heaven.

Jasper licked his lips, chasing the taste of her as he watched Fey stretch out on the mattress with a long, satisfied sigh.

She was beyond beautiful, Jasper thought, eyes roaming down the curve of her back and spine, the perfect arch of her ass. She was exquisite. A work of art. He rolled onto his side to be closer to her, fingers caressing her back and trailing patterns over her skin.

Mine.

"Fuck," Alastair panted, still struggling to catch his breath. "You did so well, Witchling."

Fey made a small noise of contentment, rolling on to her side between the two of them. Her pale skin sparkled with sweat.

They're both so beautiful, Jasper thought, eyeing Alastair. His dark hair was artfully tussled, and a sheen of sweat coated his chest.

This was *definitely* heaven. Smiling, Jasper moved even closer, nuzzling his face into the spot at the nape of Fey's neck where her scent was the strongest. He licked the skin there, savoring the taste of her. Licked up her shoulder blade, licked the fingers and the hand resting there.

Mine.

"Watch it, puppy," Alastair warned, pulling his hand away. But when Jasper glanced over, he was grinning.

Alastair stretched with a long exhale, then turned his attention to Fey.

"Are you alright, Witchling?" he asked in a gentle voice.

Fey let out a small laugh.

"I think I'm better than alright," she answered. "That was... incredible."

Alastair smiled, and he reached out to run his fingers over her arms again. Jasper nuzzled harder against her, and Fey melted against him, closing her eyes and luxuriating in their attention.

"Alastair?" Fey said, voice thick with sleep.

"What do you need from us?" Alastair asked, leaning closer to plant a soft kiss on her lips. Jasper took the opportunity to lick that perfect spot on her neck again.

"I'm starving," she answered, wriggling between them.

Laughing, Alastair rolled away, sliding off the bed and stretching his arms over his head. Jasper watched, lips against Fey's skin, as the Vampire stalked across the bedroom to grab his discarded pants. He pulled them up over his hips, not bothering with any other clothing.

"I'll get started on dinner," Alastair promised her, and his eyes flickered to Jasper's. "Maybe you'd like to have a shower?"

"I'm on it," Jasper grunted, and before Fey could protest, he scooped her up in his arms, cradling her against his body and swinging his legs off the bed.

"I can shower on my own," she grumbled.

"But where's the fun in that?" Jasper asked her, smirking as he carried her through the bedroom and into the bathroom.

Goddess save him, it felt good to hold her like this. Unwilling to put her down even for a moment, he maneuvered her until he could hold her with one arm and turn on the shower.

Alastair's shower was overly complicated, and Jasper almost lost his patience more than once as he tried the various knobs until he finally managed to get all three shower heads running. Trust Alastair to over-complicate a damned shower. He cradled Fey away from the water's spray until he got the right temperature, then gingerly set her down on her feet under the stream and stepped into the shower behind her.

Under the heat of the shower, her body relaxed, and she tipped her head back with a quiet moan as the water cascaded over her. Jasper's cock twitched to life in response.

Not now, he thought, glaring down at his body. This part wasn't about sex, this was aftercare. This was making sure Fey felt taken care of. Felt loved.

Speaking of... Jasper reached around her and opened a bottle of soap from the marble shelf.

He flipped the lid open and sniffed it, immediately pulling a face. *No, not that one.* Putting it back, he reached for another.

Yes. This one smelled like her, like jasmine and just a hint of something else, something floral. Honeysuckle?

Pouring a generous amount in his palm, Jasper set the bottle back down and stepped closer to Fey. He lathered the soap in his hands, before gently reaching out to scrub her.

"I can wash myself, you know," she told him, but there was no heat to the words, and she didn't stop him as he rubbed the soap over her skin, using it to help massage the muscles in her arms.

"And deprive me of this? You wouldn't be that cruel," he said, playfully.

"Then you don't know me at all," she answered. "I'm always cruel."

Jasper snorted.

He washed her carefully, sliding his hands from her arms to her sides and down her stomach. His cock gave another twitch as he lathered her breasts and grew painfully hard when her breath hitched in response. But he kept his touch professional, even when he got to his knees to wash her legs, fingers slipping delicately between her thighs and ass cheeks to wash away the remnants of their fun together.

When he was done, he rinsed her under the shower spray, washing all the soap away, and smiled at how languid and relaxed she was from his touch.

She stopped him when he reached for the shampoo bottle, though.

"It's not my wash day," she said, opening her eye only a fraction to scowl at him.

Jasper scowled back.

"Fine," he said, leaving the shampoo where it was and coming to stand in front of her. It always shocked him how small she was. He towered above her, her eyes barely reaching his collar bone. Incredible that someone so small could hold so much power.

Bringing his hands up to cup her face, he said, "Lean back."

"Why?" Fey asked, instantly suspicious.

Jasper bared his teeth. This would be easier if she were a Wolf. Then he could just nip her, take a bite of that delicious spot at the back of her neck and force her to submit. "Oil collects at the scalp when you don't wash it every day. Lean back and let me at least rinse it."

Still scowling, Fey did as she was told, tilting her head back into the spray and letting him run his fingers through her hair.

Truthfully, her hair was fine, but he wasn't ready for this to be over yet, wasn't ready to stop touching her. And he'd use any excuse for a little extra time to enjoy this moment.

Fey sighed as his fingers softly caressed her scalp, massaging the skin there. His cock twitched again, and Jasper gave up ignoring it, knowing there was no way she didn't feel it pressing against her.

"Sorry," he told her, continuing his massage. "It has a mind of its own. Ignore it."

Fey was quiet, but her lip twitched up at the corner.

"I'm proud of you, you know," he told her as he worked.

She opened a single eye to watch him, her gaze wary.

"Telling Alastair that you love him. That's huge. I'm proud of you, Fey."

She huffed. "Goddess, both of you are so infuriating, you know that? It's not huge. Don't make such a... thing over it."

"It is." He laughed, ignoring her glare. "You're opening yourself up, and I'm proud of you. You can let people in and still be a terrifying force of nature, gorgeous. It's okay to feel."

She glared at him but didn't respond. After a few minutes of silence passed, she started chewing her lip, as though lost in thought.

"Jasper?" she asked, finally, closing her eyes once again and tilting her head back as he ran his fingers through her hair. "What did this mean for you? For us?"

Jasper's fingers stilled.

What did it mean for him? It wasn't the first time he'd played third for a couple. Hell, group sex was so casual between some of the Shifter packs it was almost more common than being with another Wolf one on one. He'd never had any issue with it. Sex was sex.

Except when, suddenly, it wasn't.

He pulled her closer to him, wrapping his arms around her waist.

Mine.

"I care about you, Fey," Jasper answered, truthfully. "You and Alastair. This was fun. More than fun, that was mind blowing," he corrected, and she smirked. "But you're my friend, before anything else. I don't want anything to change that. I'm not looking to come between you and him."

Still holding her, he leaned down, ducking his head under the stream of water to plant a chaste kiss on her cheek.

"Of course"—he grinned, shifting to whisper in her ear and delighting in the way it made her wriggle against him—"if you and the boss ever feel like having some fun again, I would never say no."

He flipped off the water as Fey laughed.

"Stay here," he ordered. "I'll get you a towel."

"Jasper, you're dripping everywhere," Fey scolded as he stepped out of the shower to grab a towel for her.

Frowning, Jasper glanced down at the puddle he'd left on the floor, then grabbed two more towels, wrapping one around himself and throwing the other down to soak up the water. *Fixed.* Satisfied, he stepped back into the shower, wrapping her in the terry cloth and patting her dry.

Fey snorted, swatting at him playfully. But she let him finish.

When he was satisfied that she was dry enough, he stepped back out of the shower to grab a robe for her.

"That's Alastair's," Fey told him as he grabbed one hanging on the back of the bathroom door. Jasper brought the fabric up to his nose and sniffed. Sure enough, it smelled like him, like cedar wood and oak-aged whiskey. Jasper adjusted the towel around his waist, embarrassingly hard, now.

"Even better," he said, stepping close to her and wrapping her in the robe despite her protest. The sleeves were way too big, so he rolled them up on her arms until they were just past her elbows. "He's going to love seeing you in it, gorgeous. I promise."

JASPER DRESSED before joining them in the kitchen, plucking his clothing out from under Fey's and Alastair's, and made himself somewhat presentable. By the time he finished, Fey was already seated at the kitchen bar with a glass of wine in her hand and Alastair's massive robe pooling around her. Alastair was at the stove cooking, his back to Jasper as he worked on their dinner.

"Smells delicious," Jasper said, coming up behind Alastair, and ducking under his arm to sniff the pot of sauce.

Alastair swatted him away with a spoon.

"It's not ready," he snapped. "Fuck off."

Jasper ignored him to dip his finger in the pot of sauce. Popping it directly into his mouth, he hummed in appreciation. With an irritated grunt, Alastair swatted at him again, but Jasper just danced away, licking his fingers and chuckling.

Alastair bared his fangs at him as Fey laughed, her eyes sparkling. Then, dropping his voice to a low murmur, he asked, "Was the robe your idea, puppy?"

Jasper's only answer was a wicked grin.

"I like it," Alastair said. His eyes moved over Fey where she sat, taking in every inch of her. The robe was so big on her it barely stayed closed where he had cinched it shut. Where the fabric met in a deep V, the curves of her breasts were clearly visible, and the fabric shifted a little lower every time she moved.

"I thought you would," Jasper admitted, smirking at the heated look in Alastair's eyes.

"Sit," Alastair ordered, motioning to the kitchen bar. He reached for a glass of wine, taking a deep drink of it before handing Jasper an open bottle of beer.

"Yes, boss," Jasper grinned cheekily, taking the beer and sliding onto the seat next to Fey.

This was heaven, too. Jasper's heart felt light in his chest as he watched Alastair cook. By the time he dished up their food, all three of them were relaxed and chatting. Fey told them both about her day of training, filling them in on meaningless gossip about her students. Before long, Alastair and Jasper were talking about the club and some of the newer employees, and Fey's eyelids were clearly growing heavy.

The third time Fey's head drooped toward the table, forcing her to jerk herself back up, Alastair finally gave in.

"Alright, Witchling," he said, setting his unfinished wine on the table and standing. "No falling asleep in your dinner. Come on, let's get you to bed."

Fey pulled a face, propping her face up in her hand. "That's a really rude thing to say to me on my birthday."

Jasper barked a laugh, but Alastair only rolled his eyes, coming behind her and lifting her from her seat. She flashed Jasper a small smile as Alastair led her back to the bedroom.

He tried not to acknowledge the feeling in his chest as he watched them go. Tried to pretend it was like every other time he'd been a third in this situation, every other time it had gotten to the point in the evening where he should gracefully make his exit and let them return to their lives together.

Without him.

Swallowing, Jasper started gathering up the dishes. This was nice, he told himself, stacking the dishes in the sink. This had been just what he'd needed. A way to scratch an itch. And it doesn't have to be anything more than just this, more than just one night. It doesn't.

It doesn't.

Grinding his teeth together, Jasper flicked the water on and grabbed a sponge. He poured soap into the sink and started washing up, focusing on scrubbing sauce from the dishes with just a little more focus than was necessary.

He lost himself in the task, so consumed by it he didn't notice Alastair return until a dark voice spoke directly at his shoulder, making him jump.

"What are you doing, puppy?" Alastair asked.

Jasper glanced to his side where Alastair leaned against the counter, assessing him. He was still wearing only a pair of slacks, and they hung low on his hips. Distractingly low.

"Just washing up, boss," Jasper answered, painting a grin on his face. Alastair raised an eyebrow, plucking his wineglass from the counter and draining it. "I'm almost done, then I'll be on my way."

The eyebrow rose even further. "Oh no," Alastair said, curling his lip. "Our agreement was for one night. And it is…" Alastair looked pointedly at the clock on the wall. "A quarter past one. That is not *one night*."

Jasper's brain stuttered.

"You want me to stay?" he asked, certain he misunderstood.

"I don't want to be responsible for telling Fey that her birthday present cut and run the moment she fell asleep," Alastair answered.

He set his empty wineglass on the bar top and walked back toward the bedroom, calling over his shoulder. "Come on, puppy. You can sleep at the foot of the bed like a good dog, can't you?"

Grinning, Jasper dried his hands and followed.

CHAPTER 15
VEE

She had to hand it to Jayce—he'd come through for her this time. Vee looked around at the boxes stacked on the clubhouse rooftop and smiled.

"How much did this cost us?" she asked. It didn't matter, not really. Whatever it was, it would be worth it. And if they had to arrange a special score to get some more gold, they could. With her powers, they could do anything they wanted.

"Nothing," Jayce answered with a smile. He looked nothing like the little kid she had protected for all those years, not anymore. A growth spurt had taken care of that. Now Jayce towered over her, towered over everyone in their little gang. He brushed his dark blond hair from his eyes and grinned as he explained. "Jacques got a job as an apprentice at the printer's office about a year ago—he went in after hours to get these all printed up for us, free of charge."

Vee frowned. Jacques, she vaguely remembered him. But they all blended together after a while, especially the males. He was another of Jayce's strays—one of the boys he brought into their gang to give them a better chance, to give them a little safety and consistent access to food. Jayce's brother may have started the tradition, but since he'd taken over, Jayce had expanded their little gang almost tenfold. And it was paying off now that some of his strays were making names for themselves, getting jobs and gaining influence. They had resources all over the city, which meant they had a lot of favors they could call in at any time if need be.

Kneeling down and taking out his pocketknife, Jayce sliced through the tape on a box for her and flipped the cardboard open.

Vee grinned as she looked inside, squatting down to get a better look. Stacks and stacks of posters with the same image printed on them. Replicas of the ones someone else was putting up all over the city.

Fey's face looked up at her from inside the box. The Witch who had taken down an empire. The Witch who brought the Crown itself to its knees.

Just as Vee intended to.

"They're perfect!" she squealed, pulling out a stack.

"Jacques was a little confused about why you wanted them," Jayce admitted, glancing up at her before opening another box.

Vee opened her mouth to explain but was interrupted by another of Jayce's strays climbing up the ladder to the roof. The old metal ladder squeaked and moaned under the weight, but it held.

"Hey, Vee," the boy called when he saw her, his head popping up over the brick lip that lined the rooftop. Vee chewed her lip, trying to remember this one's name... he'd been around at least a year now, hovering on the sidelines.

"Hey, Seth," Jayce called back to him, shooting Vee a significant look.

Seth. Right. All these males looked the same to her, she supposed. Big, smelly, and noisy, all of them, and it made it very hard to tell any of them apart.

"What do you need, Seth?" Vee asked, standing up and watching him. She didn't bother hiding the posters from him. None of the strays would ever dare to question her or her business.

"I want to introduce you to someone," Seth said, climbing up the ladder the rest of the way and stepping up onto the roof to stand amongst the boxes.

Vee waited, watching as Seth leaned over the edge to help someone up. Finally, a girl's head emerged over the brick, no more than six or seven.

Vee forced herself to smile, but something cracked in her chest. A thousand emotions swirled inside her. Rage, pain, sadness. She kept a movie-star smile on her face, betraying nothing.

"Hey there," she said to the girl, who scrambled up the rest of the ladder and glanced around at them suspiciously. "My name is Vee. What's yours?"

The little girl stared at her with untrusting eyes.

"This," Seth said, putting a gentle hand on the girl's shoulder, "is Stella."

Vee crouched slowly, lowering herself to Stella's level. Vee was tall, taller than a lot of the gang, so it helped the younger ones trust her more sometimes if they saw her as closer to their size. She didn't bother to get any closer to her, though, didn't close that gap between them. New strays needed space, after all. "Hey, Stella," Vee said, still smiling. "Welcome to our clubhouse."

Stella blinked at her and slowly looked around at the others. It was a busy night, tonight. A few other strays were lounging around on the roof, chatting in their usual packs. Jayce ignored them all, pulling stacks of posters from the boxes and piling them around Vee.

"Pa says I shouldn't talk to strangers," Stella said, finally, breaking her stare and looking down at the ground.

That rage, again, roaring in Vee's ears, but she kept her smile. "Oh yeah? That's a good rule, Stella, it really is. But we're not strangers anymore, are we? You know my name, and I know yours." She grinned at Seth. "And you know my buddy Seth, right? So, that makes us friends, doesn't it?"

"S'pose," Stella said, still looking at the ground.

"Where is your Pa, Stella?" Vee asked, careful to keep her voice relaxed. Casual.

She shrugged a shoulder, looking away.

"Last he was seen, he was down at the south dock," Seth told Vee, eyes hard as slate.

The south dock. Vee clenched her teeth together. A user, then. No one hung around the docks unless they were looking for a fix, or they were selling one. And the only sellers in this city anymore were the Vampires.

Filthy leeches.

"Stella here is a Badger Shifter," Seth announced, clasping the young girl on the shoulder.

Vee's smile widened at the pride in Seth's voice, at the way Stella grinned, her smile stretching from ear to ear. "Is that so?" she asked. "Wow, Stella. I've never met a Badger Shifter before. Have you, Jayce?"

Jayce glanced up from his stacks of paper and shook his head. "Me? Nah. Never."

"Must be pretty rare, huh?"

"We are!" Stella said, looking at them, excited. "And we're diggers. Better diggers than any of the other Shifters, even the Rats."

"Wow!" Vee said, shifting back to sit on her ankles. "You know, Stella," she dropped her voice to a conspiratorial whisper. "Our clubhouse could really use a good digger. We have some scores coming up soon, and you might be just what we need. What do you say? Want to help us out?"

The way Stella's eyes lit up made her stomach twist, but Vee kept the smile on her face. They'd learned this together, her and Jayce. Strays wouldn't accept handouts, didn't trust that anyone would want to help them out without expecting something in return. But convince them they can pay you back, somehow? Convince them they're necessary, that they have a skill you desperately need? Well, then they'll accept your help, thinking the whole time that they're pulling one over on you. Taking advantage of a good deal.

"Are you hungry, Stella?" Jayce asked suddenly. "We've got sandwiches downstairs left over from dinner. Seth, why don't you take her down and get her something to eat, huh? We can't have our new digger going hungry."

Stella grinned, and Seth clasped her by the shoulder before leading her back down the ladder and off the roof.

Vee watched them go, the smile slipping from her face.

"They found a dead Badger Shifter by the docks earlier this week, didn't they?" she asked Jayce, voice low.

Jayce nodded. His own smile was gone, too, and his eyes were hard. "Yeah. Overdosed. He'd be about the right age to be her father, too."

Vee nodded. "Keep an eye on her. She's probably been living off scraps for at least a few days now. Keep her inside just in case she had to steal her last few meals and got on a merchant's bad side. And find something she can dig. I don't care if it's a score or not."

Jayce grunted.

Vee hated this part. Hated the first few weeks of trying to keep a new stray. These poor kids were so damaged, so used to surviving moment to moment, that it was almost impossible to help them. Convince them they were necessary, give them their freedom, and let them adjust. That was the trick to it. If they could keep her safe over the next few weeks, they could find Stella a more permanent place to stay, maybe some other Shifter pack that would take her in.

And if not? Well, they had beds here, in the clubhouse. They had food. And they had Vee to keep them all safe.

Vee sighed, trying to push all those emotions boiling inside of her away, at least for the moment. Sitting back on the cold brick of the roof and grabbing a pen, she took the top poster and scrawled a message on top of it, then set it aside.

Jayce wandered over to watch after a few minutes. He knew better than to ask what she was up to; she would tell him when it was necessary. So, instead, he sat down next to her, head cocked to the side, watching her quietly as she worked.

Vee grabbed another poster, humming to herself as she wrote.

CHAPTER 16
AMALIA

It was raining. Amalia could hear the gentle percussion of the raindrops hitting her bedroom window.

She had no idea what time it was. Her curtains were closed tight enough to not let in any light, and she couldn't remember the last time she'd bothered to open them. It could be morning outside. It could be the middle of the night or the middle of the day, she didn't know. Not that it mattered.

She should take a bath, Amalia thought to herself. Something smelled sour in her room, and she guessed it might be her. Either that or the long white nightgown she wore. Amalia couldn't remember the last time it had been washed.

She should take a bath, but... the rain sounded so comforting, tapping rhythmically against the glass. She could bathe later, couldn't she? The sounds of the rain made her tired again, and even though she'd been sleeping all day—or night, or whatever time it was out there—Amalia decided she just might fall back asleep and let the sounds of the rain carry her away.

A light knock on her door pulled Amalia from her haze, and she scrambled to sit up, rubbing her eyes.

"Linh?" she asked hopefully as the door opened.

Linh had visited every day after her mother's death, assuring her that justice would be done, that the crown would rise again, that the council would fail, and she would be queen. Amalia had never cared about being queen, not really. But she'd enjoyed the company, enjoyed the attention. Enjoyed having someone to talk to, even if Linh was much better at talking than she was at listening.

But over time, Linh's visits dropped to once a week. Then once a month. And, eventually, her visits stopped altogether.

Amalia didn't blame her. She didn't have the energy to blame her, or anyone else who had forgotten about her. Back when her mother was still alive, even she seemed to forget that Amalia existed, so that wasn't anything new. Sometimes Amalia felt like a little trinket her mother kept in storage. Every now and then she'd take her out, put her in a pretty dress, and prop her up next to her on a child-sized throne to show her off. Then, back in her box she'd go until the next time her mother wanted to show her off again.

You get used to it.

But it wasn't Linh who entered her room. It was another High Priestess, Leandra, the head of the Fire Coven. Amalia's heart fell, but she tried not to let it show on her face. Her mother had told her once that she wore her heart on her sleeve and her emotions plain on her face. The way she said it made it clear to Amalia that it wasn't a good thing, and since then she had tried as best as she could to keep her heart and emotions to herself, hidden away.

In the doorway, Leandra paused, frowning.

"I'm sorry, child," she said sadly. "High Priestess Linh remains too sick to visit the palace. Perhaps, you would like to visit her...?"

"No," Amalia answered, a little too quickly. She swallowed, and straightened her back, sitting up in bed with her shoulders back and head high, just as her mother had taught her. "No, thank you, Priestess. I am sure she will visit when she is able. It would be best not to disturb her rest."

She didn't want to see Linh and didn't want to bother her when she was sick. When Linh was better, she would come and visit again. Amalia knew she would. Had to believe she would.

"I thought you and I might go to the kitchens and have a small meal together," Leandra said, giving Amalia what she guessed was meant to be a friendly smile. It looked a little too stretched on the Priestess's face, a little too forced. "Your handmaids informed me you didn't eat your dinner tonight. Perhaps you are hungry now?"

Amalia frowned. Had she not eaten dinner? She couldn't remember. She didn't even remember anyone bringing her food. When was the last time she'd eaten, anyway?

She did feel empty, she realized. Perhaps she was hungry. She almost said yes, almost let Leandra take her out of her room—the room she'd spent the last several weeks in, leaving only to use the toilet and bathe—but something stopped her. When she opened her mouth to accept the invitation, Amalia's gaze fell on Leandra's shawl, and any hunger she felt disappeared.

Her mother had ordered the White Priestesses to give any powerful Witch they identified at their Awakening Allium, to keep them from getting strong enough to challenge their family line. Strong enough to challenge the throne. Leandra had been one of those Witches. And now, on the red shawl that marked her as a Priestess of the Fire Coven, she had two more colors embroidered there. Blue for water, and yellow for Air.

Leandra was another Witch her mother had hurt. Another Witch who had reason to hate her.

Amalia swallowed her words and chose new ones, instead. "Thank you, but no. I find myself with little appetite these days."

Leandra looked concerned, and Amalia supposed the Priestess must be a wonderful actress to make it look so real. Her mother could do that, too. She could smile, laugh, and look at the men in her life like they meant the world to her. But it was a lie, and the moment they were alone, all those emotions vanished.

"Have you been feeling ill, child?" Leandra asked, taking a step further into the room. She raised her hand, coming forward as though to feel Amalia's forehead and check for a temperature.

Amalia's heartbeat rose so quickly she felt dizzy. She didn't want someone near her, didn't want someone touching her. She was dirty, and that sour smell in the room was surely her and her unwashed night clothes. The last thing she wanted was someone touching her.

It was the last thing she wanted and yet, inexplicably, she wanted it more than anything. Wanted someone to hold her, to hug her, if only for a moment.

"Stop!" she cried out, and Leandra stopped mid-step. Amalia was breathing too quickly. She felt she might faint. "I'm fine. I have no fever, no sickness. Truly."

The Priestess lowered her hand slowly, still looking concerned.

Leandra had come by after her mother's death, too, just as Linh had. But she hadn't talked about revenge and reinstating the Crown. She hadn't talked about making Amalia queen and making the Witches who had killed her mother pay. No. She'd talked about healing. About forgiveness and growth.

She'd talked about Fey. About how the woman who'd murdered her parents was now working for the Palace, helping all those Witches her mother had hurt. It made Amalia's heart feel like it was being squeezed in a vise to hear it.

"You may leave," Amalia said, putting as much of her mother's voice into her words as she could. It must have worked, because Leandra bowed and retreated.

"Of course, Princess," she said, softly. "Perhaps next time, then."

Amalia didn't want to think about next time. She didn't want to think about why Leandra sounded so sad. She just wanted to listen to the rain and go back to sleep.

After Leandra left, that's exactly what she did.

CHAPTER 17
JASPER

It was just past dawn when Jasper finally returned home to his small rundown apartment, and he couldn't stop smiling.

He'd barely slept. *They'd* barely slept. Fey had woken up almost as soon as Jasper had crawled back into their bed, eager for round two. And, later, round three.

He'd lost track after that. Lost track of all the ways he'd touched and licked and fucked her.

Now he was exhausted and in desperate need of another shower. *Goddess*, he stank. Slipping his key into the lock, Jasper let himself into the tiny, single bedroom apartment he called home. A shower first, he decided. Then a long nap before he had to go to work in the evening. That's what he needed. Jasper threw his keys down and made straight for the kitchen. He was so thirsty he could drink a lake. Grabbing a reasonably clean glass from the counter, he poured himself a glass of water straight from the tap and drained it in one go.

More. He ran the tap again, filling up the cup and drinking another.

He was so tired and so distracted by the smell of them lingering on his body that he didn't notice he wasn't alone until Vivian spoke.

"Jeez, Uncle Jas, where have you been all night?"

Jasper choked on his water, spitting some back out into the sink.

Coughing, he whirled around to find his niece seated cross-legged on top of his small kitchen table, a bowl of cereal balanced on her lap. Her eyebrow rose as she looked him up and down, assessing.

Disapproving.

Coughing up the last of the water, Jasper shot her a glare.

"Feet off the furniture, Viv," he scolded.

Vivian rolled her eyes but complied, uncrossing her legs and dangling them off the edge of the table instead.

"What are you doing here?" Jasper asked. He glanced at the calendar he kept on the icebox, where he noted when Vivian was supposed to be staying with him. Today was blank. "Aren't you supposed to be with Nan for the rest of the week?"

Vivian shot a grin at him, chewing a mouthful of cereal. "Nope," she told him in an amused voice. "I'm staying with you until midweek, remember? We talked about it?"

Jasper groaned, rubbing at his face. *Fuck.* Somehow, with everything going on, he'd forgotten. He never would have left her alone all night, never would have agreed to stay with Fey and Alastair if he'd remembered.

Would he?

Jasper rubbed his eyes. "Sorry, Viv. I guess I forgot."

She shrugged, kicking her legs in the air as she ate, but Jasper knew immediately it was a front. Viv always did this and always tried to hide when she was upset. She always tried to act older than she really was.

"Tell you what," Jasper started, smirking at her. "Why don't we go for a nice run through the city, just the two of us? As an apology for being an ass."

Yeah, he was exhausted. And yeah, he should really get some sleep before his shift at work, but what the hell, right? One night of exhaustion wouldn't kill him.

Vivian's eyes widened. "Really?" she asked, unable to hide the excitement in her voice. Jasper grinned. Vivian spent most of her time being shuffled around the homes of the older Wolf Shifters, including her grandmother. The Shifter community as a whole had raised her more than he had, and though that was common with orphaned Wolves, it meant she spent too much of her time with Shifters who weren't able to run with her. Shifters who weren't able to keep up with a young, agile Wolf who needed to stretch her legs and paws now and then.

"Really," Jasper promised, taking a step closer to her.

Vivian pulled a face, putting her hand up to stop him. "Ew," she said, wrinkling her nose. "Take a shower first. You smell like sex, Uncle Jas."

Jasper stopped immediately, his jaw dropping. "How... how in the fuck do you know that smell, Vivian?" he asked, stunned.

The spoon Vivian was holding clattered into the bowl as it slipped out of her fingers, her eyes going wide. "Ew!" she shrieked. "Ew, I was right? I was just joking! Oh, Uncle Jas, that is revolting. Were you really out all night shacking up with someone?"

Well... multiple someones, Jasper thought, as Vivian shuddered and pretended to gag, leaning over the side of the table and heaving.

"No," he insisted. "Of course not! I just wanted to know where you got that idea from! You're only sixteen!"

"Oh, sure." Vivian rolled her eyes. "Ick, I cannot believe you. So that's where you were all night?"

"I was working!" he lied. "I'm just... stinky. That's all."

Viv wrinkled her nose at him, obviously not believing his lies, and Jasper finally gave up.

"Fine," he said. "Fine... just let me take a quick shower, okay? Ten minutes, tops. Then we'll see which one of us can run to the riverfront and back fastest. How about that?"

It had been too long since they'd run together, and Jasper could use some time in his other skin after last night. He needed to stretch his legs, to smell the city.

If Vivian had a tail in this form, she'd be wagging it. She sat up a little straighter, excited.

"Oh, I know I can beat you to the riverfront, Uncle Jas," she called after him as he left the room.

He didn't want to shower, not really, even knowing he should. He could still smell them on his skin, and he wanted to keep it that way, wanted to have their scents all over his body as long as possible. But he really did stink, didn't he? And who knew what would happen if we went to the club smelling like them tonight?

Resigned, Jasper got into the shower and scrubbed himself clean, washing those delicious scents down the drain.

Vivian had already shifted by the time he emerged from the shower, and Jasper couldn't help but smile at her Wolf form. She'd always been a little too skinny, especially around her mother's death when times were lean and there hadn't been enough to go around. She was still too thin, in his opinion, but she'd filled out enough that her Wolf was now nearly as big as his.

She was a sleek Wolf, with short, spiky auburn fur and eyes full of trouble. She looked just like her mom...

Grinning, Jasper slipped into his own room to change, reveling in the feeling as his body shifted and morphed into something new. He was a male, sure, but he was also this—a Wolf. Strong, fast, powerful...

And ready to run.

Nipping at Viv's heels, he chased her out of the townhouse and out into the streets, toward the water.

He let her beat him to the riverfront. Or, at least, that's what he told himself.

CHAPTER 18
AMALIA

Her clothes didn't fit.

Amalia looked down at the gold-and-white gown she'd pulled from her wardrobe, confusion and frustration swirling together in her chest. She couldn't remember the last time she had bought a new dress, couldn't remember the last time someone had delivered one to the palace.

But her old clothes no longer fit.

This one was—inexplicably—too large and too small at the same time. A fact that seemed to defy all reality. The hem should have reached the floor or at the very least to her ankles, but no—it fell at least three inches too short, hitting her nearly mid-calf. And the dress was uncomfortably tight across her chest, the stiff fabric digging into her ribs. But the rest?

Amalia snorted, holding her arms out to her sides. The dress was heavy and loose, everywhere but her chest. It slipped off her shoulders, and there was much more fabric than she remembered. Enough that she could grab a handful where it pooled at her waist and below her collarbones, just above her chest.

She needed new clothes. Amalia let out a long breath.

She'd wanted to start with something simple. A bath and then maybe a walk around the palace grounds. She'd opened her curtains this morning and seen the sun and the rich blue sky and felt... something. For the first time in a long time, she'd felt something, some kernel of emotion in her chest.

Not happiness or hope, or anything like that. Maybe a little sad. But it had been something, after so long of feeling nothing, and somehow that had been enough to get her out of bed and into the bath.

But now? None of her clothes fit. She couldn't go outside, not like this. Couldn't be seen wearing clothing that was so obviously not her size. She looked a mess.

You represent our entire Faction, her mother had told her, repeatedly. *Try not to be such an embarrassment, won't you?*

And Amalia *was* trying. *Truly* trying. But she didn't have other clothing, and not a single item in her wardrobe fit her anymore. Her nightclothes at least fit, but they were all dirty. She'd piled them all up outside her door, hoping her handmaids could get at least some of them washed before she went to bed tonight.

She would need to send someone out to buy her new clothing, eventually, but until then...

An idea occurred to her. She knew where there were clothes that might fit her. Most of it unworn, too.

Her mother had always bought more dresses than she could ever wear, hadn't she? And her mother had known exactly how to dress, exactly how to be the proper representative for all Witches. Surely her clothing would be good enough, wouldn't it? Wouldn't make her look like an embarrassment?

Yes, Amalia decided, though the idea gave her a flutter of fear. *That is the answer.* Still, the idea of leaving the small world around her room was almost frightening enough to send her back to bed.

Amalia poked her head out her bedroom door and looked around. No one. Perfect.

Taking a deep breath to calm herself, she stepped out of her room and into the palace.

Moving quickly, Amalia snuck through the hallways of the Northern Wing, listening for anyone who might be in the palace, walking the halls. She didn't want to be seen like this—her dress, too short and so tight around the chest she could barely breathe, and her hair still wet from the bath. She was glad she hadn't put on shoes yet. Her bare feet made barely any noise on the cold marble floors as she hurried.

No one had bothered doing anything with her mother's effects after her death. It was like everyone had forgotten her, just like they'd forgotten Amalia. Her mother's room looked just as it had that night—almost. The maids had taken the sheets from the bed and replaced them with fresh ones. There was a very thin blanket of dust on it now, and Amalia wondered how often they bothered to change the sheets for a queen who would never use that bed again.

Amalia tried not to look around at her mother's room too much, heading straight for the closet instead.

Her mother's closet was full of dresses, just as she'd predicted. Amalia brushed her hand over the shoulders of the gowns, reveling in the textures. They were even more beautiful than the ones in Amalia's wardrobe, even more well-made, more luxurious.

There were a few dresses Amalia remembered, a few she'd seen her mother wear before. Amalia didn't touch those. She couldn't even bring herself to look at them for too long. They made her want to go back to bed and forget about ever wanting to get up in the first place.

But there were others, plenty of others. Unworn. Ones her mother had never even touched. Those dresses didn't make her feel anything at all. Amalia took a few of them from their hangers, laying them out on the bed, before choosing a green gown with cream lace to try on. It was intricate, but not so much that it couldn't be a day dress. It was perfect.

Amalia struggled to remove her old dress, wincing as the fabric cut into her skin. It was a relief to toss it aside and step into the green gown.

It fit. Mostly. It was a little long, the hem brushing against the floor, though not nearly as long as she'd expected it to be. Her mother had always been so much taller than she was. Maybe this dress was meant to be worn short? And that's why—

Amalia yelped as she turned and caught sight of her reflection in her mother's mirror.

At first, she thought it was a ghost. Her mother's specter of death, trapped in her bedchamber, waiting for Amalia to come here so she could tell her what a disappointment she was one last time.

But no. That wasn't her mother in the mirror, Amalia realized, stepping closer. The figure took a step closer, in time with her.

It was her. *Her* reflection.

I look so much like her, Amalia thought, shocked. She walked to the mirror, leaning closer to her reflection. She twisted her head from side to side, trying to see herself from every angle. Not an exact copy, no. But enough like her, it was a shock to see.

Her face was so thin—much thinner than she remembered. When had she last looked in a mirror, last seen her own face? Her round rosy cheeks were gone, and their loss made her look so much older than sixteen.

She didn't have her mother's snow-white hair, and there wasn't even a trace of white in her brown curls. But she had her mother's eyes, her mother's height.

Her body looked more like her mother's, too. A little too thin, like she was being stretched, but her mother had looked the same way.

Suddenly, it was all too much. Amalia looked away from the mirror, not wanting to see herself there anymore. Not wanting to see her mother there anymore. She gathered up the dresses she'd pulled from the closet and ran back to her room, not bothering to pick up her old dress from where it lay abandoned on the floor next to her mother's bed.

CHAPTER 19
ALICE

Alice forced herself to swallow her irritation when she rounded a bend in the palace halls and found Leandra standing there, blocking her way to the throne room.

"I'm worried about the princess," the High Priestess said, forgoing any greeting or preamble.

Great. Another thing I have to deal with today. But she managed to keep the irritation from showing on her face as she met Leandra's eyes.

"You're stopping me in the middle of the hallway to tell me this?" Alice asked her, her tone skeptical.

Leandra nodded.

Just great.

"Fine," Alice said, clenching her jaw tight. She gestured for Leandra to follow her, skirting around her and continuing down the hallway. "Walk with me and talk. I don't have time to stop and chitchat. I'm on my way to the council meeting."

She'd be damned if she'd let Leandra's little worries keep her from getting there in time.

"I've been speaking with the princess's handmaids," Leandra explained, hurrying to keep up with Alice as she stomped through the hall. Leandra's silk slippers made a soft pitter-patter on the marble floor, a stark contrast to Alice's heavy steps. "She rarely leaves her room anymore. All she does is sleep. And I don't think she's eating."

"And?" Alice prompted.

"And... and what are we going to do about this?" Leandra asked, stunned.

"Do about *what*?"

"I think the princess is depressed, Alice. I think she's lonely. She never has any visitors, never spends any time outside of her room."

"If you're so worried about her being alone, why don't you go and visit her?" Alice asked. She didn't have time for this. Didn't have time to worry about one little brat when the realm was hanging on by a thread. The army had been practically dismantled after the Queen's death, and despite all of Alice's efforts to rebuild the city's forces, they were still understaffed. They were vulnerable without an army of trained Witches to rely on. Vulnerable and ripe for the taking.

Kallista's words still echoed through her mind and kept her up at night. *You have a power vacuum in this city, and I've lived through enough of those to know that they breed monsters...*

They needed an army. They needed to be ready when the monsters came.

She had to be ready.

"I have talked to her," Leandra insisted. She reached out, taking Alice by the arm and stopping her, turning the Witch to face her. "Alice, listen to me. That child is alone. Truly alone. I think she needs a friend. She needs to spend time with children her own age. To connect with someone."

Alice's teeth clenched tight. "She has been encouraged to join Fey's training classes, where there are children her own age. We have encouraged her to come out of her room and make new friends. You know as well as I do that she hasn't taken anyone up on that offer."

Leandra's voice dropped to a whisper. "Alice... Fey killed her parents. I don't think she wants to be around her. I'm starting to wonder if it might have been cruel of us to suggest it in the first place. Would you want to spend time with the Witch who killed your family?"

Had they been cruel to suggest it? The thought gave Alice pause. She had forgotten that particular lie, forgotten that the realm believed the old queen had died at Fey's hands rather than Joy's. That Leandra—that Amalia—believed it. Exhaling loudly, Alice let her head drop back.

"And what do you want me to do about it, Leandra?" she asked. "What do you expect the council to do about one sad little girl?"

Leandra shook her head. "I don't know," she admitted in a whisper.

Alice snorted and started walking again, forcing Leandra to keep up.

"I'm just worried," Leandra continued, hurrying after Alice as they reached the throne room. The rest of the council was already assembled there, waiting for her. *Great*. She was late.

Leandra was still talking, though Alice had stopped listening. "We agreed to keep her in the palace, keep her taken care of, but I can't help but think we're just caging her in here. And since no one seems to know what to do with her—"

She stopped mid-sentence. Alice stopped as well.

Kallista stood at the council table, angry shadows swirling around her. The very air around her was dark. Cold.

"We need to discuss this," the Demon snapped, pointing at a stack of papers strewn across the table.

Alice clenched her teeth together tightly, temporarily forgetting all about Leandra as she approached the council table to see what had Kallista in such a temper.

When she saw what was there, she snorted, not bothering to give the posters more than a passing glance.

"We're aware of the posters," Alice stated, moving around the table to get to her seat. "*Fey* is aware of the posters, and we've discussed what they mean for both her and the city. I think the best thing we can all do is ignore them—this is nothing more than a fringe movement to elevate Fey into a position she is, in no way, shape, or form, considering. It's a non-issue."

Goddess, she couldn't believe Kallista was still pushing this nonsense, still insisting that Fey wanted to be anything more than—

"These are different, Alice," Kallista snapped, interrupting her thoughts. "Look at them. Damn you, Witch, open your eyes and actually read them."

Startled, Alice glanced from Kallista back to the posters on the table. Grabbing one at random, she lifted it to read.

They were different. Sure, they used the same image of Fey, but...

"Goddess help us," Leandra whispered, picking up a poster and visibly paling. Alice had forgotten the High Priestess was even there.

Death to the council, read the handwritten message scrawled over the page in angry black ink. Frowning, Alice picked up another. And another.

Traitors.

Council = Witch's Pets.

"This is... much more concerning," Alice agreed. With difficulty, she pulled her eyes away from the image of her sister and looked at Kallista. "Where did you find these?"

"Everywhere," the Demon said. "They're in every district, on every damned street. Someone has put them up all over the city."

"No," Alice said, flipping through the pages. They were all variations of the same thing. Image after image of Fey's face from the day the Crown had outed her, all marred with handwritten messages. "No, not someone. One person didn't do this. This was a group. This was an organized attack."

The deSanguine gave the stack a dismissive glance. "So?" he asked. "I fail to see the immediate concern here. How is this any different from the ones demanding she be queen?"

Alice's hand paused on the final poster.

DEATH TO THE ROYAL FAMILY.

DEATH TO PRINCESS AMALIA.

"This is different," Alice whispered. Her instincts, finely honed from her years of training as a Queen's Blade, flared to life. Warning her. "This is a threat to everything we've built these last few years."

Kallista had been right. The monsters had come for them.

And they weren't ready.

CHAPTER 20
AMALIA

Amalia picked the simplest dress she'd stolen from her mother's room to wear the day she snuck out of the palace.

It was a crimson gown, with a hand-stitched skirt that cascaded off her hips in waves. It came with a matching cloak, the golden clasp fashioned to look like a songbird with a sapphire for the eye. Amalia fastened it around her shoulders.

She stood in front of her mirror, looking at herself and gathering the courage to leave. She'd asked for the mirror to be brought to her bedroom, feeling as though she had lost something by not noticing the way her face had changed over the last few months.

But staring at her reflection now, Amalia fought the urge to crawl back under her covers. Some might consider her pretty, she supposed. After all, she had her mother's nose, her mother's eyes. Her mother had been pretty—beautiful, even. Everyone said so. But somehow, Amalia didn't feel like the features fit her face as well. She felt like an unfinished painting, like there was something missing from her that everyone else had. Something her mother had.

She'd spent an hour styling her hair after her bath, trying to get her curls under some semblance of control, and even braiding crimson ribbons into her hair. And yet, after all that work, the ringlets looked flat and limp. Lifeless. With a sigh, she plucked at one of the ribbons, reaching for the sharp scissors her handmaids had left to trim it one final time.

Good enough.

Before she could chicken out and go back to bed, Amalia found her largest nightgown and put it gingerly over her mirror, covering the reflection. She was tired of looking at herself, tired of seeing a poor replica of her mother's face staring back at her. Maybe it would get easier with time.

But for now...

Amalia took a deep breath to steady herself. Then, with all the courage she could muster, she opened her window to climb out.

She'd snuck out once before when she was just a child. It had been just after her Awakening, and after the joy of finding out she possessed control over all four elements had worn off, she had felt... empty. She had expected things to change between her and her mother after she'd been officially named heir to the realm, expected that her mother would begin teaching her how to use her powers, the way the generals in Solare taught their soldiers. She had expected her mother to be proud.

But nothing had changed between them at all. Sure, Amalia was suddenly invited to public appearances and was suddenly expected to be present at all her mother's parties and meetings, a silent miniature version of the queen everyone loved. But behind closed doors, her mother behaved just the same as she always had. It was as though she knew from the moment of her birth that Amalia would be a disappointment and had decided right then and there not to waste time on her.

Unable to take it any longer, Amalia had run away.

Well... "ran away" is perhaps an exaggeration. She hadn't even made it out of the palace before she'd been caught by a guard and escorted back to her rooms. Her mother had been informed, Amalia assumed, but she'd never brought it up to her. The next time Amalia had seen her, though, she'd looked even more disappointed than usual. As though she realized that even running away was somehow outside of Amalia's skill set. Too incompetent to even accomplish *that*.

This time she wasn't running away, Amalia told herself as she hopped down from her window to the ground below, clumsily using

Air to slow her fall. She just needed to get out of the palace, just needed to see what was going on outside those marble walls in the city proper.

In the weeks after her mother's death, Linh had told her what a mess the realm had become. The city was full of riots and murder, crimes committed out in the open, innocent people being dragged into the streets. It had terrified her when she'd heard that, and somehow it seemed to get worse and worse every time Linh updated her. For a while, she'd been so sure the rioters would come for her, would pull her out of the palace to make her pay for her mother's crimes. The idea kept her up at night, too frightened to sleep.

Linh had described some of the horrible things they were doing to young Witches. Deplorable, disgusting things...

She just needed to see it for herself, Amalia resolved. Just needed to look out at the city and know how things were. Then, maybe, she could help somehow. That's what her mother would have done.

Wasn't it?

There were so few guards around the palace now. Not nearly as many as there had been when her mother was still alive. And since Solare had burned to nothing, there were no soldiers around this side of the palace to catch her and take her back to her room. Still, Amalia pulled the hood of her cloak up and kept her head down, hoping she could at least avoid being recognized, in case a palace servant saw her.

It was a longer walk to the city than she'd expected, and by the time she'd crossed the river and left the palace grounds, her legs were already complaining about the exercise. She hadn't done much more than gentle walks around the palace gardens in years. Was it any wonder she was so out of shape?

But Amalia kept walking, hood up, trying to ignore the heat of the summer day and the shaking in her legs. She could do this. She would do this.

Linh had told her the palace was one of the few safe places left in the city—perhaps in the entire realm. Linh had her believing that since her mother's death the city was crumbling under the weight of crime and horrors beyond her imagining.

A small part of Amalia wasn't at all surprised to find out it was a lie.

The city looked just as it always had, and the streets became busier and busier as she walked further into the city center and away from the imposing shadow of the palace. There wasn't chaos here. People were not being murdered in the streets, being dragged from their homes in broad daylight. No one was being tortured, no one was being violated or ripped limb from limb...

The sidewalks were full of citizens walking with their friends and family, full of people hurrying to and from work, full of people shopping, and talking, and laughing. After a while, Amalia lowered her hood, unable to stand the heat a moment longer. Her feet hurt, and she could feel herself getting blisters from shoes that weren't meant to be walked in for more than a short distance, but she didn't care.

There were more people on these streets than she'd seen in all her life.

She looked around at them all, wide eyed. She'd known, of course, that the city was full of people from all four Factions, but at the palace she'd had little contact with anyone besides other Witches. Here, there were Shifters—some in their animal forms. A Wolf prowled the street, stopping to scratch behind their ear with a long back foot. Not a single person other than her looked twice at it. There were even Demons, some with horns of various sizes and textures, but others with scales and long snake-like tails. She saw no Vampires, of course. The sun was high in the sky, and they were a nocturnal Faction by nature. But their presence was clear here, even during the day. A candy shop advertised their lollipops as "fang safe, for Vampire children," and another sign further down the walkway specifically assured patrons they were open until dawn "to accommodate all Factions, day or night."

After almost two hours of walking, Amalia knew she should head back to the palace, knew that even if no one noticed her absence she should at least go back before she was too tired to walk at all. Yet... she couldn't seem to leave. Every street brought new wonders, new shops, and new people. It was nothing she had ever experienced before, and she drank it all in, staring around at her city in wonder.

Demons were, by far, the Faction she'd had the least contact with, and the first Demon she'd seen with horns—actual horns, that curved from the side of his skull and ended under his ears, like a ram's—had smiled at her so sweetly she'd almost tripped over her skirt and fallen.

There had been no menace in his eyes, no anger. He seemed nothing at all like the creatures Linh had warned her about. Nothing at all like the savage things her mother had described.

That was another thing—her skirts. Even though this dress had been the simplest of her mother's gowns, and even though she'd worn dresses just like it every day of her life, Amalia looked around at the people on the street and felt wildly out of place.

None of them wore clothing like hers, not even the women. They wore pants, and skirts, and shorts. They wore things unlike any she'd seen before, and though their outfits weren't fancy, Amalia coveted every garment she saw.

And the clothing changed! As she walked, the neighborhoods shifted around her, and so did the people. Demons gave way to Shifters, and young student-filled neighborhoods gave way to businesses, and then to warehouses.

Amalia was so in love with the world around her, so in love with the changes and the people, that she didn't notice at first that she was lost. She had been following a song in her heart, a feeling rather than a road, and suddenly all the businesses were gone. There were people here, sure, but they looked... harder. Angrier.

Suddenly, no one was looking at her dress and smiling. There were no friendly nods or approving glances. If she'd felt overdressed before, it was nothing compared to how she felt now. Eyes followed her. And they did not look welcoming.

She had somehow managed to make her way into the shipping and warehouse district, and the workers here were not impressed with the ribbons in her curls, and her rich crimson cloak and hand-stitched dress. Amalia tugged her cloak tight around herself, trying to hide her clothing as best as she could, and began to avoid making eye contact. She looked around the streets and tried to remember where she'd been, tried to remember how to get back.

She couldn't see the palace anymore for all the tall buildings around her, but as she circled the block, she noticed that one direction seemed more uphill than the others. That should be the direction home, shouldn't it? After all, the palace sat at the highest point in the city—

surely if she made her way uphill, she should eventually find her way back to a place she recognized.

Her legs were in agony by now, and she knew her feet were bleeding from where blisters had formed and popped. She *ached*. But she had no choice now. She had to keep going, had to get home. Steeling herself, Amalia pushed the pain down. She could do this.

At least... she thought she could.

Amalia's foot caught the curb at a wrong angle, and she tripped, stumbling into a large male Shifter who was smoking outside a factory.

Instead of offering her his arm, or asking if she was okay, he gave an irritated grunt and pushed her until she stumbled away from him.

"Watch where you're going, Witch," he barked, curling his lip at her.

Amalia felt her cheeks heat. She'd never heard someone say Witch that way, as though it were an insult, not a blessing. Weren't they the greatest of the Factions, the most beloved by the Goddess? Why would anyone say it in such a manner?

She mumbled an apology and hurried away, glancing behind her often to make sure she wasn't being followed.

The Shifters didn't chase her. But they laughed as she left, and Amalia felt herself blush hard enough that she was sure her neck was the same color as her dress.

After a few blocks, Amalia wasn't sure she was going the right way, after all. Uphill was a harder concept to judge than she'd thought, and she backtracked several times, trying to figure out which direction was which.

She should just pick a direction and keep going, Amalia decided, stopping for a moment to look around once again and decide which direction was her best bet. If she turned right and then headed straight, that seemed like the best possible—

Amalia gasped as someone grabbed her arm and yanked her into an alley. They pulled at her with enough force that she lost her footing and stumbled, falling to her hands and knees.

"Well, well, well," came a voice from behind her. "Look what I caught, fellas."

Scrambling to her feet, Amalia looked around in horror.

A boy stood between her and the entrance of the alley, blocking her way back to the street. He was maybe a little younger than she was, but he was big. Tall, with dark blond messy hair, and wild looking eyes. A Shifter.

A predator.

She glanced around at the rest of the alley. There were more boys here, a whole group she hadn't even noticed when she'd been trying to find her way. She'd been so distracted, so focused, she had walked right into trouble.

Stupid, stupid, stupid.

"What brings a Witch to this side of the city, huh?" the boy asked, advancing toward her. Amalia scrambled back away from him, only to be shoved back toward him by another of the boys.

"A rich Witch, too," another said, stepping forward and fingering the hem of her cloak. His eyes fell on the golden bird clasp of her cloak and widened with a greedy hunger.

"Please don't," Amalia said, breathlessly, trying to pull out of the grip he held on her clothing. But they were all moving closer to her, surrounding her. She had to get out of here, had to find a way to escape.

"Aw, don't be like that," the first boy said, chuckling. He was clearly the leader, the oldest of them. And the scariest. "We're not going to hurt you. We're not savages. But that is an awfully nice coat you're wearing, isn't it? I'm guessing a fine noble Witch like you doesn't leave the house without some gold, huh? You're lost, aren't you? Give us what you have, and we can get you safely home. Promise."

Amalia's heart was pounding in her chest as the boy came even closer, towering over her.

"I—I don't have any money," Amalia said, looking around her desperately. She didn't. It hadn't even occurred to her to bring any since she'd never carried gold before. She had to get out of here, had to—

"Leave her alone, Jayce," came another voice. Firm and female, this time. Deeper down the alley, someone hopped down from a fire escape ladder and started toward them.

This girl didn't rush. She approached slowly, like she had all the time in the world. The crowd of boys parted to let her through.

And she was...

Beautiful, Amalia thought, heart beating hard against her ribcage. This girl was beautiful.

The boy towering over Amalia—Jayce—stepped back immediately. They all did, every single boy in the alley, heads lowered like they were in trouble, eyes on the gravel at their feet.

"Look at how scared she is," the girl said, frowning at all of them. "You should all be ashamed of yourselves. Apologize."

"Sorry," Jayce mumbled, backing away further. They were acting like scolded children.

"*Louder*," the girl ordered.

Jayce glanced up at her quickly, then looked at Amalia.

"We're sorry," he said, staring her full in the eyes. "We were never going to hurt you, and we didn't mean to scare you that badly. Honest."

"That's okay," Amalia answered, her voice a broken whisper, as she looked from Jayce to the girl.

She was Amalia's age—sixteen, maybe seventeen, with soft brown hair, and big green eyes. She was breathtaking, Amalia thought—really, truly beautiful, not like her, with her mother's incomplete face. With her too-thin face. This girl was so beautiful it almost hurt to look at her. So beautiful it made her mouth dry and her palms sweat.

"Ignore them," the girl said, stepping to Amalia and brushing her hands over Amalia's cloak as though brushing away the boys' touch. "Boys have no manners, do they?"

Amalia had no idea, but staring up into this girl's wild green eyes, she nodded. That seemed to be the right answer, because the girl smiled widely at her, and to Amalia it was like seeing the sun come out from behind the clouds.

"What's your name?" the girl asked, still smiling that warm smile at her.

"Amalia," she answered, a little surprised she could still speak.

"Amalia," the girl repeated, her smile widening. Her canines were sharp and dangerous looking, visible between her plump lips. "What a pretty name. And my! What a pretty dress!"

She stepped back to admire it, looking Amalia up and down, taking in the crimson cloak and the expensive gown.

"And your hair! You're so precious-looking, just like a little doll, aren't you?" the girl asked. She tilted her head to the side when she spoke. "I'm so sorry about my friends. I hope you can forgive them. They're just stupid boys. They don't know any better."

"Oh," Amalia said, blushing from the attention. "Oh yes, of course. I forgive them."

"Good!" the girl said, clapping her hands together, and Amalia gasped as she stepped even closer, taking Amalia's arm and looping her own arm through it, pulling her close enough that their hips and shoulders touched. Her skin was so warm Amalia could feel it through the thick fabric of her dress.

"My name is Vivian," the girl said, walking Amalia past the boys and back to the street. Back to safety.

Vivian. What a beautiful name, Amalia thought.

"It's very nice to meet you, Vivian," she said, breathlessly. The street was warm and sunny, and suddenly her feet didn't hurt much at all.

Vivian pulled her closer and glanced sideways at her with sparkling eyes. "You're so formal. It's cute."

Cute? A blush rose on Amalia's cheeks.

"But you can call me Vee. That's what all my friends call me."

Vee smiled at her wide enough that her sharp canines flashed in the sunlight. "And I can tell we're going to be very, very good friends, Princess."

PART TWO

CHAPTER 21
FEY

Fey's shoes patted rhythmically on the rough cobblestones as she ran through her neighborhood. It was just past dawn, and the early morning air held a pleasant chill, cooling the sweat that coated her skin. But the cold air could only do so much, and by the time she reached the park, a thin line of sweat had collected on her back and ran down her spine.

This was Fey's favorite trail to run in the mornings—through her neighborhood, past Regina's shop, and up through Goddess Park. It was early enough that no one was out, early enough that the only sounds around her were the chattering and singing of birds as they heralded the coming day.

Today, Fey felt at peace.

Once, she could only achieve this level of calm after spending hours in the training gym. Back then, she would push herself far past her limits, almost to the point of collapse, to feel like this. But something was changing. *She* was changing. Now, she let herself relax as she ran, losing herself in the rhythm of her breath and the repetitive sounds of her feet hitting the pavement.

She didn't see the posters until she reached the midpoint of her morning run—the Dual-faced Goddess statue. Stopping near the base, Fey took a moment to catch her breath and stretch out her legs.

That's when she saw it.

Someone had taped it to the base of the statue, as if they had put it there just for her. Frowning, Fey stepped closer, and when she saw the image on the notice there, all the calm of her morning run vanished.

It was the same posters she'd seen before, the same image of her face. But the words written over it no longer read *OUR TRUE QUEEN*.

No. This message was different. Written in a different hand.

DEATH TO THE COUNCIL.

DEATH TO THE ROYAL FAMILY.

Fey's hands shook as she took the poster from the statue and held it tight between her fingers.

There were more. Now that she'd noticed, she saw them everywhere. Nailed to power lines, taped to shop windows, they were all around her—Fey's own face looking back at her under a hand scrawled message.

KILL THEM ALL.

Fey collected all the posters she could find, but even after she'd burned each and every one, she couldn't erase that image of her own face from her mind. Couldn't keep the taste of ash from her mouth, as that inferno of rage burned inside of her.

BANG, BANG, BANG

Alice sat bolt upright at the knock, fumbling for the blades she kept next to the bed—the only memento she kept from her life under the Queen's reign. Lying next to her, Joy groaned and rolled over, pulling the covers over her face.

"You deal with it," Joy said, voice sleepy and muffled from under the blankets. "Whatever it is, you deal with it."

In the few seconds it took Alice to climb out of bed, grab one of her twin blades, and pull on a pair of pants, Joy had already fallen back asleep. Her soft, rhythmic breathing reminded Alice why she was so jumpy. Reminded her of all the things she needed to protect.

She had lost Joy once, for the good of the realm, and it had almost killed her. She wouldn't risk losing her again. Not for anything.

BANG, BANG, BANG

Blade ready at her side, Alice snuck quietly to the front door and opened it, ready for whatever monster awaited her on the other side.

Thankfully, this time the monster was one she recognized.

Fey stormed in, nearly knocking Alice over in her rage. The tension in Alice's shoulder dissipated, and she released a shaky breath of relief, closing the door behind her sister and flipping the lock back into place.

"Have you seen these?" Fey asked without preamble, shoving something toward her. Alice set her blade down against the wall before taking the piece of paper from her sister.

TRAITORS, this one read. Fey's face, wearing a near-identical scowl to the one she wore now, stared back at her.

Alice ran a hand over her face. It was too early for this. Far, far too early.

"Yes," she told Fey, handing it back. "Yes, I've seen them. You want some coffee?"

Fey bared her teeth, lip curling in anger. "No, Alice, I don't want any fucking coffee. Why didn't you tell me about this?"

Alice rolled her eyes, pushing past Fey and into the kitchen. She opened a container of coffee and scooped some into the machine. "Well, I'm going to need coffee to deal with this conversation, so you're going to have to wait. Do you want a cup or not, babe?"

Fey clenched her teeth together, crossing her arms tight against her body, but she knew better than to argue. "Fine," she snapped. "I'll have a cup."

The coffee bubbled rhythmically as it percolated, making happy conversation with itself while Alice and Fey sat in silence and waited.

"Where'd you find that one?" Alice asked, finally.

"Near Goddess Park," Fey told her. "But Alice... they're everywhere. I found them on every block, every street sign from the park to here."

Alice nodded, pouring a cup of coffee for herself and then one for Fey. When she opened the icebox to get some cream, the door to their bedroom opened and a head full of blonde, tousled hair appeared.

"Is that coffee?" Joy asked sleepily, then spotting Fey, she smiled.

"Hey, Fey! I should have known that was you trying to break down our door!"

Alice smiled at her, grabbing another mug from the cupboard for Joy. Merle appeared from out of the ether to rub against her ankles as she poured.

"What's this?" Joy asked, walking up to the counter and plucking the slip of paper up off the table. Her eyebrows drew together as she read it.

"Someone is putting them up all over the city," Alice explained as Joy's face tightened. The air in the room crackled. "Kallista brought them to our attention at the last council meeting, which means someone has also replaced all the ones she spent several hours taking down."

"You're telling me you've known about this for days," Fey said, tapping the poster with a long fingernail. "And you didn't tell me?"

"I haven't seen you since then, babe, so don't give me that," Alice explained. "Calm down. I haven't been keeping anything from you. I would have told you the next time you came over. Which, coincidently, is right now, isn't it?"

Fey pursed her lips but didn't argue.

"Who is doing this?" Joy asked, frown deepening.

"We don't know," Alice told her.

"Probably the same lunatics putting up the other ones," Fey said. "This is just the next step, isn't it?"

Alice shook her head. "No, no, I don't think so. All of those posters were about Fey. These... these are different."

"They're using her image," Joy argued. "These are the same posters as before, aren't they?"

"Yeah, but they're not *about* her, are they?" Alice looked at Fey. "Do you remember what some of the other posters you found today said?"

"Yeah," Fey answered. "*Death to the council, death to Witches*, that sort of thing."

"The ones Kallista found were the same," Alice verified. "They're not about Fey at all, they're mostly about the council and the royal family. Fey is just... a symbol, here. A revolutionary."

Fey raised an eyebrow at her, and Alice shrugged, stirring sugar into her coffee and taking a sip. "I'm not saying you are a revolutionary, babe. But to this group? Maybe that's what you represent. Change. A challenge to the system."

"But I have nothing to do with the council," Fey argued.

Alice shrugged again. "Maybe that's why they're using your image? You *haven't* had anything to do with it—but you were responsible for taking down the Queen. Maybe they see you as the solution. The one to bring down the council. I don't know, babe, I'm just speculating here. We're as in the dark as you are."

"What did the council say when you talked about this?" Fey asked.

Alice took another drink of her coffee. Sip by sip, she was feeling more awake, more herself. "Nothing, really. We decided on a wait-and-see approach. The posters are concerning, but... so far, there haven't been any real threats, no action taken against anyone. It's all just talk. Let's see if these people burn themselves out."

Fey pulled a face. "'Wait and see'? This is my face plastered all over the city, Alice. And you're not going to do anything about it?"

"What do you want us to do?" Alice asked, exasperated. "Set up a stakeout? Bring in random citizens for interrogation? We barely have an army anymore. You realize that, right? Enrollment has never recovered after... after everything that happened. Do you want me to waste what few resources we do have trying to track down whoever this is? When they haven't even done anything?"

"Do you have any idea who might be behind this?" Joy asked Fey, her voice soft.

Fey shook her head. "No," she conceded. "I have no idea. None whatsoever."

"No one has approached you about the council?" Joy pushed. "No one has tried to corner you and find out how you feel about any politics in the realm?"

Fey snorted a laugh. "When would anyone have the chance? I spend all of my time here, at home, or at work. I don't see more than a handful of people a month. You two included."

"Well, that's concerning for completely different reasons," Joy said, giving Fey an assessing look.

"What about your students?" Alice pressed. "I know you teach more than just kids now. Have any of them tried to speak to you about this, any of the older Witches?"

Fey thought back, trying to remember anything unusual, but finally shook her head. "No," she said. "Most of the work is group-focused, not individual. Leandra handles more of the one-on-one time with them. Most of our students are terrified of me, they don't try to engage in casual conversation."

Alice threw up her hands in exasperation. "You see? What are we supposed to do here, without any leads or any real threat? Where would we even begin?"

Fey scowled.

Setting her mug down, Alice gave Fey what she hoped was an understanding smile. "I get that you're scared—"

"I'm not scared," Fey said. "I'm *pissed*. This is my face, staring at me from every place I look in this city. My face, posted on every damned building I see. I don't appreciate the constant reminder of my public outing by the Queen. I don't appreciate having one of the hardest times of my life shoved back into my face every time I leave my house."

She snatched the poster from the counter, crumpling it in her hand.

"Tell me when you find something," she demanded, glaring at Alice. "The moment you find something."

Then without another word, without a goodbye, she stormed out, leaving Joy and Alice and a quickly cooling cup of coffee behind her.

CHAPTER 22
FEY

This time when she went to the gym to train, Fey made no attempt to smother her anger. She embraced it, letting it burn through her, letting it fuel her. And her body reveled in it. *Thrilled* in it.

She used that anger, that rage, to hone her training and push herself further than ever. She saw the faces of everyone who had called her queen, everyone who had knelt to her, everyone who had looked at her like she was something she wasn't. She saw her own face, scowling out at her from those insidious posters. And she used those images to power her, filling every punch she threw, every hit she delivered, with red-hot fury.

She was no queen. She was no savior, no revolutionary.

She was... she was...

Vengeance. The word flowed through every fiber of her being. That's what she had been when she took down the Queen's consort, her once mentor, what she had been when she had stormed the palace looking for blood. That's what she had been when she'd sent her own father to his death. The Goddess made her for violence, for war. She was no healer, no peacemaker. She was fury and rage, and she could bring this whole city to its knees using just a fraction of her power.

Alastair was right. No one should kneel before her.

They should cower.

Alastair. Just thinking of him soothed that roiling anger in her. The power inside her purred at the very thought of him.

Tonight, she would be meeting Alastair's family for the first time. Tonight, she didn't need to hide what she was, didn't need to pretend. She would meet them as herself. Fey, the Queen's Broken Blade. Fey, the warrior. Fey, the murderer.

By the time the sun started creeping toward the horizon and it was finally time to meet Alastair at The Last Drop, Fey was feeling blissfully exhausted and content. Let the world see her for what she truly was. Let them all see.

On her way to the club, tendrils of fire wrapped around the posters as she passed by them, leaving nothing but ash in her wake.

THE WOLF GUARDING the door to The Last Drop gave Fey a shy grin as she gestured her inside. Fey didn't recognize her, but she gave her a smile she hoped was less threatening than it felt. The music inside was already loud enough to rattle her bones, despite the early hour, but for the first time Fey found it soothed her. It fit her mood, the vibrations through the floor tuned to the frequency of her anger.

Jasper wasn't in his usual spot behind the bar when she arrived, but one of the other Wolves pointed her toward the stockroom, saying he was back there.

She rapped twice on the door frame to get his attention.

"One second," Jasper murmured, his back to her as he flipped through a few sheets on his clipboard. He made a note, frowning, then turned.

His smile was instant.

"Hey gorgeous." Jasper grinned. His green eyes slid down her body, from her neck to her feet, and the smile only grew.

"Wow," he said with a whistle. His eyes glittered as he took her in. "Don't you look good enough to eat. What's the occasion?"

Fey smiled. She gave a little spin, showing off the little black dress she was wearing. It was a simple, gauzy piece, tight across the chest with a flowy skirt, but even Fey had to admit it looked lovely on her.

"Alastair is taking me to meet his family tonight," she explained. "I thought I'd at least try to make a good impression."

"The whole family? Brother and father?" Jasper asked, arching an eyebrow.

Fey nodded, and he grimaced, turning back to his clipboard.

"Best of luck with that one, gorgeous. Alastair is always in a shitty mood when he gets back from visiting that asshole. His dad's a piece of work, so don't take it personally if he's not very... receptive to you."

A spark of anxiety ignited in her chest. Alastair had given her a similar warning. She didn't care if the Fallen King approved of her or not. The Goddess herself knew Alastair didn't care. But Fey hoped at the very least to get Callum's approval. Alastair spoke so fondly of his little brother. She doubted very much Callum would give his approval if she and the family patriarch came to blows over dinner. And tonight, that rage inside her was still bubbling just a little too close to the surface for that not to be a distinct possibility.

Eager for a distraction, Fey looked around at the stockroom. It was her first time back here, and she let her eyes drift over the space, taking in the boxes and bottles of liquor, the stacks of paper towels and cleaning supplies, and...

"What's with the laundry?" Fey asked, frowning at the corner.

Jasper turned, eyes landing on the pile of used bar towels heaped against the wall.

"Oh for...Sid, you fucker," he murmured. "It's nothing, just... just don't touch it, okay? Keep away from that."

Eyeing them warily, Fey moved further inside. There wasn't anywhere to sit, and since Alastair wouldn't be awake for a while yet, she hopped up to seat herself on a stack of boxes and keep Jasper company as he worked. Crossing her legs, she tried not to stare too hard as Jasper pulled boxes down from the shelves, his thick arms flexing as he handled them. One by one he set them near the door, returning to his clipboard to tick items off the list there.

"What are you doing in here, anyway?" Fey asked.

"Inventory," Jasper answered. "Normally I make one of the other Wolves do it, but I'm feeling charitable today."

He paused, frowning at the sheet, then turned back to the shelves, searching once more. Fey uncrossed her legs. Her feet didn't quite reach the ground, so she let them hang there, dangling.

"Ah, there you are," he muttered, crouching down and prying a box loose from the lower shelf. When he finally managed to get it out, he sat back on his heels and glanced over at her.

From his place on the ground, his face was right at knee height, and he grinned wickedly up at her.

"You know," Jasper said, turning and placing one hand on either side of her hips on the box she was sitting on, staring up at her with hungry eyes. "I think this might be my favorite place in the whole world."

"Where?" Fey asked, smiling despite herself.

"On my knees for you."

Fey laughed, kicking out at him, and Jasper grinned even harder. He rose to stand, but he kept his hands there, on either side of her.

"So," he said, moving a little closer, leaning over her. Fey's breath caught in her throat. He wasn't touching her, wasn't doing anything to her. But just having him that close to her was enough to make her blood heat. "Are you and Alastair planning on spending a little quality time together in his office before you leave tonight?"

"Why?" Fey teased, trying to ignore the things his voice did to her. She gave him a mocking grin. "Are you looking for an invitation to join?"

"Maybe," he admitted. He shifted closer, hands sliding almost to her hips, until all she could see was him. "Maybe I could just warm you up for him? Get you all wet and ready for his cock. I bet he'd like that."

Fuck, that voice. Fey swallowed. Trying to keep her voice casual, she asked, "I thought that was just a one-time thing?"

He was teasing her. Playing with her, just like he always did. It didn't mean anything—just harmless flirting.

Wasn't it?

Jasper's voice was husky when he answered her. "Maybe I underestimated how much I liked it..." Those hands moved closer, almost touching her now, almost brushing against the fabric of her dress. "Maybe I can't stop thinking about how you tasted. And what I'd give to taste you again."

Fey's tongue darted out to wet her lips.

"And Alastair?" she asked, breathlessly.

Jasper's lips hovered just above her own, close enough to brush against hers as he spoke in a soft whisper. "Maybe I wouldn't mind tasting him, too."

His green eyes were dark as he held her gaze, letting that truth hang between the two of them.

Neither of them heard Alastair enter the stockroom. They didn't even notice he was there. Not until a strong arm wrapped around Jasper's neck and yanked him away from Fey.

"Well, well, well," Alastair said, his voice thick with barely constrained fury. "Doesn't this look fucking cozy, hm?"

CHAPTER 23
ALASTAIR

Alastair was already in a shitty mood.

It started with the hunger. He needed to feed. Desperately. Raw hunger gnawed at his concentration, blanketing all his thoughts. It was keeping him awake during the day and making it difficult to get through his nights.

It was his own fault. He'd been putting it off longer and longer each time, finally pushing himself to this point. But since Fey, feeding had become... complicated. He'd been back to the family manse a few times since she'd moved in, trying to make it work, but...

He hated it. Hated every moment his mouth was on another woman. Hated it even when he insisted on feeding from their wrists, rather than their necks, wanting to keep as much distance from them as physically possible.

The thought of taking blood tonight while Fey dined with his family was enough to turn his stomach, but he had to do it. Had to fight through the nausea at being that close to another person and calm this insistent ache inside him.

And that was the other thing, adding to his shitty attitude today. Very few things spoiled Alastair's mood as much as visiting his family.

Scratch that. As much as visiting his *father*.

The truth was, he was excited to see Callum. His younger brother hadn't met Fey yet, and he'd been looking forward to tonight, looking forward to finally seeing the two of them together. Callum was going to love her.

But his father...

Alastair swore in frustration, his fingers fucking up the knot on his tie once again. He tugged it loose, unraveling the knot to start again. He'd tied this same fucking knot every night, for the Goddess only knew how many fucking years. Why was he having so much trouble with it tonight? Why were his hands suddenly fucking it all up?

A heavy knock on the open door was all the warning he got before Ferus entered his office. The giant Wolf came right up to Alastair, taking the loose ends of the tie and making quick work of the knot.

Just as Alastair opened his mouth to thank him, though, the fucker had the audacity to ask, "Nervous, boss?" in an annoyingly amused tone.

"Fuck you," Alastair snapped. He straightened the knot in his tie, tightening it so it sat perfectly between his collarbones. When had Ferus learned that? "Why the fuck would I be nervous?"

"First time bringing a girl home to the family," Ferus said in a matter-of-fact tone, ignoring Alastair's glare entirely. Alastair scowled harder. "That could make any man nervous."

"Speaking of," Alastair said. "Have you seen her?"

She was here, in the building. He could feel that pull of her power. Could feel that she was close. A different sort of hunger rose inside him.

Ferus nodded, giving an affirmative grunt. "Saw her when she came in. I can grab her for you, if you want?" he offered, but Alastair shook his head.

"No, that's fine. I'll go find her. I figure I should warn her about my father before we leave."

Ferus blinked. "You've already warned her, boss."

"Yeah, well, you can't be too warned when it comes to dear old Dad," Alastair said. He shrugged his suit jacket on, giving the lapels a shake to straighten it, and flicked a bit of lint from the shoulder.

Why had he even agreed to this? He'd avoided seeing his father for the last couple of years, only stopping by the family estate to feed and visit his brother when he knew the deSanguine wouldn't be in residence. The last message that his father had left with Callum, though, had been straight to the point. A date, and a time, with a note instructing Alastair to bring his betrothed.

His betrothed? Who the fuck even talked like that anymore?

Alastair had been sorely tempted to send the note back cut into little pieces but eventually decided against it. For Fey, he'd make an effort. For his brother Callum, he'd make an effort.

And if the old man overstepped, Alastair could just kill him, right?

Right.

Better yet… he'd let Fey do it. Yeah. He liked that idea. She would make it hurt. She'd tear him to pieces with that new, deliciously deadly power of hers.

Alastair straightened his cuffs as he approached the unmanned bar, eyes flickering over the room, before they settled on an open door.

Ah, the stockroom.

The door was ajar, the light on, and he could hear Fey and Jasper's voices coming from inside. Alastair slipped behind the bar, maneuvering his way toward them. The door made no sound when he pushed it further open, and Alastair smiled, excited to see her. Excited to spend the evening with her, even if it meant spending dinner with his asshole of a dad.

But as the door shifted open, Alastair wasn't prepared for what he saw. He froze in the doorway, the smile slipping from his face, as the scene inside the stockroom unfolded before him.

Fey, perched on a stack of boxes, leaning back, her body deliciously arched as she stared up at the male above her.

And Jasper, leaning over her, hands on either side of her body, lips hovering above hers. Close enough to touch.

Close enough that he could have kissed her.

Alastair moved without a single thought. He closed the space between the doorway and them in a fraction of a second. Wrapping his arm around Jasper's neck, he yanked him backward, pulling his body tight against him.

Jasper was a powerful Shifter in his own right, and the growl he made would have sent a lesser man scrabbling. Claws dug into Alastair's arm, tearing at his suit jacket, as Jasper's fingers shifted.

"Well, well, well." Alastair ignored Jasper's growl, ignored the confusion in Fey's eyes, ignored the sting of those claws digging into his flesh. Something hot and angry burned in his chest, and it wanted violence. It wanted *blood*. "Doesn't this look fucking cozy, hm?"

At the sound of Alastair's voice, Jasper's growl faded away, and he relaxed in Alastair's grip, the claws disappearing.

"Hey boss," Jasper said, angling his face slightly to look back at him, his voice a little breathless. "We were just talking about you."

"What are you doing, Alastair?" Fey asked. He recognized the anger in her voice. Recognized the warning there. And he ignored it.

"Oh, I think the better question is, what are *you* doing, Witchling? I'm not interrupting anything, am I?" Alastair asked, tightening his hold hard enough he could feel bones shift under his grip.

Jasper's lips curled to a smile. "Maybe," he said, holding his gaze without fear. "Care to join?"

"Let him go," Fey demanded.

Rage boiled inside him. How *dare* she be angry at him? How dare she take Jasper's side?

Goddess, he was so, so hungry. The world felt strangely distant, like he was in a dream.

"What's wrong, Witchling? Scared I'll hurt your little toy?" Alastair twisted his head to speak into Jasper's ear, his breath tickling the Wolf's skin. "She's mine, puppy. Remember that."

"I remember," Jasper gasped. He wasn't struggling, wasn't fighting. But his body had tightened at Alastair's words.

"I'm not anyone's," Fey snapped, her voice full of fury. The air around the room crackled with energy. She could kill him with one thought, could rip him to shreds without even coming to her feet.

Any control Alastair had disappeared. He dropped his hold on Jasper, shoving him away, and was on Fey in an instant.

She gasped as he took her jaw in his hands, twisting her face up towards his. His eyes flashed as he stared down at her, gaze boring into hers.

"Say it again, Witchling. Look me in the eye and tell me you don't belong to me. Look me in the eye and lie to me again."

The power filling the room grew darker, more deadly, but Alastair ignored it. He ignored the voice in his head, telling him to run. She was *his*. His goddess, his Witch. She was...

She was his *everything*.

Wrapping his hand around the back of her head, he pulled Fey's lips to his and kissed her.

Fey struggled against him, pushing away, but Alastair held her there, letting her struggle, letting her bite at his lips, letting her fight. He groaned when her teeth drew blood, opening his mouth to her, and slipping his tongue against hers.

Her struggling weakened, and the next time he slid his tongue over hers, she returned the gesture, blood on their lips as she kissed him back.

He knew she would. He knew what she liked and what she wanted. Knew her better than Jasper ever could. The hands that had been pushing against him tightened on his shirt, pulling him closer, arching against him. She wanted this. She wanted *him*.

By the time Alastair broke the kiss, she was gasping for air, eyes clouded with lust. Her tongue flicked out, licking a smear of blood from her bottom lip.

"Close the door," Alastair hissed at Jasper, not looking up.

"Alastair," Fey whimpered. There was a soft noise as the door to the stockroom shut, and Alastair glanced back to see Jasper was still there, leaning against the closed door. Staring at them.

"Alastair," Fey moaned again, writhing under his touch.

She looked so beautiful there, his blood on her lips, eyes unfocused. Needy.

For him.

"That's right, Witchling, say my name," he urged. Nudging her legs open with his thighs, he pulled her tight against him, so he could whisper in her ear. "Show him who you belong to."

Fey let out a hiss of pure fury that turned to a gasp when he licked her neck, his hand finding her nipple through the thin material of her dress and squeezing.

"Did he get you wet, Witchling?" Alastair asked, snaking his hand lower down her body. His fingers found the hem of her dress and tugged it up. Too much clothing, there was far too much clothing between them. He needed to touch her. Sliding his hands under her ass, he lifted her so he could tug her underwear off. He pulled them down her long legs and tossed them aside.

She was wet. Alastair brought his fingers to her slit, parting her easily and running the tips of his index finger over her perfect pussy. So wet already.

Fey groaned, her hips rising to meet his touch.

Alastair glanced over at Jasper, still standing by the door. He expected the Shifter to look angry, maybe even disgusted.

Lust was all he saw in Jasper's face. The Wolf's eyes were locked on where Alastair's fingers slipped over Fey's body.

"Oh, look at that—he got you all worked up, didn't he?" Alastair asked. Fey's eyes opened to look at him, her perfect mouth opening to speak, but he didn't want to hear it. He didn't want to hear anything she had to say, not now. With a groan, he pushed his finger inside her, and whatever words she was about to say disappeared with a gasp, her head tilting back.

Holding her legs open wide with one hand, Alastair pleasured her with the other, adding another finger and circling her clit with his thumb.

"Say my name, Witchling," he demanded.

"I—" Fey gasped. Her hips rose and fell with his fingers, fucking herself on his hand.

Alastair's fingers sped up. "Say it."

Fuck, she was already so close, grinding against him. He could feel her pussy tightening around his fingers, her body fighting for release.

"Alastair," Fey begged, hips rocking against his hand.

Faster. "Again," he demanded.

"Ala—" Fey's body arched, and she cried out as she came, shuddering against him and tightening around his fingers. He caught her mouth with his, swallowing her scream. Over the sounds of her climax, Alastair heard Jasper groan softly, and he waited until he had milked every second of pleasure from Fey before he broke the kiss and gently removed his fingers. Then he straightened and stalked toward the Shifter.

Jasper's chest was rising and falling quickly, his eyes unfocused. He licked his lips as Alastair got closer, tongue running across his bottom lip in anticipation.

Reaching out, Alastair grabbed Jasper's face in one hand, Fey's arousal still glistening wet on his fingers. Jasper sucked in a greedy breath.

"Remember this the next time you try to touch her," Alastair said. He pushed the Shifter back toward the wall next to the door. "Remember how prettily she comes for me. Remember how easily I can make her fall apart."

"Yes boss," Jasper answered. His nostrils flared, taking in her scent on Alastair's hand. The tip of his tongue snuck out to glide along his bottom lip again.

"Do you really think you could do that to her?" Alastair asked in a mocking tone.

He wanted to shame the Wolf—wanted to force him to back down. To acknowledge Alastair's claim on her.

To admit that she was *his*.

But Jasper only grinned, ignoring the pain of Alastair's fingers digging into his face. "I'm willing to try," he answered with a smirk.

Alastair bared his fangs, pressing his body harder against Jasper's.

He wanted him to back down. To *make* him back down.

He wanted...

The door swung open and then slammed, jolting them both out of the moment.

Dropping Jasper, Alastair whirled around.

The stockroom was empty.

Fey was gone.

CHAPTER 24

FEY

Let me out.

Rage burned through her, hot and unstoppable.

Fey made no effort to hold it back. She let that rage fill every part of her, let it burn through her from the tips of her toes to the top of her head.

Power, raw and untamed, flowed from her, filling the building. Air swirled and circled her like a vortex. It pulled dust from the ground and the atmosphere around her, a maelstrom with her at the center. Lightning arched at her fingertips, that glorious new energy that sparked and burned, crackling with fury.

There were startled sounds from the other patrons in the club, voices full of fear and panic, but she ignored them all.

She was death incarnate.

She was unstoppable.

"Fey?"

Distantly she could hear Alastair calling her name, but she didn't stop, didn't turn. The wooden slats of the club's dance floor singed under her feet as she made her way toward the exit. Ice crystalized on the liquor bottles behind the bar, and several of them shattered as she passed by, leaving icicles sharp as glass in her wake. She was fire and ice. She was wind and earth. Every element roared to life inside of her, awaiting her command. Ready to destroy.

"Fey, wait, stop!"

This time, she listened.

Fey stopped and slowly turned, fire blazing in her eyes as she faced Alastair.

Let him see me for what I am, she thought. *Let him see a goddess's wrath.*

He froze under her stare, fear flashing in his eyes. Across the bar, she heard Jasper swear. Heard the Shifter hiss a command to Ferus, "Get everyone out of the building. *Now.*"

Howling exploded throughout the club, and suddenly there were Wolves everywhere, shepherding the patrons out. Wolves appeared from all corners, herding people toward the door, racing to clear the building. In the chaos, someone screamed.

This was why she could never be queen, why she could never wear the crown. They wanted a Witch who could protect the city, a Witch to stand between them and whatever threats may come.

They couldn't understand that she was the threat.

"What the fuck was that, Alastair?" Fey asked. The electricity buzzing at her fingertips crackled louder, arching towards the ground.

"I..." Alastair stumbled back a step, lost for words.

Oh, that beautiful fury. That exquisite rage. It roared inside of her, eager to be set free. It would be so easy to burn this place down with him inside. So very easy.

"You *used* me. You don't get to touch me like that, to use me like that. I'm not your fucking prop."

"You're mine," Alastair told her through gritted teeth. "Not his. *Mine.*"

Cold. So, so cold, that beautiful anger inside her.

"When will you learn? I'm not yours, Alastair," Fey told him, lightning trailing up and down her arms, crackling with energy. "I don't belong to anyone but me."

The ground shifted just slightly, the only warning before her power rose to a crescendo.

And the world exploded.

CHAPTER 25
ALASTAIR

Alastair ducked, dropping to his knees as lightning cracked through the air. It hit the walls like a bomb, shattering bottles and exploding furniture. In its wake, it left black scars of scorched wood marring the floor and spiking up the wall.

Considering the circumstances, the blast was remarkably contained.

Somewhere in the building, something was burning. A chair, a table, hell, maybe the very foundations of his club. He could lose it all right now. Fey could burn the entire building to the ground.

The thought of losing his nightclub didn't scare Alastair. Seeing Fey in all her dark fury, seeing the extent of her power finally revealed, didn't scare him.

But in that moment, he knew he had gone too far. Far enough that he might lose her.

And that terrified him.

He rose to his feet and took a step toward her, ignoring the instincts that screamed at him to run.

"You're not mine," Alastair admitted, taking another step. That rage in her eyes was so cold. He should be terrified of her. Terrified of this dark power. But this was all just another part of her, wasn't it? Just another facet of the Witch he loved.

Goddess help him, he loved her so much.

Swallowing hard, he took another step. "But I'm yours, Witchling. Fully, completely, yours."

The icy rage thawed. Just a fraction.

And Alastair did the only thing he could think to do. He dropped to his knees before her.

Let her kill him, if that's what she wanted. Let her do with him what she will.

"I'm sorry, Witchling," he said, voice breaking as he stared up at her. That dark power around her hesitated. "I fucked up. And I'm sorry."

"Good." Fey's eyes flashed with rage and power. "You should be fucking sorry."

He reached for her hand, ignoring the power still swirling around her. She tensed like she might snatch it back, away from him. Electricity still sparked between her fingertips as he touched her, but Alastair barely noticed as he pressed her palm against his cheek.

"If you try to use me like that again," Fey warned, that deliciously deadly power scraping against his skin, "I will burn this place to the ground, Alastair. I won't even hesitate."

"I believe you," he said, turning his face to kiss her palm. Power sparked between them, but it wasn't as strong as before, not nearly as deadly. "Never again, Witchling. I promise you. You don't need to belong to me. But I'm yours. And I'll never use you like that again."

Fey exhaled, and that beautiful fury surrounding her pulled back even more. Satisfied.

"Come here," she said, voice rough. She pulled him to his feet. "Get up. You can be so dramatic sometimes, you know that?"

It was more forgiveness than he deserved.

Wrapping his arms around her, Alastair pulled her tight against him. That energy still pulsed between them, raw and angry. But softer, now. "I'm sorry, Fey. Truly, I am."

She smelled divine. Even with the faint hint of ozone in the air, she smelled so wonderful. He squeezed her tightly and pressed a soft kiss to the top of her head, the tension in his chest loosening as she relaxed in his arms.

"I thought... I thought he was going to kiss you," Alastair murmured. "And I lost it. I thought I was losing you."

"He was just being Jasper," she said, sounding irritated. Good. Irritation beat homicidal rage any day. "He wasn't going to kiss me. And if he had, I would have handled it. No one is going to take me away from you, Alastair. No one, not ever."

He exhaled slowly, pulling her tighter against him.

"I love you," she told him, voice muffled against his chest. "But that won't stop me from killing you, you know."

His chest rumbled as he laughed, and the sound reverberated through the empty bar.

"I love you, too, Witchling. More than you could ever know."

Fey snorted against his chest.

Glancing around at the damage around them, he couldn't help but admire her restraint. Sure, he'd have to replace some of the tables and chairs, and half the bottles in the lower bar were probably a write off, but as far as foundational damage? The club would survive. He probably wouldn't even need to put up any new walls.

They stood like that, wrapped in each other's arms for a while, Fey letting him hold her, his hands tracing idle patterns over her back and shoulders. And for those few moments, it was just the two of them, alone in the world. But the night wasn't over, and the world was still out there, waiting.

Fey broke the spell, leaning back slightly to look him in the eyes.

"You should go let Ferus and the others know it's safe for them to come back in. We need to get going. We're already late."

Alastair shook his head, furrowing his brow. "To the dinner? Witchling...we need to cancel. You really want to go see my family after that?"

"No," Fey admitted. "But you're just looking for an excuse not to go."

Alastair grumbled.

"I don't want this to define our night, Alastair." Fey told him, almost reluctantly. "I don't want to go home and have this be... it."

The emotion in her voice surprised him. Fear. Seeing her lose control hadn't scared him, no, but... it may have scared her.

Gripping her shoulders softly, he forced his smile. "Fine," he told her. "We'll go."

He'd give her anything, after all.

Anything at all in the world.

CHAPTER 26

JASPER

Frankly, they were lucky no one was killed.

Standing in the wreckage of the dance floor, Jasper couldn't decide if it were a miracle from the Goddess, or just Fey's good aim.

Ferus and Mara were already opening the place back up, not that many patrons remained. Jasper couldn't blame the ones that fled. Few casual club goers are likely to stay at a place where they'd been pushed outside, mid drink, by a pack of Wolves. Even if they had been doing it to save their lives, it was the type of experience that left a bad taste in a customer's mouth.

By the time Alastair had calmed Fey down, only the regulars had remained waiting outside the club. And a few others Jasper was sure would be new regulars. If the prospect of being ripped to shreds by a powerful Witch, and herded by a giant Wolf Shifter, wasn't enough to scare you, then it was probably a selling point. Jasper was pretty sure those who had stayed would come back, night after night, chasing that high.

Heading back to the stockroom, Jasper started sorting the boxes he'd picked out, carrying them behind the bar and getting ready to resume his stocking duties. He had to add a few more to the list, cringing as he took inventory of the bottles Fey had shattered. She couldn't have aimed a little lower, for the ones on the bottom shelf?

He pulled a few more boxes out, adding them to the stack and noting them on the inventory list. Ferus came up with the idea of constantly updating their inventory lists, and Jasper was pleased at how easily they could keep their stock organized now. The Wolf was a business genius. Who would have thought?

He was almost done when he spotted something in the corner. Something... lacy?

Blood rushed out of Jasper's head so fast he felt dizzy as he plucked the small piece of fabric from the ground and realized what it was. Fey's thong, barely more than a slip of lace.

Jasper bit back a groan as he held them. They were soaked, and the scent all over them was intoxicating.

He straightened and walked to the storeroom door. It barely made any noise as he shut it. Leaning back against the closed door, Jasper replayed the scene in his head.

Fey, back arched in ecstasy, as Alastair's fingers brought her closer and closer to that edge. And Alastair... holding her legs wide open for him to see. Alastair, locking eyes with him, his fingers buried in Fey, his gaze burning hot.

And then he was thinking about Alastair, holding him in place, Fey's arousal on his skin, pressing his body against Jasper's. Feeling just how hard watching them had gotten him.

Fuck it.

Someone else could tend the bar for a while. Someone else could make the drinks.

Jasper's breath was quick and erratic as he undid his pants, slipping his hand down to stroke himself.

CHAPTER 27

FEY

"You don't have to do this," Alastair said, looking down at Fey as they stood on the doorstep to his family home. The double doors loomed before them, made of wood so dark it was almost black.

In all her years serving the Crown, all her years of living in the Eternal City, Fey had never set foot in the Vampire district. Few ever had, outside of their own Faction. The Vampires were notoriously secluded, separating their district from the others with tall black iron gates.

She had heard stories of the deSanguine estate, of course—the place all Vampires who lived in the city called home. Every Witch in the realm had heard the stories. But seeing it was another matter entirely. And even the most outrageous stories fell woefully short of the real thing.

The Vampire district took up almost a full quarter of the city, nestled in the southeastern tip and bordering the river that separated the city from the second octant. The towering black mansion that housed the deSanguine family took up the vast majority of that space. Fey's entire neighborhood could have fit inside that building. And there were other mansions, scattered on the grounds, built in clusters. They must house the other Vampire families, Fey suspected.

"I mean it, Witchling. Especially with what an ass I've been tonight. We can turn around and go home right now."

"I know, Alastair," she answered, trying to keep the bite from her voice. He wasn't off her shit list, not yet. "You've only mentioned that about a hundred times already."

Alastair flinched and shoved his hands into his pockets. "I just mean that you shouldn't feel obligated to have anything to do with my family. They're my bullshit, not yours. Loving me doesn't mean you have to put up with them."

"And what about your brother?" Fey asked, raising an eyebrow at him.

Alastair smirked. "My little brother is the only one I'm excited to introduce you to," he said. "He's the only one worth knowing out of all of them."

Fey nodded. "I want to meet him, Alastair. He means a lot to you. I want to get to know that part of your life." She sighed. "You said you wanted me—*all* of me. And I want to know all of you. Even the bad."

"Okay." Alastair let out a long breath. "Okay, then."

Satisfied, Fey raised her hand to knock, but the door clicked before she'd even touched it, swinging inward, as though beckoning them inside.

The interior hall of the deSanguine manse was even more opulent than the palace. Fey's eyes widened in wonder as she took it all in—the ornate patterned rugs, the heavy rosewood furniture. Paintings hung from every wall, nestled between lit candelabras that supplied the hallway's only illumination. There was so much to look at, so much demanding her attention. It was overwhelming.

"Master Alastair," came a clipped voice.

Fey jumped. A man stood just inside the door, head bowed, in a crisp black uniform lined in white. He was old, his skin paper thin and sagging with age. His voice was crisp, with just a hint of an accent Fey couldn't place. An accent she was sure she'd never heard before in her life.

"And Mistress Fey," the man continued. He kept his eyes down as he addressed them, as though speaking to their shins. "I will take your coats, if you wish?"

Alastair was already shrugging off his suit jacket, the sleeves marred from Jasper's claws, and handing it to the strange man, who took it and folded it over his arm in a swift practiced motion.

"I don't have a coat," Fey told the man. She didn't get the sense he was a Vampire, but... she couldn't place his Faction at all. He was... nothing. A husk.

"Of course," the man said, inclining his head, addressing her feet instead. "Your bag, then?"

She didn't have one of those, either. Suddenly, she wished she'd brought her blades, just to give him something to shut him up. Two steps inside, and she already felt out of place, already felt like an imposition in this crowded opulent space.

"She's fine, Winston," Alastair insisted. He placed a hand on Fey's lower back, and instantly her body relaxed, just as it had at the club. *It's okay,* that touch told her. *We're okay. And I'm yours.* "Do you know where my brother is? We're running a little late, and—"

"No, you're not running a *little* late," came an amused voice from a doorway to their left. "You are running *very* late."

Fey turned, watching as someone familiar walked into the room. Her heart skipped. Alastair stood with her, his hand pressed to the small of her back, and yet... Alastair walked into the hallway from that room. A near-perfect replica of the man she loved.

Behind her, Alastair—her Alastair—ran a hand through his hair.

"Fey, this is my little brother, Callum," he said, gesturing to the man approaching them. "Callum, this is Fey."

Little brother. That's how Alastair had always referred to Callum. Somehow, Fey had forgotten that their Faction aged so differently. She had expected a kid, maybe a teenager.

Not the tall, elegant male who stepped forward to take her hand.

"Fey," Callum said with a kind smile. He put her hand to his lips, placing a gentle kiss on her knuckles. "It's such a delight to meet you. I'm only sorry my brother hasn't brought you to meet us sooner."

They could be twins, Fey thought, as Callum rose to stand before her. They looked nearly identical.

Except... there were differences, weren't there? Now that she looked closely. Now that he had stepped closer to the light.

Callum was shorter by a fraction of an inch. Slimmer, too, in the shoulders. And his hair was a softer shade of black, more of a dark brown, and worn in a different style, long in the front and cut shorter in the back. It fell around his face in soft waves.

Their eyes were where all similarities ended, though. Callum had the same golden eyes as his brother, but they were... soft and friendly. Kind. That anger, that barely restrained violence in Alastair's eyes, was completely missing in his brother's.

"You are even more beautiful than my brother said," Callum told her, still holding her hand.

Fey couldn't help the blush that rose to her cheeks, no more than she could help the smile she offered him in return.

"If I didn't know better, I'd say you were flirting with me, Callum," she teased.

Hand still on the small of her back, Alastair laughed. "Don't let his attention get to your head, Witchling. You're not his type."

"True," Callum said, his eyes sparkling. "But who knows? Maybe I could always make an exception for the right woman." He winked at her.

"Alright, back off," Alastair warned him, stepping forward. Callum threw back his head and laughed, a sound so full of joy it brought a smile to Fey's face immediately.

"Forgive me, Fey, I can't help it," Callum told her. He let go of her hand and took her elbow instead, guiding her down the hallway and away from the strange man that still stood there, holding Alastair's jacket. "I'm a shameless flirt. Please, come and sit. Let me pour you a drink."

He led them to a sitting room, with a long velvet green couch and matching armchairs. He didn't let go of her until he brought her to the couch himself, guiding her to sit.

"Wine?" he asked, crossing the room to a small bar and pulling out a glass for her. "Or we have liquor, if you would prefer? I could mix you something—anything you'd like."

"Wine is fine," Fey told him, watching as Callum selected a bottle.

"Ah, this is a good one," he told her, eyes skimming over the faded label. "Over five hundred years old. Grown over the mountains past the eighth octant."

Fey laughed, not sure if he was teasing her or not. "There's nothing past the eighth octant but wastelands," she said.

"True," Callum said, pouring a generous glass of wine from the bottle. "But five hundred years ago there was. And the grapes they grew there were delicious."

Alastair joined him at the bar, smirking, and reached for a bottle of scotch. Callum's hand shot out, rapping his brother on the knuckles.

"Oh no, none for you, yet," Callum chided. "Father wants to talk to you. Before dinner."

Alastair bared his fangs. Slapping Callum's hand away, he grabbed the bottle and a glass and poured himself a drink, anyway.

"We don't have anything to talk about," Alastair said, filling his glass with whiskey.

"Don't tell me that," Callum shot back at him. He plucked the wineglasses from the bar and approached the couch, holding one out for Fey. "Tell him that."

She took the wine from him with a smile, and Callum sat next to her, knees angled toward her, but with plenty of space between the two of them.

"Fuck. Fine," Alastair said. He drank the whiskey in one go, setting the empty glass back on the bar. "Fey, I leave you in my brother's capable hands. Callum? No more fucking flirting."

Callum chuckled, holding his hand up in mock surrender. "I wouldn't dream of it, brother."

Alastair scowled at him, crossing the room so he could give Fey a quick kiss on the cheek.

"I'll be back before you know it," he murmured to her. The closeness of him, the feel of his lips on her skin, made her body purr like a contented cat. The memory of his touch earlier was still fresh on her skin.

Then he was gone, and it was just her and Callum, and the most delicious glass of wine Fey had ever tasted.

"What did he mean?" Fey asked, taking another sip of wine and glancing at Callum over the rim of her glass. "About me not being your type?"

It was a personal question, perhaps too personal for their first conversation together. But Callum answered it with a quick, genuine smile.

"Let's just say you lack the prerequisite parts." When she raised an eyebrow, he laughed. "I like men, Fey. And only men. Which makes me one of the few males in this realm I bet my brother feels comfortable leaving you alone with."

An image of Jasper immediately jumped into Fey's head, and she blushed, taking another sip of her wine to hide it. It might surprise Callum to learn just how comfortable his brother was with other men.

"So," Callum said, leaning forward and taking her empty hand in his. It was a loving gesture and done so completely without artifice that it brought a warm feeling to her chest. "I've been absolutely dying to meet you, Fey. I want to know all about you. Please, tell me about yourself."

Fey shrugged, looking down at the wine in her glass. "Not much to tell, really," she told him.

Callum raised his eyebrows. "Oh?" he said in a sarcastic tone. "I can't imagine that's true, love. Aren't you the same Witch who brought down the Crown? The same Witch your Faction is trying to make queen?"

Fey made a face at that, mouth twisting in disgust.

Callum cocked his head to the side, watching her face intently. "Oh, that's certainly a reaction. Interesting. I take it you don't appreciate those trying to make you queen?"

"I just think they're wrong," Fey told him. She took her hand from his and pushed her hair back behind her ear. "I don't think the Goddess gave me these powers to be queen."

"Oh? So why did she give you these powers?"

"To be her vengeance," Fey said, unthinking.

Callum sat back, watching her. "Interesting," he said again.

Fey shrugged. She hadn't thought about it, since the thought had occurred to her earlier that day, but it felt true. She had been the Queen's Blade, and was, in part, a sword delivered by the Goddess. She was destruction, not creation. And no one needed a destroyer on the throne.

"I just think I'm better at killing than I am at leading," Fey told him, and it felt good to say it aloud, to be honest with someone she had barely met.

"I don't doubt it," Callum told her, and the way he said it didn't make her feel like he was judging her at all.

"It's funny," Fey said with a smile. "The way Alastair talks about you... I didn't expect..."

"Didn't expect what?" Callum asked, smirking. "Didn't expect me to be quite so handsome? So charming?"

Fey laughed. "No, I mean... you're so similar, much more than I expected. But at the same time, you're like night and day."

Callum's smile turned slightly sad. He looked down at the wineglass in his hand, swirling it. "I lack his brooding nature, I think you mean."

"A little," she admitted with a laugh.

Callum settled further back against the couch. "That's Delilah's doing. Our sister," he added quickly, answering Fey's question before she could even ask. "I was just a child when she died, but Alastair... she meant the world to him, you know? I think it broke a part of him when she died. And I don't know if that's something that he can ever heal from."

"Alastair never talks about her," Fey admitted.

"I don't doubt it," Callum said, running a hand through his hair. "He's not exactly the paragon of an emotionally available male, my brother. He's better at bottling it up until it eats away at him like a poison."

"Tell me about it," Fey said, rolling her eyes.

Callum laughed.

"But I'd love to hear about her," she assured him.

"Where do I even begin? She was powerful, I'm sure he's told you that at least. She would have been the first female head of this family if she was still here. The first female deSanguine. We're traditionally patriarchal, as I'm sure you already know, but she broke the mold when she came into her power. There wasn't a single Vampire from any of the families who would have even considered standing in her way."

The silence that followed his words was heavy. "What happened to her?" Fey asked, finally.

Callum sighed sadly. "She overdosed. She'd been... going down that path for a while. It caused a rift between the two of them—Alastair and Delilah, the first rift of what would be many. After she started using, he did everything he could to stop her. To help her."

He took a long drink of his wine.

"She liked to get her blood from users and get high that way. Said it was like smoking cigarettes with a filter," Callum said with a smirk. "We didn't even know she'd started using on her own until after... Well. Until after it was too late."

"I'm so sorry," Fey said, putting her hand on Callum's.

"Thanks," he said, giving her hand a squeeze. "But, like I said, I was just a kid. I barely remember her, so for me it's like... like she's this ghost haunting our home, you know? This specter of death and loss that lives in every room here and in everyone's minds. A ghost everyone can see but me."

Fey nodded.

"Her death hit Alastair hard, though. They were so close when they were young, practically inseparable. When she died, it just about broke him. And he blamed our father, of course. He left the estate within the week and never looked back..."

Fey frowned, brows drawn together in confusion. "I don't understand. Why would he blame your father for it?"

Callum winced. "Where do you think she got the drugs, Fey?"

CHAPTER 28

ALASTAIR

Alastair didn't bother knocking when he reached his father's study. He stood in the doorway, leaning against the door-frame with his hands in his pockets, and waited. His father sat at his heavy wooden desk, back to the door, while the pen in his hand skimmed across the paper with practiced speed.

"Callum says you wanted to talk to me. Alone," Alastair said.

His father stopped, the pen coming to an immediate halt as he stilled.

Cassiel Salvatore deSanguine was a man used to intimidating others. He wielded his power like a weapon, demanding people defer to him and bend before his strength. Once, when he was young, Alastair had done just that, bending to his father's will just like everyone else in his life. He had existed in the orbit of his father's power, his very existence revolving around his father's whims.

But that was a long time ago. Now Alastair only smiled as his father's power filled the room and space between them. Smiled, because he knew long, long ago that his own power eclipsed his father's. The old man was just too blind to see it.

"It's customary to knock before entering someone's chambers, Alastair," his father chided, turning.

"Well…" Alastair shrugged. "Maybe if you weren't such an ass, I would actually bother with what's customary."

Cassiel curled his lip in disapproval.

"What did you want?" Alastair prompted.

"What do I want? I want to talk to my son," Cassiel said. "Is that such a crime? To want to speak to you, to know what is going on in your life?"

"You've never wanted that before."

"This 'woe is me' act is past tiresome, Alastair," his father told him. "I have wanted that, have always wanted that. I wasted years when you were younger trying to get you to be a part of this family."

"So sorry it was such a waste, Father," Alastair sneered. "But you know where I stand when it comes to this family."

"It doesn't always have to be this confrontational, Alastair," Cassiel said, sounding almost a little sad. "We're not enemies, son."

"But not friends, either."

Cassiel's eyes narrowed. "You know… there will come a time when I'm gone, and you'll be expected to take over this family. A time when my title as deSanguine will pass on to you. And it will make it much easier if you stop fighting me every step of the way."

Alastair laughed. "Yeah, well," he said, his words dripping in disdain, "there's no chance in hell that's going to happen."

"And why not?"

"Well, first off, fuck that," Alastair said. "Secondly, I'm not your heir. Never have been, so the title is never going to pass to me. And third, fuck that."

"You already said that one."

"It was important enough to bear repeating."

Cassiel exhaled loudly, drumming his fingers on the arm of his chair in irritation. "Alastair… your sister was my heir, yes. But she is no longer with us. Delilah is gone. That makes you next in line to inherit the family title."

"No, it doesn't," Alastair insisted. "Callum will inherit your title. Whether you like it or not."

Cassiel scoffed. "Oh please, son. No matter what you say, I don't believe your brother is more powerful than you are. The title won't transfer to him, Alastair. It will go to you."

"That's always been your problem," Alastair said. "You've always seen him as weak. You think strength means being cruel, and Callum doesn't have a cruel bone in his body. You've never bothered to consider that his kindness is what makes him stronger than me. Stronger than either of us."

"Enough," Cassiel said, waving Alastair's words away. "I didn't call you here to rehash this fight again, son."

"Then, pray tell, why did you call me here, Dad?"

"I wanted to talk about that Witch of yours." He waved his hand toward one of the heavy armchairs seated near his desk, motioning for Alastair to join him.

"I think I'll stand," Alastair said. "I don't think this will take long..."

Irritated, Cassiel rolled his eyes. "Just sit down, for God's sake, Alastair. I want to talk without you looming over me like this. It's unproductive."

Alastair took a deep breath and walked to the chair, sinking into it. *There*, he said to his father with a look, *happy now?*

"I was... surprised when you first told me about her," Cassiel said. "Not unpleasantly surprised, mind you. I hadn't thought you were capable of..."

"Of what?" Alastair interrupted. "Of love?"

"Of commitment," his father answered, shooting him a glare. "With all the rumors, and with you fucking everyone from every family we ever brought here over the years, I hadn't thought you capable of the maturity necessary for a committed relationship."

He hadn't fucked everyone from every family who visited the estate, Alastair thought sourly. Hadn't even fucked all the women, let alone the men, and anyone else in between. Though, he supposed, he'd fucked enough of them that the rumors weren't entirely untrue... A few of the men, too, come to think of it. He wondered if his father had ever heard about that. He hoped so. He hoped it made him choke.

"I was happy to hear of your relationship with her, is what I am trying to say," Cassiel continued. "Happy again to hear that the two of you are still together after so many years."

"Two," Alastair clarified. "Two years."

"Even still." Cassiel shifted in his seat. "I approve, Alastair. I saw her when she came before the council, you know. And she has... a fire inside her. Power. I think she is a good match for you. A good match for my son."

Something softened in Alastair's chest. His father approved of Fey. Liked Fey. It made him feel... good.

Huh.

"Thank you," Alastair said, and he meant it. He'd never sought his father's approval, never cared much whether it was given or withheld. But, somehow, hearing his father voice his approval of his love for Fey... it felt nice.

Maybe he was being too hard on him. Maybe his father had been trying, in his own way, to connect with him over the years. They hadn't always hated each other, after all. Maybe his father did want to connect with him, want to know him and his life.

Cassiel leaned forward, placing a hand on Alastair's shoulder. And it felt like just the right amount of parental affection. Alastair almost smiled.

Almost.

"I think we should talk seriously about marriage," Cassiel said.

Too shocked to do anything else, Alastair barked out a laugh. "Marriage?" he repeated incredulously. "You must be joking..."

"Not at all," Cassiel said, staring into his eyes. Goddess damn him, he was serious, wasn't he? "I think it's the obvious next step for the two of you, don't you agree?"

Alastair shook his head slowly from side to side. "No, no. Fey and I haven't discussed marriage. I don't even know if she wants to get married."

"Of course she does," Cassiel said, sitting back with a bemused smile on his face. "All women do, Alastair. Some are just a little more obvious about it than others. But it's something they all want, at the end of the day."

Alastair laughed. "Yeah, I don't think that's even remotely true. I think you're way off the mark on that one."

Marriage? He hadn't thought about it, he realized. He supposed if it was something Fey wanted…

But why? What would even be the point? It was an archaic ritual, one rarely practiced anymore, and certainly not one their Faction put much stake in. That had always been a Witch thing, and even then, it hadn't been in vogue for centuries. Alastair didn't need a mindless ceremony and a ring binding Fey to him. He loved her, heart and soul. They would spend the rest of their lives together, he had no doubt about that.

Marriage just felt unnecessary, given that. It felt insignificant compared to how he felt about her.

"It's important," Cassiel continued, "to acknowledge her ancestry. Consider it a way to pay homage to her ancestors. Wars were once fought over marriage, you know."

"Oh please, her Faction knows so little about their ancestors, Father. I doubt they even remember that. And it's not something she's ever mentioned. I really don't think marriage is something she's even thought about."

"Well, maybe you should be thinking about it, then." Cassiel said, voice dropping slightly. "After all, once she becomes queen—"

"Fey doesn't want to be queen," Alastair interrupted, frowning.

Cassiel waved away his words. "Of course she does. And she will, trust me. There's enough chatter about it around the city to guarantee it will happen, eventually. Sooner rather than later, most likely. And once she does become queen, well… you would want to have some sort of contract binding the two of you, wouldn't you? Something that would ensure you take the throne as her equal, and not just… not just a consort, or some such thing."

So that was it, Alastair thought, sitting back until his back hit the chair's cushion, a familiar feeling of disgust forming in his gut. That was what this was all about, wasn't it?

His father wasn't interested in Fey at all. This wasn't some visit to bring her into the family, to get to know her. To spend time with her.

This was another chance for him to put a Salvatore on the throne—to finally guarantee his lineage turned royal. This was just another path that he started three hundred years ago when he'd crowned himself the Vampire King.

"I can't fucking believe you," Alastair said, stunned. "I can't fucking believe I almost fell for your shit again."

"And what on Earth are you talking about this time, Alastair?" Cassiel asked in a frustrated tone.

"Fey doesn't want to be queen, Father," Alastair said, and when Cassiel opened his mouth to argue, Alastair spoke over him. "And even if she did, I don't want to be king. I don't want a fucking contract ensuring that we're equals. Because we're not."

He stood, staring down at his father, and bared his teeth.

"In every possible fucking way, I am not her equal," he continued. "She is better than I am on every level. More powerful than me. Stronger than me. And if you only see her as a means to an end? If you can only see her as a way to get what you want, what you've always fucking wanted, then stay the fuck out of our lives."

Alastair didn't wait to hear his father's response. He simply turned on his heel and left.

CHAPTER 29

FEY

Fey blinked, stunned, and Callum sighed.

"I guess Alastair never told you that, either, huh?" He drank the last of his wine and set the glass back on the table in front of them. "Okay... well, you ever wonder where my father's money comes from? Where all of this"—he motioned at the room around them, the mansion around them—"comes from?"

Fey shook her head. She hadn't, not really. The Vampire Faction having riches beyond imagining was just a universal given. Like how the sky was blue, and the sun rose in the east. It wasn't something she had ever bothered to question.

"Our family is responsible for almost all the drugs circulating through the city, Fey," Callum said sadly. "Devil dust, delirium, haste, you name it. Our father is the one who oversees all manufacturing and sale, throughout all eight octants of the realm."

"Holy shit," Fey whispered, thinking of all the time she'd spent as a Blade trying to fight that very specter of drug dealings. That all of it, all of that seemingly endless stream into the city, came from one source?

"Yeah," Callum said, tucking a lock of his hair behind his ear. "After Delilah started using... Alastair blamed our father. Tried to force him to stop, to put an end to the business."

"And he wouldn't?"

"Couldn't, if you believe Father. Wouldn't, if you believe Alastair."

"And who do you believe?" Fey asked.

Callum groaned. "You know how to cut right to the bone, don't you, love?" he asked, giving her a lopsided smile. Then he grimaced, rubbing his face. "Alastair. I believe Alastair, I suppose. Father could do it if he truly wanted to. He could put a stop to it, as the family patriarch. He has the power to make us all fall in line, so who could stop him, really?"

"So that's why Alastair hates your father?"

Callum nodded. "They fought about it constantly, but then Delilah died and... that was that. Alastair made one last attempt, demanding he stop all manufacturing and sales of any drugs everywhere in the realm. Father refused, and Alastair left. They didn't speak for years after that. Tonight is one of the few nights they've even agreed to be in the same room together, you know?"

Fey considered this. Considered what Alastair had put himself through to bring her here tonight. "When did Delilah die?" she asked finally, taking a sip of her wine to wash the taste of this new knowledge out of her mouth.

"Oh, fifty or so years ago..."

Fey spat out her drink. "Fifty years ago?"

Callum smirked at her. "I take it you have no idea how old my brother is, then?"

"He told me he was still young, for your Faction, but... How old is he, Callum?" Fey asked. She felt a little dizzy.

"Oh, he is young, for one of us. That's not a lie," Callum assured her. "He's just barely over two hundred."

"I think I'm going to faint," Fey whispered, and Callum threw back his head and laughed. "I had no idea... wait—you said I was the first woman he's brought to meet your family?"

"I did, yes," Callum said, grinning. "And that's true, Fey. Two hundred years, and what I can only imagine was countless women from the rumors I've heard over the years, and you're the first one, in all that time, he's actually seemed to care about."

It was almost sweet, Fey thought, hiding her face from Callum and taking another deep breath.

"I had no idea your family was so long-lived," she admitted.

"Understandable," Callum said. He stood and walked to the bar to grab the bottle of wine, pouring himself another glass and refilling hers without asking. "We do look good for our age, don't we?"

"I know your father is old," Fey said. "He was there for the War of the Fallen. That's not just a myth, is it?"

"It is not a myth," Callum answered, smirking.

"He's over three hundred years old, then," Fey said, breathlessly. "I knew, but it never really... sank in."

Over two hundred. Alastair was over two hundred years old.

The room was spinning around her. Fey set her wineglass on the table and leaned forward, nestling her head between her knees.

Callum chuckled and rubbed comforting circles over her back and shoulders.

"I think our father is closer to five hundred, at this point," Callum said. "But I doubt that makes it better, does it?"

Fey just groaned.

"He wasn't at all surprised by you, you know," Callum continued. "Our father. It made perfect sense to him that you would be the one to steal his son's heart. After all, they've always been more alike than Alastair ever wanted to admit."

"What do you mean?" Fey asked.

"A powerful Witch? Capable of tearing down an entire regime almost entirely on her own?" Callum asked. "Cassiel fell in love with a woman just like that over three hundred years ago, Fey."

"You don't mean..." Fey sat up, twisting toward Callum, open-mouthed. "Callum, you cannot be telling me that your father was in love with the Witch Queen. The First Queen."

Callum's eyes sparkled with amusement. "You Witches really don't remember a lot of your own history, do you? Yes, Fey." He smiled. "He was in love with her. And she was in love with him, too. But, sometimes, love isn't enough. He was furious with her when she crowned herself queen, you know. That's why he did it, why he made that stupid proclamation declaring himself king. And I can only assume the fact that she loved him was why she didn't kill him outright for the sheer audacity of it..."

"Goddess," Fey whispered, putting her head back between her knees. "Callum, this is all a little too much for me."

He laughed again but continued to pat her back. "I am sorry, Fey. I had no idea you Witches had forgotten that bit of your history. I assumed you knew."

"We're not taught a lot about the First Queen," Fey murmured, her voice muffled by her legs. "We're not even taught her name..."

"Thea," a voice said softly from the door. "Her name was Thea." Fey sat up. Alastair stood there in the doorway, looking in at the two of them. His eyes looked... sad. Hurt.

"Father still talks about her. I think she might have been the only woman he ever really loved," he continued sadly.

"So, your family has a type?" Fey asked.

"I guess we do," Callum told her with a wink. "Let me know if any of the males in your Faction ever develop powers. I am single, after all."

"Come on, Witchling," Alastair said, approaching the couch where they sat. "It's time to go."

The smile slipped from Callum's face.

"I take it your meeting with Father didn't go well, then?" he asked, gaze locked on the ground rather than meeting Alastair's eyes.

"That's the understatement of the century." He held out his hand for Fey and she took it, letting him help her to her feet. Callum stood, brushing his hands over the rich fabric of his dress shirt self-consciously.

"I'm sorry we didn't get to spend more time together," Callum said softly to Fey. He took her other hand, kissing the back of her fingers again. "It was a pleasure to meet you, Fey. I truly mean that."

Fey smiled. "It was a pleasure to meet you, too. And thanks... for clearing some things up for me."

He grinned. "Of course. Evil thrives in ignorance. I think truth is the only thing that can drive it away, don't you?"

She didn't know, so she kept quiet.

"Please, do come and visit us again," Callum said. But the pain in his eyes, and the way Alastair's grip tightened on her hand, made Fey think neither of them believed that would be happening anytime soon.

CHAPTER 30
AMALIA

This is a disaster, Amalia thought.

She frowned at the rapidly cooling tea on the table, at the teacup Vee hadn't even touched.

This was such a stupid idea, she thought to herself, slouching over her own teacup and taking a sip. She should have known this was a stupid idea.

Stupid, stupid, stupid.

Of course Vee wouldn't want to have a tea party. What in the name of the Goddess was wrong with her, thinking this was a good idea?

"So..." Vee asked, looking around at the entertaining room, clearly uncomfortable. She looked so out of place in this room, surrounded by gold baubles and intricate furniture. Another mistake, Amalia realized. She shouldn't be hosting her in a receiving room like she was some sort of diplomat. *Stupid, stupid.* "What do you do for fun around here?"

This, Amalia thought miserably, looking down at the tea tray stacked with cookies and treats. At least those Vee had touched, stuffing two of the strawberry macarons in her mouth, one right after the other, the moment the tray had been set. Amalia couldn't imagine how she kept so thin with the amount of food she ate.

"Oh, you know..." Amalia tried to sound demure, setting her teacup down so gently the porcelain didn't make a single noise. "This and that…"

She glanced up, and noticing Vee's bored expression, Amalia quickly added. "I, uh, I read. A lot. And I have been known to cross stitch, from time to time…"

Vee propped her elbow on the armrest of her couch, and as Amalia spoke, she brought her feet up onto the velvet seat next to her, tucking her legs underneath her. Amalia quickly hid her wince, swallowing the urge to chastise her for putting her shoes on the furniture. It was Amalia's furniture, after all, wasn't it? Who cared if her friend put her shoes on the furniture?

Resting her head on her hand, Vee gave Amalia a long, assessing look.

"That doesn't really sound like fun," Vee said.

No, Amalia realized. *It really doesn't, does it?*

She hunched her shoulders, folding in on herself. She didn't want to care about Vee's feet on the furniture, didn't want to drink tea and nibble on biscuits and talk about her cross stitch. She didn't want to pretend.

"Truthfully," she said in a voice so quiet she wasn't sure Vee could even hear her. "I can't remember the last time I had any fun…"

Vee blinked at that, leaning forward a little more.

"I'm sorry," Amalia told her. Her body felt like it was made of lead, heavy and useless. She wanted to go back to bed. "I'm sorry, this whole thing is a disaster, isn't it? There's not a lot to do here in the palace. You don't have to stay. You can go, if you want."

But instead of leaving, Vee laughed. "Go?" she asked, smiling. "Why would I go? You can't just tell me you haven't had fun in ages, and then expect me not to do something about it."

Vee sat up, putting her feet back down on the ground. "Look, you don't have to do this sort of thing for me. The like… rich nobility, thing. We can just hang out, you know? That can be fun, spending time together."

Amalia felt the corners of her mouth twist up in a smile. "Okay," she said. "I'd like that, if we just hung out."

She picked her teacup up again and frowned. It was cold. Calling a small tendril of Fire, she pushed a little heat back into the cup and took a sip. *Much better*. Fire had never been easy for her, but recently it hadn't seemed to fight her like it once had.

Vee watched her, and then picked up her own cup of tea, as though determined to make an effort. Eyes on Amalia, she took a sip. Immediately, Vee's face twisted, and to Amalia's horror, she spat the liquid back into the cup before setting it down on the table with a look of disgust.

"I think your drink has gone off," Vee said, voice serious. "It tastes like dirty plants."

"That's how it's supposed to taste," Amalia said in a quiet voice.

"Oh." Vee frowned at the cup. "Well... at least the cookies are good." She plucked another macaron from the plate and popped it into her mouth.

Amalia nodded, relieved Vee at least liked something of the spread. "Oh yes. Macarons are the cook's specialty. He makes them fresh every morning for me. They take about two hours to set, so he has to get up at dawn to start."

Vee froze mid chew.

"Two hours?" she asked. Pink crumbs flew out of her mouth as she spoke, and Amalia couldn't help the small wince that crossed her face. "These cookies take two hours to make?"

"Two hours to set. I think it's about three hours total, from start to finish."

Vee looked horrified, her eyes darting from Amalia to the plate, and then back again. Then, finally, she swallowed.

"Well," she said, slowly, thinking. "Best not to let any of them go to waste, then, right?"

She plucked another from the plate and stuffed it in her mouth, then grabbed the entire plate with her other hand. Opening her bag, she dumped the cookies inside.

Amalia let out a shocked laugh.

"What?" Vee asked, smiling. "Trust me, this is for the best. Can you imagine spending so long on something and it doesn't get eaten? This way, none of them will go to waste, I promise."

Amalia hadn't considered that. In fact, she'd never thought about it before, never considered all the days she'd let those macarons be taken back to the kitchen untouched. Thinking about it now made it feel like there was a lead weight in her stomach.

"You should try the cucumber sandwiches," she said, motioning toward the small triangular pieces on the table.

Vee didn't need to be told twice. She took one from the stack and gave it a suspicious sniff. Then frowned.

"It's just... it's just salad, is it?" she asked.

"Well, it's... it's cucumber," Amalia tried to explain.

Vee set the sandwich back on the plate gently and wiped her hands on a napkin. Amalia couldn't help but think it was probably her best impression at being polite.

"I'm not a big fan of salad," Vee said patiently, as though speaking to a child. "Wolves prefer meat."

"And cookies," Amalia added with a slight smile.

Vee rolled her eyes. "Well, obviously, and cookies." She then shot Vee a grin, reaching into her bag and popping another macaron into her open mouth.

Amalia giggled.

"So, that's what sort of Shifter you are? A Wolf?" she asked. She sipped her tea, then frowned at it. It did taste a bit like dirt and leaves, didn't it? For the first time, Amalia wondered whether she actually even liked tea.

Vee nodded, chewing. "Mhm," she said, mouth full of cookie crumbs. "There's a lot of us in the city, you know. We might even be the single biggest group of Shifters in the realm." She licked crumbs from her fingertips.

"Could I... could I see, maybe?" Amalia asked, nervously. "Your Wolf form, I mean?"

Vee gave her a wicked smile. "Oh, you could," she said in a teasing voice. "But I'd have to get naked first."

"Oh," Amalia blushed, looking down at her hands folded in her lap. Her heart hammered in her chest. "Never mind, then. I'm sorry for asking. That was rude of me."

"Don't be sorry," Vee said with a shrug. She picked the tea up again as though to drink and then, giving it a long look, put it back down again. "You couldn't have known. I'm guessing you haven't had a lot of dealings with my kind, right?"

Amalia shook her head. "No," she said. She shrank further in on herself. "I haven't had a lot of dealings with anyone, truth be told."

Vee just looked at her, head tilting to the side.

"My mother..." Amalia swallowed the lump that suddenly appeared in her throat. "My mother didn't let me out of the palace much. And hardly anyone but our own Faction ever came to visit, or petition her for anything, so..." She let the sentence die, suddenly embarrassed by her own ignorance.

"I like your outfit," Amalia said, looking at Vee's clothing and desperately wanting to change the subject. She was wearing a simple long-sleeved shirt and jeans, ripped and worn with wear at the knees. It looked... cool. Comfortable and effortlessly pretty.

Just like Vee.

Vee just laughed. "My outfit?" she said, grinning. "I wouldn't call it much of an outfit, not next to what you're wearing."

Amalia winced and looked down at her dress. She had dressed in one of her mother's fanciest gowns, dressed as though she were attending an official tea party with someone of note.

Stupid, stupid, stupid.

"I think I need some new clothes," she said, pulling a face. Even after supplementing her wardrobe with her mother's clothing, she realized she owned nothing that wasn't either a dress or a skirt. She had no pants, no simple tops like the ones Vee wore. Nothing like what the people she saw in the city were wearing.

Feeling suddenly self-conscious, Amalia looked down at all the ruffles and lace on her skirt and wished she'd chosen anything else to wear. She tugged at the fabric, as though trying to smooth the lace enough to make it less noticeable.

When Vee reached out, placing a hand over her own, Amalia froze.

"Hey," Vee said in a low voice, and Amalia looked up at her. She had the most beautiful green eyes she'd ever seen. And her hand was warm, so warm, against Amalia's. "I like your dresses, okay? You're so... fancy," she finished with a smile.

Amalia blushed and looked away.

"Thanks," she said. "But I think I'd like to be a little less fancy, sometimes. I didn't know there were so many different types of clothing out there. So many different ways to dress. This? This is all I've ever known."

"Well, I know a ton of the stores in the city," Vee said, letting go of her hand and sitting back on the love seat. Amalia immediately wished she would hold her hand again.

Suddenly, Vee's face lit up, and she sat straight up at attention. "Hey—do you want to go shopping?"

Amalia blinked. "What? Like...now?"

"Sure, why not? You're not like a prisoner here, are you?" she asked.

Aren't I? The words jumped into Amalia's head unbidden, and she shook them away. She wasn't a prisoner, was she? So she could leave whenever she wanted. After her last trip into the city, no one had yelled at her, no one reprimanded her. Her handmaids hadn't even said a word about it, except to replace her bloodied shoes with new, near-identical ones.

"Yes," Amalia declared. She sat up a little straighter, feeling suddenly very confident in this decision. Feeling brave. "Yes, let's do it!"

The smile on Vee's face in answer was enough to make her giddy.

CHAPTER 31
VEE

The bell chimed a friendly greeting as Vee opened the shop door and stepped inside.

"Welcome, welcome!" The Demon behind the counter turned to greet them with an unctuous smile, spreading his arms wide. "How are we today, my lovely—"

His face darkened, his smile turning into a scowl as he recognized her.

"You," he hissed, pointing a scaly clawed finger at Vee. "Out! I want nothing to do with you and your group of thieves, you miserable—"

Vee simply stepped aside, smiling sweetly at the shopkeeper as the Witch behind her entered the store. The princess glanced around her curiously, taking in the racks of clothing, the wooden forms modeling various wares, and the swatches of fabric hanging from the walls.

The shopkeeper stumbled, words dying on his tongue and his eyes going wide as saucers. Vee could practically see him counting gold as he recognized the royal heir and realized the gold mine that had just walked into his store.

"M-my princess," he cooed, that unctuous smile plastered back on his face as he bowed his head to her.

"My *friend* here," Vee put emphasis on the word, smirking at the

Demon, "is in need of some new clothing, and I thought to myself—who do I know that has the best wares in the whole city, hm? Why, my dear buddy Franky, of course!"

The scowl Franklin shot Vee's way disappeared the moment the princess looked at him. For her and her money, he was all smiles.

"Of course, of course," Franklin said, coming around the shop counter to greet them properly. "I would be simply delighted to help in any way that I can."

Delighted? Vee almost laughed. The only thing that delighted Franklin was the thought of more gold in his pocket. Which was probably why he looked ready to skin her alive.

After all, the last time she'd seen him was three years ago when she and Jayce had managed to make off with about half the gold in his till. It didn't surprise her that he still held a grudge. Dear old Franky never forgot anyone who cost him money.

Vee gave Franklin a wide grin, flashing her canines at him and walking into the shop like she came here all the time. There were plush armchairs near the dressing rooms, set up as a comfortable place to rest for attendants and mates, and Vee slid into one of them, dangling her long legs over the armrest.

"Franky, dear, could you get the princess and I a drink? We're simply *parched* from the walk from the palace."

The scales that bordered Franklin's hairline quivered with rage at having to wait on a mutt like Vee, but he bowed and said in a perfectly well-mannered voice, "But of course, ladies. What can I get you?"

"A glass of sparkling water would be just fine," the princess answered casually. She was distracted by the clothing, picking a few items from the rack and examining them.

"Tea for me, Franky," Vee said, her smile smug, as the shop owner kept scowling at her. "The fancy stuff."

"Of course, I'll be but a moment."

By the time Franklin returned with their drinks, Vee could tell the princess was starting to get overwhelmed. Perhaps she'd never gone to a shop like this, never had so many options available to her. Luckily for the princess, forcing Franklin to wait on her as though she were a highborn lady was only one of the reasons Vee had picked this shop. The truth was, Franklin was damn good at his job.

The princess probably had people to shop for her, Vee reasoned. Hell, she probably had people to do everything for her. What she needed was someone who could take control, who could help her out. Hence, Franky.

Right on time, as though sensing the princess's discomfort, he swept in, his smile less oily and more subdued.

"If I may be of assistance?" Not waiting for an answer, Franklin stepped around the rack, removing a few items of clothing. "I would say these would be a good fit for Your Highness. I have some truly magnificent gowns, fresh in from the second octant, in the back that I could bring out as well, if you would like?"

"She'd like some pants," Vee called from where she lounged. Meeting Franklin's eyes, she took a big sip of tea, trying not to gag. *Goddess, this stuff was simply awful. How did those rich Witches stomach it?* "Casual clothes, only. No gowns."

"Ah, but of course, then I have just the thing."

Franklin was a sartorial force of nature, moving around the store, holding fabric swatches up to the princess's face to judge coloring, pulling items seemingly at random. He skillfully took charge, and Vee couldn't help but appreciate how at ease he made the princess.

By the time Franklin had shepherded the princess to the dressing room, Vee had given up on her tea, setting it on the small table next to her chair. Who cares if fancy people drank it? It was clearly some sort of trick. A joke that people low born like her weren't in on. Vee abandoned it and instead got up to look at the clothing herself.

She picked a few items from the racks. A tan leather jacket, some new boots, a few pairs of pants. She piled them all on the shop counter, knowing a princess wouldn't think twice about a few extra gold added to the bill. It had been too long since she'd had any new clothes, and Vee deserved a little treat. And it's not like someone swimming in gold would notice. Hell... the princess could probably feed every stray in their gang for life and not even bat an eye at the cost.

The thought made her chest tighten a little in anger.

"Vee?"

The voice coming from the dressing room sounded lost. Vee set the bag she was admiring down and turned. The princess was there, face poking out from behind the dressing room door, looking terrified.

Had Franklin said something to upset her? Something roiled in Vee's chest, something white and hot she didn't recognize. Had Franklin done something to hurt her?

"I... I don't know if I can wear this," the princess told her quietly. "It's...well, it's quite scandalous."

"Oh, come on, you can show me." Vee flashed her a smile. The princess liked her smile. Vee could feel the way it made her heart beat a little faster, the way it brought blood to her cheeks. It worked. With a grimace, the princess stepped out of the dressing room and turned to look at herself in the tall mirrors.

Wow.

Franklin knew what he was doing. The pants were a fine, expensive linen, light and flowy in a pale cream that complemented her skin tone perfectly. They were high-waisted, which was good because the top he'd paired it with in matching cream cut just below the ribs, revealing two full inches of smooth midriff.

Amalia twisted and turned, looking at herself from all angles in the mirrors.

"I look..." she frowned.

"Beautiful," Vee finished, her voice husky. Amalia's eyes snapped up to hers in the mirror, and a soft blush rose to her cheeks, even though Vee hadn't been smiling at all.

But it was true. She did look beautiful. Without the layers and layers of lace from those ridiculous gowns, Princess Amalia looked... older. Not so much like a girl, but a woman. The outfit showed off her thin frame and long legs, while still looking like something a highborn aristocrat would wear.

"I was going to say powerful," Amalia admitted, glancing down at herself and smiling.

Powerful? Vee considered her, cocking her head to the side.

Yes. She did look powerful, didn't she? She looked like a proper queen.

Instinctually, Vee reached for that power. She hadn't considered

Amalia to be powerful before. Everyone in the city already knew the princess had just a fraction of her mother's power, knew she was barely a proper heir at all...

And yet... yes. There it was, that pulse of power under her skin. Power was a force like gravity, pulling lesser beings into its orbit. Alastair had that pull. So did Uncle Jas. Fey's pull was like a vortex, drawing everything that existed closer to her.

Vee was surprised to feel Amalia had it, too. It was... muted, somehow, muffled so much she hadn't noticed before. Even as she stood there watching Amalia admire herself in the mirror, that pulse grew a little stronger.

Huh...

Amalia's fingers traced the visible skin of her belly self-consciously. Vee frowned. No, that wouldn't do. Heading back to where she'd found her new leather jacket, she flipped through the clothing, pulling a piece out and jogging back to where Amalia stood.

"Here," Vee held the jacket out for her to try, and Amalia gave her a curious look before slipping her arms inside and letting Vee straighten it on her shoulders.

"Perfect," Vee said, giving her a big wolfy grin as they looked in the mirror.

The jacket was the same cream coloring as the rest of the outfit and fell to mid-thigh on her. It was fitted, but it managed to give the outfit just a modicum of modesty.

"Wow," Amalia murmured, looking at herself.

Wow was right. The woman in the mirror was someone to be reckoned with, a powerful, beautiful Witch on the cusp of adulthood. Amalia twirled, giggling as the jacket spun, showing off the lilac lining that added the perfect feminine touch. Something felt stuck in Vee's throat as she watched Amalia spin, laughing for the first time since they'd met. That pulse of power grew a little more.

"Ah, yes! Yes, you are a vision!" Franklin exclaimed, returning from the back with even more clothes. He clapped his hands together, excited. "The jacket is an excellent choice, Your Highness."

Amalia paused, smiling, and Franklin's claws picked at the fabric, pinching places. "It will need some minor tailoring, I think. Yes, we can bring the shoulders in just a bit. And the pants, we can hem them, if you would like to forgo heels?"

"Yes," Amalia said, breathlessly. Her smile was so wide it looked like it might hurt. "Please. I think I'll do away with heels for a while."

"Very good, very good," Franklin murmured. A pen and pad of paper appeared in his hand, and he began to sketch out numbers, his eyes roving over the outfit and calculating.

"We'll take the set," Vee said, smiling. "And a matching set in any other colors you might have."

Franklin paused, raising his brows at Vee, before glancing back to the princess.

"Yes, I think so," Amalia grinned. "You can charge it to the palace."

This time, when Franklin looked at Vee, there was no scorn in his eyes, no more scowl. His eyes were wide, glistening with thoughts of gold. "N-naturally, Your Highness! Ah, yes, I believe I may have some similar styles you may enjoy as well. And, perhaps, shoes?"

"Shoes are a must," Vee confirmed, smirking as she settled back into the armchair. "Don't you agree, Princess?"

Amalia turned to smile at her, and for just a moment Vee forgot how to breathe, and the smug, satisfied smirk on her own face disappeared completely.

CHAPTER 32
VEE

Was there anything in the world more beautiful than stars?

Vee stared up at the night sky, ignoring the cold, sharp brick that dug uncomfortably into her back. Ignoring the soft murmurs of voices all around her.

Stars had to be the most beautiful thing in existence, she imagined. The sky, a deep black velvet, so perfectly accentuated with all those pretty little lights. Sure, the moon was pretty, shining up there all on its own like a big silver coin, but the *stars*. They were something special, little gems caught in the air, sparkling forever. What were they? Were they reachable? She wondered if one of the flying Shifters knew, wondered if they'd ever touched one...

Footsteps reverberated on the brick next to her head, coming closer and closer, and suddenly Jayce was there, standing above her, his face blocking her view.

Vee stared up at him.

"Some of the gang are talking about you," Jayce told her in a low voice. "They're worried about the princess. About what you're planning."

Vee's good mood dimmed.

"Who?" she asked.

Jayce laughed. "Who do you think?"

Tom. Vee clenched her jaw tight.

He was one of the oldest boys still here, and even though he was nothing but a Coyote Shifter, he had been itching to challenge her leadership among the strays. Uncle Jas once told her that was common among their kind. Whenever groups of different species got together, they were always scrambling to prove who was better, who was top dog.

How annoying that he thought, even for a second, that he was on her level. He was an insect compared to her.

They all were.

"Hey, Tommy," Vee called, still staring up at the stars. The roof went quiet as a grave in an instant, every conversation stopping the moment she spoke. "Can I have a quick word?"

Vee didn't need to look up to know where he was.

Ba bump.

Ba bump.

Ba bump.

There were twenty or so of them gathered on the roof tonight. A few more in the building below that served as their clubhouse. Vee could feel every single one of them through the tangled webs of their heartbeats. She'd never tried to hold them all at once. She sometimes wondered if she could.

Tom froze from where he was sitting, his back against the short brick lip that lined the rooftop. His hand, which had been stroking Kayla's leg where she sat next to him, stopped immediately.

Ba bump.

Ba bump.

Ba bump.

He's scared, Vee noted, smiling.

Good.

Tom took his time. He stood up slowly, dusting debris from his pants and straightening his clothes. A power play, taking longer than necessary to answer her summons.

Vee's smile only grew.

He crossed the roof with slow, deliberate steps, and Vee waited patiently. Only when he came to a stop, standing just by her head, did she sit up.

She loved the stars, loved staring up at the night sky. But Goddess, it did hurt her neck to lie like that for so long. Vee groaned, rolling her head on her shoulders and stretching her arms.

"I hear you have something to say about me and the princess," Vee said, rubbing a knot from her shoulder. She turned her head, angling it to look up at where Tom stood over her.

Another power move. And such an obviously male one. As though looming over her like that was power. Like size meant anything to someone like her. It was funny.

Everyone was the same size when you could make them crawl.

Tom's amber eyes snapped over to Jayce and he bared his teeth in a challenge of dominance. Jayce only shrugged, unfazed and unapologetic. It wasn't a secret to anyone that Jayce told her everything. Only an idiot would think otherwise. He was loyal to her. The way they all should be.

"If you have something to say," Vee prompted, "you can say it to me. Now."

"You've been spending a lot of time with her," Tom said. "Some of us are worried—"

"Not some of us, Tommy," Vee interrupted. He clenched his teeth together, visibly annoyed. Tom hated being called Tommy. "I'm asking you if *you* have something to say."

Tom swallowed. "You're spending a lot of time with her."

Vee waited. When Tom didn't continue, she prompted him.

"And?" Vee asked.

"And... and what's the plan?" Tom asked, frustrated. "A few weeks ago, we were talking about how that whole family had to go, and now it's like... it's like you're friends with her or something."

Boys. They were all so, so stupid. Vee tucked her feet underneath herself and stood.

She felt a little vindication in the way Tom immediately took a step back away from her, putting a little distance between them.

"Do you know what being friends with the princess gets us?" she asked.

Everyone was watching them, hanging on her every word. Excitement and fear and dread pulsed in their blood.

Ba bump.

Ba bump.

Ba bump.

Tommy shook his head, just the slightest movement from side to side.

She took him so quickly he didn't even have time to gasp.

It didn't matter that he was bigger than she was. Didn't matter that he was stronger, physically. None of that mattered when she could kill them all with a flick of her wrist.

Wordlessly, she called to the blood in his veins, commanding him to his knees, and forcing him to kneel at her feet.

"Of course you don't know," Vee said, staring down at him. His body shuddered and went still. "Because you're nothing but a stupid boy. I don't need to tell you what plans I have, and I don't need to explain anything to you, *Tommy.*"

He was perfectly still under her hold. Unnaturally still.

"Does anyone else have a problem with how much time I'm spending with Amalia?" Vee asked, looking around the roof. She made sure to look at each of them, one by one, meeting each set of animal eyes that gazed at her.

No one spoke.

"Good," Vee said simply. She let go of that hold over Tom. Suddenly free, he gasped for air, scrambling away from her.

Oh, Vee realized, as Tom coughed and spluttered, trying to catch his breath. *Breathing. Right.*

She forgot, sometimes, when she took full control like that. It was a lot to keep track of, after all, keeping the heart beating, the blood circulating through the body, and keeping the lungs going.

Oops!

"For the record," Vee said, raising her voice so they could all hear, "access to the princess gets us access to the palace. To the council. And maybe you could see that, if you weren't so busy trying to get into Kayla's pants."

There were snickers of laughter from around the rooftop. Kayla's lips thinned, but she at least had the pride to raise her chin, unashamed.

"And we need access to the council. We don't even know who's on it, for Goddess's sake. We don't even know who's meant to be representing us."

"My uncle says it's one of the Lions," one of the younger boys said. "Kellos maybe, or his sister."

"Your uncle is an alcoholic, Kevin," Vee snapped. "He doesn't know shit. But neither do we, which is why we need access to the palace. So, let me ask you all again—does anyone else have any issues with me spending time with the princess?" Vee asked, looking around.

No one said a word. No one even moved.

They were scared. Maybe it had been too long since she'd put one of them in their place. Maybe she should start doing it more often. Only Jayce's heartbeat was steady. No fear, no doubt. Forever confident in her decisions.

Vee smiled.

"Good," she said. "That's settled then."

CHAPTER 33
AMALIA

Amalia chewed on her lower lip, twisting to look at herself in the full-length mirror in her bedroom.

She looked...

Beautiful. That's what Vee had called her. Beautiful.

Staring at the reflection of herself, Amalia almost felt it. Beautiful. She smiled and ran her hands over the fabric of her new clothes. The fabric was luxurious, soft and silky under her fingers.

She'd decided to ditch the jacket, if only for the moment, wearing just a short midriff top in a lovely turquoise color and matching pants. It felt scandalous, showing so much skin, but... in a good way. It was thrilling. Her fingers trailed over the exposed skin of her stomach, leaving goosebumps in their wake.

Her mother would have hated this, Amalia knew, turning and looking over her shoulder to admire herself from a different angle. Goddess, she would have thrown such a fit if she had seen her daughter in an outfit like this. But these clothes. They looked incredible on her, made her look powerful. And the way they made her feel...

"You look really hot," came a voice from the open window.

Amalia squealed, twisting around so quickly she almost fell. Vee sat on her windowsill, legs dangling off the frame. Her eyes sparkled as she looked Amalia up and down.

Amalia brought a hand to her chest, heart hammering.

"Vee, you just scared about five years off my life," she gasped.

Vee laughed, hopping off the window and into her room. She flung herself down on Amalia's bed, giggling as it bounced under her weight.

"How did you get up there, anyway?" Amalia asked. "Didn't anyone try to stop you?"

Vee laughed. "Like who?"

"Like the guards?"

"What guards?" Vee answered with a wide smirk. "There aren't any guards patrolling outside the palace, not anymore. I can come in and out whenever I want, and no one would stop me."

She rolled over on the bed, propping herself up on an elbow, and stretched her legs out.

"So..." Vee said, smirking. "What're you up to, anyway?"

Amalia blushed. She wished she'd worn the jacket, now. But the way Vee was looking at her, the way her eyes sparkled, somehow made her even more embarrassed than being caught admiring herself in the mirror.

"I was... I was just trying on my new clothes," she admitted, giving her reflection another glance. Swallowing her embarrassment and putting on her bravest face, she held her arms out, posing for her friend. "So... what do you think?"

"I think you look ready to break a few hearts," Vee said, smiling.

Amalia laughed. She turned back to the mirror.

"Oh please," she said. Yeah, the clothes were great, and she loved the freedom she had in them much more than those stupid gowns. But she was still just... her. She wasn't going to be capturing anyone's attention, let alone breaking anyone's heart. Even displaying a little skin, she wasn't going to draw anyone's eyes. "No clothing is that good."

"I wasn't talking about just the clothes," Vee said.

Amalia's cheeks heated, and as her gaze met Vee's in the mirror, her heart skipped a beat.

"I brought you something," Vee said, suddenly.

"A... a gift?" Amalia blinked, shocked. This girl brought her a gift?

Vee chuckled. "Yeah, something like that." Sitting up, Vee pulled her bag off her shoulder and reached inside.

"I kept thinking about you stuck here, eating cookies and sandwiches with only salad in them, you know?" she said as she searched. "And I thought... well, we can't have that, can we? A princess deserves a proper meal. Ah! Here they are!"

Vee pulled a parcel from her bag, wrapped in paper, and held it out to Amalia with a bright smile.

"Go on," she urged when Amalia just stared at the paper, confused. "Take it!"

"What is it?" Amalia asked, taking it from Vee's outstretched hands. It was warm under the paper. Amalia unwrapped it, frowning in confusion at the white circle of dough hidden inside.

"It's a pork bun, from Regina's. Do you... know Regina's?" When Amalia shook her head, Vee smiled like she'd expected that answer. "Well, she makes the best buns in the city. Trust me, these things are more valuable than gold out there on the streets."

Amalia raised the bun to her nose and gave it a delicate sniff. It didn't smell like anything she'd ever eaten before. Not wanting to appear rude, or like a snob, she took a small, hesitant bite.

Oh. My. Goddess.

It was incredible.

"See?" Vee smirked, watching her. "Better than gold."

The noise Amalia made when she took her next bite was vulgar enough she was sure her mother must be rolling in her grave, but she couldn't bring herself to care. The spices! The meat! Even the strange, spongy dough that held the whole thing together.

It was sensational.

"This is the best thing I've ever eaten in my life," Amalia murmured, not caring even a little that she was speaking with her mouth full.

"I'm glad you like it," Vee said. "The stuff they keep giving you here, it's all... sweet, you know?"

Amalia swallowed. "What's wrong with sweet?" she asked.

Vee shrugged. "Nothing. But..." She fiddled with the strap on her bag. "The world out there? It's not always sweet. Maybe it's time you experienced a little more of it."

Amalia considered this, staring at the last bite of pork bun in her fingers.

"Yeah," she said. "I think maybe I should."

She offered the bite to Vee, who took it with a grin.

CHAPTER 34
JASPER

"Excuse me?"

Jasper glanced up, smiling brightly at the Witch who approached the bar. He had heard her walk up, even over the heavy bass of the music. But when he gave her that surprised smirk, as though she'd snuck up on him, she blushed so prettily.

They always did.

"What can I get you?" Jasper asked, setting down the glass he was polishing and leaning toward her, his palms flat on the bar.

There was a time before Fey, when having a Witch in the Last Drop was practically unheard of. Sure, they were close enough to the university to attract a few college kids, but most of their clientele come from the Fallen Factions. Witches had their own bars and their own clubs, where they didn't have to rub shoulders with the riffraff in the lower city.

Fey had changed all of that. Hell, Fey had changed a lot of things.

Now the club's clientele had a broader range. And it had been months since Jasper and Ferus had been forced to beat the shit out of anyone. He almost missed it some nights.

Almost.

The Witch gave him a flirtatious smile, batting her lashes at him.

Behind her, the group of women she'd come in with watched their interaction and giggled.

"I heard you have a specialty drink? One you make for... for the Broken Blade?"

Jasper widened his smile just enough to flash his sharp incisors as he straightened. The Witch's eyes went to his teeth immediately, and her breath hitched. Fear was a powerful aphrodisiac in small doses, and the Witches who had started coming here (always in groups, always giggling) enjoyed a bit of danger to spice up their evening.

And Jasper was happy to oblige them. Up to a point, of course.

"A Witch's Temple," he told her, grabbing bottles. "Of course. And for your... friends?" He glanced at the table, raising an eyebrow and smiling at the four Witches there.

"The same, for them," the Witch answered breathlessly. Jasper gave her a wink and set to work making them.

"Is... is she here tonight?" the Witch asked, and Jasper glanced up to look at her. "The... the Broken Blade?"

"Fey?" he asked. "Nah, not tonight. Not yet, anyway. But later?" He shrugged, like she came in all the time. "Who knows? She might show up."

And if she did, he'd be sure to give her a talking to about her aim. Sure, the scorch marks on the wall were barely visible in the dim light of the club, but they'd lost about half their top-shelf stock to her temper. Next time, maybe he could convince her to aim just a little lower.

Jasper lined the finished drinks up on the bar but shook his head when the Witch reached into her pocket for her coin.

"Oh no, darling, this round is on me," he told her, dropping his voice to a husky whisper. Her blush was delicious.

Thanking him, she gathered the drinks and ran back to her table to tell her friends everything. Jasper grinned. That free round, and his little white lie implying Fey might come by that night, would be enough to keep that group around and drinking up a huge tab until closing time. They'd more than make up for the cost of the free drinks, and next week he'd bet his whole paycheck he'd see them, and even more Witches like them, after they told all their friends what a great time they'd had.

Whistling, Jasper went back to polishing glasses. It was a slow night, and for once, it seemed like they might be over-staffed. Sid was cleaning the stockroom, but Jasper had given him the task mainly to give him something to do. Well, that, and because after the last few weeks of use the stockroom probably needed a good deep clean. With bleach.

He had just put down a glass and picked up a new one when the club door opened and Alastair walked in.

The Witches whispering at their table went dead silent, jaws dropping as the Vampire moved across the dance floor. He had that effect on the patrons. Hell, if half of the Witches who came in tonight were hoping to see Fey, the other half was probably here to see Alastair. The Vampire Prince who was drop dead gorgeous enough to capture the heart of the Broken Blade? Now that was something people wanted to see.

Jasper reached under the counter and pulled out a bottle of Alastair's favorite whiskey. Flipping one of the freshly polished glasses up, he grinned at Alastair, expecting him to stop for his usual.

"Hey boss," Jasper called, uncorking the bottle.

But Alastair didn't look up. Didn't acknowledge him at all. He walked, head down, straight past the bar and up the stairs to the VIP section, heading toward his office.

Something tightened in Jasper's chest. He corked the bottle as the smile slipped off his face. He stared down at the empty glass on the bar for a few long seconds before putting it back with the others.

Once upon a time, before he started working for Alastair, Jasper had tried his hand at being a thief. It was a common line of work for most Shifters when he was growing up, and Jasper figured if some of his friends could do it, so could he.

He was, without a doubt, a really shitty thief. Sure, he could blend into a crowd, and he could pick pockets with the best of them, but a good thief always knows when to cut and run.

And Jasper never ran from a fight.

After getting into one too many scraps after being caught in the act, and after drawing way too much attention to himself, Jasper had given up on picking pockets and managed to get a job as hired muscle.

All these years later, and he still didn't know when to back down. Still never ran from a fight.

Grinding his teeth together, Jasper went to the stockroom to find Sid. He needed someone to cover the bar while he and Alastair had a chat.

CHAPTER 35

ALASTAIR

I was a fucking idiot not to promote Ferus earlier, Alastair thought, looking over the order sheets from the last few months. Who would have thought the Wolf he'd brought in to run security would be so damned organized?

In the two years since his promotion, Ferus had turned The Last Drop into a perfectly oiled machine, meticulously tracking their earnings, spending, and the workers' schedules. The damned Wolf was not only saving him a fortune every month, but he'd also managed to do everything so efficiently that Alastair didn't have any work to do most nights.

And now, when he needed a distraction, when he needed something, *anything*, to get his mind off the hunger gnawing at his guts, now was when everything was running perfectly smooth. Just his fucking luck.

Alastair took a sip from the glass of whiskey on his desk and nearly spat it back out.

Fuck the Goddess, that stuff was awful. He scowled at the label, turning the bottle toward him to read it. It was top shelf, aged, and the Wolf running the VIP bar last night had said it was spectacular. One of their most expensive bottles.

Why did it taste like backwash to him, then?

A knock on his open office door made him glance up. Jasper. Great. And his luck officially just got shittier. Swallowing his rising anger, Alastair looked back down at his paperwork.

Jasper didn't wait to be invited in. He walked right in without a word and closed the office door behind him.

"I have that open for a reason, you know," Alastair grumbled, not looking up from his paperwork.

"Yeah. And now I've closed it for a reason," Jasper answered. He took a few steps into the room and stopped before Alastair's desk. "We need to talk."

Alastair raised an eyebrow, glancing up just long enough for Jasper to appreciate it. "Shouldn't you be at the bar?" he asked.

Jasper shrugged. "It's a Thursday night, boss. The place is empty. Sid and Mara can handle it. And since when do you care, anyway? You used to be fine with me taking a few minutes off to play with a pretty girl if she caught my eye."

Alastair grunted, turning back to his paperwork.

"You're avoiding me," Jasper said.

He was. Had been ever since that night in the stockroom when he'd lost control.

"Don't be ridiculous," Alastair said, adding a notation to the ordering form.

"I'm not being ridiculous," Jasper insisted. His voice was infuriatingly calm. "You're avoiding me."

"I've been busy, Jasper. I don't always have time to swing by just to chat."

"Oh, really?" Jasper snatched the paper out from under Alastair's pen, ignoring his snarl and flipping it around to read it. "Busy annotating... the liquor orders from two quarters ago?" He raised an eyebrow at Alastair in challenge. "Yeah... I can see why such an important piece of work has been keeping you locked up here. And why you can't even stop by the bar for one drink."

Jasper's gaze fell on the bottle on Alastair's desk, and he curled his lip in disgust. "*Blended whiskey*, boss? You can't stand blended whiskey."

"I've developed a taste for it," Alastair lied. Leaning back in his chair, he lifted the full glass to his lips and took a gulp.

It tasted so awful he almost couldn't swallow it.

"Delicious," Alastair purred.

Jasper rolled his eyes.

"Ferus says you've had him triple check the last month's orders already. But here you are, doing it again. You don't come down to the main bar anymore, you only go to the VIP bar and *only* if I'm not working it. Because you're avoiding me. Just admit it."

Alastair stood. He was only a fraction taller than Jasper, but he used every bit of that height to his advantage now, straightening his back and staring down at the Wolf across his desk.

"And why," Alastair asked in a deadly voice, "would I be avoiding you?"

Jasper didn't back down. "That's what I'm hoping you'll tell me," Jasper said, staring back at him and crossing his arms over his thick chest. "And I don't plan on leaving here until you do."

"You're being ridiculous, Jasper, and if this is all you came up here for—"

"Is this about what happened?" Jasper interrupted. "Is this about what we did together? You, me, and Fey?"

The world tilted around Alastair, and something very dark was rising inside of him. It was getting harder to hold it back.

"Because that's when this started," Jasper continued, tapping the desk between them. "That's when you started avoiding me. So, what is it, Alastair? Was it seeing me with Fey? Was it watching someone else touch her?"

Alastair snorted a laugh. "You know very well that wasn't my first threesome, Jasper, and I doubt it will be my last, considering how much Fey enjoyed herself. You can take your paranoid fantasies somewhere else."

"And it can be different when it's someone you love," Jasper insisted. He rounded the desk, coming around to Alastair's side to face him. "I've known Shifters who won't let anyone touch their mate once they've found them. It bothered you, didn't it? Is that why you freaked out in the stockroom?"

"Fey and I have discussed what happened that day, and I have apologized."

"Not to me," Jasper said. He held Alastair's gaze, seemingly oblivious to the danger lurking there. Oblivious to the anger roiling through the Vamp standing in front of him. The hunger. "You never said one damned word to me about what happened."

Alastair bared his fangs. "I didn't realize I had to apologize to my *employee*." He spat the words at Jasper, pushing him to back down, but the Wolf refused.

"Don't give me that shit. I wasn't just your employee when you finger fucked her in front of me, was I? You did that to her to teach me a lesson," Jasper continued. "So, if it wasn't jealousy, then what was the lesson, boss? Because if the three of us are going to work, you need to—"

"The three of us?" Alastair asked incredulously, temper flaring. "Let's get one thing straight, puppy, there is no three of us. There is me and Fey." He stalked closer. "And then there is *you*. Off in a completely different stratosphere."

Jasper blinked slowly. "I didn't mean it like that. I didn't—"

"But you *did*. That's the fucking problem, Jasper. You did mean it that way. Because that's how you're starting to see it, isn't it? *The three of us*."

This time, Jasper didn't deny it. "You can't tell me that night didn't mean anything to you, Alastair," he said in a low voice.

Alastair's answering laugh was nothing short of cruel. "Listen to me very closely when I tell you that's exactly what it meant. We had fun. But you? You were there as a toy, never forget that. Hell, you were nothing more than a dildo with a pulse."

"You're lying," Jasper told him, anger filling his voice. "You're fucking lying."

"And why the fuck would I—"

"She's my mate, Alastair," Jasper breathed, eyes screwed shut. Like admitting it hurt him, somehow.

Alastair wasn't sure he heard him right over the sudden roaring in his ears.

"What the fuck did you just say to me?" he asked.

Jasper groaned, running a hand through his hair in frustration. "It's not... not just her. I think... I think it's both of you. Together."

Meeting Alastair's cold stare, Jasper gave a halfhearted smile.

"Surprise?" He shrugged.

"Fuck you," Alastair snapped.

"Look, it's not a big deal," Jasper explained with a placating gesture. "You and I have always been—"

"You and I have never been anything," Alastair interrupted.

"Sure." Jasper rolled his eyes. "Right, there's never been anything between us at all. Tell me something, boss—those three times you walked in on me with a woman in the stockroom, how many times did you join in?"

A dark and violent rage was brewing inside him, and Alastair wasn't sure how much longer he could hold it back.

Twice. The answer was twice.

"Does Fey even know?" Jasper asked. He shifted a little closer. Close enough they were standing chest to chest. "Does she know that's not the first time we've done that together? Shared a woman?"

Alastair shoved Jasper away so quickly the Wolf stumbled back against the wall.

"Don't you fucking touch me," Alastair warned.

Anger, hot and fast, rose in Jasper's eyes. "Why not?" he pushed. "Are you scared you'll like it?"

Alastair's temper snapped. One moment he was staring at Jasper, and the next he had him pinned to the wall, hand around his throat.

"Say that again," Alastair ordered, pushing down on Jasper's throat. "Say it again, puppy. I fucking dare you."

Jasper stared up at him, teeth bared, with only the briefest flicker of fear in his eyes. "Make me."

Baring his sharp fangs, Alastair loosened his grip around Jasper's throat and crashed their lips together.

He hadn't meant to. He'd meant to drag the damned Shifter over to the door and throw him out on his ass. He'd meant to beat the shit out of him, to remind him who was in charge around here. He'd meant to tell him he was wrong.

But... he wasn't.

Jasper froze under his kiss, shocked. Then Alastair felt his hands come up to grip him by the hair, pulling him closer with a moan. Alastair pushed closer, pinning Jasper against the wall.

How long had he wanted to do this? How long had—

Hunger, raw and angry, burned underneath his skin.

He desperately needed to feed.

Alastair pulled back with a jerk, breaking the kiss. Jasper stared at him with wide, wild eyes before bringing his fingers up to his own lips reverently, touching where Alastair's lips had been.

"Fuck," Alastair said, screwing his eyes shut. He felt a little breathless. "I shouldn't have done that."

"I knew it," Jasper murmured. He licked his lips. "I fucking knew it. I can't believe you... you had me thinking this was all in my head."

"That was a mistake," Alastair hissed. But he didn't move. He kept Jasper pressed to the wall, kept himself pressed against him.

"Oh, really?" Jasper asked, smiling. He rolled his hips, and Alastair groaned as Jasper's body rocked against his. There was no hiding what the kiss had done to him. "That right there? That doesn't feel like you think it's a mistake, boss."

"Fuck," Alastair said again. He pushed himself away from the wall, turning away from Jasper. He needed some distance, needed to catch his breath. He needed to think without this fucking hunger clouding his mind.

"You need to leave," Alastair said, gesturing at the door. "This shouldn't have happened. This can't happen."

Jasper laughed. He hadn't moved, still leaning smugly against the wall, smirking. "What are you talking about? This is a good thing, isn't it? You want me, too." His eyes were bright. "I was right, wasn't I? I can't believe it. This is... the three of us we're—"

"Don't you dare finish that fucking sentence."

Jasper laughed again, shaking his head. "Alastair, are you really that repressed?"

Alastair shook his head. "I've fucked men before, Jasper. That's not... that's not the problem."

"Then what?" Jasper closed the space between them, reaching up to clasp the back of Alastair's neck. "The three of us could be so good together," he whispered. "Goddess, just imagine it."

Alastair angrily slapped Jasper's hand away. "There's no *three* of us. There's no us. I love Fey. I can't lose that. I can't lose her."

Jasper frowned. "So? I'm not trying to get between you and her. Don't you get that? It's *us*. The *three of us*. And once she hears about this—"

"No." Panic flooded his chest. "No, she can't know what we just did. She can't know any of this. I can't risk losing her if she… if she doesn't understand."

Jasper's face went cold, eyes darkening.

"This shouldn't have happened. I shouldn't have touched you like that."

"But you did," Jasper said, voice dropping to a low growl.

"You fucking provoked me!" Alastair shouted. Enough. He'd put up with enough.

"Get out," Alastair snapped, pointing toward the door. "Get out of my office. You're fired."

Jasper snorted a laugh, and Alastair ground his teeth together so hard his jaw cracked.

"I'm not kidding this time, Jasper," he said, looking up. "You crossed a line. Get your shit and get the fuck off my property. You're officially unemployed. Ferus can take you off the roster, but I don't want to see you here again."

Jasper's smile slipped from his face, and the look of hurt that filled his eyes shattered something in Alastair's chest.

"Fuck you," Jasper said. Then he turned around and walked out of Alastair's office, slamming the door behind him.

CHAPTER 36
AMALIA

This time, when Vee came through the window, Amalia was ready. Despite what she'd said about there being no guards, Vee never seemed to bother with entering the palace properly, like she was a guest. No, she liked to come to Amalia's window. Liked to surprise her.

But ever since she'd eaten her evening meal, Amalia had been waiting eagerly. And when she heard the soft click of claws on glass, she wasn't surprised.

Amalia tried not to look too excited as she pushed the window open to let Vee in.

"Hi," Vee greeted her, smiling.

"Hi," Amalia whispered back.

Their faces were mere inches from one another, almost close enough to touch...

Clearing her throat politely, Amalia stepped away from the window to let her in. "I... I wasn't sure you would be coming tonight," she said, twisting her hands together. "I didn't have anything planned for us, I'm sorry to say. What—what did you want to do?"

Vee shrugged, hopping down from the window. "I don't know, really. What's there to do in the palace, anyway?"

"Oh." Amalia frowned, feeling awkward. "Not much, really. Most of the palace is empty."

They used to have visitors, she remembered. Her mother loved having visitors from all over the realm, loved being wined and dined by the aristocrats from every octant. She'd had the whole Western Wing converted to bedrooms, so there was always room for guests. Now, those bedrooms were all empty. No one bothered to visit the palace anymore.

"Why don't you show me around?" Vee pressed. "I'm sure you and I could get up to some trouble somewhere around here…"

Something in her tone, something in the way her eyes traveled over Amalia's face and lingered on her lips, made her pulse jump.

She nodded, quickly.

"We'll have to be quiet," Amalia warned her, working to keep her voice careful and calm. "There are still a few guards around the palace. I'm not sure if we're really allowed to be wandering around, especially at night."

"Oh, don't worry," Vee said, her eyes sparkling mischievously. "I can be very, very sneaky."

She stepped closer to her as she said this, stopping right in front of Amalia. Their noses bumped.

Amalia swallowed loudly.

"Okay," Amalia whispered, feeling dizzy as she stared at Vee's smile.

THEY HIT THE KITCHENS FIRST, giggling as they pulled snacks out of the pantry, eating whatever looked good until Amalia felt fit to burst. Then they swung through the Western Wing, creeping into long-empty bedrooms, cooing and laughing over some of the things old visitors had left behind.

Amalia found a cat-o'-nine-tails stashed under one bed, frowning in confusion over the leather pleated whip while Vee howled with laughter.

Truthfully, Amalia didn't really know much about the palace. She didn't even know how to find the Eastern Wing, where the Queen's Blades had once lived. Her heart had broken at how disappointed Vee had looked when she'd admitted that to her.

"I could show you the throne room?" Amalia heard herself saying, wanting to give her friend something. "That's where it all... you know, it all happened."

She didn't want to talk about the night of the Blood Moon. Didn't want to even think about it.

But Vee's eyes had gone wide when she'd said it. "Really?" she gushed. "That would be amazing!"

She wrapped her arms around Amalia, and suddenly it was too late to back out.

Amalia didn't want to go to the throne room. She hated that room and had only been there twice since her mother's death. The first time was to oversee the clean-up. The second time was to take her place on the council. The idea of going back made her feel a little nauseated.

But Vee... Vee wanted to see the throne room. Vee looked so excited. Swallowing her own feelings and pushing them as deep down into her stomach as she could, Amalia managed to paint a smile on her face.

"Sure," she said. "It's this way."

The smile vanished when Vee reached out to take her hand, interlocking their fingers. Amalia stood there, dumbly, looking down at their intertwined hands, her heart pounding.

"Lead the way," Vee said, smirking.

THE THRONE ROOM was designed to be an entertainment space—a long singular room, made to accommodate large groups of people coming to pay homage to the Queen. There were four entrances—the main entrance leading into the palace proper, two side entrances, and the back entrance closest to where the throne had been placed. This was the entrance her mother had favored—preferring a private method of coming and going that allowed her the freedom to leave whenever she chose. It was also the entrance the council members used.

The eastern side entrance was closer, so Amalia led Vee there, holding her hand the entire time. She felt lighter than air as they raced through the halls, giggling.

This was... fun. And Amalia couldn't remember the last time she'd had fun before Vee. If she'd ever had fun...

As they approached the throne room, all that vanished though. The room had been designed to hold large crowds of people, yes, but it had also been designed to carry voices from one end of the hall to the other—the acoustics such that anyone sitting on the throne would merely have to whisper and still they could be heard all the way at the other end of the room.

Amalia froze when she heard the voices, coming to a halt so quickly Vee almost ran into her.

"What's wrong?" Vee asked, head cocked to the side.

Amalia shook her head. "The council," she whispered, listening to the gentle rumble of conversation drifting out from the throne room's eastern entrance. Someone had left the door ajar slightly, and she could make out Alice's voice.

Alice. The Dead Queen's Blade. The one who had started all of it, everything that led to her mother's death. The one who had stormed the palace that night with a pack of Shifters. Amalia had felt numb when she'd found out that was who the council chose to replace her, but now...

Now she felt angry. Disgusted.

Why did it have to be her, of all people? Why couldn't the Priestesses have held her spot on the council? Until she was ready? Why hadn't anyone even talked to her before they decided, even mentioned it to her?

They hadn't even thought about her, had they? Hadn't even considered how it might feel for her to be replaced on the council by the woman who had ruined her whole life...

"Amalia?" Vee prompted. "What's going on? What's wrong?"

She was hyperventilating, Amalia realized. She inhaled slowly, trying to calm her breathing to a normal level.

"The council is meeting right now," she explained in a quiet voice. "We can't go in there."

She'd expected disappointment. Maybe even anger, since she couldn't show Vee the Eastern Wing either. She hadn't expected Vee to get even more excited.

"You're serious?" she asked, releasing Amalia's hand to clap her own together excitedly. "They're meeting now? At night?"

Amalia nodded. "They always meet at night now," she explained. "For the Demon and Vampire Factions. It's easier for them..."

She trailed off. Vee wasn't listening anymore, she was tiptoeing closer to the door and pushing it further ajar.

"Vee," Amalia hissed. "Vee, stop, we can't go in there!"

"Why not?" Vee asked, turning to look at her over her shoulder. "We can just watch, right? It's not like they're hiding anything, are they?"

Amalia blinked.

"I guess..." she answered, considering. Why couldn't they just watch, after all? No one had ever said she wasn't allowed to watch the meetings... no one had ever forbidden her from coming, either. Wasn't she, of all people, allowed to see what they were doing?

Wasn't she supposed to be *on* the council?

Vee shot her a grin and turned back, nudging the door open a little more so they could peak inside.

"We don't even need to go inside, see?" Vee whispered to her. "We can just watch from here. They'll never even know we were here, trust me."

Something felt off. Wrong. But Amalia shook the feeling off, moving closer to the door with Vee. Vee took her hand again, smiling at her, and despite everything, despite the feeling in her gut, despite being right outside the last room she ever wanted to see again, Amalia found herself smiling back at her.

Her hands were so different from Amalia's. Calloused, where Amalia's were soft. Scarred, where Amalia's were flawless and perfectly groomed. Vee's fingernails were rough and jagged, and a little dirty. She liked that. Liked the contrast. Liked the way their hands looked with their fingers laced together. She liked the darker tan of Vivian's skin against her golden hues.

"Shhh," Vee whispered to her, even though Amalia wasn't talking. "I want to hear what they're saying."

"—send someone to request a meeting," Alice was saying. "*Request*, Cassiel. Not demand. Repeat that back to me, so I know you understand."

The Vampire's reply was so full of venom, Amalia felt herself shrinking away from him, instinctively.

"I'm not in the habit of making requests," the deSanguine said. His voice held so much menace, so much violence, Amalia wanted to turn and run. But Alice... Alice didn't flinch. She didn't cower away from him even a little. From their vantage point in the doorway, they had a perfect view of her as she turned to the deSanguine and raised a single eyebrow.

"Repeat it back to me, Cassiel," she said, slowly, as though talking to a child. A child, and not a deadly blood sucker who could snap her in two in an instant.

And to Amalia's shock, the Fallen King—one of the worst of the bogeymen from the stories told to her when she was a kid—laughed. He didn't cackle, didn't snicker villainously. He simply... laughed.

Holding his hand up as though swearing an oath, he spoke. "I, Cassiel Salvatore deSanguine, will request a meeting with *l'enfant de sang*. Not demand," he said in a clear, amused tone.

"Excellent," Alice said.

They weren't scared of him, Amalia realized. None of them were scared of him... and he didn't seem scared of Alice. He wasn't terrified of the ex-assassin at the table. The Blades had been her mother's greatest weapon, the strongest and most deadly Witches in the realm. They should be terrified of her.

They were all peers, Amalia thought suddenly. That's why they weren't scared of each other. And that's why she hadn't fit in among them. She wasn't their peer, was she? Wasn't strong like they were, wasn't powerful... The realization left an uncomfortable lump in her throat.

"How is our wheat farm in the fourth octant fairing?" Alice asked, looking down the table at an attractive man in his twenties.

"Good!" he answered. "Two families have settled onto each farm, and it sounds like the vast majority of the crop from this year can be salvaged. By next year, the Elk are confident they can have the realm's wheat supply back to expected levels."

"Who's that?" Vee asked Amalia, frowning at the man at the table.

"I don't know. I don't recognize him," Amalia answered. "He's sitting in Kellos's seat, so I guess he's representing the Shifters tonight?"

Vee's head jerked sideways to look at her.

"Kellos?" she asked, and something in her eyes made Amalia uncomfortable.

"Yeah," she said. "He's, uh, he's a Lion Shifter. He's usually the Shifter representative. Do you... do you know him?"

"I know him," Vee answered, looking back into the room. Her voice was strangely quiet, strained. "I just didn't know he was our Faction's representative, is all."

"Oh," Amalia answered, not sure what to say. Were the council members supposed to be a secret? Had she broken some rule by bringing her friend here, by showing her this?

Vee stepped back from the door, and for a moment her face was hidden in shadow, so much so that Amalia couldn't make out her expression at all.

Then it was gone, and Vee smiled at her.

"Come on, let's go back to your room. This is boring anyway, isn't it?"

Amalia smiled back, relieved.

"Yeah, okay," she said, reaching out to take Vee's hand again. This time, when they walked through the halls together, she let her thumb caress Vee's. And Vee didn't stop her.

CHAPTER 37

FEY

I f Fey had been expecting the morning rain to dissuade her students from attending her lessons this morning, she was woefully disappointed.

There must be six hundred Witches here, she thought in shock, staring at the groups gathered on the palace lawn. *Maybe even more.*

Where were they all coming from? And why, for Goddess's sake? Why were they all here, all so eager to learn from her?

"These are all Witches who were given Allium?" Fey asked Leandra, staring in wonder at the crowd gathered in the steady rain. They looked uncomfortable and mostly wet, though a few had managed to make their own makeshift shelters and umbrellas out of Air.

Leandra pulled a face. "Well, actually, no," she admitted quietly. "Your lessons have become rather popular, if I'm being honest, and the other covens asked if we wouldn't mind accommodating a few other students from their temples. Ones who might, not necessarily, have had any of their powers taken away from them by the Queen, but who want to attend your lessons for other reasons."

Fey cast a sidelong glance at her. "And why do they want to do that?"

Leandra's lips twitched. "Fey... whether you recognize it or not, you

218

are an effective teacher. You've taken Witches with barely any powers at all and turned them into forces to be reckoned with. I think you'd be surprised at how many Witches in this city want that for themselves."

Frowning, Fey looked out at them all again. Witches willing to brave the freezing rain just for a chance to learn from her. "Clearly," she said.

She pivoted to face the class. But before she could begin, Leandra stopped her.

"May I ask you a personal question, Fey?"

Fey paused, turning to regard the High Priestess with narrowed eyes. She gave her a brief nod.

Leandra took a breath. "Sana informs me that you have... stopped attending her sermons. Your absence has been noted by the congregation."

Fey waited. When Leandra provided nothing more, she said with a quirked eyebrow, "I don't think that was a question."

Leandra gave an exasperated sigh. "You know Sana, likely as well as I do. She overthinks. She's concerned about you. About why you've stopped coming."

"Again, is there a question coming or—"

"Why have you stopped?" Leandra asked, bluntly. "A few months ago, you told me yourself that your visits to the temple were good for you. That they helped you feel grounded. More in control. So why did you stop?"

Fey considered it.

She could lie. She could say it was because of the congregation. The swirling voices that called her queen. The Witches who looked at her and dreamed she was something more.

Or?

"I don't need to visit the temple to feel in control anymore," Fey admitted. Fire and Earth pulsed beneath her skin, constant and familiar companions to her now. "I hold the Goddess inside me wherever I go, now."

After a moment of scrutiny, Leandra nodded.

"I'm glad," she said, giving Fey a tight smile. "And I'll pass along the message to Sana to save her worries for someone who needs it."

Fey nodded her thanks, before turning back to the wafting crowd.

Time to begin.

"Alright," she called, voice traveling over the lawn. The effect was instantaneous. Conversation died immediately as they turned toward her. Hundreds of Witches, young and old, watching her expectantly.

"Since it's raining, I figured this is a perfect day for my favorite element." Fey paused, waiting long enough to let them grow a little restless. Then, calling Water, she reached out to the falling rain...

And stopped it.

She could only hold it for a few seconds, and only for a small area. But it was enough to cover the entirety of the group, enough to earn gasps and murmurs as the Witches looked around the lawn in wonder. They stared at the tiny beads of water, halted midair, glimmering like stars.

Releasing a shaky breath, Fey let her hold drop, and the raindrops fell to the ground with an audible splash.

"Water Witches, you're with me today," Fey called, raising her voice to be heard over the gasps and murmurs of the crowd. The Witches were all talking now, chattering excitedly to one another. Shooting Leandra a quick grin, Fey continued. "And the rest of you? The High Priestess will be taking over your instruction. Let's begin."

It was an exhausting day.

By the time the palace bell tolled the late afternoon hour, signaling the end of their daily lessons, Fey felt on the verge of collapse. Goddess save her. She could run five miles a day, and usually trained for hours with Alice and Joy each week, but she never felt this worn out, this exhausted.

Thankfully, the clouds had finally broken, and the sun came out just in time for Fey to enjoy it on her walk to her sisters' place from the palace. It made the walk infinitely more pleasant, and she took her time, deviating from her normal route to slip through a new neighborhood.

Jasper would be proud, she thought with a smile as she walked.

This neighborhood was a little fancier than her own, and even with the desegregation of the city, almost all the people she passed were from the Witch Faction. Fey recognized a few of her students walking back to their own homes. She smiled when they waved at her excitedly.

Maybe she'd stop by one of the stores here and grab herself something to eat from a new bakery. She had plenty of time before Joy and Alice expected her at their place for family dinner. And she was hungry. Famished, even. She could—

Fey froze, staring at the man nailing something to the wooden signpost at the end of the block.

She recognized him. An aristocrat who had frequented the palace back when she was a Blade. A sniveling coward of a man, always a little too effusive in his praise for Queen Edelin. But, more importantly, she recognized the poster he was putting up.

"What are you doing?" Fey asked in a hollow voice. A dark storm formed in her chest as she stared at the image of her own face.

OUR TRUE QUEEN, the poster said.

The man turned, ready to tell her to mind her own business. But when he saw her—recognized her—he did the most peculiar thing.

He smiled.

"Your Grace!" the man greeted her, his grin stretching ear to ear. The same unctuous, pandering grin he'd given the old queen. It made her feel ill. It made her feel angry. "How good to see you on this beautiful day!"

"Are you the one putting these up?" Fey asked, fingers flexing. She felt so cold, suddenly. Like ice had started to creep down her spine, and through her nerves.

"One of many," he told her, dropping his voice to a conspirator's whisper. "You have many fans among the old guard, believe me, Your Grace."

"Don't call me that," Fey whispered. But the man wasn't listening.

He reached out to grab her wrist, thick clubbed fingers holding her. Touching her.

The gentle breeze that had been moving through the city streets stopped. A stillness hung in the air, unnoticed by the aristocrat before her.

"When you are ready, we will fight for you," the man told her. Something uncoiled in Fey's chest, something dark and dangerous. "We will drive these Fallen scum out of the palace, and you can take your rightful place on the throne."

Her skin felt hot where he held her. Hot and cold all at once.

"Take your hands off me," Fey warned him in a dark voice.

Her words were lost on the man, who turned toward the crowded streets and shouted, "Our queen! Our queen has come! Salvation is at hand!"

The crowd of people on the street turned to stare. Some smiled at Fey and this fat aristocrat. This disgusting man who thought he had the right to touch her. To put his hands on her. Others looked from her to the poster and scowled. But many, far too many, came closer, their eyes hungry.

These were the Witches who wanted her to take the throne.

Deep in the crowd Fey spotted a Shifter girl, barely knee high, who hid behind her father's legs. He led her away, shooting fearful glances at Fey over his shoulder.

Fey's stomach twisted.

There were murmurs in the mob gathering around her, growing louder and louder by the second. Their words felt sharp. Dangerous.

Our queen.

Our savior.

"She will save us from the growing Fallen influence!" the man holding her arm continued. He squeezed his hand tight around her, shouting with joy. "She will right what the council has done to our city! She will—"

"I'm not your fucking queen," Fey interrupted. She felt that rage rise in her chest, unleashed and raw.

It took no effort at all to grab the man's arm and snap the bone, releasing herself from that sickening touch.

The voices of the crowd went dead silent as he screamed, and Fey let all that delicious rage out.

Alastair was right. They shouldn't kneel to me.

They should cower.

The ground around her crunched as she fractured it, the stones under her feet splintering outward like a spiderweb.

"How dare you touch me," Fey told the mewing man. Those fractures grew, fissions forming in the street, spreading through the stone and concrete. Clutching his arm, pale-faced and scared, he stepped back away from her.

"My queen, he only—" someone else said in the crowd, and Fey turned, rage flashing in her eyes.

"Queen?" she asked. Fire came to her, pouring from her skin and down her arms. It danced over her hands. She took a step closer to the crowd, smiling as they shrank back. The stack of posters lying forgotten on the ground caught fire, vanishing into ash.

"I told you I'm not your queen," she said, venom dripping from her words. "I killed your queen. And I'm no one's savior."

The fire turned to lightning, sparking from her fingertips and leaping to the ground around her, striking the fractured stones at her feet. There was shouting and panic from the crowd.

"I'm not your salvation."

She took another step, the very ground shaking beneath her.

"I'm your *fucking reckoning*," she spat.

It was oh so satisfying to watch them run away. To hear their screams.

To know that—this time—they saw her for what she really was.

CHAPTER 38
JASPER

Jasper hadn't bothered grabbing his things when he stormed out of the club the night before. And when Ferus had spotted him coming out of Alastair's office and called out to him, Jasper had turned on him savagely enough the other Wolf had whimpered like a frightened pup and quickly moved out of his way. Jasper hadn't bothered to stop even for a moment until he was out of the club, kept going even after he'd made the change and shifted to his Wolf. Then he was running, running through the city, leaving all that anger and pain behind him.

He'd run for hours. Run until he'd barely been able to make it back home, almost too exhausted to shift back and change into fresh clothes.

And now?

The evening sun was still hovering far above the horizon, but Jasper couldn't wait any longer. He had to do something to fix this, had to restore whatever balance they still had. If there was a chance, even a remote chance, that he could make this right...

Come on, you stupid sun. He glared up at the sky as though he could threaten the sun to set a little faster. But it took its time, tendrils of light clinging to the day as though fighting against the coming night. Finally, when the very last tip of the sun's orb rested just above the horizon, Jasper steeled himself.

Close enough.

Raising a hand to Alastair's front door, he knocked. And knocked again.

No answer. Was he still asleep? How long after sunset did it take for Vamps to wake up, anyway? How long was he going to have to wait out here, standing awkwardly on their doorstep?

Jasper raised his hand to knock again, but before he could, the door clicked and opened.

"Boss?" he called, poking his head into the dark room.

"Come in. Close the door."

Well, Alastair hadn't immediately told him to fuck off. That was something, at least. A good sign, maybe. Jasper ducked inside, trying to let in as little of the remaining sunlight as possible, and shut the door behind him. It took a moment for his eyes to adjust to the dark of the townhouse.

With the sun barely dipping below the horizon, it was a surprise to find Alastair fully awake. In the dim light, with the blackout curtains drawn tight against the sunlight and only one lamp lighting the room, it was hard to see too well. But it looked as though Alastair hadn't been to sleep at all.

He sat on the couch, still dressed in the suit he had worn to work the night before. His shirt was unbuttoned and opened to the waist, and his belt lay on the ground at his feet, as though he'd attempted to get undressed and simply stopped. He held a glass of amber whiskey cupped tight in one hand. An empty bottle sat on the table in front of him.

"Hello, puppy," Alastair said, raising the glass in greeting before taking a long drink. "Let me guess—you're here to beg for your job back?"

"I wouldn't say beg," Jasper answered with a shrug.

Alastair smirked.

"Good," he said. "You won't need to. You're not fired."

The stiff knot in Jasper's chest loosened a fraction.

"And," Alastair continued, staring into the amber liquid in his cup as he swirled it, "you'll be happy to hear that I no longer have the authority to fire you, starting today. Ferus, and Ferus alone, now holds that power."

His stomach sank.

"Are you leaving The Last Drop?" Jasper asked.

Alastair glanced up quickly.

"Fuck's sake... *no*. I'm not leaving my fucking club. But as far as your employment goes, only Ferus can fire you from this point on. Officially, he's your new boss. Since apparently I can't be trusted with it, according to him."

Jasper snorted.

"So.... If that's all you came here for, you can go now," Alastair said, gesturing toward the door. "Run on home, puppy."

Jasper didn't move.

"Where's Fey?" he asked, shoving his hands into his pockets and looking around the empty townhouse. Her scent was nowhere in the air tonight.

"Family dinner," Alastair answered, reaching up to run a hand through his hair. Jasper noticed it trembled, ever so slightly. "With her sisters. She'll be back later tonight."

Jasper frowned, staring at the Vampire on the couch before him. His hand was definitely shaking. And he looked gaunt. Paler even than normal. "No offense, boss, but you look like shit."

Alastair smirked. "Such a flatterer." The smile faded so quickly Jasper could have convinced himself he imagined it. Alastair ran a hand over his face, groaning. "I need to feed. I was supposed to the night we went to see my family, but..."

Jasper raised an eyebrow. "Wait you... you don't feed from Fey?"

The look of disgust that flashed in Alastair's eyes before he shook his head was very curious. Very curious indeed.

"I just assumed that you did," Jasper explained with a shrug. "That's what Vampires do, right?"

Alastair kept shaking his head.

"It's complicated," he muttered. "This whole thing is too fucking complicated."

"She won't let you?" Jasper asked.

Alastair's laugh was entirely devoid of humor.

"No, puppy. She'd let me. But I won't do it." He sighed, tipping his head back. "We don't feed on anyone stronger than we are. I can't feed from Fey. But I can't..." He paused and took a long drink, draining his glass. "I can't bring myself to feed from anyone else, so..."

"So, this is your solution?" Jasper asked, raising an eyebrow and glancing around the dark room. "You're going to sit in the dark and, what, starve yourself to death?"

Alastair didn't answer.

Right. For a moment, there, he'd forgotten how stubborn the Vampire could be.

With a frustrated sigh, Jasper reached down to grab the hem of his shirt and pulled it up over his head.

"What in all hell do you think you're doing?" Alastair asked, raising an eyebrow as Jasper folded his shirt and placed it on the couch.

"This is my last clean white shirt," Jasper explained. "And I don't want to get blood on it."

Alastair's face remained impassive. Blank.

"That doesn't answer my question, puppy," he said.

"I'm not as powerful as you are, right?" Jasper asked. It wasn't even a question that needed asking. No Shifter in the realm could rival a Vampire. Especially not a Vampire like Alastair.

Alastair just blinked in response.

"So." Jasper spread his arms wide and grinned. "Why not feed from me?"

The seconds ticked by as Alastair stared at him, his face giving away nothing. Each passing second standing there, shirtless, got a little more humiliating.

"I'm not going to beg, if that's what you're waiting for," Jasper told him.

"You don't know what you're offering," Alastair said, finally.

"Does it matter?" he asked, rolling his shoulders. "You need to feed. And... here I am. You can feed from me, right?"

Alastair shifted forward on the couch, setting his glass down heavily on the table.

"Why are you doing this?" he asked in a low voice. "Why offer this?"

Jasper sucked in a breath. He could make a joke, like he always did,

He could shrug it off again. He could keep pretending, keep ignoring that pull he felt. Or he could finally face it and stop burying it in a tipsy haze.

"You know why," he said, finally.

Mine. The word rolled through his mind, through his entire being, again and again as he stared at the Vampire before him.

Alastair stood.

For a second, Jasper thought he might kick him out. Or, at the very least, try to fire him again. Alastair approached him slowly, eyes locked on his. It was pure instinct that had Jasper stepping backward, moving away until his back hit the wall.

"Are you sure about this?" Alastair asked. He commanded such a presence standing in front of him like this, and Jasper now regretted taking off his shirt. Maybe getting it a little bloody would have been preferable to this. To feeling this exposed. Not trusting himself to speak, Jasper nodded.

Why was his heart beating so quickly? Alastair reached out and traced a single finger down the side of Jasper's neck, and his heart hammered unfathomably loudly in his chest.

"It will hurt," Alastair told him. Jasper nodded, his mouth dry.

"I can take a little pain," he said. His voice hitched as he said it.

The corner of Alastair's lips twitched up into a smile.

"Good to know," he said, reaching out to hold the back of Jasper's head. Then, fast as a viper, he struck, fangs sinking into Jasper's throat.

The force of the bite was a shock. Jasper sucked in air. And it *did* hurt, initially. Two sharp points of pain, where Alastair's fangs sunk into him. But then...

Jasper's hands clenched at his sides, back pressed hard against the wall, and a shudder went through him as Alastair began to feed.

This wasn't pain. Jasper swore and squeezed his eyes shut on the next swallow, the sensation going straight through his body and down his cock.

This wasn't pain at all.

Every instinct in him screamed to touch the Vampire feeding from him. He wanted to reach out and run his hands over Alastair's chest and down his back. He wanted to grip his shoulders and pull him even closer.

He wanted...

Alastair's hand on the back of his head tightened, pulling Jasper closer to him, pressing him back against the wall with a force that was almost painful.

Jasper swore as their hips touched.

There was no hiding how hard he was as Alastair pressed against him. No hiding his body's reaction to this. To him.

But Alastair didn't stop. He didn't even seem to notice. Mouth pressed tight to Jasper's neck, he growled deep in his throat, moving against him, rolling their hips together.

Too much. Too much sensation, too much pleasure, and Alastair just kept feeding, mouth pulling long, slow gulps of blood from Jasper's body.

It was all too much, and he was going...

"Stop," Jasper gasped.

The response was immediate. That wonderful sensation suddenly gone as Alastair pulled his head back, releasing his neck.

"Are you alright?" Alastair asked in a husky voice, looking concerned. There was blood on his lips.

Jasper almost laughed.

"I'm fine," he said, swallowing hard. Alastair's hand still cradled the back of his head, his touch almost gentle now. "I just... I need a second."

Alastair frowned, confused. "Did I hurt you?" he asked.

Jasper closed his eyes, shaking his head. He couldn't look Alastair in the eye and say it aloud.

"Then what—"

"If you keep going, I'm going to come," Jasper interrupted with a nasal laugh. "I just... I just need a second to calm down, okay?"

Alastair stilled, then glanced down, seeming to only now realize how they were standing. Jasper, who he'd clutched tight against his body, their legs entwined. Jasper's cock, hard and pulsing against Alastair's thigh.

"I see," Alastair said. He licked his lips. He didn't move away.

Instead, to Jasper's horror, he leaned back down, mouth hovering over the bite.

"Boss, please," Jasper whimpered.

"You're still bleeding. I need to seal the wound," Alastair told him, sounding amused. His tongue traced the bite, and Jasper bit back a groan.

"Oh," Jasper murmured. He'd gripped the back of Alastair's shirt without realizing, and slowly forced himself to let go when Alastair began to move away.

"Was that..." Jasper swallowed, hard. "Did you get enough?"

"For now," Alastair answered. He already looked better, face flushed, eyes bright. He traced the bite on Jasper's neck, now sealed, with the tip of his finger.

"Is it... is it always like... that?" Jasper asked.

Alastair chuckled darkly. "No, puppy. No, it's not. That was... different from what I'm used to."

Mine, that voice insisted inside him. Goddess, he was a mess. He needed a drink. He needed to come. He needed to get the fuck out of here.

"I should go," Jasper said. "I'm probably late for my shift tonight, and my boss is a real asshole, so—"

Alastair leaned down and kissed him. A soft, chaste kiss that tasted metallic and left him dizzy.

"Thank you, puppy," Alastair whispered, against his lips. "You have no idea how much I needed this. From you."

Heart beating too fast, too many emotions to understand swirling in his head, Jasper could only nod.

"Of course, boss. Anytime."

CHAPTER 39
VEE

"Hey... Vee? You doing ok?"

Vee didn't bother looking up at Jayce. She frowned harder, watching the rat in front of her. It rose clumsily on two legs, jerking and spasming, as though her command required too much effort.

"Yeah," she answered. "I'm just thinking, is all."

The rat shuddered. It stood like she told it to, but it was... unnatural. Wrong. She furrowed her brow.

"*Dance,*" she commanded.

The rat shuddered again but didn't move.

"*DANCE!*" she said louder, pushing all her power into the word. The rat twitched and bent under the command, but still just stood there.

Disappointed, Vee sighed.

"I don't understand why it's not working," she said, putting her face in her hands and rubbing at her eyes. She was tired. She'd been spending too many nights at the palace, too many early mornings here at their clubhouse. Eventually someone was going to notice she wasn't at Nan's, wasn't where she was meant to be. But she would solve this problem today. She could get the rats to dance—easily really—when she was orchestrating the moves herself. Why couldn't they do it when she commanded it?

Why wouldn't they just do what they were told?

One of Jayce's strays looked up, glancing between her and the rat.

"Rats don't dance," he said helpfully.

Vee's lip curled. Stupid fucking boys. "I know rats don't dance," she said mockingly. The boy flinched away from her. "I'm not an idiot like you. But—"

She stopped. Stopped and thought about what he'd said.

Rats don't dance...

Watching the rat under her control, Vee frowned, considering what that really meant. Was it really that simple? That obvious?

She stared at the rat and released the hold she had on his hind legs that kept him standing. The rat dropped to four feet, shaking off her influence like a dog shaking off water. He twitched his whiskers in irritation but didn't run.

None of them ran anymore. They learned quickly they couldn't escape her. Now, they tolerated her toying with them. Some with more annoyance than others.

"*Groom*," she commanded.

He obeyed instantly. Sitting up on his haunches, the rat began to clean himself, running his front paws over the fur of his face and ears. It was frantic, much faster than their usual grooming. But it was what she'd asked for.

"*Stop*," Vee commanded, and the rat froze, completely still.

Vee's heart leapt in excitement.

"Rats don't dance..." she repeated, a smile blossoming over her face. She turned to look at the stray who had said it. "What's your name?"

"Paul," he answered nervously. "My name is Paul."

"You're not as dumb as you look, Paul," Vee said with a smile.

"Uh... thanks?"

"You're very welcome. Rats don't dance. So... what do rats do?" Vee looked around at the pack of boys lounging in the clubhouse around her. "Well?"

"They like to chew," one boy offered hopefully. "That's why they're such a nuisance, right? They'll chew through anything, even if it's not food."

Vee nodded.

"*Chew*," she commanded the rat.

Influencing a creature's mind was infinitely harder than controlling their body, Vee was starting to realize. And every time she'd thought she'd gotten the hang of it, something had gone wrong. She could make her rats dance, moving their limbs herself and pulling their strings, but she couldn't convince them to dance. She could make them run, but they wouldn't strut.

Was it really this simple? Vee wondered, as the rat grabbed the corner of the poster he stood on and began gnawing on the paper with abandon. He chewed the material like a glutton, ripping and tearing with sharp teeth. Vee didn't care that he destroyed it, didn't care as he bit through the photo of Fey's face and the words written underneath it. They had plenty of them, after all. And it didn't matter how many times they had to put them up around the city, replacing the ones that kept getting torn down, they could always print more...

"I can't convince them to dance, because rats *don't* dance," Vee said excitedly. "They don't have a concept of dancing. I can't ask them to do something they don't know how to do. Something they don't understand."

Paul was nodding, sycophant that he was. "That makes sense, yeah," he said.

But Jayce shook his head. That's why she kept him around. That's why he had so much more power in their gang than the rest of the strays, why he was her second in command. He stood up to her, didn't just automatically agree with everything she said. He made her think, challenged her, and sometimes she needed someone who was willing to do that.

"How do you know, though?" he asked. He was the only one who ever questioned her. She didn't mind, most of the time. After all, she'd known him the longest. He'd earned it. "It's just one rat... how can you tell if that's why it won't dance?"

Vee considered this.

"We need to test it. And we need a bigger target," she said, finally.

"Something with more range. Something that can dance, that can do whatever I tell them to do, with no limits…"

When the idea hit her, Vee smiled widely. It was perfect, a perfect way to kill two birds with one stone.

Or one Lion at least.

"I think I know the perfect test subject."

CHAPTER 40
KELLOS

Traitor...

Kellos woke slowly. His eyelids were like lead weights, fighting to stay closed. The painless comfort of sleep awaited him, and he wanted to return to that blissful realm.

What time was it? He wondered, looking around his room. It was dark, his room pitch black and empty. No Med Witch in sight. Late then, he reasoned. Groaning, he forced himself to sit up in bed. His joints hurt. Everything hurt.

After this latest bout of pneumonia, it was finally time to admit he was too old to keep up with the others. He would need to abdicate his role on the council, and soon. He was too old, too weak to keep making the trek to the palace every other day in the middle of the night. And the stress of his position was slowly killing him. But Sam and the others hadn't settled on a permanent replacement yet. Silas was a little too young, a little too rash to be a permanent representative. The Shifters needed someone with more experience, more foresight.

Looking around the dark room, Kellos frowned. What had woken him up? Had there been a noise? Something moving—

Traitor...

Kellos blinked. Was that a voice? Where had that come from? The room was empty; he was sure of it. And... It didn't sound like a voice, not really. It was more like a thought... something loud inside his own mind.

Traitor...

Kellos winced. It was louder this time. A sound rattling in his skull. He shook his head, trying to dislodge the voice.

It sounded...

It sounded like *his* voice.

Get up.

His legs stiffened, and reflexively he stood, lurching from the bed and to his feet. The muscles in his legs quaked and shook from the effort, and the pain in his joints flared into an inferno.

Something was wrong, something was very wrong. Kellos's heart was pounding like a drum. He had to get to someone, had to get some help. Where was his sister? Maybe she could—

Walk.

He was nothing but a puppet. Kellos hissed in fear and horror as his body disobeyed his own commands to stumble forward.

No, no, no.

He needed to yell for help, needed his pride of Lions to hear him and come to his aid. Needed them to know something was very wrong.

Walk.

He stumbled forward, his atrophied legs barely able to hold his weight. Something inexplicable pulled him forward, yanked him toward the bathroom.

Even in the dark, he could see the fear in his eyes as he looked in the bathroom mirror. Abject terror.

Something roared in his mind, and he fought against it with what little strength he had, but it was like fighting the tide. He had no defenses against this, no walls to protect him from this force. The world around him darkened and swayed, as a body no longer his own jerked and twisted, caught between obeying commands not his own and collapsing under his own weight.

He'd been too sick for too long. He shouldn't be standing like this, shouldn't be...

Traitor.

Rage filled his mind. Rage... at himself. He was a traitor, wasn't he? He'd joined the Witches on their stupid council, he'd abandoned his own kind, he'd betrayed them, betrayed them all. They had a chance to take the throne, and he'd thrown it all away. He'd gone to the Witches like a kitten, mewing for its mother, begging for a saucer of milk. He was a traitor to his own kind, a worthless, irredeemable traitor—

No... No, that's not right. Kellos shook his head, trying to clear his thoughts. He was no traitor. His spot on the council was a win for Shifters everywhere. Already they had seen some remarkable changes in the city, shifts in the poverty, shifts in the regulations that favored one faction over all others—

TRAITOR.

The voice screamed inside his head so loud that Kellos briefly lost consciousness, waking a few seconds later on the cold tile floor of the bathroom. Goddess, he hurt. His body, his mind, everything hurt.

Get up, traitor.

Kellos moaned as his body obeyed the command, forcing him upright despite the agony in his atrophied muscles and swollen joints.

Find the others.

What others? Kellos didn't understand, and for a moment his mind was his own, that icy grip gone and his legs nearly collapsing without that voice urging them to stand.

Find the other traitors. Find the others who sold us out.

His body lurched forward again, and an image filled his mind. Silas, Ben. Sam. The other powerful shifters who supported him, who offered him advice, and worked to hold their faction together.

No, Kellos thought, but he was slipping away, slipping into darkness as the voice filled his mind, pushing him further and further from consciousness. The world in his view narrowed to pinpoints, then vanished entirely as he disappeared into the dark.

Find the traitors.

Hunt them.

Kellos hadn't shifted in months, preferring the pain of his human body to that of his Shifter form. But as the voice filled him and pushed him deep into the darkness, his body began to shift and morph.

Commanded, no longer in control of his own body, Kellos felt himself shift into his Lion skin.

It was the last thing he felt before everything went black.

Hunt them.

Hurt them.

Kill them.

Regina was just getting up for work when Kellos found her.

Ever since his joint inflammation had become severe enough to affect his mobility, she had taken to sleeping on Kellos's couch, wanting to be nearby in case her brother needed anything in the middle of the night. It wasn't much of an imposition for her, which she consistently reminded Kellos every time he complained about her staying over. After all, her bakery was just down the street from her brother's house—closer, even, than her own place.

Her day started before dawn, and like clockwork, she awoke, ready to get started. She didn't notice anything amiss as she got ready, sorting out her clothing and brushing her teeth in the downstairs bathroom.

She was in the kitchen, putting together a simple lunch for Kellos to enjoy later, when she heard the growling.

A Lioness is first and foremost a huntress. Keen eyes, sharp hearing, and lethal reflexes. Regina was no exception. There was a reason the Shifters had sent her and her pride to the palace the night of the Blood Moon. They were predators—far deadlier than their male counterparts.

And it is remarkably hard to sneak up on a predator.

The moment she heard the growling, Regina spun around, putting the kitchen counter at her back.

The house was dark. But not still. Something crept in the shadows, something big.

"Brother?" Regina called into the dark.

There was no answer but that growl, guttural and dangerous. A warning and a threat.

When he pounced, he did so without so much as a sound. Six

hundred pounds of Lion came from the shadows at Regina, claws extended, and fangs bared.

She barely had time to grab the knife from the counter before he was on her.

CHAPTER 41

JASPER

He could ignore the first knock on his door. He could even ignore the second round of knocking that started a few minutes later.

But when the knocking continued, Jasper realized he couldn't ignore it forever.

With an irritated grunt, he rolled out of bed, pulling on whatever clothes he'd thrown on his floor the night before.

"I swear to the Goddess, Viv, if you lost your key again, I am going to murder—"

He wrenched the door open and stopped, frozen.

Fey leaned against his doorway.

Mine.

"Hey," she said, smirking.

"Hey, gorgeous," he murmured, too stunned to even smile. He stepped back, welcoming her inside, and—

Wait. This was a terrible idea. His place was a mess. Wincing, he shut the door behind her and started grabbing empty beer bottles from the kitchen table. What was he thinking, letting her come in here? He only had two chairs, and one was covered in a pile of Vivian's dirty clothes.

Fey just smiled, watching him carry an armful of rubbish to the kitchen.

"Sorry, it's a mess," he told her. "I'd give you an excuse, but... this is pretty much what it's always like."

"It's fine," Fey said with a laugh. She looked around. "I like your place... it's cozy."

Jasper snorted. *Cozy, right.* It was a dump. But it was close to his mom's place, and an easy walking distance from The Last Drop, so he didn't mind it too much.

Usually.

"Can I get you a drink?" he asked, opening the icebox to check what he had to offer her. "I have... beer."

"It's ten in the morning, Jasper."

He grabbed two beers, anyway, tossing her one and grinning.

"So? You have to start drinking at some point, right? Why not start now?"

"Hard to argue with that logic," Fey said, lifting the bottle to her lips to take a drink. As she did, the light caught her wrist, and Jasper's eyes leapt to the bruises there. A growl rose in his chest.

"Who did that?" he asked, stepping toward her. He reached out, touching the purple skin gently, a feral anger rising inside him. "Who hurt you?"

"It's nothing," Fey said, dismissively and trying to tug her hand away. Jasper held firm.

"It's not nothing," he snapped. His Wolf pressed against the skin, wanting out. Wanting blood. Someone touched his mate. Someone had hurt his mate.

Someone needed to pay.

Fey gave him a strange look.

"It was a man," she told him. "When I was walking home. He called me queen and... grabbed me." Fey held his stare. "I broke his wrist for it. And I would have done worse if he hadn't run."

The Wolf inside him huffed in satisfaction, retreating. Jasper dropped her wrist.

"Good," he said. "I'm glad you hurt him."

Fey's lips curved up in a small grin.

Feeling suddenly awkward, he moved back, giving her space. "So... what brings you here, gorgeous?"

"Alastair told me to come," she said with a shrug. "He said you helped him with something. And that we needed to talk."

Fucking Alastair. Of course, he didn't tell her anything.

"But he didn't tell you what I helped him with, I take it?" Jasper asked. Or... anything else?

Mine.

He wasn't ready for this, not yet. Wasn't ready to tell her what... what he thought they might be. Fey liked her independence, liked belonging to herself. And... he didn't want her to think he was trying to take that from her.

Fey shrugged, toying with the label on her beer bottle.

"So, I'm guessing he also didn't mention firing me?" Jasper asked with a grin.

Fey's eyebrows rose.

"No. He did not," she said. "But it wouldn't be the first time, would it?"

That was true. Rolling his eyes, Jasper set the beer bottle down on the table and reached up to his shirt collar.

"This is what I helped him with," he explained, moving the collar aside to show her.

There wasn't much of a wound, not anymore. Shifters are quick healers, and with whatever was in Alastair's saliva that stopped the bleeding, it was almost gone now. Just two tiny puncture marks were all that was left. A reminder of the moment they'd shared.

Fey's eyebrows rose so high on her forehead they almost met her hairline.

"He fed from you?" she asked, sounding shocked. And maybe even a little jealous.

Huh.

"Sure did," Jasper said, letting go of his shirt collar. He picked up his beer again and took a deep drink.

"How..." She swallowed, hard. "What was it like?"

She was jealous. Goddess, what a fucking mess.

Fingers gently touching the bite mark on his neck, Jasper wet his lips. "It was... intense. Like everything he does. It was raw, and... and intense."

Fey bit her lower lip.

"Intense how?" she asked. He didn't miss the breathy tone in her voice. The hunger in her eyes.

Setting his beer bottle down on the table next to her, Jasper moved a little closer.

"Intense as in... hot enough I almost came in my pants, like a teenager." Fey's pupils widened, and he continued. "Intense as in, I'd let him do it every night to me if he wanted. If he asked. Intense enough that I want to go over there, drop to my knees and beg him to do it again."

"Oh," Fey said. Her lips were a deep ruby red, begging to be kissed.

He moved a little closer.

"Almost as intense as burying my cock inside you," he told her, nudging her thighs apart so he could get even closer. He needed to feel her pressed against him. He wasn't sure he could stand to have any distance between them, not right now. "As feeling you come on me."

"Jasper..." Fey started, breathlessly.

"I never lied to you, Fey. I'm not trying to get between the two of you," Jasper said, the words coming out rushed. "I told Alastair that. That's not what I want. But... but I don't mind sharing you with him, and—"

"And him with me?" Fey asked.

He swallowed hard.

"If... if he wants that," Jasper said. He moved a little closer. "But what do *you* want, gorgeous? Because whatever it is, whatever you're feeling, I can handle it. I can back off, I can give you some space to think, I can—"

"Kiss me," Fey said, eyes locked on his lips.

The Wolf inside him threw back its head and howled in victory.

MINE.

Jasper didn't need to be told twice. Taking her face gently in his hands, he lowered his mouth to hers.

Kissing Fey was like kissing lightning. The moment their lips touched, he felt a jolt of electricity course through his entire body. He loved it. He loved the way she let him take control, let him set the pace.

When he slipped his tongue into her mouth, she groaned so deliciously he couldn't keep his hands to himself.

He wrapped his arms around her, pulling her against him, letting her relax against his chest. His tongue moved against hers, dancing in her mouth. He could have kissed her forever. But when her hands tugged at his shirt, urging him to remove it, wanting to touch his bare skin, he didn't hesitate to release her. He pulled his shirt off, tossing it on a pile of clothes.

"I need you," he told her, pulling her close again and kissing his way down her neck and toward her chest. Her shirt came off next, and he eased the straps of her bra down over her shoulder to free her breasts. His fingers went to her pants, deftly unfastening them and starting to pull them open. "Fuck, Fey, I need to taste you. I need you on my tongue, I —"

The sound of the front door opening and closing was almost lost in the commotion.

"Uh... Hi, guys," Vivian said in a strangled voice from the doorway, as Jasper swore, jerking backwards and struggling to catch his breath. Fey scrambled to cover herself, pulling her bra back into place and grabbing her shirt.

"I... uh... didn't expect to see you here," Vivian continued. Her eyes were locked on the ceiling, as though actively trying to avoid looking at either of them. Her hands fiddled with the straps of her shoulder bag nervously. "Both of you. Like... this."

"Viv, we were... were just talking," Jasper tried to explain.

Vivian's lips twitched. "Talking, huh?" she asked, barely contained laughter in her voice. "I don't know, Uncle Jas, that didn't look like talking to me..."

Fey pulled her shirt back over her head, hopping down from the table.

"Hi, Vivian," she said breathlessly. Her cheeks were flushed and pink. "Sorry for that."

Viv smirked and tucked her hair behind her ear nervously.

"It's fine. I mean... you're adults, right?" she laughed. "And Uncle Jas has been in love with you for, like, *years*, so—"

"That's enough, Viv," Jasper said.

Fey moved toward the door, running her fingers through her long red hair to smooth it. "I should go," she said, and even though it broke Jasper's heart to hear it, she was right.

She smiled at Viv on her way out.

"Nice seeing you again, Vivian," she told her. Vivian's eyes lit up as she grinned. "And Jasper?"

The smile Fey gave him over her shoulder before she left was full of promise.

"We'll see you soon, okay?"

"Yeah," he replied, voice husky. "Real soon."

Mine.

When the door closed behind Fey, Vivian squealed.

"Uncle Jas!" she laughed, slapping him on the arm. "You dog!"

"Wolf," he corrected.

"I can't believe you. On the table? We eat at that table!" she scolded. But she was grinning, ear to ear, as she said it. Her hands came up to fiddle with the strap of her bag again. "So, are the two of you a thing now?"

He ran a hand through his hair, suddenly exhausted. Were they? "No. Maybe. I don't know yet. We have to talk about some things. You know it's... it's complicated."

She nodded, eyes bright.

Jasper chewed his lip. "But... would that upset you? If we were? If Fey... came around here, more often?"

Vivian grinned. "Upset me? To have the most badass Witch in the realm as my aunt?" She scoffed. "Uncle Jas, you have no idea how great that would be for me."

"Yeah..." Jasper wet his lips, imagining it. "It would be great... wouldn't it?"

CHAPTER 42
ALICE

"H e's claiming she broke his wrist," Sana said with a frown, reading the rather vulgar letter that had been hand delivered to the palace earlier that day. "And there were... witnesses. All of them saying the same thing, that the Broken Blade flew into a rage, in the middle of the street. And her power... well, I've never heard of powers like this before."

Alice closed her eyes, her irritation brewing.

"Fey wouldn't have attacked anyone without just cause," she said, tapping her finger on the table. *Though she at least could have given me a heads-up about this.* "And if all he got from an encounter with her was a single broken bone, he should be thanking the Goddess herself. But I'll talk to her. And I'll make it clear she can't just go around assaulting citizens, anymore. Send a letter back, telling them that—"

"Kellos is dead," a quiet voice interrupted.

Alice looked up from her conversation with Sana and met Silas's gaze over the expanse of the throne room. She hadn't even heard him arrive. The others had come early this evening, and the council meeting hadn't officially started yet, each member attending to their own matters while they awaited the last representative. The Falcon Shifter looked

246

haggard, like he hadn't slept in days. It made him look several years older than she knew he was.

Grief could do that, though.

Setting her pen down slowly, Alice swallowed. "I'm sorry for your loss, Silas," she said. And she meant it. "Kellos was a fine council member. A great representative. He will be missed."

Death is always a struggle. Even when it's expected, even when it might be welcomed, it's never easy. Death leaves a hole in the hearts of all those left behind, a void that never fully disappears, even with time.

The others at the table murmured their own condolence. Even the Fallen King managed to make it sound sincere. Though, she supposed, when you live as long as he has, you must be well acquainted with death, and the pain it brings to a community.

A shame, Alice thought with a heavy heart. Kellos *had* been a great leader, and he had made tremendous strides on the council. Not just for the Shifter faction, either. And even knowing it had been coming, even knowing he was growing more ill and older by the day, it still was a great loss to—

"No." Silas's voice was harsh, and he shook his head quickly from side to side. "No, you don't understand. He didn't just die. Kellos was *killed* last night."

The room paused. Alice looked at Silas again and saw something in his eyes she hadn't noticed before. Not grief.

Fear.

"Killed?" the deSanguine asked, sitting up straighter. "Who on God's green Earth would want to kill that old bag? Wasn't time doing it quick enough for them?"

"What happened?" Alice demanded, attention laser focused on Silas.

"We're still trying to figure that out," Silas told them. His bird of prey eyes sought them each out, one by one, assessing them. "He... Goddess, he attacked his sister last night. Out of nowhere."

"Regina?" Alice asked, blinking in shock. She knew the Lioness, knew her well in fact. They'd spilled blood together, side by side.

Silas nodded. "He had no reason to hurt his sister, none at all. But he... Regina says he wouldn't stop. He just kept coming for her, over and over, until she... until she put him down."

Alice winced.

"I think the council should speak with her," Silas insisted. "She... something is wrong. *Was* wrong with Kellos. He wasn't violent, wasn't a fighter. The male Lions aren't even hunters. He had no reason to do this, and he wouldn't listen to her. It was like he wasn't even there."

"Age takes a lot from us," Kallista said, her voice surprisingly compassionate. "I have seen more than one friend turn violent as they grow older. They become confused and lash out at the ones they love."

Silas shook his head. "No. No, he wasn't confused. He wasn't Kellos." When no one offered aid, he continued, incredulous. "Kellos was sick, yes, but he was still sharp. He wasn't losing his mind. Goddess, I spoke to him less than a week ago and he was fine."

"Perhaps I'm the one who is confused," Cassiel said, irritation plain in his voice. "Why would he attack his sister, then?"

"I think this has something to do with the threats. With those posters," Silas said. Alice fought against rolling her eyes. "I think he was drugged, or being controlled, or... or... I don't know what. But that wasn't Kellos, he wouldn't have done that. He wouldn't have put his sister through that."

"We have no proof the group behind those posters pose any real threat," Alice said. "Nothing has happened aside from someone putting up those damn messages."

"*This*," Silas insisted. "This is proof! The council was threatened, and now a council member is dead!"

"Enough," Alice cut him off, and stood. "Council member Silas, you are out of line. There is nothing to investigate here. And we have other matters to discuss. Do you have even one speck of evidence for your claim?"

Silas's eyes grew dark as he watched her, unblinking. But finally, he shook his head.

"Good." Alice gathered her papers, shifting through them before taking her seat again. "Then I suggest we move on."

"I just—"

"When you get proof," Alice snapped, interrupting Silas, "you can bring this matter back up to us. But until then, you will take your seat and do your job."

Silas did so slowly, stalking to his chair and taking his seat.

But Alice didn't miss the anger in his eyes. Didn't miss the scorn.

Swallowing her own anger, Alice picked the first item on the agenda and began the meeting. They didn't have time to chase wild theories down rabbit holes. They had a realm to rule.

CHAPTER 43

JASPER

He played that moment over and over in his mind for the rest of the day.

She'd asked him to kiss her. She hadn't objected when he mentioned sharing her. Maybe... maybe this could actually work. Hope blossomed in his chest at the thought of it.

Eventually, he'd have to tell her. Witches didn't have a concept of mates, not the way some Shifters did. He would have to explain it to her at some point, make her understand what it meant...

But Fey? Gorgeous, independent, *fierce* Fey? Telling her now, so early... it might be a mistake. Maybe he should wait. It had to be her choice, didn't it? Her choice to let him into her life. Into *their* lives. If he pushed too soon, sprung it on her before she was ready...

She might pull away from him forever.

And he couldn't let that happen.

The smell of her still clung to his clothes when Jasper showed up at The Last Drop for his shift that night. He couldn't bring himself to change into something else. They smelled too much like Fey, and to Jasper, it was the sweetest perfume he'd ever known.

He really should have changed. Going into work smelling so strongly of her was bound to raise questions. But... he couldn't do it.

Couldn't stand the idea of not being coated in her scent. He wanted her mark on him, wanted that ownership.

The touch of her skin was still fresh in his mind as he nodded a greeting to Mara at the door to The Last Drop, standing a little downwind, just in case.

But rather than greeting him back, Mara just frowned at him, looking puzzled.

Crap. He must smell even more than he'd thought.

"What are you doing here?" she asked, brow knit in confusion. "I thought you were off tonight."

Jasper paused. "It's Saturday, right?" he asked. He always worked on Saturdays.

"Yeah, but... Ferus pulled your shift tonight and gave it to Sid," Mara told him, chewing the inside of her cheek. "Didn't anyone tell you?"

Jasper's stomach sank.

"No," he answered, an acidic anger rising inside of him. "No one told me."

He pushed past Mara and into the club, emotions swirling a little too close to the surface.

Sid? Why would Ferus pull his shift and give it to Sid? And without telling him? Had something happened, something—

A laugh came from the upstairs bar, and Jasper turned toward the sound, growling.

Alastair.

He knew it was too good to be true. Knew it was too much to hope that things would just... work out. He should have known whatever moment they'd had together, whatever that feeding had meant, Alastair would run from it. The fucking coward.

With a snarl that had the other employees backing quickly away Jasper stalked forward, taking the stairs to the upper level two at a time. Alastair stood next to the VIP bar, a sharp grin on his face as he chatted with Ferus. And he looked so damned relaxed, so damned at ease...

"What the *fuck*, Alastair," Jasper shouted as he advanced. The Vampire turned with a casual grace, eyebrow raised and a drink in his hand. At his side, leaning against the bar, Ferus straightened to his full height as though preparing for violence. Jasper didn't miss the way the other wolf sniffed the air between them and tensed.

Yeah, there was no question that they could smell Fey on him. All around the place, the other wolves were pausing in the middle of their tasks, turning toward him.

And Alastair.

"Am I fired or not?" Jasper asked, baring his teeth as he stalked toward his boss. "Make up your fucking mind!"

He must be going crazy. There was no way Alastair was smirking at him right now. No way he looked this fucking *amused*.

"Ferus," Alastair said calmly, turning to smile at the Wolf next to him. "Have you fired Jasper and not told me?"

"No boss," Ferus grunted. His eyes were narrowed and locked on Jasper, clearly expecting trouble.

Jasper gave the other Wolf a low growl, warning him to back off. Ferus didn't so much as blink.

"Then explain why I'm not on the schedule tonight. Explain to me why I have to hear from Mara that my shift was given to Sid." Jasper gestured toward the Wolf, who was currently pretending to wash a glass behind the bar.

Not looking up, Sid polished the glass a little faster.

Alastair's lips quirked up a little more. He turned toward Ferus again. "Ferus, would you—"

The words were cut off as Jasper shoved him, forcing Alastair backward a step. Ferus immediately moved forward with an angry grunt, but Alastair just shook his head slowly. Reluctantly, Ferus backed down, eyes on Jasper.

"I'm not talking to him. I'm talking to you, asshole!" Jasper shouted.

"And I told you yesterday, Ferus is the one in charge of your employment now, puppy. So, if you have a question about—"

"This is because of Fey, isn't it? You jealous motherfucker, this is because she came to see me today, isn't it?"

There was no pretending they weren't paying attention anymore. Every employee in the building was watching them both. They weren't even bothering to hide it.

He was increasingly aware of how much he must smell like her. Maybe like both of them. But right now, he didn't fucking care.

Alastair exhaled slowly, raising his hand and running it through his hair. He was so calm, so fucking collected...

Jasper shoved him again, ignoring Ferus as he tensed to intervene. Alastair barely moved from the impact. His drink didn't even spill.

"Or is this because of us?" Jasper asked, closing the distance between them. "One fucking kiss and you're running scared."

Behind the bar, Sid made a choking sound somewhere between a cough and a laugh. Ferus did a small double take between the two of them.

"Two," Alastair said with a slight grin.

"Fucking coward." Jasper showed his teeth, ready to fight. "Fire me, then. Fight me, fuck me, whichever, but make up your fucking mind."

Someone, somewhere, laughed nervously. Mara, Jasper thought. He didn't give a shit, let them hear it. He was done pretending, done drowning the truth in alcohol. He'd gotten a taste—one glorious fucking taste—of what it would be like to be with them, either of them, and there was no turning back now. He wasn't going to back down.

"Jasper," Alastair said, exasperated. He spoke in a calm, measured voice, ignoring the growl rising in Jasper's throat. "Where did you leave your phone?"

Jasper's growl sputtered and died.

That... wasn't the response he'd expected.

"My... my phone?" His hands went to his pockets, but he already knew they would be empty. Jasper struggled to remember when he'd last had it, when he'd—

"Here," he realized, suddenly. "I left it... I left it here, behind the bar." That must have been after his confrontation with Alastair in his office, when he'd left in the middle of his shift. He hadn't bothered to grab anything he'd brought in that night. Hadn't picked up his phone after his next shift, either.

Alastair nodded, as though that was the answer he expected.

"If you'd had your phone," he said through slightly clenched teeth, "you would know that Ferus called you. How many times did you call him, actually?" he asked, turning to look at the other Wolf.

"Five," Ferus grunted, arms crossed over his chest.

"Ferus called you five fucking times, Jasper. To *inform* you that your request for a night off was approved."

"I..." His brain skipped. "But I didn't ask to take tonight off."

"No, puppy." Alastair smiled. "I did."

He set his drink on the bar and stepped closer to him. Jasper was only vaguely aware that everyone was watching, every Wolf in the club giving up the pretense of not openly gaping at them, as Alastair reached out to cup the back of his neck.

"Fey wants you at our place tonight," he said in a velvety voice. "For dinner. She tried calling you, but..."

"But I didn't have my phone," Jasper finished for him, awkwardly. Goddess, he was an ass.

Alastair smiled. "But you didn't have your phone," he confirmed.

He shouldn't be doing this, Jasper thought, as Alastair's thumb stroked his jaw. Not in front of the other employees. He shouldn't be touching him so openly, like they were... like they were...

"Will you join us tonight, puppy?" Alastair asked, eyes locked on his.

Jasper nodded.

"And this makes three," Alastair said as he leaned down to kiss him again.

CHAPTER 44

ALASTAIR

For the first time in months, Alastair felt like his old self. Living on the verge of starvation, caught on the knife edge of falling to bloodlust, his mind had started to crumble.

And then Jasper, that infuriating fucking Wolf, had come along.

Feeding from him hadn't been anything like feeding from the Vampires he'd conscripted since he'd met Fey. There had been no oily disgust filling his stomach, no intense need to keep physical distance.

Feeding from Jasper had felt *right*, in a way nothing else had in a long, long time. In the way being with Fey had felt right.

And he'd be fucked if he was going to let that go now.

By the time they left the club and made their way back across the city to his townhouse, Jasper was practically vibrating with excitement. The little pup had gotten himself all worked up into a frenzy, willing to shout at him. Hell, willing to shove him.

How fucking adorable it had been.

"She told me about your kiss this morning," he told the Wolf as they reached their front door. "Tell me... what would you have done with her if your niece hadn't interrupted?"

Jasper grinned.

"Anything she wanted," he responded in a husky voice.

Right answer, Alastair thought. But to Jasper, he simply leaned down, close enough his lips touched against the shell of his ear as he whispered, "Naughty puppy."

The shiver that went up Jasper's spine was positively delicious. Smiling, Alastair pushed the front door to their town house open and—

Smoke.

Why did he smell smoke?

Jasper sneezed loudly, scrunching his nose against the smell as they stepped inside. Alastair could barely smell it, just a hint in the air, but for a Wolf, it must be overwhelming. A quick glance around showed nothing amiss, but from the kitchen, where the smell was coming from, he could hear the sounds of someone moving around and... swearing?

"Fey?" Alastair called out, concerned, striding swiftly to the kitchen. "Are you hurt? What is that awful smell? It's—"

"Dinner," Fey informed him, turning toward him with dangerously narrowed eyes. "And it's going to be delicious."

As she spoke, she lifted a dish from the oven, dropping it on the counter with enough force to make him wince. Goddess, she hadn't even put down a potholder, or anything at all to protect the countertops. And that dish? The smells coming off it certainly didn't smell like food.

"I thought you were picking up dinner tonight," Alastair said, keeping his voice as polite as possible. Jasper appeared at his side, tactfully breathing through his mouth.

"I was going to," Fey explained as she pulled plates from the cupboard. Alastair's stomach rolled. "But Regina's was closed when I went by, and we just had pizza the other night. So I thought, why don't I cook instead?"

Goddess spare them. She wasn't actually going to make them eat that, was she? As if in direct answer to his thoughts, Fey grabbed a knife and cut into the dish.

"Witchling, we've talked about this," Alastair said gently. "Remember what happened last time you cooked?"

"Oh, please," Fey snorted. "It was one tiny fire. Get over it."

That "tiny fire" had required replacing the wooden doors on half his kitchen cupboards.

"What, uh… what is it?" Jasper asked, stepping forward. It was a very good question, Alastair thought. The… thing in the glass casserole dish appeared to be yellow and orange, at least the parts that weren't burnt. Maybe some sort of cheese?

"It's a lasagna," Fey told them. She clutched the knife handle a little harder as she cut. "Joy gave me the recipe yesterday, and I figured I would give it a try."

"Lasagna," Jasper repeated, skeptically.

"I can follow a recipe, you know," Fey spat at Alastair, heaping a slice of horrors onto a plate and thrusting it at Jasper's chest. "It's not that difficult."

It shouldn't be, no. But in the years they'd been together, Fey had only cooked a handful of times. Not one of her concoctions had been edible.

"I don't mind cooking for us, Witchling," Alastair assured her. "Why don't you sit down and rest, and I'll…"

Jasper took a bite.

Alastair watched in horror as the Wolf chewed, face perfectly blank. It seemed to take forever, like he was chewing a sponge. When he finally swallowed, he did so with a barely perceptible shudder.

"See?" Fey shot Alastair a satisfied smile. "It's fine. He likes it."

"There's, uh…" Jasper swallowed hard. "What is the sweet taste?"

"Well…" Fey looked away, chewing her lip. "We didn't have all the right ingredients, so I had to improvise. I couldn't find any ground beef in the icebox, but there were some chicken sausages with apple bits, so I used those instead."

"Did you make any other substitutions?" Alastair asked, terrified of the answer.

Fey shrugged. "Just a few spices. You didn't have oregano, so I used cumin. You had plenty of that."

Alastair thought he might faint. His stomach roiled, his nose starting to tease apart the disparate scents of the monstrous dish in front of them. No one could eat that, no one could survive that. He had to—

Jasper took another bite.

"What the hell are you doing?" he hissed before he could stop himself.

"It's not bad, it's..." Jasper swallowed an obvious gag, clamping his teeth together tightly until it passed.

"Puppy, put it down, you don't have to—"

The last of it went into Jasper's mouth.

"He doesn't have to, what?" Fey asked, turning on Alastair, eyes flaring. He was acutely aware of the knife still clutched in her hand.

Jasper, sweet stupid Jasper, swallowed hard, his eyes watering. And then he did the most remarkable thing.

He held out his plate for seconds.

"More," he requested, unshed tears in his eyes. "Please."

"For Goddess's sake," Alastair muttered, watching in horror as Fey took the plate, grinning. She shot him a smug look before turning back to the dish, ready to serve up another slice. "Witchling, have some compassion. You cannot make him eat any more of that."

"You are such a brat," Fey informed him. "He liked it. And it's not bad at all. I'm sure it's fine."

To demonstrate, she took a fork from the counter and cut a bite off for herself. "It's just a little burnt, is all."

She brought the fork to her mouth, and the moment her mouth closed around it, her face changed. A shudder went through her body before she pivoted, leaning over the sink to spit it out.

"It's revolting," she gasped, turning on the tap to wash her mouth and spit water back into the sink. "Jasper, you ate that?"

He did. He ate an entire slice. Alastair watched, amazed, as the Wolf just shrugged.

"You made it," he said, by way of explanation.

Fucking remarkable.

Still leaning over the sink, Fey groaned. "Why was it so salty?"

"I wondered about that, too," Jasper admitted.

Sighing, Alastair scooped up the meal, glass dish and all, and dropped it in the trash. He needed a drink. Uncorking a bottle of red wine, he poured a glass for himself and a particularly full one for Fey.

She took it from him with a small murmur of thanks, gulping some down immediately to wash the taste from her mouth.

"There's beer, if you'd like," he informed Jasper, nodding toward the icebox. The Wolf didn't hesitate. Tearing the cap off, he downed his first one in one go, stopping to catch his breath for a moment before opening another.

"Alastair, you'll need to cook later, but my appetite is ruined," Fey said, taking a sip of her wine.

Alastair chuckled. "Anything for you, Witchling." He set his own glass of wine down, reaching out to take hers as well. "But I can think of a way we can work up an appetite..."

He pulled her toward him, brushing her hair out of her face.

Goddess, he loved the way she responded to him. Fey's pupils widened and her breathing quickened. Just a few touches were all it took to have her panting for him.

"What did you have in mind?" she asked, licking her lips in anticipation.

"Oh, I have all sorts of things in mind," he promised her. "Provided you haven't actually poisoned our guest."

Leaning against the counter, Jasper chuckled.

"Oh, don't worry about me, boss, I'm fine," he said, eyes sparkling.

"Good," Alastair said. Running his hands over Fey's body one last time, he stepped back, turning toward Jasper. "Because you owe me an apology, puppy."

"For what?" Fey asked, irritation in her voice.

"Stay out of this, Witchling," Alastair warned, ignoring Fey's exasperation. He took a step toward him, enjoying the fear that crept into Jasper's eyes.

"Did you think you could call me out like that, in my own club, without any consequences?"

Jasper's breath caught in his chest as Alastair loomed closer.

"I want an apology, Jasper. And you better make it a good one."

Jasper swallowed audibly. "And what kind of apology were you looking for, boss?"

Alastair smiled.

"I think you should put that mouth to good use," he said, stepping close enough that his chest pressed against Jasper's. The Wolf licked his lips, heart hammering in his chest so loud Alastair could hear it. Leaning down, Alastair let their lips brush together as he spoke. "Use that tongue to make her come, puppy. I want her dripping wet and satisfied before I fuck her tonight."

Jasper's lips curved up into a grin. "I think I can manage that," he answered.

CHAPTER 45
FEY

Fey heard the words Alastair said to him, heat jolting through her body at the command. Jasper's eyes met hers over Alastair's shoulder as he grinned, eyes sparkling with sinful promise.

It was still a shock when he moved forward so quickly and lifted her. He moved with the savage grace and speed of a predator. Fey let out a shout of surprise, wrapping her legs around his waist.

"I've been waiting all day to taste you," Jasper murmured, burrowing his face in her neck as he carried her to the living room. He laid her down gently on the couch, and Fey glanced over to see Alastair seat himself at the other end, arms spread on the seat back as he watched them.

Settling himself between her legs, Jasper kissed his way up her body. He took his time, kissing and licking at every available inch of skin before he reached her neck, nuzzling his face into the space between her ear and her jawbone.

When his teeth grazed against her skin, Fey gasped, arching against him.

Jasper chuckled. He balanced on his forearms to keep his weight from crushing her beneath him and lowered his hips down enough to press against her.

"Do you feel that?" he asked, and Fey sucked in a breath as he rolled his hips against her. "Do you feel how hard you've gotten me already? Fuck, Fey, I could come just looking at you."

Fey moaned, but it turned to a gasp of pain as he bit down on her skin, holding those sharp teeth against the flesh where her shoulder met her neck. He groaned into her, biting down nearly hard enough to draw blood.

It was nothing like the ecstasy she'd felt when Alastair had sunk his fangs into her neck all those years ago, but it still felt incredible. Arching against him, Fey moaned his name, her hands coming up to wind through his hair.

"Oh no," Jasper said, pulling back and sitting up. He took her hands off him delicately by the wrists. "The boss didn't say anything about you getting to touch me."

Fey swallowed as he put her arms back on the couch above her head.

"Keep your hands there," he said, staring down at her. "And don't move."

She narrowed her eyes at him but obeyed, fingers gripping into the cushions of the couch as Jasper leaned back down over her.

When he started touching her, hands sliding over her clothing, she didn't notice the claws at first. Writhing under his touch, she didn't notice them at all until a sharp claw slid across her chest, leaving a slight red line on her skin before it reached her shirt and ripped through the cloth as easily as a knife.

"Jasper!" Fey gasped. The shirt fell away, parting easily under his claws.

"Shhh, gorgeous," he said. "I warned you not to move."

She was breathing so quickly, too quickly. When that claw slid back up to her bra, she whimpered.

And then the bra was gone, too, slit up the middle. Jasper used his hands to peel the fabric aside, revealing her breasts.

"Fuck me," Alastair cursed, leaning closer from where he watched.

"Not yet," Jasper laughed. He traced one of her nipples with that sharp claw, and Fey wasn't sure if the noises she was making were out of fear or pleasure.

Smiling at her, Jasper lowered his mouth to her breast and nipped at her nipple, dragging his teeth over it.

She could go mad from this, Fey thought, gasping for air as his mouth teased her breast. She could go mad, and happily so.

Finally, he released her. He pulled the ruined shreds of her shirt and bra from her chest slowly and reached for her pants.

"Stop," Fey gasped. His hands froze. "I like these pants. Don't you dare ruin them."

Jasper grinned. The claws retreated slightly, and his fingers undid the clasp before he peeled them off her legs.

The claw that slipped over her underwear felt very sharp, though.

Fey whimpered, fighting to hold still as he surgically sliced through the fabric, leaving nothing but bare skin and scraps of lace.

For a moment, Jasper just stared down at her as though mesmerized, his gaze burning hot as he held her legs open.

Then wordlessly he stood, eyes sliding up her body to hold her gaze as his hands reached down to pull off his shirt. He tossed it aside, eyes still on her, but when his hands went to his own pants, he paused.

Glancing over at Alastair, Jasper winked.

Fey twisted from her place on the couch. Alastair was leaning forward, arms on his knees as he watched Jasper. His gaze was heated.

Jasper popped the button on his pants open and reached his hand inside, gripping himself.

"Like what you see, boss?" he asked in a breathless voice.

Alastair's eyes shot up to Jasper's face, and he was on him in an instant. Hands gripping Jasper's hair, Alastair held him in place while he kissed him, groaning against Jasper's lips.

"Enough teasing, puppy," he said when he broke the kiss. His hands were still fisted in Jasper's hair. "Make her come *now*."

Jasper nodded, licking his lips as he settled himself between Fey's legs on the couch.

"Fuck, she's already so wet," Jasper told him, his breath tickling Fey's skin. She gasped when she felt his tongue against her, a single soft sweep over her center.

"Wetter," Alastair ordered. He peeled off his own shirt and slacks, stroking himself and coming over to where Fey writhed on the couch. "I want her dripping down her thighs when we fuck."

Jasper groaned in answer, sucking and licking at Fey while his hands held her legs spread.

Fey cried out as his lips closed around her clit. Alastair took advantage of the moment, slipping the head of his cock between her parted lips.

The angle made it difficult. Her lips were barely sliding down two inches of his length, but still Fey moaned, tilting her head toward him and trying to take him deeper. He groaned as she swirled her tongue around him, his eyes glued to where Jasper's tongue lapped at her.

Jasper's claws had left red marks on her skin, stark lines against her pale flesh, and Alastair's finger traced one of the lines down her chest and up to her nipple. His fingers closed over it and pinched, just as Jasper moaned, the vibration coursing through Fey's body.

"That's right, Witchling," Alastair praised, rolling her nipple expertly between his fingers. "Imagine all the things the two of us can do to you... the things we *will* do to you."

And she did. She let herself imagine every depraved thing the three of them could do together, every possibility. Every position. Jasper's hands gripped her harder, his pace quickening as though he were imagining it too.

Her mouth still wrapped around the head of Alastair's cock, and with Jasper's face buried between her thighs, Fey bowed off the couch and gave a muffled scream as she came.

"Fuck," Alastair hissed. He pulled himself from her mouth, and Fey gasped for breath, her body still quaking.

With one last soft lick, Jasper untangled himself from her legs, grinning. Her arousal glistened on his lips and chin.

"Come here, puppy," Alastair said breathlessly. Gripping Jasper's shoulders, he pulled him close enough to lick Fey's wetness from his jaw. Jasper moaned as Alastair's tongue slid up further, tracing his lips before pulling him into a deep kiss.

Fey went still, watching them. She didn't expect that seeing them together would bother her, but she hadn't expected to... to like it. Alastair held Jasper so completely still as they kissed, possessing him completely. When he finally broke the kiss, Jasper looked dazed, his eyes unfocused and a little unsteady on his feet.

"Roll over, Witchling," Alastair said, his eyes moving over to where she lay on the couch and flaring as they looked up and down her body. "Get on your hands and knees."

She was liquid, muscles nearly unresponsive. But somehow, she managed it, her arms shaking with the effort and her legs trembling as she rolled to her stomach and came up to her hands and knees.

"That's our good girl," Alastair praised her. He pushed Jasper toward one end of the couch, then positioned himself behind her. The head of his cock slid over her, once, twice. Then he slipped it up to her entrance and braced himself there.

Fey whimpered, muscles shaking, as Jasper knelt on the couch in front of her. He held himself, stroking his cock as he tilted her head up.

Fey didn't need to ask what he wanted. The answer was written in his crooked smile as he looked down at her, fingers gently sliding over his length. Wordlessly, Fey opened her mouth.

They entered her together, Jasper slipping between her lips and Alastair filling her dripping pussy in one hard thrust.

She tried to scream, the pleasure of having Alastair stretching her so soon after coming almost unbearably good. But she could only make a sound like a whimper, deep in her throat, her mouth wrapped tight around Jasper.

She couldn't think, could barely breathe as they took her together. Alastair fucked her hard, the sound of flesh against flesh filling the room as he pounded into her. Jasper was gentler, but not by much. He held her head in place as he moved himself in and out of her mouth, pushing deep enough to hit the back of her throat and holding himself there long enough she thought she might choke.

"Do you like this, Witchling?" Alastair asked. Fey couldn't speak, couldn't make a single noise with Jasper so deep inside her, but it didn't seem to matter. Sweeping his thumb over her clit, Alastair wet it with her own arousal before bringing it up to her ass.

Fey made a strangled noise as Alastair rolled his thumb over her hole, teasing her with it.

"Such a shame we can't fill every hole," he said, voice hitched as he pounded into her. "Maybe you need a third male, Witchling?"

"No," Jasper said. His grip on her hair tightened, and Fey moaned around him as his pace quickened. "No one else... She's *ours*."

Alastair laughed. "That's right, puppy. All ours."

Pausing with his cock to the hilt inside her, Alastair held her in place for a moment, not moving. Fey barely had time to wonder what he was doing before she felt a warm drip of saliva as he spat on her ass, sliding it toward her hole.

This time, he did more than tease her. Alastair's thumb slipped inside her, moving in and out in time with him as he began to fuck her once more. Fey let out a shriek, and Jasper swore.

"There," Alastair said, voice guttural. "All full."

She didn't have a chance to decide if she enjoyed it, to decide if she liked having them filling her so completely. The orgasm that took her came out of nowhere, slamming into her with so much force her whole body shook.

Her throat opened wider, and Jasper pushed himself further into her mouth. She couldn't breathe, couldn't speak, could only shudder over and over again as she came.

Just when she thought she might be on the verge of passing out, Jasper moved back, pulling his cock from her mouth. Fey gasped for breath, body shaking. He let her catch her breath for just a moment before pushing back between her lips.

Alastair's hands gripped her hips, rocking her back against him as he slammed into her, entirely focused on chasing his own pleasure now.

"Are you close?" Alastair asked through gritted teeth. With a groan, Jasper nodded.

Alastair reached out, wrapping Fey's long red hair around his hand and gripped it hard. Suddenly, Fey's head was yanked back, Jasper's cock popping out.

"Open your mouth," Alastair gasped from behind her. "Stick your tongue out, Witchling."

Body arched and head thrown back from his grip on her hair, Fey obliged. She opened her mouth wide, tongue out, and Jasper gripped himself, staring down at her.

"Fuck," he said, hand moving quickly over his swollen cock. "Keep that mouth open wide, gorgeous." He swore and gave a startled bark as he came, shooting over her tongue.

Fey moaned, and Alastair roared from behind her, burying himself deep inside her and shuddering his own release. She could feel every pulse as he filled her.

Alastair had been right. He knew exactly how to work up her appetites, each and every one of them.

CHAPTER 46
AMALIA

Seated on her bed, watching her reflection in the mirror, Amalia made a face, twisting her mouth in distaste.

"I was thinking about cutting it," Amalia admitted, touching her brown curls. She ran her fingers through the ringlets, trying to straighten them, but they just bounced back into place as they always did. Amalia sighed and glanced at Vee, with her shorter hair, enviously. "I don't know if long hair is really... me."

Vee cocked her head to the side, considering.

"I don't know," she said, scooting closer until their knees were touching. Amalia sucked in a breath, as Vee reached out and touched one of her ringlets, running the hair through her fingers. "I kind of like it long, you know?"

"You do?" Amalia asked. Her voice sounded too high pitched, too breathless.

Vee tucked the ringlet behind Amalia's ear. Her fingers stayed on Amalia's skin longer than necessary.

"Yeah, I do," she said, moving forward a little more. Their noses were almost touching, and Amalia was too scared to breathe, too scared to move, in case it made Vee back away.

"I think it makes you look cute," Vee said. Then she tilted her head to the side, leaned forward, and kissed her.

Amalia froze, eyes open. Vee was kissing her. Those were Vee's lips pressed against hers. She couldn't believe it, couldn't believe it was actually happening. She had hoped, had dreamed, but...

The kiss was over almost as soon as it started, and Vee moved back, smiling.

"Goddess," Vee laughed, seeing her face. "You are blushing so hard!"

"I..." Amalia brought her hand to her cheek, feeling how warm she was. "I've never... I've never kissed anyone before."

"Seriously?" Vee asked, looking shocked.

Amalia nodded.

"Well." Vee lowered her head and looked up at Amalia through her lashes, grinning. "Did you like it?"

"Oh yes," Amalia squeaked, and Vee smiled.

"Would you like to do it again?"

Her voice was so inviting. *Yes*, Amalia thought—she did want to do it again. And again and again and again. Vee leaned closer, and this time Amalia let her eyes flutter closed, let herself lean forward, let herself—

Someone at the door cleared their throat loudly.

Amalia jerked back immediately, mortified. But Vee didn't move, not for several seconds. Then, when she shifted away, she did so slowly, leaning back from her as though unwilling to be startled away.

Linh was in the doorway, frowning at the two of them. She glowered as she took in the scene, the two of them seated close enough to be touching on Amalia's bed, both flushed.

Amalia scrambled to her feet, barely able to contain her excitement. "Linh!" she squealed excitedly. "You're here!"

But Linh wasn't looking at her. Linh was looking past her at Vee. And she was scowling.

"Oh!" Amalia said. Goddess save her. She'd spent barely any time with Vee, and she'd already forgotten all her manners. "I'm sorry, please pardon me—Vivian, this is the High Priestess of the Air Coven, Linh. And Linh, this is my friend, Vivian."

"It's a pleasure to meet you," Vee said, but the way she said it made

Amalia frown. Her voice didn't sound like it was a pleasure. It sounded... venomous. Angry.

"I'm sure," Linh sniffed. Her attitude, at least, was not unexpected. Though Amalia had enjoyed her visits and company after her mother's death, she didn't have any misconceptions about how... difficult Linh could be. She was a sour woman, with a sour disposition.

"I thought Leandra was going to find you some appropriate friends your own age," Linh said to Amalia, ignoring Vee entirely. "Some *Witch* friends."

A growl rose from Vee's throat, and Amalia felt a rush of anger on her friend's behalf.

"Vivian is my age," Amalia heard herself say to Linh, in a voice she barely recognized as her own. "And I think she is a very appropriate friend."

Linh inclined her head, her eyes betraying just what she thought of how *appropriate* their friendship was. "As you wish, Your Grace. Is she responsible for this... new look of yours?" She said with an undeniable sneer, gesturing down at Amalia's new clothes. Vee's hands clenched at her side as Amalia looked down at her pants and sweater.

There was nothing wrong with the clothes she was wearing. Nothing at all.

But the way she'd said it made Amalia feel a little sick. During Linh's absence, she'd found herself wishing every day that she could come and visit. And now that she finally had... Amalia didn't want her here. She found herself wishing she would leave.

"I think you are being very rude, Linh. I think you should apologize to my friend," Amalia said, surprised at the steel in her own voice. "And I think you should leave."

A look of disgust passed over Linh's face, but still, she mumbled something that sounded like an apology. And she left, casting a suspicious look at Vee as she did.

When the door shut behind her, Amalia sat heavily on her bed, suddenly unable to continue standing. Her heart thumped hard in her chest.

What had she just done? Linh had been like a mother to her, even more than a mother, really. And now that she had finally come to visit after so long, Amalia had treated her like that?

"I can't believe I just did that... I think I might be sick," Amalia said, putting her head between her knees. "Could you pass me the waste bin, please? I don't want to make a mess."

Vee laughed. "What are you talking about? That was incredible. You sounded so... so..."

"Like a princess?" Amalia muttered.

"No," said Vee, sounding amazed. "You sounded like a *queen*."

Amalia almost smiled. If she didn't know better, she'd say Vee was proud of her. Maybe she wouldn't throw up, after all.

"What was her problem, anyway?" Vee asked, tugging at the ends of her hair. "*I thought Miss So-and-so was going to get you appropriate friends,*" she said in her best Linh impression. "*Not some... scoundrel mutt!*"

Amalia laughed. "She's not normally that bad," she lied.

Vivian pretended to shudder. "What a monster."

Amalia sat up, hugging herself. "She was nice to me after my mother passed, you know. Well... not *nice*, but... she was there for me, at least. I think she figured I was going to be queen one day, so she might as well get on my good side."

"You think she really believes that?" Vee asked. "That you'd be queen?"

Amalia shrugged. "I guess. I think a few of them did. Linh didn't like the idea of the council at all. She's the one who insisted the other High Priestesses act as my advisors when I was the representative."

"She's on the council?" Vee asked, sounding disgusted.

"Yes. I mean, no, not really." She struggled with how best to phrase it. It was hard to explain, wasn't it? "She and the other High Priestesses were meant to... well, meant to help guide me as the Faction representative. But none of them are really on the council. The Witches only get one vote, same as all the others."

"One vote, but many representatives?" Vee said. It sounded like she was teasing, but there was something hard under the words that sounded a bit too much like anger. "Doesn't sound very fair to me."

"I guess," Amalia said with a shrug. "Anyway... I haven't seen Linh for ages. She lives at the Air temple, just down the way, but she got sick, and... I guess she just stopped coming after a while."

Vee reached out and took her hand. "Hey," she said softly. "I'm sorry. But you don't need that bitch, okay? She's just... just awful."

Vee shuddered again, and Amalia laughed. Maybe Vee was right, she thought. Linh had always been rude and critical, just like her mother. Nothing like Vivian. Maybe she didn't need her anymore.

After all, she had Vee, now, didn't she?

Why would she need anyone else?

CHAPTER 47
CASSIEL DESANGUINE

He was late. And Cassiel deSanguine, the self-proclaimed Fallen King and patriarch of the most powerful Vampire family in history, hated being late.

This was Alice's fault. He'd nearly forgotten all about the meeting with *l'enfant de sang* that she had insisted he set up. Why should they even bother with the other Vampire families? It wasn't like their bloodlines were even a fraction as strong as the deSanguine family. But Alice had insisted.

Alice. He sighed, thinking of the young Witch. They were all young, though, in his mind, compared to him. All children in the eyes of time, regardless of their Faction.

But Alice? She was the worst of them all. A child and an idealist, all in one. And God damn her, she made even him believe in these foolish ideas she had. Like this one, uniting the heads of all the Vampire families together, bringing their Faction together, finally, under one singular representative. It was insane. Too ridiculous to even consider.

And yet... Alice made him believe they could do it. Shifters, too. She wanted a council that truly represented everyone, every citizen in the realm, regardless of Faction or octant. And despite himself, despite the

273

cynicism time had drilled into him over his hundreds of years of life, Cassiel found himself wanting it, too.

Maybe it wasn't so crazy, after all.

A shame. A shame Alice wouldn't live to see if it worked or not.

She had to die, of course. They all would have to die, eventually. The rumblings in the city were growing stronger, not weaker, and Cassiel knew the sounds of a revolution in the making. The city would start actively calling for Fey to be crowned queen soon enough, and it wouldn't be long before those calls turned to violence.

It had been a stroke of genius on his part to start putting up those original posters. A stroke of genius to start the rumor mill going, to plant the idea of Fey being queen directly into the minds of the few aristocrat Witches who still remained. Revolution left people frightened, left them wanting to return to a world they knew—a world where they felt safe. A new queen would give them exactly what they wanted.

What he had always wanted.

It was almost time for him to make his move. Alastair couldn't remain this foolish forever. Even he would see the value of sharing the throne, of ruling the realm with Fey at his side, eventually. Cassiel liked Alice's idealism. Truly he did, but he had learned many hard lessons over his centuries of life. And one lesson history had taught him time and time again was that idealists never held power for long. No. Dictators held power. Those who were willing to bring waste to their enemies, to those who disagreed with them, those were the sort who ended up in power, time and time again.

Thea had been a dictator. She'd had to be, to finally end the war.

So, tonight he would meet with the leaders of the other Vampire families, weak though they may be. Tonight, he would play the part of an idealist. But tomorrow? Tomorrow, he would start the next phase on his own plans. Tomorrow, the right amount of coin in the right hands would see another resurgence in the push to put Fey on the throne. To put his son on the throne.

Tomorrow, his revolution truly began.

Cassiel glanced at the clock on the wall and sighed heavily. He should eat. It had been over a month since he'd last fed, and he was feeling the effects of it. At his age, he needed to feed frequently to keep his strength up. It felt like a mistake to go into this meeting at a fraction of his power, but he was already running behind schedule. He didn't have time, now, to have a woman brought to him to feed on her.

Distracted, hungry, and full of schemes, Cassiel was completely oblivious to the power that reached through the walls to threaten him. And when the voice in his head first started speaking, it was so quiet he barely even heard it.

It was a gentle murmur, just a whisper over his consciousness. A fly buzzing around the room would have captured more notice.

"Have a bottle of that Riesling I like sent to the formal sitting room in the South Hall," Cassiel told Winston, gathering a few papers together from his desk. "And if *l'enfant de sang* is there already, tell her I'm—"

This time, the voice was a shout. The sound was so loud it exploded in his skull, wiping away all thought. Cassiel cried out, knees buckling. *Pain.* His entire world was reduced to pain as the noise pounded through every cell in his brain.

"Master?" Winston was saying, voice tight with fear. It sounded distant, and strained, like it was coming from underwater. Reality suddenly felt so far away. "Master, what is it? What ails you?"

The sound vanished as quickly as it had appeared, and Cassiel gasped. He was bent over his desk, hands clasping the surface hard enough his nails had dug rivulets in the wood. His mind was his own again.

Wasn't it?

Something was wrong. His body felt strangely far away, and his mind? His mind...

Leech...

It was his voice. His own voice, speaking in his head. Cassiel shook his head violently, trying to dispel the sound.

"Something is wrong with me," he said out loud, for Winston. The human wouldn't be able to do anything, weak and ancient as he was, but he needed help, needed someone—

Leech.

False King.

Witch's Pet.

Cassiel snarled, baring his fangs as the words crashed through him. What was happening? He was no Witch's pet. No leech. He was—

Kill them.

There was a straight razor in his desk drawer, hidden beneath the files he kept in there. Almost the second the image of it formed in his head, something took hold of him. His hand shot out, fumbling for the drawer handle, reaching for the blade.

Kill them.

The Falcon was right, Cassiel realized distantly. It had been so long since Cassiel had last felt fear, it took several seconds to recognize the symptoms. The sour taste of adrenaline in his throat, the sudden and quick beating of his heart.

This was what had happened to Kellos, wasn't it? What was it the Falcon had said about his death?

It was like he wasn't even there... like he was being controlled...

Kill them, the voice commanded. His own voice, coming from inside his own head.

Focusing his power, throwing every bit of strength into it, Cassiel fought against his body as it moved against his will. The hand that reached for the drawer slowed but didn't stop.

No. His fingers fumbled with the latch of the drawer.

"Get out of here," Cassiel ordered Winston. Kellos had attacked his sister, tried to kill her. He hadn't managed to do it, of course, weak as he was. But Cassiel wasn't weak.

And he...

"Get my son," Cassiel gasped, fighting with everything inside him as the voice filled his mind, as his hand pushed papers aside and his fingers grazed the silver-handled razor. "Get Callum as far away from here as you can. *Now.*"

Kill them all.

Every leech you can find.

The voice was loud enough he barely heard Winston as the human fled, barely heard him shouting for help in the hallway. All he knew was that voice, that horrible voice disguised as his own, shouting through every cell in his brain. All he knew was the urge to *kill, kill, kill.*

Cassiel had lived through centuries. He knew this world, knew the world that existed before it. He had lived through monarchs and democracies, through revolution and strife. He had lived on this Earth a long, long time. And he would leave it on his own terms.

He wouldn't let them use him. He wouldn't let them hurt his son.

Callum. Sweet, gentle Callum. Callum, who'd inherited Delilah's smile. He could almost convince himself Delilah was still here when he saw that smile.

The metal handle was cold in his palm as Cassiel held the razor.

Kill, that voice in his head mimicking his own demanded.

He would. He would answer that command. But on his own damned terms.

Flipping the blade open, Cassiel placed the razor to his own throat and fought against the voice as hard as he could to *push*.

CHAPTER 48

FEY

The sound of a ringing phone pulled Fey from a gentle sleep and thrust her into consciousness.

She groaned, attempting to stretch. Her muscles were wonderfully sore after her night with Jasper and Alastair, and it felt so good to stretch out under the soft, cool sheets of Alastair's bed.

But the moment she moved, an arm wrapped around her waist, and with a gasp of shock, she found herself being pulled flush against a warm, hard body.

"Good morning, gorgeous," Jasper murmured against her neck, folding her against his body. Somewhere, that phone continued to ring.

She opened her mouth to tell him to fuck off, but Jasper's tongue slid over the juncture of her neck and shoulder and her curse turned to a soft moan.

"Who the fuck is calling me at this time of day?" Alastair asked from the other side of the bed. The mattress shifted as he stood to pull on a pair of slacks and stalk toward the dresser where his phone sat.

"Let it ring," Jasper called out, briefly glancing over at Alastair before burying his face back into Fey's neck.

"Jasper," she protested, struggling against him, to no avail. "Get away, you're sticky," she complained.

Jasper nuzzled into her even harder. "So are you." His teeth grazed across her skin. "Let's drag Alastair into the shower, hm? Get all nice and clean so we can get dirty again."

Goddess, the way his breath tickled her skin, and the way his canines barely whispered over her skin... Fey wriggled against him, breath hitching.

"After," she whispered, rolling in his grasp to face him. She took his face in her hands, grinning before lowering her mouth to his.

Jasper's answering moan was full of encouragement.

"What?" Alastair spoke angrily into the phone. A moment passed, and he went still, body frozen. His face showed nothing, no emotion at all, as someone on the other end of the phone spoke. Fey couldn't hear who was on the other end, or what they were saying, but Jasper could.

Jasper stopped suddenly, breaking their kiss as his head whipped up to watch the Vampire.

"Oh, Alastair," he said quietly. And the heartbreak and pain in his voice turned Fey's blood cold. She scrambled to sit up.

Without another word, Alastair took the phone from his ear and stared down at the screen. Then he ended the call.

"What is it?" Fey asked.

"Cassiel deSanguine is dead," Alastair said in a hollow voice. "He slit his own throat."

PART THREE

CHAPTER 49

CALLUM

It should be raining, Callum thought, gazing up at the clear night sky. It was only fitting that it would be raining at a funeral. But the sky around the tombs remained stubbornly dry. Not even a single cloud was visible. The night was a soft velvet, a near-perfect match to the color of the suit he'd chosen to wear.

This wasn't Callum's first funeral. Not by far. They had opened the tomb only two years ago, when his cousin Santiago had been found murdered in his apartment. He could even remember Delilah's funeral, though he had been just a child at the time and didn't yet understand what death meant to an immortal. But he had been a background player in those funerals, a participant at best.

Not like now. Not like tonight.

Callum shut his eyes tight and prayed for rain. He hadn't cried yet, hadn't been able to still the emotions roaring inside him long enough to find any tears. Maybe he had hoped the sky would do his mourning for him, if only for the night.

Tonight, with his father's body laid on the black onyx slab inside the family tomb, Callum was more than a mere participant. He was the face of the Salvatore family, the strongest Vampire family in the realm.

Tonight, he would stand vigil by his father's side all night while the other families came to pay their respects and offer their condolences.

Tonight, he would represent them all. At least until...

"Has he arrived yet?" Callum asked, eyes still closed. He knew Winston was at his side without the human even uttering a single word.

The crowd around the tomb had grown with each passing hour since the sun had set. Callum had expected representatives from all the major families to come, of course, but it looked as though every member of their Faction had answered his invitation. Every single Vampire, from every octant in the realm.

All except one. The only one who mattered.

"He has, sire," came Winston's answer, his voice like dry parchment. "He just arrived. He is with your father now."

Callum took a deep breath to center himself. He could do this. It was time.

The crowd parted before Callum as he made his way through them, toward the tomb. They parted, but not before each Vampire he passed offered their condolences, pressing their fingers to their lips and murmuring prayers.

So sorry for your loss.

Our family mourns with you.

He was a great man.

Was he? Calum wondered when he heard that. Even now, he wasn't sure what sort of man his father had been. Likely, it didn't matter now.

But he accepted the words graciously, thanking those in attendance, as he made his way across the lawn.

The tomb where they'd laid his father's corpse was empty, save for one lone figure, when he reached it. The others had filtered outside to give him space to mourn.

"Hello brother," Callum said softly as he approached.

Alastair didn't answer. He stared down at their father's body, laid out on the slab of stark black stone as though resting. They had dressed him in white, the color of death, and Callum himself had selected the silk scarf that wrapped around their father's neck, hiding the death wound. Hiding where he had slit his own throat open with a razor blade.

His steps sounded obscenely loud on the stone floor as he came to stand at Alastair's side.

"Is Fey...?" Callum began to ask, looking around for signs of the Witch.

"I didn't want her to come," Alastair answered. "I don't want her involved in this. This isn't her world."

Oh. It hurt to see his brother here, alone. Hurt more to know that he wanted to share so little of his life with his family.

Callum liked Fey. He had wanted her to be here tonight, to share in their mourning. To help bridge the gap their father had made between Alastair and the rest of the family.

As always, Alastair was drawing a line in the sand, with his family on one side and himself on the other.

But that would have to end, eventually.

"We need to talk, Alastair," Callum started, in a calm voice. "About what happens next."

Alastair didn't look up when he answered.

"No."

You can't ever make things easy, can you, brother? Callum thought with a frustrated sigh. "You can't just say no, brother."

"Okay," his brother said, voice flat. "Then how about fuck no?"

Callum's temper flared. "Stop it. Stop this foolishness right now. We're at his funeral, for Goddess's sake. You can't hide anymore, Alastair. The deSanguine title will pass on to you whether you like it or not. You're going to have to step up and lead this family, brother. You can't just keep pretending it won't happen. We need you."

I need you. Callum thought. He swallowed the words down.

Alastair smirked, still staring down at the body of their father, and for a moment Callum wondered if this was how their father had looked when he was young. So cold and so angry.

"It already has passed, Callum," Alastair said, interrupting his thoughts. "It passed the moment he died. It always does. You're the only one stupid enough to not have noticed, you know that?"

Callum frowned. No, no, that couldn't be right. If the title had passed, he would be feeling it right now. But, standing here, directly next to his brother, he didn't feel anything. He didn't feel that pull, that draw his father had commanded, coming from Alastair. That whirlpool of power. Alastair felt… just like Alastair, like he always had, to Callum. Which meant he was wrong. The title hadn't passed.

"I don't understand," Callum said, suspicious.

"Who did the other families call first, when his body was found?" Alastair asked.

Callum's breath caught.

"That doesn't mean anything," he told Alastair, refusing to even contemplate it. "Everyone knows how you felt about him."

"Yeah, that's true," Alastair conceded. "But that's not why they called you first. Not why they looked to you to arrange his funeral. And you know it."

No. Callum shook his head. There was no way Alastair was right in what he was suggesting… no possible way…

"No," Callum insisted. "You're his heir. Father knew that. Hell, everyone knows that. The title follows power. Father, Delilah, you. You are the next head of this family, Alastair. You are the next deSanguine."

"Look around you, brother," Alastair said, almost gently.

He did. Callum looked around the grounds, where the most powerful Vampires in their family were gathered. The most powerful Vampires in the realm, representatives from all the Vampire families. They were all looking at him, all gathered here, under the stars and the sky that refused to weep, so they could see *him*… not his father.

Not Alastair.

"I kept telling you that you would be stronger than me," Alastair was saying as Callum looked around at the faces of the crowd. Looked at how they had positioned themselves to face him, to watch him. As though the universe itself held him at its center. "I told you over and over, but you never really believed it, did you?"

No. He hadn't. It was impossible to even consider he could be stronger than Alastair. No one was stronger than Alastair.

And yet…

"Congratulations, Callum Salvatore deSanguine," his brother said, putting a hand on his shoulder. And smiling at him. "Don't fuck it up."

CHAPTER 50
ALASTAIR

It was almost dawn by the time Alastair finally returned home.

He should feel something. Relief, maybe. Or anger. Something, at least. Anything.

He should want to cry. He should want to scream, to break something. His father was dead, the worthless bastard was finally gone, and he should feel... something.

He didn't. He felt nothing at all.

And wasn't that the biggest fuck you ever? Wasn't that the biggest middle finger in existence? A small part of him hoped there was an afterlife, hoped Cassiel was down there in hell right now, realizing that his death meant absolutely nothing to his eldest son.

Delilah had once told him that the opposite of love wasn't hate, it was indifference. Standing over his father's body, trying to imagine the wound under that stupid fucking scarf, Alastair couldn't even summon up the strength to hate him.

All he'd felt was indifference.

Grimacing, he pushed the door to his home open and let himself inside. It was late, and he was exhausted. He needed to spend a few hours of the coming day in bed, actually sleeping, instead of—

The two figures sleeping on the couch roused, awakened by his return.

Of course. Of course, they'd tried to stay up.

Alastair shrugged off his suit jacket and hung it by the door. "I told you to get some sleep, Witchling. You didn't have to wait up for me. Either of you."

Jasper rubbed at his eyes, yawning. "That's what I told her. But she insisted."

It was actually a surprise to find the Wolf here. He had been on the schedule to work tonight. He must have come over right after his shift ended, to keep Fey company. And to be here when Alastair returned from the funeral.

He was... strangely happy to see him, though. Happy to come home to the two of them.

"How was it?" Fey asked, uncurling herself from the couch and sitting up. Concern quickly overtook the exhaustion on her face.

Alastair shrugged.

"It was fine," he answered emotionlessly.

"And Callum?" Fey prompted.

Alastair's lips curved into a grin.

"Callum deSanguine will be an excellent patriarch," he said, not bothering to hide the pride in his voice. "Just as soon as he stops living in denial and starts believing it. He's exactly what our Faction needs. Exactly what the realm needs."

"Do you... do you want to talk about it?" Fey asked. At her side, Jasper tried to stifle another yawn.

And looking at the two of them, Alastair finally felt something. Not about his father's death, but about... this.

He felt lucky. Happy to have them both.

Mates, Jasper had called it. Vampires didn't have mates, not like Shifters did. But...

Home. Tonight, looking at Fey and Jasper, Alastair finally felt like he had a home.

"No, Witchling," Alastair assured her, pulling Fey to her feet and wrapping his arms around her. "I don't want to talk about it. I just want to go to bed. With both of you."

"Of course," Fey whispered against his chest. "We should get some sleep—"

He tightened his hold on her.

"I'm not interested in sleeping, Witchling," he told her, luxuriating in the way she wriggled against him.

He was a very, very lucky man.

CHAPTER 51
CALLUM

Callum had been to the palace only once, back when he was a small child.

It had been for a party of sorts, though after so many years he couldn't recall the reason behind the celebration. Father had dressed him in black, lined with a deep red. Delilah used to go to these events with him, dressed in a gown of the same colors, but Delilah had just died, and Alastair was gone more often than he was home, leaving Callum as the only one who was left. That, more than any other reason, was why his father had taken him that night.

Even then, Callum had known he was something like a consolation prize, but that night he hadn't cared, not even a little. He had been so excited to dress up, so excited to see the palace, to meet Witches. He never saw much of anyone, aside from Winston, who never wanted to play with him, and Alastair, who grew quieter and quieter, angrier and angrier as the days went on.

Witches were the Faction closest to the Goddess, or so everyone said. Callum wanted to know what that meant. Wanted to meet these holy creatures, so blessed by the divine, wanted to share in their joy.

Father had told him to stay close at his side, that night, but Callum couldn't help himself. He'd run off the moment he'd seen a group of other children, eager to meet new friends.

"Hi!" he'd said, delighted, when he'd approached them.

And they'd smiled at him, big welcoming smiles, and greeted him right back. They'd told him their names, and some of them even told him the names of their families, as though that conveyed some special piece of information to him. They'd seemed so nice, and he was so excited to play with them.

But when he'd smiled back at them and started to tell them his name, they'd paled. They'd gone from happy to scared so quickly, and he hadn't understood that sudden change until one of them had hissed it at him like a curse.

"*Leech*!"

That was the first time Callum knew what it meant to be hated.

Callum stayed by his father's side for the rest of the night after that, hiding behind his legs and keeping to himself. He'd been glad when his father went to the next party alone.

And now, as Callum waited outside the entrance to the palace throne room, he couldn't help but remember the fear he'd seen in those children's eyes when they'd seen him.

How different would the realm be today if he'd stayed and played with them that night? If he'd shown them that he wasn't all that different, wasn't scary, wasn't the monster they thought his father was. How different would things be if his father had kept bringing him, if he'd been allowed to spend time with the Witches at those parties, to make them laugh, to tell them stories?

What would the world be like if they had gotten a chance to know him?

A noise from behind him startled Callum from his revery, and he turned to see a dark-skinned Witch stalking toward him. She was handsome and built like a fighter, all muscles and sharp angles. When she spotted him standing there, she froze, mouth opening in shock.

"Alastair?" she asked, a mixture of surprise and disgust in her voice.

Callum nearly laughed.

"Sorry, no," he said, giving her a welcoming smile. "I'm the other one."

"Oh." Readjusting her attitude, the Witch approached, eyeing him warily. "You must be the new deSanguine. We haven't met, yet. I'm Alice, the representative of the Witch Faction."

She looked him up and down, assessing him.

"Please, call me Callum," he told her, offering her his hand. "I'm still not used to the title."

Alice nodded, taking his hand in her own and shaking it. Then, seemingly as though she had to, she added, "I'm sorry for your loss."

"Are you?" Callum asked, more curious than anything. "Are you, really? I'm not naïve to my father's reputation, Alice. Especially amongst your Faction. Especially to an ex-Blade."

The Fallen King. To the Witch standing before him, his father would have represented something terrible. An enemy. A constant threat to the crown.

Already, Callum was so, so tired of it all. Tired of living in the shadows of wars he'd never fought.

The Witch before him gave him a long, assessing look before she answered. "Whatever your father was," Alice said, "he was committed to this council. He did a lot of good over the last few years. I might not have called him a friend, but—" She took a deep breath. "But in the end, I don't think I would have called him an enemy. I am sorry for your loss, Callum. Sorry for the realm's loss. He will be missed."

Callum swallowed hard against the sudden lump in his throat.

"Thank you," he whispered. "I appreciate hearing that."

Alice turned away, allowing him a moment of privacy with his emotions.

"Have you met the other council members?" she asked, motioning toward the throne room.

Callum shook his head. He cleared his throat, pulling himself together. He was the deSanguine now. He wasn't some child, yearning to play with the others.

"Come with me, then," the Witch said, stepping forward and opening the door.

There were more people there than he expected. Callum glanced around, curious. Each Faction supposedly only had one representative.

With him and Alice representing two of the four Factions, shouldn't there only be two more people here?

"Leandra. Linh." Alice greeted the two older Witches waiting next to the long oak table wearily. "This is an unexpected surprise."

Unexpected and unpleasant, her tone suggested. Callum watched the Witches closely.

"Who is this?" the oldest of the women asked, looking Callum up and down. He may as well have been a piece of animal shit Alice had tracked in on her boots.

"The new deSanguine," Alice announced.

"Is he?" a delicate voice asked from the table, and Callum turned to regard the speaker. This was no Eternal City accent. This voice was older, older even than some of the eldest Vampires. The woman who spoke was the only one seated, though she stood gracefully as he turned his gaze to her.

"Welcome, new deSanguine," she said. "I knew your father for many years. Not all of them unpleasant."

Her voice was like a poisoned sweet, and something in the aura around her sent a shiver of fear down his spine. From somewhere deep in the banks of his memory, he pulled out the name.

"Kallista," Callum said, and her mouth curved to a slight smile. "My father spoke of you. Often, and with great respect."

"Liar," the Demon whispered, but her smile perked even more.

"We need to talk," the older of the Witches—Linh—was saying to Alice. "Without all of these..." She glanced over at Kallista and Callum coldly. "These spectators."

"Actually, you're the spectator here, Linh," Alice answered, walking around her to come and sit at the council table. Callum did the same, following her only to pause before the remaining two chairs.

Which one was his?

A barely perceivable nod from Kallista indicated the chair to her right, so Callum took the hint graciously and sat, inclining his head to her in thanks.

"They are members of the council," Alice continued. "But you, and you as well, Leandra, are the spectators here."

"We are advisors to—"

"No. No, you're not," Alice cut her off quickly. "You *were* advisors to the princess, and you *were* advisors to me. Before you abdicated your duties, just as she did, and left representing our Faction to Sana and myself. You haven't been advisors to anything for months, and I'll be damned if I'll let you claim the title now, just because it benefits you to do so."

The other Witch, Leandra, had the decency to look ashamed, but the older woman's fury only grew. She opened her mouth but was interrupted as the door to their back opened, and a Witch near to Alice's age stepped into the room.

This Witch, wearing a soft blue robe, blinked in surprise, looking at first to Callum, then to Leandra and finally to Linh.

"I'll get more chairs," she said, decidedly, and then turned and practically fled from the room.

Alice sighed.

"You forget, Alice, that we are the ones who gave you this seat on the council," Linh said threateningly. *And we can take it away*, her smug face seemed to finish saying.

"And you forget that you had to practically beg me to take it," Alice answered in a cold voice. "I doubt much has changed since then."

"Is this what they're always like?" Callum asked Kallista loudly, earning a glare from Linh and a wince from Alice. "These meetings?"

"Oh no," Kallista assured him. "Sometimes they're much worse."

"We have an issue to bring up with the council," Leandra said, diplomatically placing a hand on Linh's arm while giving Alice a measured look. "We wish to have our concern heard, that is all."

"I do not wish to bring up my concerns with the council, I wish to bring it up with her," Linh spat, pointing a finger at Alice, who snorted and rolled her eyes.

The door behind them opened once again, and two servants appeared, carrying extra chairs to place around the table. The blue Witch appeared with them, gave them a gentle smile of thanks, and took a seat in one of the spare chairs next to Alice.

"Please, Linh, Leandra, have a seat," Alice said, sounding exhausted. "Callum, I apologize. The council has been under a lot of pressure, and I let my temper get the better of me. Let me introduce you to everyone."

She motioned to each of the women in turn as they took their seats. "This is Leandra, head of the Fire Coven, and Linh, head of the Air Coven. Sana here is head of the Water Coven and also keeps records for all of our meetings."

Sana smiled pleasantly at him, and Callum returned the gesture easily. She, at least, didn't seem too bad.

"Ah," Alice said, turning as the throne room doors opened and an attractive male entered. "And here's the last of us. Callum, this is the Shifter representative, Silas."

"Not for long," the male said, mouth tight with anger as he approached. Alice straightened in her chair, clearly thrown off, and in her moment of confusion, the Shifter crossed the floor and thrust an envelope at her.

"What is this?" Alice asked, taking it from him. She held it lightly between her fingers, making no move to open it.

"My resignation from this council," the Shifter announced. "Effective immediately."

CHAPTER 52
ALASTAIR

Alastair sighed in irritation as he turned the page, eyes roving over the text of his book. It was early, hours and hours from the sun rising, and Fey was fast asleep on the other side of the massive bed they shared. The gentle rhythm of her breathing was the sweetest song he'd ever heard.

But Jasper?

"What do you want, puppy?" Alastair asked, annoyed, glancing from his book to the Wolf on the bed next to him.

Head still on the pillow, his body nestled beneath the sheets, Jasper grinned.

"How did you know I was awake?" he asked.

"The same way I know you've been watching me for an hour. I can hear your breathing," Alastair said. "Go to sleep."

Jasper propped himself up on his elbow, frowning.

"Why? You're not sleeping."

"I'm nocturnal. I don't sleep at night, and this? This is my afternoon."

"And you're spending it in bed? Reading a book?" Jasper asked incredulously.

It was hard to fight back his smile. "I always read in bed when Fey is sleeping. I find it calming. Go to sleep."

"I can't," Jasper complained.

Alastair ground his teeth together. "You could. If you actually fucking tried."

"Nah. I'm too restless. Why don't we wake her up?" Jasper's grin turned mischievous. "I bet you she wouldn't mind going again."

"Don't even fucking think about it," Alastair snapped, slamming his book shut. "She needs her rest. And if you wake her up, I will throw you out of here so fast it will make your head spin."

Jasper's grin only grew. "Well... we could have some fun, just the two of us," he offered, eyes sparkling.

Teeth grinding together hard enough he might break a fang, Alastair shot Jasper a lethal glare before setting his book on the nightstand.

Great. He wasn't going to get any fucking reading done tonight, was he?

Jasper seemed to take the action as blatant approval, and his grin grew even more wicked as he shifted closer to the Vampire.

"Tell me, puppy," Alastair said, speaking quietly. He wouldn't risk waking Fey, not for this. Not for anything. She was pushing herself too hard with her classes and her training, and she deserved a proper night's sleep. He was serious about her needing her rest. "Is this a game to you?"

Jasper's smile faltered, slipping ever so slightly.

Alastair took the time to really look at the Wolf shifter laying next to him. Goddess knew he was attractive. That tan, flawless skin, the hard muscles. He was naked under the sheets. They all were. And Alastair's cock twitched at the thought of what lay under those covers.

Jasper's eyes grew hooded as Alastair reached out with one hand, sliding his fingers over the Wolf's chiseled jawbone, over the coarse stubble that grew there.

"Fey is everything to me," he said, thumb tracing over Jasper's bottom lip. He felt a jolt of satisfaction at the way his breath hitched and eyelids flickered. His hand traveled lower.

"Do you understand what you're getting into here, puppy? Truly understand it?"

Jasper's breath quickened as Alastair's hand traveled lower, down the plane of his chest and down the hardened muscles of his abs.

"She's not one of your Wolves. She's not one of your conquests." His hand dipped below the sheets, sliding over the soft curls of Jasper's pubic hair. "She is everything. If you hurt her..."

He gripped the base of Jasper's quickly hardening cock tightly and was rewarded by a deep, guttural noise from the Wolf's chest. Jasper's head rolled back, his hips jerking forward.

"She comes first. Always," Alastair told him, sliding his hand up and down Jasper's shaft.

Jasper smirked, opening a single eye, but his breathing was ragged. "Figuratively? Or literally?"

Alastair swore, gripping tighter. Jasper gasped, hips jerking under the touch. "Both," Alastair told him. "We don't wake her up when she needs to sleep. And you don't come until she does. Ever. You understand me?"

"Yes, boss," Jasper murmured, breathing hard.

"Just because you have this nice cock doesn't mean you know how to use it," Alastair mocked. "Can you satisfy her? Can you make her come?"

Jasper groaned, cock jerking in Alastair's grip. He nodded.

Leaning closer to him, Alastair slid his tongue out, licking the shell of Jasper's ear before asking, "And can you make me come?"

Without hesitation, Jasper reached for him, his breath coming in swift pants. Alastair rolled back to give him access, sucking in a breath as Jasper's hand reached down and gripped him.

Jasper had a reputation around the club—so Alastair wasn't surprised that he was skilled with his hands. But even still...

He hissed as Jasper's hand slid up his thigh, rolling over his balls lightly before stroking up his shaft. His fingers barely touched as he gripped Alastair by the base of his cock, sliding his hand up to the head.

"Like this, boss?" he asked breathlessly.

Fuck the Goddess, that felt good. Alastair sucked in a sharp breath between his teeth.

"Harder," he demanded. Jasper obeyed without hesitation, gripping him harder and continuing to touch him with long, measured strokes.

Alastair's hand continued to move over Jasper, stroking him gently, teasing him. From the way his cock twitched in Alastair's hand, and the bead of precum dripping from him, it was clear the Shifter liked it.

"Harder?" Jasper licked his lips as he watched Alastair's face.

So eager to please. Alastair smirked. One hand still playing with Jasper, he reached down with his free hand and wrapped it around Jasper's fingers, forcing the Shifter to grip in even more.

"Harder," he said, and Jasper groaned softly. Jasper's hips were moving, shifting forward and back ever so slightly as Alastair stroked him. Using Jasper's hand to grip him, Alastair stroked himself, gripping tight.

"Yes, boss," Jasper whispered, watching Alastair's hand over his own as they stroked Alastair together.

Alastair shifted until his body lay against Jasper, their chests touching. He brought his lips to Jasper's cheek, licking a line to his ear. Jasper shivered under his touch, cock jerking in his soft grip.

"Do you like touching me?" he asked.

The Shifter nodded, licking his lips, hips bucking under Alastair's grip.

"*Say it*," he ordered. Jasper groaned in response.

"I love it," he answered, the words tumbling from his mouth. "I've wanted to touch you since..."

Jasper's mouth clamped shut and blood rushed to his cheeks. Alastair squeezed both hands tighter, chuckling at Jasper's answering moan.

"Since when, puppy?"

"Since I first met you," he gasped out. There was no subtle movement now. Jasper's hips rocked back and forth, thrusting in Alastair's grip. His breathing was growing erratic.

Alastair gripped them both tighter. Shifting his head, he dragged his lips over Jasper's cheek, then stopped, their mouths almost touching.

"*Come*," Alastair ordered, his lips brushing Jasper's as he spoke.

Jasper let out a small whimper and shuddered. His cock jerked in Alastair's grip, shooting his release over Alastair's stomach.

With a quiet groan, Alastair followed him, biting his lip to keep from making too much noise and waking Fey. His come shot between them, mixing with Jasper's and coating them both.

Fuck, Alastair gasped for breath, his cock still twitching under Jasper's grip.

Goddess, they were a mess. Still catching his breath, Alastair peeled his hand away. He was coated in them both. He rolled toward the edge of the bed, reaching for something to clean himself with. His fingers brushed over fabric—his shirt. Well, expensive silk worked just as well as anything, he supposed. Rolling onto his back, he began to wipe off his hand and chest.

Jasper moved without warning, sliding down between Alastair's legs before he had a chance to stop him. Eyes glued on Alastair's, he bent his head down and ran his tongue over Alastair's still hard cock, lapping up the mess there.

"Again," Jasper whispered, taking Alastair in his hand.

Alastair groaned as Jasper's lips closed around him, sucking him deep into his throat. Alastair dropped the shirt, forgetting the mess entirely, hand coming up to grab the headboard behind him. Jasper pulled him from his mouth, tongue rolling around the head of his cock.

"Again," Jasper pleaded before taking him into his throat once more.

Alastair was all too happy to oblige.

CHAPTER 53
ALICE

The night of Fey's initiation into the Queen's Blades, the night she had first become their sister, Fey had run away.

And it had been Alice's fault.

They'd never spoken about it, not once, but Alice knew. When Fey had received her mark and sigils, not making so much as a sound through the ordeal, Alice had felt an uncontrollable surge of love for her. Had wrapped the young Witch in her arms the moment they were alone, in adoration. In love.

And she'd felt that small flinch from Fey when she'd done it. Felt the Witch pull back from her.

It had been her fault that Fey had run away from them, that the Blades had almost collapsed. Her fault that she couldn't keep her family together.

And now it was happening again.

Alice clutched the letter Silas had given her so tightly her knuckles hurt. She didn't open it, didn't read it. Her head spun, a dizzying volume of emotions swirling inside her. A thousand thoughts were vying for her attention, a thousand words she wanted to say, to spit, to *scream*.

"Why?" she said, finally, pushing the words out from between clenched teeth.

"Why?" Silas laughed nastily. He glanced around at all of them, seated at the council table before him, and Alice realized she'd made a terrible mistake in dismissing him so flippantly at the last meeting. He no longer looked at them like they were allies, or like they were working toward a common goal. The way he had looked at them before. No. He looked at them now like they were his enemies. "Because I'm not even supposed to be on this council, Witch. I was here as a favor to Kellos. And now he's gone."

"You would leave your Faction unrepresented?" Alice asked, searching, desperately, for anything to keep the council together.

Couldn't they see? They were all in danger, threats coming from all sides. They had to stay together, had to stay united.

She did this. It was all falling apart around her, and it was her fault. She'd alienated him when she needed him. When the council needed him.

"Not my problem," Silas told her. "Offer the position to someone else. This isn't my fight."

"What is that supposed to mean?" she challenged.

"It means exactly what I said. This isn't my fight, Witch. I never agreed to form this council, and I sure as shit won't die for it. Find someone else who will."

Alice blinked at the envelope.

He was scared. He really, truly thought someone had killed Kellos, and he was scared they were coming after him.

"You're a coward," she said, voice flat. Emotionless.

Silas snorted. "Yeah, maybe. Maybe I am a coward. But I'd rather be a coward than a corpse."

The letter crumpled into a ball in Alice's hand as she clutched it harder, her fingers curling around the words she would never dignify by reading.

"What did you mean by that?" Callum asked. There was no anger to his words, no judgement. His voice was curious and gentle. "About not dying for the council?"

"Someone is killing council members," Silas said. "Haven't they told you? First Kellos, then the Vamp, and who knows who's next?" Then, as though realizing who he was speaking to, Silas glanced away.

"I'm sorry for your loss," Silas said, more to the ground than to the new deSanguine seated at the table. "But you're a fool if you don't see the connection. Two council members dead in under a week isn't a coincidence. It's a pattern."

"Stranger things have happened," Kallista offered. But even she sounded skeptical, now. Alice's heart beat a little too hard in her chest.

"My father killed himself," Callum said, frowning. "He wasn't murdered. He... he slit his own throat."

Silas's laugh held no humor at all. "And you believe that?" he asked, sneering. "Yeah, because that's such a normal way to commit suicide, isn't it? Tell me something honestly, Vampire. How was he acting before he killed himself? What was he doing?"

Callum blinked.

"He had a meeting with the *enfant de sang*," he told them, voice distant, pain weighing heavy in his words. "He was running late... Winston said... Winston said he collapsed and started acting strangely. He wasn't making any sense and... he ordered him to leave, to find me. To protect me."

"And does that sound like a man about to kill himself?" Silas asked, voice cold.

"This is ridiculous," Alice interrupted, not giving Callum a chance to answer. "No one is killing members of the council. You have no evidence to support any of this."

Silas turned those sharp, yellow eyes on her.

"Then I hope you're next," he said, lip curling in disgust. "And I hope whatever Witch replaces you isn't so blind to the truth."

No, not disgust, Alice realized, finally recognizing the emotion in the Shifter's eyes.

It was hate.

Her chest tightened in panic. How had she misjudged him so completely? How had she let it get to this?

Silas turned, moving toward the exit, and Alice quickly leapt to her feet.

"You can't do this," she objected, taking a step toward him. Her fingers twitched, reaching for a blade she no longer wore.

Silas stopped in his tracks. "What are you going to do to stop me, Witch?" he asked, voice low and dangerous. He turned and took a step toward her, and for the first time since meeting him, Alice could see the predator under his skin. "Will you arrest me? Kill me?"

Power roiled inside of her, drawn by the challenge in his voice, but Alice fought against it. He was right. There was nothing she could do.

She'd already lost this battle.

Silas smirked, staring her down. "That's what I thought."

He turned to go but paused, glancing back at Callum.

"Get out while you can," Silas warned him. "Don't put your life on the line for them. Their Faction never cared about the rest of us. And I see no evidence that's changed. Don't make the same mistake your father did."

Then he was gone, his footsteps echoing on the marble walls until he was out of sight.

Alice couldn't breathe. It was all coming down around her. She sat back down heavily, in shock.

At the table, someone snorted.

"Well, good riddance to bad rubbish," Linh said. "If you ask me—"

"No one asked you, you old bag," Alice murmured. She couldn't even summon the energy to put any heat behind the words.

"Do you really believe these two deaths aren't connected, Alice?" Kallista asked.

Alice looked up, glancing between Kallista and Callum, the last of her council. Was she really so sure? Was she being blind here? Were their lives at risk, all because she was being stubborn?

"I don't know," she admitted, finally. "I truly don't know."

"Then we should find out," Callum said decisively. He held her gaze, his eyes serious but unafraid. And for a moment, hearing the sureness in his voice, Alice felt a little hope bloom in her chest. He had his father's strength.

"We should make finding a new Shifter representative a priority, I think," Sana said, pen moving quickly over the notes in front of her. "Silas was right, I am sorry to say. He wasn't meant to be more than a stand in for a few meetings. Maybe we expected too much from him. The Shifters deserve a real representative, one fully committed to the role.”

“Sam,” Alice heard herself say, before she’d even realized she’d started forming a plan. She felt a shift in her emotions, felt her wits begin to gather. They needed someone trustworthy, someone the Shifters would listen to. “He’s a Hare Shifter, well respected by his Faction. I’ll reach out to him tomorrow morning and see what he can do to help repair this.”

They couldn’t lose the Shifters, couldn’t risk alienating so many citizens because of her anger. Her failure as a council member.

Sana jotted it down.

“Perhaps we could extend the invitation to Regina, Kellos’s sister? Or at least make the suggestion to Sam?” Sana added. “Silas wanted us to interview her, after what happened, but maybe she would appreciate being offered the seat on the council?”

It was a good idea. One with merit. Yes, this could work.

“We should reach out to her anyway,” Leandra added in a calm voice. “Whatever she has to tell us about her brother’s death... we should listen to her.”

Yes. They should.

And for a moment, Alice was grateful that the other Priestesses had shown up tonight. She was grateful for their support. They could do this, together. They *would* do this. The council would not fall.

Not while she still lived.

With a renewed sense of surety, Alice began to plot. She could make this work. She could salvage this.

Further down the table, Linh made a noise, deep in her throat, like a cough.

“What was that, Linh?” Sana asked, not bothering to glance over at her as she wrote in her ledger. Her pen made a playful scratching sound as she wrote. “I didn’t catch that.”

Linh’s only answer was a gurgle, strained, and almost sickeningly wet.

Goddess, is she still ill? Alice wondered, looking over at the High Priestess. She did look pale, and her eyes were glazed, unfocused...

"Linh…" Leandra started, frowning at her. Linh's head jerked slightly, more a twitch than anything. "Are you ok? You look—"

WHAM.

Leandra screamed, leaping away as Linh slammed her own head down against the council table.

Every head in the room turned in shock to watch as Linh straightened in her chair again, blood dripping from her nose.

"Linh, what—"

WHAM.

Linh slammed her head down against the wood again, with a sickening crack. When she sat back this time, there was blood smeared over the table. It was dripping down her face, coating the front of her robes.

Alice was on her feet, a hand pressed to her chest in shock.

"Linh STOP!" Leandra screeched, reaching for the Witch. But her hand barely touched the sleeve of Linh's robe before the woman twisted away, slamming her head back down on the table again and again.

And again.

"Merciful Goddess save us," Sana gasped, hands over her mouth.

"Someone stop her! Grab her!" Alice screamed, pushing her chair away and racing toward her.

Kallista was faster. Shadows snapped around Linh's shoulders, jerking her backwards out of her chair and away from the table. Alice glanced over at the Demon, who now stood, her own chair knocked over backwards behind her and her face just as shocked as theirs.

"I've got her," Kallista said, voice frantic, edged in panic.

Linh fought, struggling against the shadow bonds that held her.

"What in the name of the Goddess was that?" Leandra asked in a shaky voice.

"Something's wrong with her," Callum said, stunned. He hadn't stood, but he looked at the older woman with obvious fear in his eyes. "Why would she—?"

Snap.

Sana screamed as Linh's head twisted violently on her shoulders, her neck breaking with a crack like a whip.

Goddess help us all, Alice thought, hand over her mouth, as Linh's head lolled forward.

Dead.

Linh was dead.

"What did you do to her?" Leandra screeched at Kallista.

"I didn't do anything!" Kallista snapped back. Her shadows immediately disappeared, and Linh's body slumped to the floor, lifeless and heavy. "I was just stopping her from hurting herself! Something you should have been capable of doing!"

"This is it," Callum whispered, eyes wide, as he looked around the room, at them, yes, but also at the corners, the ceiling. "This is what killed them, isn't it? Kellos, my father..."

"That's ridiculous, this—" Leandra began, but Alice held up her hand to silence her.

"Talk," she demanded, eyes on Callum.

He looked at her, pupils blown wide with fright.

"Winston, my father's servant...he said my father tried to get him to run," Callum told them. "Tried to get him to hide me, as though I were in danger. As though *he* were the danger. He wasn't acting right. It was like he wasn't in control of himself."

Alice stared at Linh's body, puzzle pieces falling into place as she weighed everything. Had she really been this blind?

Kellos, attacking another Shifter, a Shifter he loved. The sister he'd spent his life protecting.

Cassiel, ordering his guards to protect his child, before taking his life by his own hand...

"If I were being controlled by something," she said, the reality of what was happening finally hitting her. "If I were at risk of hurting the people I love? I would hope I would have the strength to slit my own throat, as well."

Callum's head whipped toward her, a look of horror and pain flashing over his face.

She didn't want to believe it,

No. It couldn't be.

Please no.

"I know what this is," Alice whispered, horror creeping through her veins at the realization. Silas was right. She'd been so, so blind. "I've seen this before."

A Blood Witch.

In the hallway, hidden behind the heavy palace door, Vee smiled.

It served the bitch right after the way she'd spoken to Amalia. She knew enough now from the princess to know that particular Witch had been one of the few who had clung to the idea of the Witch Faction keeping all the power in the city to themselves. She'd wanted to put another Witch on the throne, wanted to keep everything the way it had always been. Maintain the status quo.

The same status quo that had gotten so many people in Vee's life killed.

The Witch got what she deserved, Vee reasoned. She wanted the city to go back to the way it had been. The way it was before Vee discovered her powers, when strays were dying in the streets every night. When the Shifters were treated like nothing but vermin in their own city.

Popping a macaron in her mouth, Vee hummed in appreciation. Goddess, these things were good. She licked sugar from her fingers, slipping off quietly down the hall, listening to the chaos and sounds of the throne room grow distant behind her.

She was glad she'd stopped by the kitchens before coming here tonight. It had been easy to sneak in and steal some sweets. Just as easy to sneak back to the throne room to watch the council meeting.

Controlling that Witch had been easy, too, almost comedically so. A weak mind, with a weaker body. She'd barely needed to use any power at all.

She'd been even easier than the rats.

But the others? Vee popped another cookie into her mouth and chewed, frowning as she walked. They weren't going to be easy. Even Kellos, old and weak as he was, had been hard, and the Vampire? It had taken more than she'd thought possible to sneak into his mind, more effort than she'd ever had to use before. He'd *fought* her, somehow. Pushed her out of his mind over and over. Every time she felt like she had a hold on him, he slipped out of her grasp. It had been like trying to hold water in her hands.

No one had ever broken her hold on them before. And that worried her.

Was it a power thing? she wondered. After all, he was the Fallen King, supposedly the most powerful Vampire alive. Maybe it was just more difficult, the more powerful they were?

That complicated things. Vee wanted to get rid of the whole council, wanted all of them gone. Every last traitor. But if power would be a problem...

That council Witch, Alice, was strong. Maybe too strong. And she was worried about trying the Vampire's son, after how difficult controlling his dad had been...

Vee weighed her choices as she left the palace, humming to herself. She was worried, sure, but not enough that it bothered her. With the lights from the palace disappearing behind her, and the taste of sugar on her tongue, she found herself in a better mood than she'd been in weeks.

And now that she had Fey on her side? Now that they were practically family?

Well... she was unstoppable now, wasn't she?

CHAPTER 54

JASPER

"**H**ey, Mom?"

Jasper rapped on the door and waited. When there was no answer, he didn't bother knocking again, just pushed the door to the tiny studio apartment open and walked in.

One glance around the room had him swallowing an annoyed sigh.

His mother was there, sleeping on her armchair, wrapped in a tattered old blanket one of the other older Wolves had knitted for her. The fabric was threadbare and moth eaten from years of use. He'd tried to replace it once, when he was a kid, had saved up for months to buy her the most expensive blanket from the most high-end Witch shop in the city. But she'd never used it. She preferred this one, old and ratty as it was.

"Mom," Jasper said, voice barely a whisper, as he stepped closer. The place was clean but could use a full scrub down, he noticed as he glanced around. He'd have Mara arrange to have her sister visit again, to clean the place properly from top to bottom. His mother hated relying on anyone else to clean her place, but maybe he'd stretch the truth just a tad for her. He could tell her Mara's sister was down on her luck and needed the money, maybe? Yeah. Mom would like that, would like to think she was helping someone in the community.

Jasper reached out and shook her shoulder, gently.

"Mom, wake up," he said softly as he could. Finally, she opened her eyes, blinking up at him with caramel-colored eyes.

"Oh! Jasper!" she said, face splitting into a warm grin. "What are you doing here, so late?"

Jasper bit back his own smile. "It's not late, mom. The sun only rose a few hours ago. Hey—have you seen Viv? I thought she was supposed to be here last night."

Blinking hard to ease the sleep from her eyes, his mother looked around her apartment.

"She's not here?" she asked, confused.

"Nope, not here. Unless you've tucked her into the icebox."

"Oh." She reached out and swatted at him. "You and your jokes, Jasper. Well, let me think, let me think. I don't think she's supposed to be here, not tonight. And she wasn't supposed to be with you?"

Jasper shook his head.

"What's going on? Is she in trouble?"

"No, Mom," Jasper said. "I just... I feel like I'm seeing her less and less, you know? I just want to make sure she's okay, keeping out of trouble. I thought she was here, and maybe we could go for a run, but..."

He motioned around at the clearly empty apartment.

His mother sat up further, and Jasper recognized the subtle shift as she swung into problem-solving mode.

"Well, she can't be at Karla's because that old bat is out of town visiting family for another week."

"You shouldn't call your friends names, Mom," he chided her.

"Why not?" she asked. "Honestly, you should hear what she calls me, the old bat. It's much worse. I'd have to cover your ears."

Jasper chuckled.

"Have you tried that little warehouse she and her friends are always hiding out in?"

"The clubhouse?" Jasper's smile widened. The place brought back memories of when he was young, and he and his friends spent their days there, getting into trouble. He should have known his mom knew about it, even back then. "Yeah, actually, that was the first place I checked. Declan's younger brother was there. You remember him?"

"Jayce." His mom smiled. "Ah, he is a good lad."

"Yeah, Jayce. He said he hadn't seen her."

His mother frowned and looked at him, really looked at him—the look that made him feel like she could see through him to every sin he'd ever committed.

"You're worried," she declared.

"I... yeah, I guess I am. I am worried."

His mother reached out and gave his arm a comforting pat. "She'll turn up," she assured him, smiling. "Trust me, they always do. Sometimes you just have to wait for them to get out of whatever mess they've gotten themselves into first. But they always turn up."

JASPER CONSIDERED her words on his walk home, back to his own apartment. It had been a surprise not to find Viv at the clubhouse. He'd hoped whatever trouble she was getting into, at least she had the rest of the pack around her. This worried him, her going off without them, doing only the Goddess knew what.

He spent the last few nights with Alastair and Fey, and would gladly have stayed there even longer if guilt over Viv hadn't set in. It had been days since he'd last seen her. He didn't want to be just another male in her life who vanished, just another family member who treated her like a stray pup. He wanted to be her Uncle Jas, the one who was there for her no matter what, the one who she could trust.

He just wasn't sure how.

The deadbolt made a heavy sound as he unlocked his door and stepped inside.

Goddess, maybe he needed Mara's sister to come clean his place more than his mother did. It was a mess, pizza boxes piled next to the sink, beer bottles he hadn't taken out to the recycling...

And his niece, sitting cross-legged on his kitchen table, stuffing her face with cookies.

"Feet!" he said, almost instinctually, even before the relief of seeing her set in. "Shoes off the furniture, Viv!"

She smiled at him, scooting forward and unfolding her legs from underneath her to let them dangle off the edge of the table. A few crumbs slipped out of her mouth, falling to the floor, when she grinned.

"What in the world are you eating?" Jasper asked. He stepped forward and plucked one from the open box on her lap, frowning at it. Some sort of... purple round thing? He gave it a sniff.

Vivian smiled at him. "They're called macarons. And they're delicious."

He'd never even heard of a "macaron" before.

"Where did you even get these?"

"None of your business," Viv told him. She reached up as though to snatch the cookie back from him, but Jasper quickly popped it into his mouth and chewed it with a smile.

It was... odd. A little too sweet. He wasn't sure he liked it. And the taste...

"What is that flavor?" he asked, frowning.

"Lavender," Vivian told him smugly.

Jasper blinked. "That's a smell. Not a flavor."

"Well, rich people think it's a flavor, and I think it's nice, okay?"

Jasper sighed. Rich people, huh?

"Viv... did you steal these?" he asked, exasperated.

Vivian snorted and kicked her legs. She didn't answer.

Okay, time for some tough love.

"Viv?" Jasper repeated, voice harder.

"No, I did not steal them," Vivian said. But she looked away a little too quickly. "Not technically, anyway."

"And what does that mean, 'not technically'?"

"I was told I could have as many as I wanted, whenever I wanted, alright?" Vivian insisted. "Just because no one was around when I took this particular batch doesn't mean it was stealing. I had permission."

He wasn't sure he could argue with that one, so he let it slide. Triumphant, Vivian popped another cookie in her mouth.

"Hey, I'm glad you're here," Jasper said, rubbing at the back of his neck. "I've been wanting to talk to you. Have you been...uh.... How are you doing?"

Goddess, he wasn't good at this.

Vivian chewed her cookie, cocking an eyebrow at him. "What do you mean, Uncle Jas?"

"I'm just..." Jasper ran a hand through his hair, suddenly awkward. "I spoke to Nan today." Viv froze for a moment, then began chewing more quickly, a sure sign she was hiding something. She was a terrible liar. Just like her mom.

Jasper took a breath. "She hasn't been seeing you around much. And she seems to think you've been spending your time here."

"Well." Vivian swallowed her bite. "You know Nan, Uncle Jas. She gets confused, doesn't she? Half the time she doesn't even remember where I'm supposed to be. Or even what time it is."

Jasper thinned his lips. "I'm not looking for an excuse, Viv. Or even an explanation. I'm just... I'm worried about you, okay?" He gave her a smile. "I just want to make sure that you're doing alright."

"Just alright?" Vivian repeated, smiling broadly at him.

His smile grew to match hers.

"More than just alright," he assured her. "I want to make sure you're happy. Healthy."

Vivian popped the last piece of cookie in her mouth and patted his arm consolingly. She gave him a crooked smile, so like her mother's. "Don't worry about me, Uncle Jasper... I've never been better."

CHAPTER 55

FEY

The sudden knock on the door was so loud and so forceful, Fey almost went to grab her blades.

It was early. Early enough the sun hadn't risen, so when the knocking woke Fey up and she sat up swearing, Alastair was still next to her, awake, reading in bed.

"Who the fuck is that?" he asked, as though she had any more idea than he did.

"I've got it," Fey told him, throwing the covers off herself and getting to her feet. She grabbed a robe on the way, tying it around her waist.

Whoever it was better have a damn good reason for getting her up, Fey thought angrily, as she unlatched the door and opened it.

It was Alice. Alice, standing at her door, fist raised to knock again. Alice, who stared at her with so many emotions flickering over her face that Fey couldn't focus on any singular one.

"Have you been here all night?" Alice asked, voice too hurried, too frantic.

Fey's lip curled. "What in the fuck is that supposed to mean?"

"Just—" Alice took a deep, shuddering breath, as though to calm herself. "Just, please, Fey. Answer me. Have you been here all night? Since the sun went down? Here, and nowhere else?"

Fey mentally retraced her steps before nodding.

"Yeah," she said. "I've been here since... two this afternoon, or thereabouts. So, all day, all evening, all night. What is this, Alice? What is this about?"

A small look of relief passed over Alice's face. She stepped inside, and Fey closed the door behind her.

"And the Vamp?" Alice was asking, looking around. "He's been here too?"

"That Vamp has a name," Alastair reminded her, coming out of the bedroom and glaring at her. "So lovely of you to stop by, Alice. Now kindly fuck off."

"I'm not asking you, I'm asking her," Alice snapped. She turned back to Fey. "He's been here with you all night? All evening? He can verify that you've been here?"

Anger filled Fey's voice as she answered. "Yes, Alice. He has been here, with me, all night."

Alice nodded, almost absently. "Good," she murmured. Her hands came up to hold her arms, hugging herself tightly. "That's good."

"Alice, what the fuck is—" Fey had taken a step toward her sister but was stopped. Alastair was there, suddenly, between the two of them, his outreached hand blocking her from moving forward another step.

"She smells like blood, Fey," he told her, his voice a dangerous warning. "Someone else's blood."

"I need to ask you something, babe, and I need you to be completely honest with me, okay?" Alice looked almost crazed, eyes frantic. Fey had never seen her like this.

Fey had never seen any Blade like this.

She pushed Alastair's hand aside and stepped closer to her sister.

"Fine. Complete honesty." Fey promised. She crossed her arms over her chest. "And then I want the same from you."

"Tell me you can't use the fifth element," Alice said, taking a step toward her. "I need to hear you say it, Fey. Please."

Alastair's temper frayed even further. "Alice, what the fuck—"

"Swear it to me, Fey!" Alice insisted, ignoring Alastair entirely.

"I can't do Blood Magic, Alice," Fey answered in a dark voice.

"Swear it!"

Fey's lip curled, anger twisting her words. "On the Goddess, I swear it. On my life, Alice, I swear to you that I cannot do Blood Magic."

Tension washed away from Alice's muscles.

"Thank you," she whispered. The hands clutching her arms loosened their grip, and her shoulders eased lower. "Thank you."

"No." Fire and rage roared in Fey's chest. "You don't get to come in here asking questions like that and then thank me. What the fuck, Alice? What the hell is going on?"

With a groan, Alice put her face in her hands.

"I think... I think the council is in a lot of trouble, Fey... I think..." She let out a long breath and looked up at Alastair, eyes narrowing. "Does he have to be here for this?"

"It's my fucking house!" Alastair said in a raised voice.

"Yes," Fey said over him. "He does have to be here. Talk."

"Fine." Alice threw him one last reproachful look. "But he might not want to hear this."

"I'm very quickly running out of patience, sister," Fey said, voice low and dangerous. "Tell me what the fuck is happening."

Alice's jaw tightened. "I think someone is attacking the council members, one by one. I think they've been killing them."

"The council?" Fey asked, frowning.

Alice nodded. "First Kellos. And then..."

Alastair shifted. "My father?" he asked, voice raw.

Alice nodded again.

"And whoever it is..." Fey paused, putting it together. "You think it's a Blood Witch, don't you? Someone who can use the fifth element?"

"I don't just think it, babe. I know it," Alice said. "They got to Linh, tonight. Someone killed her, right in front of us."

Fey hissed out a breath.

"It was..." Alice looked down at her hands. "She was like a puppet, being controlled by something we couldn't see. She was fine just a few minutes before, and then suddenly." Alice shuddered. "I've seen that before. When I was first inducted into the Blades, we were sent to hunt down a rogue Blood Witch. One the White Priestesses must have missed during her awakening. And she was…"

Alice looked up, staring into Fey's eyes. There was no trace of the strong, confident Witch Fey knew in those eyes. Alice looked terrified. "She was horrifying. She captured one of ours, used that… magic on her. And it was like, she was a doll suddenly, like she was just a shell with nothing inside." She swallowed, eyes growing distant, lost in the memory. "Only two of us made it out that night. She took down two Blades before we could stop her, Fey."

Fey's eyes flashed. "And tonight, you thought it was me?" Rage rose, suffocatingly hot inside of her. Alastair stared at Alice with obvious disgust on his face. "Me? Attacking the council?"

"Can you blame me?" Alice asked. "You walked away from the antidote with all four pure powers. What if you had them all, Fey? You would have known how we would have reacted to that. How I would have reacted. You would have hidden it. Don't lie, you know you would have."

"Fuck you," Fey snapped. But she didn't deny it.

Alice groaned, stepping back away from her and looking around helplessly. "It could be anyone, couldn't it? Any of the Witches we've given the antidote to."

"New Witches, too," Fey added, thinking. "Now that there aren't any priestess overseeing the Awakenings, there's no way of knowing how many are out there."

Fey took a measured breath, trying to gather her thoughts.

It really could be anyone. Any Witch in the city. And they had no way of finding them.

"I need you to come and speak to the council, Fey," Alice said, voice low, as though asking it pained her.

Anger, hot and fast, surged through her.

"Why?" Fey asked. "I just told you this isn't me."

"I believe you," Alice said, meeting her eyes. "Truly, Fey, I do. But you have to understand how this looks. Someone has been threatening the council, and now they're killing them. And it's your face on those posters, babe. The council is already scared of how much power you have, but if you just let them talk to you… question you…"

Fey curled her lip in a sneer. Alastair placed a comforting hand on her shoulder.

"Please, Fey," Alice said, her voice breaking. "They'll need to hear it from you. And you... you can help with this. If there's a Blood Witch out there, someone going after us?" Alice swallowed. "Fey, imagine something strong enough to take down two Blades in their prime. Something strong enough to take down the Fallen King. I can't take someone like that on my own. You know I can't."

Fey suddenly understood what Alice was really asking.

"You want me there, with the council, in case she strikes again?" she asked, voice cautious.

Alice nodded. "We need to stop her now. Whoever she is, we need to stop her before she goes any further. Before she..." Alice blinked, a new realization hitting her. Her face twisted in horror. "Fey, what if she goes after our families? What if she goes after Joy?"

Joy. Something rolled through Fey, strong enough to push her anger aside. A sour, sickening emotion. Fear.

What if she goes after Joy? But it wasn't Joy's face Fey saw. It was Willow's. Willow's face, her mouth open in shock, her throat slit open while Fey watched, unable to do anything but scream.

Willow. Who she should have been able to protect.

Never again.

"When is the council meeting next?" Fey heard herself ask as Alastair's grip tightened on her shoulder, grounding her.

"Tomorrow night," Alice answered.

Fey nodded. Under Alastair's bed, kept in a decorative wooden box, her Queen's Blades sat, waiting for a moment like this. Maybe it was time to get them out again.

"I'll be there," Fey promised.

CHAPTER 56
ALICE

Joy had been furious.

"Our own sister, Alice?" she'd said, disgust and anger swirling in her beautiful blue eyes. The air in the apartment had turned so cold it had stung Alice's skin. And she'd endured it without complaint. "You accused our own sister of this? Of hiding it from us?"

It did nothing to eclipse the shame she already felt inside. Nothing to eclipse the disgust she felt in herself.

But she'd had no choice, had she?

"I had to be sure," Alice told her, trying to hide the pain in her voice. Joy had turned her back on her, then, and gone to the bedroom alone, slamming the door behind her. She didn't bother saying goodbye to her when Alice left for the council meeting that evening.

We can spend our whole lives fighting for balance, fighting for stability, but eventually everything falls to chaos, no matter how hard you try to stop it.

Was Kallista right? Was Fey—was *Joy*—just another thing she might lose to that chaos?

It felt like the tighter she tried to hold on to the things around her, the tighter she gripped the stable things in her life, the quicker they vanished.

Alice tried to shake those thoughts away.

There was no time for thoughts like that.

It was time for the council to convene again.

FEY WAS the last to arrive.

To Alice's surprise, the other members of the council were already there and waiting by the time she'd entered the throne room. All of them, despite the danger, despite the morbid specter of Linh's death hanging over them all, had shown up. Even Sana, pale-faced and trembling, sat in her usual seat, straight backed and looking determined.

The Water Witch had more courage than Alice gave her credit for, clearly.

Someone had cleaned Linh's blood from the table. Alice couldn't help but stare at the spot where it had been, wondering who it could have been. A servant, maybe? Or Sana herself?

An oppressive silence hung over the room as they waited.

Callum was the first to break it.

"Tell us about these Blood Witches," he said, and though he, too, stared at that spot on the table, Alice knew he was speaking to her.

"Blood Witches are the most dangerous of our entire Faction. They hold power over every living creature," Alice answered, voice rote. "They can reach inside your mind and command you to act and bend you to their will."

"Do they need to be close by?" Sana asked, voice a frightened whisper. She glanced around the room as she spoke, eyes bouncing between the doors all around the throne room. Too many doors.

Alice had long known how indefensible the throne room had been, with so many avenues of ingress. She'd placed soldiers in the halls tonight, to guard the doors. But the palace hadn't had many to spare, and she almost hadn't bothered.

If the Blood Witch came tonight, it's not like a few guards could stop her.

"It's harder with distance," Alice answered. "But not impossible."

"You really believe this could be the work of your sister?" Kallista asked, tapping her painted fingernail absently against the wood of the table.

Alice shook her head.

"I thought... maybe. But now, no. No, I don't think it's her."

Callum shifted in his seat.

"And you're sure it's only Witches with this power?" he asked. Something in his tone tugged at Alice, and she turned to look at him. Unlike Sana, Callum didn't look scared. He looked... sad.

Before Alice could tease that mystery apart, the front doors opened, and every head pivoted toward the door as Fey walked in.

Head held high, blood-red hair cascading down her back, Fey entered the throne room like a queen. Alice couldn't help but glance toward Kallista. But if the Demon thought anything at all of Fey, or the danger she might pose the council, she hid it behind a mask of cold indifference.

Fey stopped before the council table, eyes sweeping over the members of the council one by one, before finally landing on Alice.

"I'm here, sister," Fey said, eyes flashing. "Let's get this over with."

Maybe Joy was right. Maybe she had crossed a line by accusing Fey. Her chest felt unnaturally tight.

But it was too late to change that now.

"Tell the council what you told me," Alice demanded.

Fey took a deep breath. "I was home all yesterday evening and night," she stated with barely contained anger coloring her voice. "And my partner Alastair can confirm that. I have not set foot here, or anywhere else in this palace, since the last time this council summoned me. And I'd have happily stayed away forever, if you'd let me."

"And?" Sana prompted. She sounded almost frightened to ask.

Fey raised her eyebrow and somehow made that simple act look like a declaration of war.

"And what?" Fey asked, rage flashing in her eyes.

Sana took a steading breath. "Do you have access to the fifth element, Fey? I... I have to record your answer for our meeting notes, so please. We need a verbal answer. Are you a Blood Witch?"

Fey's lip rose in a sneer. "If I were a Blood Witch," she said, voice dripping with violence, "Queen Edelin would have slit her own throat long before she'd had a chance to lay one finger on me or my sisters."

It was, all things considered, a terrible choice of words giving what had just happened to Alastair's father. Alice glanced over quickly to see Callum's face, to see if the imagery had bothered him.

But he didn't look upset. Instead, he was frowning at Fey, eyes still inexplicably sad.

"If that's all?" Fey prompted, looking around at them. "I had nothing to do with any of the council member's deaths. And I swear to the Goddess herself that I cannot use Blood Magic. I'm not the one you're looking for."

"I believe you, Fey," Callum said, suddenly. Alice frowned, watching him closely. Why did he sound so heartbroken? "I believe you when you say you can't use Blood Magic."

He stared straight into her eyes, like she'd shattered his heart.

"But my brother can, can't he?"

CHAPTER 57

FEY

The blood drained from Fey's face at Callum's words.

No.

"We call it Persuasion, not Blood Magic," Callum explained. "It's rare, now. Our father always thought it was a genetic throwback to when Witches and Vampires still... bred with one another. Like they left a gift of their magic behind in our bloodline."

"You're wrong," Fey said.

"I'm not," Callum answered. "Alastair might have tried to hide it, tried to keep it from his family... but I know, Fey. I know what he can do. Father knew, too."

No. She could see it in his eyes. She could hear it in his voice. He really thought Alastair could be a murderer.

"Callum... You can't honestly believe your brother did this? Killed your father? Why?"

"He hated our Father, Fey. You know that."

"Not enough to kill him," Fey insisted.

Callum laughed, a hollow, unamused sound.

"Then you really don't know him at all, do you?" he said softly.

"What are you saying, Callum?" Alice asked, voice sharp.

He shook his head.

"I'm not really sure what I'm saying," he admitted. "I know that I believe Fey when she says she has no Blood Magic. But she doesn't have to have it, don't you see? Witches aren't the only ones who can do this. *We* can. Just a few of us, but..."

"Are you accusing your brother of killing two members of this council?" Kallista asked, voice low.

Fey stared at him, pleading with him to meet her eyes.

"Callum, don't do this. You're wrong," she hissed. "Alastair had nothing to do with this. He was with me the night your father died. With me and—"

Fey swallowed the other name, keeping it close to her chest. She wouldn't bring him into this.

"I don't know if I am accusing him," Callum admitted to Kallista. He stared at the table in front of him. "I wish I could tell you that he didn't do this, but... I just don't know."

"Why?" Fey asked. "Why would he kill Kellos?"

"I think that's a question we need to ask him," Alice said, voice dark.

Fey's eyes snapped to her sister.

No. She knew that voice. Alice believed him, believed what Callum was saying.

"You have to see how this looks, don't you?" Alice continued. Her calm, rational voice. Alice didn't believe her anymore. Fey's heart raced.

"Alastair had nothing to do with this. With any of this," she insisted. "He has nothing against the council."

The members of the council exchanged heavy glances.

"Alice, look at me," Fey said, desperately. She didn't.

"Alice, *look at me.*" This time, Alice did glance up. Those warm, soft eyes weren't so soft anymore.

"You're making a mistake," Fey said. Fear gripped her throat, poisoning her words. When Alice had accused her, she'd been furious. But accusing Alastair? Her heart raced with panic. Something white hot and unstoppable rising inside of her.

Fey didn't need blood magic to take this city to its knees. And she would. If they threatened him, if they made one move to hurt her Alastair?

Power crackled at her fingertips at the thought.

Fey took a breath, letting her rage burn through her, letting it build. "He didn't do this," she said in a voice full of violence. "And if any of you try to—"

Fey stopped. The world stopped.

The air seemed to shift around the room. It crackled with energy for a single second, little more than the space of a heartbeat. They felt it, too, the members of the council. Everything stilled.

And just like that, the feeling was gone. Vanished.

A moment later, the world went black as night.

CHAPTER 58

FEY

Panic swelled in Fey's chest as the world around her went completely, impossibly dark. The throne room, the council members, they all disappeared in an instant, swallowed by an unbearable blanket of darkness.

Is this it? Fey thought, twisting to look around frantically and seeing nothing but solid, black void around her. *Am I being controlled?*

Panic filled her. Coming here was a mistake, a terrible mistake, Fey realized suddenly. All she and Alice had done was manage to give the Blood Witch access to one of the strongest weapons in the realm. If the Witch could use Fey's powers against the council...

Her sister. Alice was in danger. Callum, *Callum* was in danger. If she were being controlled, she wouldn't be able to protect them, wouldn't be able to save them...

From herself. From her own power.

But... no. The world was black, Fey realized, but not empty. Somewhere in the dark, she heard Sana gasp in shock. She heard Alice swear. There were sounds around her, distant and muffled, but still there. The crash of a chair falling over as someone stood too fast. Their frantic intakes of breath.

Not controlled, no. They were still there, all of them, still in the throne room. She could feel the ground beneath her feet. Her body was her own, her mind was her own.

So where had all the light gone?

A low, dangerous laugh came from the darkness around her, and Fey felt the blood in her veins turn to ice.

"Oh, you stupid, stupid thing," came a soft, sensual voice. Bitter laughter followed the words. It was everywhere in the dark, swirling all around her, coming from all directions. It echoed in the empty void around her.

No. Not empty.

Full of shadows.

Kallista, Fey realized, heart pounding. The taste of fear was bitter on her tongue.

"Did you really think you could control *me*?" the Demon was saying, and suddenly there was something more in the darkness around them, something dangerous. Something ancient and wild.

Something undying.

The shadows were alive. Full of something awful and vicious and hungry.

RUN, screamed that voice in Fey's head, an instinct so deep it recognized this threat around her.

But Fey wouldn't run.

"Fight it, Kallista!" Fey called into the dark. "Don't you dare let her control you!"

Goddess save them, if she'd been panicked to think about what the Blood Witch could do with her own powers...

What about the powers of a Demon stronger than anything Fey had ever seen? What could she do with this creature, so strong it drove every instinct in Fey to run, run, run, and never look back?

"I don't need to fight it," came Kallista's answer, full of rage and power. It came from the surrounding shadows, from everywhere the light couldn't touch. Someone was crying in the dark, scared, gasping sobs. Sana, maybe. "Insignificant insect. You think you have the power to control me? I'm older than you could possibly imagine."

Fey drew a quick frantic breath as the darkness vanished, shadows pulling away from the walls and coalescing, swirling like a vortex.

Kallista stood in the middle of the throne room, shadows dancing around her, twisting and turning like smoke.

"I have her," Kallista whispered, eyes unfocused and head tilted to the side. "She's running. But she can't escape me now. Not for long."

CHAPTER 59
VEE

Death comes in many forms.

But Vee never thought it could come from the shadows.

She stumbled through the hallway, nearly tripping over the body of an unconscious guard as she rushed to get away. *Sleep*, she'd told him when she'd come across him earlier in the dark. His body didn't move as she stumbled over it.

She'd fucked up. She'd broken their first rule, the most important rule.

Don't get caught.

It had never occurred to her that the council would suspect Fey. How could they? She could have killed them all in an instant, with all that power she had inside her. Why would she have needed to take them out one by one like Vee had?

Listening at the door, Vee had been furious at them. And terrified that they wanted to punish Fey for something she'd never done. Punish Alastair for something he'd never done. She just wanted to scare them, just wanted to show them it couldn't be Fey, that they could let her go, leave her and Alastair alone.

The Demon hadn't showed any powers, and she hadn't felt like the others, so Vee had thought...

Controlling the Fallen King had been like trying to hold water in her hands, his power seeping away from her no matter how hard she tried to hold it. But the Demon?

The moment she'd reached to control her, Vee knew something was wrong. Terribly, terribly wrong. Her blood felt like ichor, thick and terrible, and when she'd reached into her mind, there was only darkness.

Deep, cold emptiness.

Now Vee ran, but that darkness was all around her. Following her.

There were shadows, on the wall, reaching for her, stretching toward her.

Hissing, she leapt away as a tendril of shadow snaked out from the wall and reached for her ankle. The bright torches around the palace seemed to be keeping the shadows away, for now. She didn't want to think what would happen if they touched her, if they got her...

She needed to escape. She needed to go somewhere safe, where she had the advantage. She needed...

Leverage.

Something in her chest tightened as a plan formed, some part of her screaming out in pain, demanding another answer, another solution. But Vee pushed it down, swallowing it whole.

She was a survivor. And she would survive this.

Whatever it took.

"Hey, Vee," Jayce called out, smiling as he watched her storm into the clubhouse. She slammed her hand over the light switch on the wall the second she arrived, turning on the bulb that hung from the ceiling. "Check out the score we got tonight. Paul found a mansion near the border that hasn't been occupied in months, and we—"

He stopped and stared at her. Vee was panicked.

And Vee never, ever panicked.

"Vee?" he asked, scrambling to stand up. "Vee, what's going on? What's wrong?"

"I messed up," Vee muttered. She looked around frantically, her breaths quick and panicked. She rushed from the light switch to the lamp they kept in the corner, turning it on. Scowling, she tore the lamp shade from it, flooding the room with even more light. "I got caught."

"Vee—" Jayce started.

"No time," she interrupted. "Do we still have those massive lights on the poles? The ones we took from that factory by the docks?"

Jayce blinked. "Flood lights," he told her. "And yeah. We have three of them, down in the basement."

"I need them. And I need you to set them up. All of them, up on the roof." She was manic, her head twisting as she looked around the warehouse. She positioned herself in the center of the room, directly under the overhead light. "And they need to overlap, do you understand? All of them pointed at the center of the roof, no ... no shadows between them, okay? And then I need you to get everyone out of here. Take them to my Nan's, take them to Jasper's place. Take them anywhere, I don't care, but they all need to be gone."

"Vee," Jayce said, voice soft. "I can help. We can help. Whatever it is you did. Just talk to me."

Vee growled so furiously Jayce took an involuntary step back.

"It's too late, Jayce," she snapped. "I told you, I got caught. There's no fixing this anymore. I need you to get everyone out. I can't let anyone else go down for my mistake. I can't let anyone else get hurt."

"What happened?" Jayce pressed.

Her power hit him so quickly he had no time to react. One moment he was taking a step toward her, and the next he was on his knees, kneeling.

"*No more questions,*" Vee ordered. "Get the lights up and get everyone out, Jayce. As soon as you can. Do you understand me?"

As quickly as she had taken him, she let go, and that power that held him in her grasp was gone. Jayce blinked, heart pounding.

"I understand," he said. "I'll do it. But, Vee, you're not alone anymore. And we're not little kids. We can help, we can..."

He looked up, but the room was empty.

She was already gone.

CHAPTER 60

JASPER

Jasper awoke to the sound of someone ransacking his kitchen.

It had been so long since anyone had been stupid enough to break into his home, the sounds didn't fully rouse him, not right away. For a moment he just lay in his bed, lost in the fog that exists between sleep and consciousness.

Then something shattered, and that fog dissipated in an instant. Jasper was awake, snarling as he barreled out of his bedroom and into the kitchen.

But it wasn't a thief who awaited him there. It wasn't a thief who had ransacked the place, upending drawers and digging through his cupboards.

It was Vivian.

"Viv?" Jasper asked, looking around at the mess. His floor was covered in a hodgepodge of junk. Tools and kitchen utensils. He tried to step around it all, pushing aside a ladle with his foot to make room.

Vivian was buried in a lower cabinet, on her hands and knees. She whipped her head out to scream, "Don't turn off that light!" before immediately diving back in, digging through his emergency supplies. She tossed items out behind her, leaving them in a pile on the ground.

"She can move through the dark," Vivian was muttering, her voice so low Jasper could barely hear her. "I don't know how, but she can. Dark and shadows. She controls them, somehow."

"Who are you talking about?" Jasper asked, pushing more junk out of the way to take another step forward.

Vivian didn't answer. With a squeal, she scrambled backward, back onto the kitchen floor, an emergency lantern clasped victoriously in her hands. It was a crank operated light, something he only kept in case the electricity went out.

Vee ignored him as she began to charge the lantern, cranking the lever so fast Jasper worried she might dislocate her arm.

"Hey, slow down," Jasper said. "Here, I can help you with that—"

He reached out, but Vivian scrambled away from him, frantic.

There was an organization to the chaos in his kitchen, Jasper suddenly realized, looking around. Sure, the kitchen floor was covered in junk, but...

On the counters were every flashlight and candle he owned, carefully set aside. Matches. Lighters.

"Viv... what's going on?"

She didn't answer.

"Vivian, whatever is happening, I can help you, I can—"

The emergency lantern flared to life when Vivian flipped the switch, and in the soft glow of the kitchen lamp it blazed like a small sun. Jasper quickly looked away, blinking.

"You can't help me," Vivian told him. She sounded a little sad. But she didn't look at him as she stood and clipped the lantern to her waist. Didn't even glance his way as she scooped batteries and flashlights off his counter, shoving some into her pockets and securing others to her arms and legs with rubber bands.

"Please. Viv—"

She stopped. Staring down at the mess on the floor, she frowned, as though only now noticing what she had done.

"Hey, Uncle Jas?" Vivian asked softly. "Can you tell Nan I'm sorry?"

"Stay right there, Viv," Jasper told her, heart sinking. He ducked back into his room, grabbing a pair of pants and pulling them on. Shirt, where was his shirt? "Whatever this is, you can talk to me. We can deal with it together."

There—a shirt, not clean, but clean enough. He grabbed it, rushing back to the kitchen. "Sit down, and just tell me what—"

"*Sleep*," Vee said, the word echoing through Jasper's skull like a bell.

He was unconscious before his body hit the ground.

CHAPTER 61
AMALIA

At first, she thought it was a dream.

"This is your fault, you know," a voice told her. A voice she recognized. A voice she trusted.

Amalia was slow to wake, her eyelids fighting against opening. Sleep was a warm comfort, and something was pulling her up, up away from that wonderful emptiness and into consciousness.

She blinked tired eyes, squinting around her bedroom.

A figure. A person, standing in her doorway, surrounded by a halo of bright white light.

"Vee?" Amalia asked, her voice heavy with sleep.

"You were just so trusting. So eager to please, to be seen."

Amalia blinked. What time was it? What was Vee talking about? Rubbing the crust from her eyes, she forced herself to sit up, that warm blanket of sleep giving way to a cold reality.

It was Vee standing there. Vee, with flashlights strapped to her, taped to her clothing. Amalia frowned, squinting against the blinding light.

Was she crying?

"Why didn't she kill you that night?" Vee was asking, and it took a long moment for Amalia to process the words. Like her brain wouldn't let her understand what was happening. "When the Blades killed your parents, why didn't they kill you, too? Why were you spared, Princess?"

"Vee... what's going on?" Amalia asked, fear creeping into her voice.

"It's not fair, you know," Vee was saying, ignoring her entirely. Amalia couldn't see her face, the light hurt her eyes too much to stare at it for long. "I hated you. Hated you for so long..."

Finally, something clicked, and the words began to sink in. Amalia's mouth went dry.

"Why do you get all of this?" Vee asked. Through the blinding light, Amalia could have sworn Vee was crying, tears flowing down both cheeks. "Fresh cookies every morning. Clean clothes. All of these *stupid fucking dresses*. Why do you get all of this when the rest of us get nothing?"

"Vee, what are you talking about—"

"You have no idea what it's like to suffer, do you? No idea what it's like to be hungry, to be left behind? No idea what it's like to have to scrape and steal and work for every little thing in life? All of this was just... just handed to you, wasn't it?"

Amalia couldn't seem to draw enough air to breathe.

"I didn't want to hurt you. I didn't want to *like* you," Vee was saying. "But I did. I did like you. And now..." A sob. Or maybe a laugh. "Now... now everything is fucked, isn't it?"

She should run. But this was her friend, and her friend was in pain. Amalia reached out to her, wanting to comfort her.

She didn't make it.

Pain shot through her. Amalia let out a gasp as her arm froze, just a centimeter from Vee's, pain coursing down her body.

Finally, Vee looked at her, and there was nothing friendly in those beautiful green eyes.

"I didn't want it to go down like this," Vee said, and Amalia let out a soft gasp as her knees buckled, as her body twisted and bent until she was on the ground, on her knees before Vee. Before her friend. "But sacrifices have to be made, don't they?"

She opened her mouth to say something, anything, but her body wouldn't respond, wouldn't listen to her. There was a roar in her ears, like a storm.

Terror gripped her.

"It's finally time for you to suffer for a change, Princess. Time for someone else to take charge of this miserable city."

CHAPTER 62

FEY

The throne room was filled with quiet terror after the attack on Kallista.

"She's running. Trying to hide from me," the Demon told them. "But she can't run forever."

"It's not...?" Callum began.

"This is no Vampire," Kallista assured him. The visible relief in Callum's eyes was nowhere near as strong as the flash of guilt Fey saw there. He'd really believed it, if even for a moment. Believed his brother was capable of this.

Fey met Alice's eyes. No more doubt there, not from either one of them.

"Keep searching, Kallista," Alice said, eyes still on Fey.

A Blood Witch. A real Blood Witch, in the city, hell bent on bringing them all down.

"I think it's time to get your blades, sister," Alice told her.

FEY HADN'T WORN her blades since the night of the Blood Moon. For weeks after, she'd kept them at the foot of her bed, just in case. It had been hard, back then, to think there would be a time in her life without them. Hard to put up that mantle and put that part of her to rest.

Joy had helped. One day she'd come home with a decorative cedar box, just large enough to fit both her blades. The weapons remained next to her bed, carefully nestled in that box until she'd moved in with Alastair.

It had been easier to put them away for good, then, tucking the box under his bed and out of sight. She'd felt okay leaving that part of her behind.

Now, storming into their home, her powers thrumming to life inside of her, Fey felt those blades pulling her toward them like a beacon.

She had expected Alastair to be working at the club tonight. He wasn't. And he wasn't alone. Fey stopped for just a moment, staring in surprise at Jasper on their couch, hunched over himself as though in pain, leaning against Alastair's chest.

"What's going on?" she asked, throat constricting. "Is he hurt?"

Alastair shook his head.

"It's Vivian," Jasper said. He looked up at her, fear in his eyes. "Something's wrong with her."

Guilt twisted in Fey's stomach. She didn't have time, not even for him, not now. She was on a mission, and her sister needed her.

"I'm sorry," she told him. "I'm so sorry but...but I can't stay."

Alastair's gaze sharpened.

"What happened?" he asked.

"The council was attacked by a Blood Witch," Fey told him. When Alastair opened his mouth, the sharp look in his eye replaced with fear, she shook her head quickly. "Your brother is fine. They all are. But I have to go. Kallista is tracking her, and... they need me. The realm needs me."

Jasper nodded, slowly.

"Go," he told her. "Do what you need to do."

They knew who and what she was. And they understood, both of them.

Fey moved past them toward the bedroom, kneeling before the bed and reaching under it blindly. *Where was it, where was it?*

There. Her hand clasped the wood, and she pulled, yanking it out triumphantly. It was just as beautiful as she remembered, just as beautiful as the day Joy had brought it home for her. Her fingers trailed lovingly over the carved wood gently before she opened it.

The twin blades felt almost warm in her hands as she took them out.

As her fingers worked to attach the familiar sheaths to her thighs, Jasper's voice carried from the living room.

"I just don't understand what happened. One second, we were talking, and the next... nothing. Like I passed out."

"And she was just gone?" Alastair was asking.

"Vanished," Jasper answered, pain lacing the words. Fey's heart twisted in her chest. She would help him. Would help Vivian, too, as soon as she could. But not now. Whatever was happening with his niece could wait.

The danger to the realm couldn't.

"That's not even the weirdest part, though," Jasper continued. "She kept talking about... about *shadows,* and someone controlling them. She had to get away from the shadows. She wasn't making any sense, but—"

Fey's heart stuttered. In a numb haze, she stood, blades clasped in her hands, and slowly she stalked back into the living room.

"What did you just say?" she asked Jasper, praying she'd misheard.

Jasper blinked. "About Viv?"

"About shadows," Fey answered, her voice strained. Let her be wrong. Please let her be wrong.

"Viv... she said shadows were chasing her. Someone was controlling them, and... she needed to get away from them..."

No.

No, it couldn't be.

"Vivian's father..." Fey whispered. "The male who sired her. He was a Witch, wasn't he?"

Jasper's eyes narrowed. "I don't know what that has to do with—"

"Answer the fucking question," she ordered, baring her teeth. Jasper swallowed hard.

"Yes," Alastair answered for him. "He was a Witch."

No, no, no.

"It's her. She's the Blood Witch," Fey murmured, feeling the world tilt around her. "It's Vivian."

Jasper shook his head. "What? No. No, she's a Shifter, not a Witch. I've seen her Wolf, Fey."

"She's a Shifter with Witch blood," Alastair said, considering it. "It's... rare. But—"

"But she *could* be a Witch. She could have powers, couldn't she?" Fey finished for him. This was bad. Goddess, this was so bad. "Callum said something in the council meeting about shared genetic traits..."

She had to find her. Find her before Kallista did. Vivian was in danger. Her Jasper's Vivian.

"Where would she go, Jasper?" Fey asked.

He was panicked, his gaze unfocused, eyes so wide she could see too much white.

"She's not a Witch," he insisted, shaking his head. "She can't be. She would have told us, would have told her family. She would have told *me*."

"Focus." Fey snapped her fingers in front of his face. "Jasper, we need to find her. Now. She is in danger and every second counts. Where would she go?"

Kallista would find her. And Kallista would kill her.

Unless Fey could get to her first.

This time, when the memory of Willow's death jumped to her mind, her sister was wearing Vivian's face.

Jasper blinked. Finally, his eyes focused. First on Fey's hand, and then slowly rising to look her in the eyes.

"There's a warehouse," he said finally. "She and her friends hang out there. She thinks we don't know about it, but..." He took a deep breath. "It was Declan's hideout first. *Our* hideout. Declan's younger brother, Jayce... he's Vivian's best friend. That's where she'd go."

Fey slid her blades into place on her thighs. Their weight was a familiar comfort.

"Then that's where we're going," she said.

CHAPTER 63
ALICE

Joy was awake when she got home. Waiting up for her, like she always did, even when they fought. Even Joy's anger held a kernel of love, always.

Looking at her where she sat on their shared bed—seeing her beautiful soft blonde hair, her bright intelligent eyes—looking at her *hurt*.

I have to protect her, Alice thought, her heart twisting in her chest. She looked away quickly, bending down next to their bed and reaching for her blades.

No matter what... I have to protect this.

Joy took one look at Alice's face as she searched and knew something was wrong.

"Alice? What happened? You look... you look terrified."

"It wasn't Fey," Alice told her. Joy's gaze hardened, and she opened her mouth, probably to remind Alice she'd said so from the start. Alice raised her hand to silence her. "But it... it is a Blood Witch. Kallista is trying to find her now. I'm going after her. Fey and I are going to stop her."

Fear of what could happen if they weren't careful colored her next words. "I need you to hide, Joy. After I leave, I need you to lock the door, and —"

The air crackled with power.

"How dare you," Joy hissed. Her voice was cold as ice. "How *fucking* dare you."

"Joy—" Alice started, turning to look up at her. The power in the room roiled, a wild, untamed thing.

"I am not your pet," Joy said in a voice full of power. "I am your partner, Alice. I am the last of the Queen's Blades, and you will not treat me like... like a *liability*. You won't leave me here like I'm some powerless *thing*. Not when I can help."

Her eyes were so beautiful. So, so beautiful, even when she was angry.

And Alice loved her so much.

"Whatever this is, whatever you're chasing. We will do it together, Alice," Joy told her. "Don't you dare try to sideline me."

It hurt so much to look into those beautiful eyes.

Hurt so much to remember how it had felt to lose her.

"I can't lose you again," Alice admitted, the words catching in her throat. Her vision swam with tears. "I... it would kill me to lose you again, love. I wouldn't survive it. I know I wouldn't."

Joy gave her a small, beautiful smile. With a little sigh, she hopped off the bed and reached underneath it. She found Alice's blades with no effort at all and pulled them out.

"Then don't lose me," she answered, placing the weapons in Alice's outstretched hands. "You don't need to do this alone. You never did. Whatever this is... we will face it together. You need me, Alice. We need each other."

It was true. They did need her. Fey was powerful—maybe the most powerful thing in the realm other than Kallista.

But Joy?

Joy was a force of nature.

Somewhere along the way, Alice had forgotten that. Had forgotten that the last time she'd been responsible for protecting the realm, she hadn't done it alone. She'd never done it alone.

Swallowing her fears, Alice nodded.

"Get your blades, sister. The realm needs you," she murmured, setting her blades down and reaching out to squeeze Joy's hand in hers. Together... they would do this together.

Joy grinned and bounced to her feet, heading toward her dresser. Alice watched her, love blooming in her heart, when—

Something moved in her peripheral vision, and Alice turned, frowning. Shadows, in the corner, writhing like living creatures. Before she could consider what that meant, before she could decide what to do, the shadow struck, reaching out for her and wrapping around her mind.

Dark. A void so deep it felt like the pits of hell, like staring into oblivion.

Then a voice. Delicious and deadly, like poisoned sweets.

"I found her," Kallista's voice echoed through her head. Then the darkness shifted, changing, and images flooded her, fluttering before her eyes. The Western River. A factory—no, a warehouse. Two figures on the roof, surrounded by light.

"Come," Kallista commanded. And then the images were gone, the void was gone, and Alice gasped as she returned to her body, blinking hard, the dim light of their bedroom suddenly seeming so bright it was blinding.

"Alice?" Joy asked. "What happened? The shadows... it's like they took you away..."

"Kallista," Alice gasped. Her head throbbed from the invasion. "She's found the Blood Witch. I know where we need to go."

Then she shuddered, trying to shake off the feeling of that dark, empty void. Wrapping her arms around herself she murmured, "Goddess, that woman terrifies me."

Joy was already moving, scrambling with something in her dresser. She pulled a box out, flipping it open. Her blades—and her uniform. Alice hadn't realized she'd kept them.

"She showed you where to find her?" Joy asked, pulling off her nightclothes and slipping into her black leathers.

When she finished, Alice couldn't help but admire the creature who stood before her. The last Queen's Blade. The realm's most powerful weapon.

A weapon she'd forgotten.

How could she have forgotten this side of her? This beautiful, deadly Witch she'd fallen in love with?

"Yeah, she did," Alice said, placing a soft kiss on Joy's cheek, savoring the feeling of the mask under her lips. "It won't be hard to find. From the looks of it, they've set up a beacon to welcome us."

THEY FOLLOWED THE SHADOWS.

Kallista made it easy, directing them through the city streets, her dark shadows leading the way. But the Blood Witch made it even easier.

The lights from the top of the building were visible from half a city away.

When they finally reached the building, Joy didn't speak. She simply raised her hands, and a gentle current of wind lifted them both into the sky and toward the roof.

CHAPTER 64
AMALIA

Amalia was cold.

It felt stupid, at a time like this, to feel something as ordinary as *cold*. But kneeling on the brick rooftop, dressed in nothing but her flimsy white nightgown, there was no protection from the cold night breeze. Amalia shivered violently, wrapping her arms around herself.

The lights did nothing to keep the chill of the night air away. Amalia glanced up at the towering flood lights above them, casting near blinding white light over the rooftop.

A few feet away, Vee paced. Gone were the lights she'd strapped to herself. She didn't seem to need them now. Gone, too, were the invisible binds that had held Amalia immobile on their journey here. Gone was the invisible gag that had kept her quiet.

Her body was her own again.

"Aren't you worried I'll scream?" Amalia asked, watching Vee pace. She walked the same path, over and over again. Vee paced forward just a few feet, turned, then stalked back over the same steps. She never ventured too far from where the lights intersected. Like she was scared of getting too close to the dark areas of the roof.

Vee shrugged, not bothering to look at her. "You can scream, if it'll make you feel better. But it doesn't matter now. If they don't know where we are, they will soon enough."

Amalia swallowed.

"Why are you doing this?" she forced herself to ask. Her voice wavered as she spoke. "I thought ... I thought we were friends."

Goddess, she sounded pathetic, didn't she?

"You thought what I wanted you to think," Vee snapped. She did look at her, then. But all too quickly her eyes darted away, and her pace faltered.

No, that wasn't true. They were friends. Vee had been nice to her. They'd had fun together, they'd...

Kissed.

"You're lying," Amalia said, steel rising in her voice. "You do like me, you even said so yourself. I know you do. I know—"

"Do you want to know what your problem is, Princess?" Vee asked, stopping her endless march and turning around to glare at her. "You're so trusting. You're like a newborn fawn—so awkward and clumsy, and just so sure that no one in the world would ever hurt you."

Tears stung the corners of Amalia's eyes. She tried to blink them away.

"You don't mean that," she insisted. But she didn't sound as sure this time.

Vee laughed, harshly.

"You're right, Princess, I *don't* mean that. You're not a fawn at all." Vee stalked toward her, and there wasn't a trace of that laughing, relaxed girl in her eyes. No trace of the girl Amalia had called her friend. "You know what you are? What you *really* are, Princess?"

She tried not to cry, she really did. But as Vee knelt down, angling her face until it was right above hers, Amalia blinked and the tears that had been clouding her vision slipped out, spilling down her cheeks.

"You're nothing but a little doll," Vee told her. "You're just there to look pretty and play dress up and stay nice and safe up on your shelf. But you're not even a real person, are you? You're just their little toy—something for people to dress up and pamper. What are you, under all that frilly lace? What are you, without anyone there to pull your strings and tell you what to do?"

Something inside of her chest cracked open, and Amalia shut her eyes against it all, not caring anymore about the tears flowing down her cheeks, not caring if Vee saw her cry.

"You were so eager to think someone cared about you, weren't you? The real you. You made it so easy, you know that? You would have given me anything I wanted."

Eyes squeezed shut, shoulders shaking as she cried, Amalia didn't notice how close Vee was until she touched her chin, angling her face back up. Startled, she opened her eyes to find Vee's face directly above hers.

"Wouldn't you have?" Vee asked. Her lips brushed against Amalia's, gently. A mocking, hate-filled kiss.

Then Vee was pushing her away, and she fell back against the ground with a wet sob.

Amalia couldn't bring herself to look at Vee anymore. Couldn't face the fact that Vee was right. She would have given her anything.

Happily.

And because she didn't look up, she didn't see Vee quickly wipe the tears from her own face.

"Get ready, Princess," Vee said, drying her face on her sleeve and tilting her head to the side as though listening to something Amalia couldn't hear. "They're almost here."

CHAPTER 65

FEY

"It's here," Jasper said as he pointed. The tall brick building loomed in front of them, the roof illuminated like the rising sun.

Jasper frowned as they stared up at it. "The lights are new," he said.

"She's trying to keep the shadows away," Fey told him. *Clever girl.* Fey wished she could have left Jasper at home with Alastair, wished she hadn't needed him to show her where Vivian's clubhouse was. He shouldn't be here, not for this.

"You should go back," she told him as they approached the building. A fire escape ladder dangled against the brick wall, tucked in an alley, inviting them to climb. But Fey hesitated, her hand gripping the metal. "Go home and wait with Alastair," she told him.

Jasper shook his head.

"I'm not going, Fey," he insisted.

"Jasper—"

"She's family," Jasper said, voice tight with pain.

She should send him away, Fey knew. She should knock him out if he wouldn't go on his own. There was a good chance his niece was going to die tonight.

But she couldn't do it.

When Fey started up the ladder, she knew Jasper was right behind her.

CHAPTER 66

AMALIA

When the shadows at the corner of the roof began to move and twist, Amalia thought she must be dreaming. Surely, this was all some horrid nightmare and here was the proof. Any moment now, she would wake up back in her bed in the palace. And all of this would finally be over.

But she didn't wake.

Amalia watched in horror as the shadows coalesced before her eyes, morphing together to form the figure of a woman.

A Demon.

Kallista. Vee sucked in a quick panicked breath as the Demon formed from shadows and rose to stand before them.

Please let me wake up, Amalia thought, panicked.

Let it be just a dream.

Just another nightmare.

Now fully formed, Kallista cocked her head to the side, gazing around the roof with wry amusement. Her eyes trailed over each of the three blinding flood lights, raised high on metal legs, before finally settling on Vee.

"Cute," she purred. "But I don't need my shadows to hurt you, little Witch."

With a deadly smile on her face, Kallista stepped forward, toward the center of the roof.

"We can do this the old-fashioned way," she cooed, advancing without fear, arms stretching out at her sides. "It's been a long, long time since I've felt someone's blood running through my fingers. I imagine I'll quite enjoy it, tonight."

Amalia screamed.

She couldn't help it. The pain that suddenly took her, twisting her spine violently backwards, was such agony she couldn't hold the sound inside. She'd screamed before she'd even realized what was happening.

"One more step and I break the princess's neck," Vee told Kallista.

Fear replaced the pain in Amalia's chest as she felt Vee's hold on her vanish. Vee should know that wouldn't stop her. Amalia was nothing to Kallista, nothing at all. The Demon would never stop to protect her. She had no reason to keep her alive...

But... the threat worked. Eyes flaring with rage, Kallista stopped her advance.

"I can do it, too," Vee continued. "You've seen it yourself, Demon. So step back, if you want her to live."

Remarkably, the Demon did. Glancing quickly over at Amalia as though to ensure she was still alive, Kallista took a step backward, toward the edge of the roof. And then another.

"That goes for you too," Vee said, pivoting.

Amalia hadn't heard the Witches arrive. But they stood there now. Near the top of the ladder that Vee had made her climb.

Alice. Alice and...

Amalia swallowed a sob.

Alice and a *nightmare*, dressed in black leather.

Please, merciful Goddess, let me wake up.

"We won't move," Alice assured Vee, palms raised. "There's no need to hurt her."

Amalia's chest tightened.

Alice had no reason to want to help her. And at her side, the Witch in the Blades uniform, blonde hair streaming down her back, that was the last Queen's Blade, wasn't it? The only Witch with an intact Blades mark left alive.

These Witches didn't come here to save her, Amalia knew, with a sinking realization. That's not what the Blades did. They had come to kill. And despite everything, despite the pain and the fear and the betrayal, Amalia felt more fear for Vee than for herself.

"Why don't you tell us what you want," Alice continued, speaking slowly. "And we can all help each other."

"Are you okay?" the blonde Witch asked. It took Amalia a long moment to realize she was talking to her. "Did she hurt you?"

"No," Vee told her, stepping between them, blocking her from view. "I haven't hurt her. But I will. If any of you makes one move against me, I swear I will."

"What do you want, Witch?" Kallista asked, voice cold.

Vee turned toward her, baring her teeth.

"Don't call me that!" she snapped.

Kallista shrugged. "Why not? It's what you are, isn't it?"

Shaking her head, Vee curled her lips in disgust. "I'm a *Wolf*. Witches destroyed this city. Witches are the ones with their boots on our necks, holding us down while we starve. I'm not one of them. I'll never be one of them."

Kallista huffed a small laugh.

"What do you think that power is, that you tried wielding against me, hm?" she asked, quirking a brow.

If she was trying to get a rise out of her, it didn't work. Vee simply smiled, all irritation gone from her voice in an instant.

"It's *mine*, is what it is. I don't care where it came from. It's *mine*."

A sound filled the air, like metal twisting. Someone was coming up the ladder. Alice and the last Queen's Blade moved aside, careful not to move closer and risk Vee's wrath, as someone emerged.

Someone with blood-red hair.

Vee threw back her head and laughed.

"Oh, you're all really fucked, now, you know that?" she asked Kallista, grinning widely. "You might not be scared of me, Demon, but you should be scared of her."

Amalia watched in horror as Fey, her mother's murderer—her Broken Blade—stepped onto the roof.

CHAPTER 67

FEY

Fey took in the scene quickly as Jasper scrambled up the ladder behind her. Kallista and her sisters were already here, and thankfully, it looked like no one had been killed. Yet.

Her eyes narrowed when she looked across the roof and saw...

The princess?

What was she doing here?

"Fey," Vivian said, excitedly, grinning at her. Fey's heart sank as she stared across the roof at the young girl. A part of her had hoped she had been wrong. That they would find someone else, *anyone else* on the rooftop waiting for them. "I knew you would come. I knew you'd help."

"Took you long enough," Alice grumbled. Joy reached out, fingers wrapping around Fey's hand and giving her a comforting squeeze.

Vivian saw. Eyes locked on Joy's hand, her face fell, that smile slipping away in horror.

"You came here with them," she murmured, almost in disbelief, as her eyes drifted up to stare at Fey. "You didn't come here to help me, did you? You came here to stop me."

"I came here to stop you from making an even bigger mistake," Fey insisted. "Listen to me, Vivian. You can let this go. Let *her* go."

Rage. Cold, dangerous rage flooded those green eyes. Those eyes so like Jasper's.

"Let it go?" Vee asked, voice icy. "How... How can you take their side? After everything they've done?"

"I'm not taking anyone's side—"

A sharp scream burst from Amalia, and her back arched painfully as she twisted under Vee's control.

"*You are taking their side*," Vee shrieked. She didn't even look at Amalia as she twisted her body unnaturally far, her eyes burning into Fey's instead. "How could you? You were the one who took them down in the first place. We had a chance, Fey. *You gave us a chance*! A chance to make it all better, a chance to take power for those who've never had any. Those who have been left behind, who have been hurt for all these years under the Queen. To make it better."

Her voice was breaking, pained. She sounded desperate. And desperation made people dangerous.

Fey tried again.

"The council is trying to make it better," Fey started to tell her. "They're—"

Vee growled. "They're nothing but puppets for the Witch Faction to control. What has changed? What has gotten better, for any of us?"

"It takes time," Alice interjected. "And we're trying, we—"

"We don't have time!" Vee screamed. Amalia was shaking, shuddering on the ground, but the Wolf didn't seem to notice. "We're *dying*. Shifters, Demons—we're dying out here in the city, all on our own. Why do we need to wait? Where's the justice in that?"

"It doesn't work like that," Fey tried to reason.

"Someone needs to pay," Vee told her, fists tight at her sides. There were tears on her cheeks. "Someone needs to pay for our suffering. For our deaths. So many of us have died, and the council isn't doing anything to stop it. They're keeping everything the same, and *no one is paying for what they did to us*."

Another shudder from Amalia, and this time everyone noticed, even Vee. They all turned to look toward the princess, bent and powerless under Vee's control.

Her face was pale and her lips were blue as she convulsed.

She wasn't breathing.

Vee took a sharp breath and dropped her hold on the princess.

Amalia gasped, drawing a deep, painful breath into her lungs. The force of it made her cough, body shaking as she tried to restart her breathing.

"I'm sorry," Vee whispered, looking horrified. She swallowed hard, staring at Amalia. "I forgot. I didn't mean..."

"Viv... please," Jasper said, stepping forward. "Please let her go. Don't hurt her again."

"I didn't mean to hurt her," Vee whined. She glanced between Jasper and the princess, her eyes pleading. "Sometimes I forget about the breathing, that's all. I didn't mean..."

Jasper took another step toward her, and Vee tensed.

"Don't do it, Uncle Jas," she warned in a dark voice.

He ignored her.

"Let her go," he said softly. "Please, Viv. No one else needs to get hurt. Please, just listen to me. We want to help you. But you need to trust me."

Vee took a step backward, shaking her head slowly from side to side. Crying.

"Viv, look at me," Jasper continued, coming even closer to her. "If you let her go, we can fix this. We can—"

He stopped, and the words caught in his throat. He made an odd sound, like a gurgle.

Vee wasn't looking at him. With her head still down, she stared at the ground beneath her, at the ring of light there. But her arm was extended, her hand pointed toward him.

"There is no fixing this," she said, and she curled her fingers toward her palm. "There's no going back. Not anymore. Not until this is finished. Not until they all pay."

It's never easy to watch the transformation—to see a Shifter move between forms. It's a monstrous process, horrifying to witness. And it's even worse when it's forced.

Jasper let out a guttural scream as his bones twisted, breaking and reforming. He screamed as his muscles extended, his face elongating and fur sprouting all over his body. Screamed, until it turned into a howl, and suddenly there was a Wolf where he had once been, a huge golden-brown Wolf cowering on the roof.

It was too much for Fey to take.

Drawing her blades, Fey stepped into the light.

CHAPTER 68

JASPER

It was agony. Agony, being forced into his Wolf form and pulled from his human body against his will.

Agony to see his sister's little girl standing there, so lost and alone and afraid. So hurt.

Agony to see Fey dive for her, going for her throat. Her blade glittering in the bright lights.

And the worst agony imaginable when Fey fell, crashing to the ground and crying out in pain as Vee's power reached out and took control of her body.

Jasper whimpered, trying to stand, but that same power held him down as well, pinning his four legs hard against the rough brick of the roof. He couldn't get up, couldn't even move.

"You were supposed to be on our side," Vee shouted, standing over Fey's body. She flexed her hands, and Fey let out a pained groan, her body twisting. "Don't you get it? They need to be punished for the suffering they caused! For the people they've killed!"

How had he missed this? How had he missed her suffering, her pain?

How had he been so blind?

His sister's death had nearly killed him. For years, he couldn't even look at Viv and not see the sister he had loved. The sister he had lost.

Vivian had been alone, so alone, all those years. Surrounded by family, sure, but had anyone ever gotten close to her? Had anyone ever managed to make her feel loved? Cared for?

No one had even known about this side of her. No one had even known she was a Witch.

They'd let her down. No father, no mother, and passed from elder to elder, house to house. They'd fed her scraps of their affection.

And they'd turned her into this.

Jasper's heart was breaking for her. She'd seen so much death in her short life, hadn't she? So much suffering. Caught in a system designed to keep her down.

And given the power to change everything. Given the power to even the scales.

With effort, he stood, whimpering. Vivian was so focused on holding Fey down, and Fey was fighting, fighting that power that was trying to overtake her.

Jasper took a step forward, dragging his front paw along the ground, unable to even lift it fully. And then another. And another.

He had to reach her. Had to save her. Vivian had no one on her side, no one left to protect her. But he wouldn't turn his back on her, not now. Not ever.

He just needed to reach her, somehow. To let her know she wasn't alone.

Another step. Another.

He was less than ten feet away from Viv when Fey shook off her control. Less than ten feet away when she scrambled across the brick, grabbing her long and deadly blade, and shifted into a crouch. Less than ten feet away when Vivian noticed him there, looking away from Fey and staring straight into his eyes.

He didn't recognize the Witch staring back at him.

"*Kill her,*" Vee commanded, and with horror, Jasper found himself turning away from Vivian, his muscles tensing and bracing to attack.

Turning away from her, and straight toward Fey.

CHAPTER 69
FEY

Fighting Vivian's control was like fighting a storm.

It was torture, having someone twist your own body against your will like this. But Fey had known torture, before. She had known suffering and pain. And she'd survived.

This was nothing new to her. And when everything else failed her, when everything else turned away, she had the powers the Goddess had given her.

Earth answered her call first, filling her with strength. Her rage came next, Fire coursing through her body. Then Air, pushing back against an invasion.

And finally, her body called Water.

Vivian's power was an infection, a foreign body invading her own and seeking to control her. And all that delicious power inside of Fey came out to fight it.

She could feel when Vivian began to slip, and she started to lose control. She pushed even harder, forcing Fey's body to bend, trying to break her.

No.

Fey didn't even try to fight that influence. Her power was enough to do it for her.

And suddenly her body was her own again, and Fey found herself on the ground, her muscles back under her command. Her body ached. There was blood in her mouth, and Fey was fairly confident she'd bitten off part of her own tongue.

Propping herself up on her elbow, Fey spat out a glob of blood onto the bricks and scrubbed at her mouth with the back of her hand.

Time to end this.

Fey reached for her blade and was crouching down to make the kill when she heard the command.

"Kill her."

Oh, no.

Jasper. His Wolf was a giant, beautiful thing, full of powerful muscles. It was glorious to see. And under Vee's command, that glorious monster turned, lips curling in a snarl, as he advanced toward her.

"Jasper," Fey warned him, gripping her blade so tight her hand felt numb. "Fight it, Jasper."

The snarl only grew, lips pulling back to reveal long, deadly teeth. She knew exactly how dangerous those teeth could be. She'd fought more Wolves than she could count. *Killed* more Wolves than she could count. And she could kill him, too.

Jasper stalked closer, closing the distance between them.

"Please," she said. "Jasper, please don't. Don't make me do this."

But there was nothing of the crooked grin she loved in that face. No trace of the warm, friendly eyes that made her feel so safe.

She thought of Alastair, then. The way he smiled at Jasper. Teased him. How happy he had been in the short time the three of them had been together. Would he survive this? Losing Jasper to her hand?

Her heart twisted.

"Jasper," she tried again, staring into those wild eyes and hoping some small part of him could hear her.

A stranger looked back at her.

Fine. Fey squared her shoulders and made her choice. She hoped the Goddess would forgive her for what she had to do tonight.

She hoped Alastair would forgive her eventually, too.

Steeling herself, Fey stared into those eyes and let her blades fall to the roof with a clatter.

"Just make it quick," she told him.

Something in his eyes faltered. Two steps away and advancing, some of that wildness in his eyes broke, and for a second, she thought she could see the male inside.

Then he snarled even louder, a bone chilling sound that Fey could feel deep inside herself before he crouched to leap.

Fey closed her eyes.

His fur was soft as it passed over her. Soft, as Jasper leaped straight over her head, and threw himself off the roof.

CHAPTER 70

FEY

There was screaming. Everywhere around her, there was screaming.

Vee, racing forward, arm outstretched for her uncle as he fell, screaming in shock. Alice, screaming just once, a single startled gasp before her hand came up to cover her mouth.

And Fey. She was screaming, too, she realized. A heartbroken, inconsolable sound full of fear and rage.

"No!" she screamed, stumbling toward the edge of the roof, reaching for him...

A blur of black and gold whipped through the air, next to her, fast as lightning toward the ground as Jasper fell. Fey would never reach him in time, had no chance at all.

But maybe—just maybe—Joy could.

Even with a burst of air from Joy cushioning his fall, the sound of Jasper hitting the pavement was enough to turn her stomach. It was too dark to see him. But he was hurt down there, and she had to get to him, had to help him...

"I'm sorry." Vee was on her knees at the edge of the roof, looking stunned. Twin rivers of tears ran down her cheeks. "I didn't mean to, I didn't..."

Vivian.

Now was Fey's chance. Scrambling back over the rooftop, she reached for her blade to finish this, once and for all.

Alice must have thought the same thing. She moved forward, raising her hand to call Fire, her face a mask of cold fury.

Vee looked up, eyes widening when she realized what was happening, but it was too late. Fey was already holding her blade, Alice by her side.

It hurt even more this time, when the Blood Witch took control of her body. Her powers rose inside her, fighting that influence, but it was too slow.

Fey swallowed a scream as her body twisted, bones close to shattering.

Vee stood.

"I'm done playing nice," she hissed, taking a step toward them as Alice collapsed to the ground.

Back bending, Fey's neck twisted painfully on her shoulders, threatening to break.

In her peripheral vision, she watched Princess Amalia rise to her knees, hands pressed firm against the brick underneath them.

Amalia had been forgotten in the fight. And, somehow, with the effort to control Fey and Alice, Vee had let her concentration on the princess slip. Maybe she'd done it on purpose. Maybe she hadn't wanted to risk hurting her accidentally again.

Lips set in a thin line, Princess Amalia reached inside herself and called Earth.

The rooftop shuddered. A sharp wave of power tore through the bricks, rippling outward from where the princess knelt. It rolled underneath Fey, rolled toward Vee, who stumbled, barely staying upright while the ground bucked beneath them. And it rolled to the edges of the roof, to where the flood lights stood, looming over them all.

"No!" Vee screamed. She dropped her hold over Fey and Alice in her panic, stepping toward the closest light as it teetered.

Too late. It fell, smashing into the one next to it. The lights shattered as they hit the damaged roof, their bright light suddenly extinguished. Vee pivoted, racing toward the one light that still remained standing.

Amalia was faster. Her hand shot out as she called Air.

The cyclone that exploded toward the flood light was more than enough to send it tumbling off the building.

"No," Vee murmured, watching the light fall further and further away. "No, no, no, no."

Darkness returned to the rooftop. Fey almost thought she heard a light laugh as the shadows began to descend, flowing over the bricks like smoke and racing toward one solitary figure.

Vee screamed as the shadows consumed her.

And then, a moment later, she was gone.

CHAPTER 71
VEE

Death had finally caught her.

But she wouldn't go down without a fight.

Vee snarled, lashing out with a clawed hand. The blow didn't land. There was nothing there, just endless, formless dark. It felt cold, the emptiness an icy chill all around her. Filling her.

She reached out with that bright power inside of her, reached for a heartbeat, reached for blood, reached for *anything*.

But there was nothing. Emptiness. Nothing around her but the dark.

Desperate, Vee shifted, bones snapping and reforming. A Wolf emerged from Vee's skin, with long fast limbs built for running.

If she couldn't fight, she would run.

Vee raced into the darkness.

Endless. The black was endless and formless, and she ran and ran and ran...

"Where are you running, little Wolf?" a cold voice asked from the void.

Vee turned, snapping her powerful jaws. The voice was behind her. In front of her. All around her.

Come out and fight, she thought, turning her head side to side, looking for something, anything, in the dark. *Come out and face me. I'm not afraid.*

"There is nowhere left to run," said the voice.

Vee dove into the darkness.

Nothing.

She snapped her teeth and flailed. She bounded and fought.

Nothing.

The voice was everywhere and nowhere, and in frustration Vee threw back her head to howl.

"Come out and fight me!" she cried, the words garbled and strange coming from her muzzle.

"I don't need to fight you," came that voice, that horribly cold voice. "You've already lost."

Vee growled.

"You think you know suffering, little Wolf?" the voice mocked.

Claws sunk into her mind, and Vee whimpered, dropping to her belly. Pain. So much pain. Something was in her head; something was digging around in her skull. She whimpered again, shaking her head from side to side, trying to shake off those horrible claws.

Images came to her, unbidden and unwanted.

Memories of her past.

Flash.

Her mother's face. Smiling. Happy.

Flash.

Her mother's face. Bloody and beaten. Dead.

Flash.

Jayce's brother. Bloody and beaten. Dead.

Flash.

A Shifter she'd never known, never recognized. Starving to death on the streets. Eyes vacant and hollow, flies crawling over his flesh.

Flash.

She and Jayce, barely more than kids, running from three men, knowing they were going to die. Her standing above those same men, holding their lives in her hands with this new, glorious power.

Flash.

Vee had shifted again, without realizing. She huddled on the ground, her hands gripping her head.

"Stop it," she pleaded. "Stop doing that."

Flash.

Kellos, struggling against the hold she had on him. Kellos, jumping toward his sister, blood on his paws. Kellos, who had felt so scared under her control. So... sad.

Flash.

The Vampire. He fought so hard against her. His thoughts were full of thoughts of his son. Full of horror. Full of pain.

Full of noble sacrifice.

Flash

Amalia.

"No," Vee sobbed.

Amalia.

Amalia the first time she'd ever seen her, in that ridiculous red dress, lost and alone in the city.

Amalia smiling at her.

Amalia spinning in her new outfit, her power growing. Growing every day since Vee had met her, with no sign of stopping.

Amalia's face crumbling.

Amalia crying.

"Stop," Vee pleaded, her entire body shaking. "Please stop."

"You have suffered," the voice said. "And you have caused so much suffering. Was it worth it?"

Flash.

Her mother's face.

Flash.

Amalia's face.

Flash.

Flash.

Flash.

THE IMAGES WOULDN'T STOP. The memories wouldn't stop.

"You think you understand suffering?" Kallista asked, her voice coming from everywhere and nowhere. She was the darkness, she was the voice surrounding them, she was the cold and infinite void. Vee whimpered. "You think you have any idea what that word means?"

This was the Demon's world. Her realm.

Kallista stepped forward, out of the dark, kneeling before Vee while she shook with fear and pain.

She touched Vee's temple, gently.

"You don't know anything about suffering," the Demon told her. "Let me show you what suffering really is, mortal."

Four thousand years.

Four thousand years of war, and pain, and death. Kallista took that pain, took those memories—*her* memories—and pushed them into Vee. Flooding them into her mind.

Vee screamed.

She begged.

She cried.

But the pain wouldn't stop.

And eventually, when nothing else worked, she gave into the darkness and let it take her away.

CHAPTER 72
FEY

When the sun finally rose the next morning, it bathed the sky in a pink so dark it was almost red. Fey watched it from a window in her sisters' apartment, watched the colors bleed over the city, tinging everything in a rose-colored haze.

Behind her, she heard the sound of a door opening, followed by light footsteps on the carpet. Her sister's footsteps.

"You can see him now," Joy told her. She sounded completely drained. Exhausted. Fey wasn't surprised. Joy had put everything that she'd had into that healing. And even then, even with all her power, it almost hadn't been enough.

"Is he..." Fey swallowed. The light from the sunrise looked a little too much like blood to her. "Is he going to be okay?"

Joy's hand landed gently on her shoulder, turning her away from the window. Exhaustion lined Joy's face. But so did hope.

"He'll be fine, sister," Joy assured her, smiling. "Back to normal before you know it."

An awful weight that had been pressing down on Fey's chest lifted, ever so slightly.

"Thank you," Fey murmured. "For saving him, and for... for everything."

Joy's answering smile was full of understanding.

"You love him, don't you?" she asked, gently. "You and your Vampire?"

Unable to speak, Fey just nodded.

"I saw. On the rooftop, when you let your blades fall." Joy closed her eyes and took a deep breath. "Sister... If I hadn't made it in time? If he had passed into the afterlife? I promise you—I would have reached into the beyond and pulled him back with my own two hands if I'd had to. For you."

Fey let out a laugh.

"You know, I almost believe you could, sister," she said, shaking her head.

"Thankfully, it didn't come to that. But he needs to rest. I healed the worst of it, but—" Joy rubbed a hand over her face. "I need to rest, too, before I can finish the rest of the healing. I'm tapped out. His hip is still broken, and he has multiple contusions that aren't life threatening, but..."

"But you both need to rest," Fey finished.

"I should be able to heal everything else in a day or so," Joy said. "Until then, yes—lots of rest. And no... no funny stuff."

Fey raised an eyebrow, and Joy responded with a huff and a roll of her eyes.

"No sex. And I mean it. That broken hip is a problem, and if you —or Alastair—do anything to make it worse, it'll be a nightmare for me to heal, okay? There's no guarantee I can repair the bone fully as it is."

"I'm sure I can control myself," Fey assured her.

Joy just laughed.

"See that you do. I'm going to call Sana and see if she can come and help with some of the injuries in the meantime." Joy's eyes were kind as she smiled. "Go in and see him, sister. He's waiting for you."

Intentionally or not, they'd put Jasper in Fey's old room when they'd rushed him here last night. She smiled as she closed the door behind her, looking around at the place she'd once called home. Then her gaze landed on Jasper, deep asleep on the bed, and her smile fell.

Bruises covered half his face and continued in a molted purple down his body. Joy had made a cast for his hips until she regained enough strength to finish mending the bones there. But...

Fey let out a shaky breath. He was alive. Seeing him lying there for the first time since he'd gone off the edge of the roof, Fey allowed it to really sink in. Jasper was alive.

She wouldn't cry. She promised herself she wouldn't cry...

Taking a shuddering breath, Fey wrapped her arms around her own shoulders and curled in on herself. She'd come so close to losing him. Come so close to losing everything. She screwed her eyes shut tight, fighting against the tears she refused to cry.

"Hey," came a voice from the bed.

Fey looked up.

Jasper was awake, watching her. He tried to lift himself up on his elbow, wincing as he did so.

"What's wrong, gorgeous?" he asked her, frowning. "Are you okay?'

A startled laugh broke through her lips.

"Okay?" she asked. She shook her head. "Jasper... you're alive. I'm much, much better than okay."

He grinned.

"But if you don't lay back down, I'll call my sister back in here, and she will break something non-vital until you do," Fey warned him.

Chuckling, Jasper lowered himself back onto the pillows.

"Come here," he beckoned her closer, opening his arms and patting the bed next to him. "Lay down with me. Then I'll have no reason to move, will I?"

Wiping a hand over her face, she moved closer and crawled into bed next to him, curling on her side to press against him. His heart was slow and steady in his ribcage.

I'm alive, it said with every beat.

We're alive.

"I was so scared when you went over that ledge," she admitted, burrowing her face in his chest. "I thought I'd lost you."

"Me too," he responded, voice thick. "When I couldn't fight it, I thought..." He trailed off.

He didn't need to say it. His arm pulled her toward him a little tighter.

"Is Alastair here?" he asked.

Fey shook her head. "He was, before the sun came up. Alice sent him home. We're lucky she didn't murder him. He didn't want to leave your side, and she kept saying he was getting in Joy's way... one of them threw a lamp. It was a whole thing..."

Jasper laughed.

"How are you holding up?" he asked. His hand stroked down her back, rubbing soothing circles over her.

"Jasper... you're the one who was hurt," Fey reminded him. "Not me."

"Well, sure," he huffed and shifted on the mattress. "But that doesn't mean you don't get to be hurt, too. We already know I'm hurt. But... How are you? Are you okay?"

"No," she admitted, cuddling closer to him. "But I will be. When you're better."

She lost herself for a while in the feeling of him pressed against her, in the comfort of his touch along her back.

"Do you know..." Jasper trailed off, voice breaking. "Do you know what happened to Vivian?"

Fey swallowed.

"She's alive," she told him. Jasper released a shaky breath. "Kallista did... something to her. I don't understand what. But she's safe, for now. They have her in a cell, in Lunairea."

His confused frown almost pulled a smile from her. "The soldier's quarters, behind the palace. She'll be safe there. Until... until the council figures out what to do with her."

Jasper nodded slowly.

"Do you think they'll let me visit her?" he asked.

"I don't know," Fey admitted.

"This was all my fault," Jasper whispered. Fey sat up to protest, but he kept going, lips set in a thin line. "I should have known something was happening with her. I should have helped her; I should have done... something."

"You did everything you could, Jasper," Fey said. "You didn't know—"

"I *should* have known," Jasper insisted. He swallowed hard and closed his eyes. "I was supposed to protect her, Fey. And... I fucked that up. She needed me, and I didn't even notice."

His chest shuddered as he took a trembling breath.

Fey didn't know what to say. Curling up against him again, Fey just held him and let him mourn.

After a while, his arms came up to circle her again. He squeezed her tight against his body. They lay there together, holding one another, as the silence stretched on and on.

"So..." Fey said finally, sliding her hand over his chest. "Mates, huh?"

Jasper stiffened, ever so slightly, under her touch. The only indication he'd heard.

"Alastair told me last night," Fey murmured, drawing patterns over his chest with her fingertip. "Shouted it, really, when Alice threatened to make him leave. Said he'd break her neck if she tried to keep your mates from you. But... he didn't really explain it. Or what it means."

Jasper remained tense under her touch.

"It's a Shifter thing," he told her in a gruff voice. "Not all of them, but... Wolves, and... some of the others."

Fey waited for him to continue, her hands stilling.

"And?" she prompted.

He shifted uneasily against the mattress. "And... it's hard to explain. It's like... being made for someone. Like you're a part of them, a piece of them that was missing."

He went quiet again.

"Is that how it feels for you?" Fey asked, curious. "Like you found a missing piece?"

Jasper laughed.

"No, not really. It feels like home," he said in answer. "With you... with Alastair. When I look at the two of you, it feels like home."

Home.

Her chest tightened.

"I know you Witches don't feel anything like that," Jasper told her, softly running his palms over her back. "I don't mind. And I'm sorry for not telling you."

"For not telling me that I belong to you?" Fey asked, a hint of anger coloring her voice.

Jasper shook his head quickly.

"That I belong to *you*, Fey," he told her softly. "To *both* of you. I'm not a missing piece of *you*...you're both a missing piece of me."

His hands felt so good on her, so comforting. And it did feel like home, to be laying here with him, didn't it?

Letting go of that small flicker of anger, Fey let herself relax further into him.

"Is it common to have more than one mate?" she asked.

"Not common, no," Jasper answered. "It's unusual, but it happens. But having a mate who's a Vampire? Or a Witch?" Jasper laughed. "Now that... that's rare. That's something I've never heard of happening before."

"I'm... glad," Fey admitted. "I wish you had told me, but... I'm glad I know now. Now I understand what makes this so special. The three of us."

Jasper raised her hand to his lips and pressed a gentle kiss to her fingers. Then to her palm, and her wrist. By the time he'd begun to kiss further down her arm and to the crook of her elbow, a guttural moan had started in his chest.

"Jasper," Fey warned him. His eyes met hers and they flashed with lust.

"Oh no." She smirked, pulling her arm away. Jasper pivoted, kissing her neck and up to her cheek. "I promised Joy. No funny business."

"No funny business at all," Jasper promised. But his hand moved further down her back, to cup her ass. "I won't move, I swear. I'll stay right here. Just... let me touch you, Fey. Let me taste you."

His hand roamed over her curves, and it was tempting, so, so tempting, to let him keep going.

"Sit on my face," he said. "I'll be still, I promise. I won't—"

Someone's fist banged hard against the door.

"What did I say?" Joy's voice was angry through the thin wooden door. Jasper's hand finally stilled but his shoulders shook with silent laughter.

"The walls here are very thin," Fey told him, grimacing. "Trust me."

When the bedroom door opened, Joy didn't seem at all surprised to find Fey curled against Jasper's chest. But she did shoot her an irritated glance.

"Get up," she said, shooing Fey out of the bed. "I had an idea. Sana's here now, and we want to try something."

"Shouldn't you be resting?" Fey asked, quirking an eyebrow.

"I can rest later. But, right now, I need to test something. So, shoo."

Fey gave Jasper an apologetic grin as she shimmied off the mattress. A moment later, when Sana entered, she was glad for the space between the two of them.

The Water Witch glanced between Fey and Jasper, who was still looking at Fey with raw lust in his eyes, and she flushed red.

"That girl, Vivian?" Joy asked Jasper, stepping forward. "She's your niece, right?"

A flicker of pain flashed in Jasper's bright green eyes before he nodded.

"By *blood*, right?" Joy pressed, and again Jasper nodded. "Good... that's good."

"Does that matter?" Jasper asked skeptically.

"For this? Oh yes. It matters." Joy smiled.

"Shifters and Witches have produced children before," Sana explained, fiddling with the sleeve of her robes. "Many times, over the history of the realm. But... we've never heard of their offspring possessing both sets of gifts, one from each parent. And if Alastair really does have the gift of Blood Magic—"

"He what?" asked Jasper, frowning.

"—and if that gift did come from breeding with Witches," Sana continued, unabated. "Perhaps our Factions have more in common than we once thought."

"That got me thinking," Joy started to say. Sana shot her a look, and Joy quickly rephrased. "Got us thinking. Maybe... maybe these gifts only appear after several generations of interbreeding between the Factions. Maybe Vivian's power doesn't just come from her father being a Witch, but from *multiple sources*, coalescing in her family line. In *your* family line. And if that's the case... Fey, if that's the case, there's a chance —a small chance—Jasper may be the same. And there could be many more like him, Shifters with Witch blood. Maybe Demons, too."

Jasper blinked, slowly. Then he chuckled, shaking his head.

"Hang on... you're not suggesting I'm a Witch? Like... like all of you?" he asked with a wry smile.

Sana shook her head. "Not a full Witch, no. But you—and others like you—might share enough genetic similarity with us that, well... certain things may be possible. Things we never considered, before. Like..."

"Like healing sigils," Joy finished, beaming.

Clearly, the conversation was lost on Jasper, who looked at each of them blankly.

But Fey's mind roiled with the possibilities. If that were true... if there was enough Witch blood in the Shifter factions...

"Do you really think he—?" Fey began.

"Only one way to find out!" Joy grinned. She held her hand out, palm open, to Sana, and after a moment of hesitation, Sana pulled a thin, silver knife from the pockets of her robes and handed it to her.

"This is probably going to hurt," Joy told Jasper, with a sympathetic glance, as she set a bowl of black ink on the nightstand. A lick of flame shot down the knife as she held it, hovering over the tip.

"But if this works?" Joy's eyes flashed. "If this works, this could save countless lives."

———————

THE EFFECT WAS INSTANTANEOUS.

The moment Joy finished the last line of the healing sigil on his shoulder, stepping back to admire her work, Jasper drew a deep breath. He stared around at them in shock.

And the bruises marring his body started to fade.

CHAPTER 73
AMALIA

Amalia stared into the mirror. A poor proximity of her mother's face stared back. Incomplete. Still lacking something she couldn't quite figure out.

Vee's words played in a loop through her head.

You're nothing but a little doll.

A little doll.

A little doll.

Vivian was right. That was all she was, wasn't she? Nothing but a plaything. Something molded by others, manipulated by others.

Used by others.

The piece of brick she'd taken from the rooftop that night was sharp and jagged in her hand as she squeezed it tight.

That's what she'd been to her mother, after all. A doll. And not even a doll her mother had wanted. No—that had been the problem, hadn't it? Her mother had wanted a miniature version of herself. An ice queen, powerful and untouchable. Cold and aloof.

And Amalia wasn't any of those things, was she? She didn't have her mother's cold nature. Didn't have her mother's disdain. She felt everything—maybe a little too much.

Still... she'd tried. She'd let her mother dress her up. Prop her up before the citizens of the realm with a smile painted on her face. She'd been well-behaved. Cordial.

A *perfect* little doll.

And then, just like that, her mother was gone.

And Amalia had let it happen again.

She'd become Linh's doll. Something the High Priestess could prop up for the council and speak with her voice. Something she could mold into another queen, just her mother. Something she could set up on a throne, to replace the monarch she'd lost.

Nothing but a little doll.

Vee had been the first person to actually make her feel... special. Make her feel like...

Amalia gripped the shard in her hand even tighter, savoring the flash of pain.

Vee had made her feel like a real person. Like she could be something more. Made her feel like she wasn't incomplete, like she wasn't missing something. Like who she was had been enough.

But she'd been a toy for her, too, this whole time. And Amalia had been too stupid to recognize it. Too stupid to even realize she was being used.

Vee had used her to gain access to the palace. Used her to gain access to Kellos. To The Fallen King.

To Linh...

Amalia was responsible for their deaths, just as much as Vee was. If she hadn't been so blind, hadn't been so easy to manipulate.

Nothing but a little doll.

It should hurt more than it did, Amalia realized.

Setting the shard of brick down, she traced a finger down the side of her cheek, turning her head in the mirror.

It should hurt more, to know that she had caused this. And yet...

Nothing but a little doll.

Something inside of her that had cracked that night finally split open. Her power swirled under her skin like a tempest.

Amalia didn't want to be a doll anymore. She didn't want to be weak, didn't want to be anyone's plaything.

She wanted to be free. She wanted to be...

To be *herself.*

Maybe she was an incomplete version of her mother. But she didn't have to be, did she? She didn't have to be *any* version of her mother. She didn't have to be anyone's doll, anyone's plaything. She could be whatever she wanted.

Couldn't she?

Amalia fingered her long curls, soft and brown. Her father's hair. In the mirror, a version of her did the same.

Gently, she gathered those curls in her hand, bundling the locks together at the base of her neck.

It was amazing how much hair she had. She could barely hold it all.

The cold night air tickled the delicate skin of her neck as she pulled the hair away from her skin.

With her other hand she reached out, taking hold of the sharp metal scissors her handmaids kept next to her bed, to cut the ribbons they used to braid in her hair. Back when she was someone the realm cared about dressing up. Back when she was a princess.

The metal was cold against the base of her skull as she positioned the scissors against her skin.

And with one quick snip, she freed herself from all those soft curls.

CHAPTER 74
AMALIA

The cell in Lunairea would be cold.

Amalia considered bringing her jacket. But Vivian had been the one to choose it for her, hadn't she? That memory had stayed her hand when she'd reached for it this morning.

She could handle the cold.

Her silk shoes made very little noise on the stones as she made her way down the stairwell and into the dungeons.

Amalia hadn't been sure what to expect. She'd never been to see the prisons housed underneath Lunairea. Maybe she'd expected the prison cell to be dirtier, to be nothing but a pile of straw in the corner of a muddy room and a bucket. Maybe she'd expected it to be a miniature version of the guest rooms in the Western Wing of the palace, opulent and garish.

Whatever it had once looked like, Vivian's prison cell was now destroyed.

There had been a mattress. And what Amalia could only assume was a chair, or maybe a wooden table. It was nothing but splinters now, scattered amongst the shredded bed sheets on the ground.

The mattress had been shredded. Long claw marks marred the soft cushiony top, and feathers and padding had been pulled from the corpse of what looked to have once been a rather decent bed.

Otherwise, the room was unremarkable. Just another room if you could ignore the bars that lined one wall. Thick, iron bars, set mere inches apart. Close enough together that even Vee couldn't fit her way through them.

Vee.

She was sitting on the ground when Amalia approached, knees pulled against her chest, head down. For a moment, Amalia thought she might be sleeping.

"Good morning, Princess," Vee greeted her, lifting her head and smiling.

Amalia's gait stumbled as they locked eyes. Vee's eyes...

Shadows. Dark, twisting beasts made of shadow danced in Vee's eyes as they stared at one another. A swirling abyss, with no bottom.

She's gone insane, Amalia thought, suddenly frightened. Her resolve faltered.

But then Vee blinked, and suddenly those shadows were gone, and her eyes were that perfect green once again.

"You cut your hair," Vee said suddenly. She sounded almost sad.

Amalia resisted the urge to reach up and touch her short curls.

"I did," she confirmed.

"You said you were thinking about it, before—"

The shadows came back, filling Vee's eyes for just a moment before they cleared away once more.

"Why are you here, Princess?" she asked, twisting her head to the side and picking at the hem of her pants, almost nervously. "Have you come to gloat? The big bad Wolf has been captured, and all the little Witches are safe again. You've won."

There was so much hate in her voice, so much resentment. But this time, at least, Amalia could understand why.

"No," Amalia said, drawing her shoulders back. "I didn't come to gloat. I came to tell you that you were right."

Vee looked up and blinked, and Amalia took a deep breath to steady herself.

"You were right," she said. "About me being nothing but a doll."

Vee didn't say anything, so she went on.

"I've been a doll my whole life. I didn't even realize. What you told me that night? How I was just a puppet? You were right. I've always let people use me. Including you."

Vee opened her mouth to speak, but Amalia cut her off, quickly. She needed to do this, needed to get the words out.

Not for Vee, but for herself.

"I came down here because I wanted to thank you," she said, staring into those beautiful green eyes.

"Thank me?" Vee asked, sounding amused. Her lips quirked up into a smile.

"Yes," Amalia insisted. Her stomach twisted. Vee had the most beautiful smile she'd ever seen. Even now. Even when it hurt to look at her. "Thank you for telling me and thank you for helping break me free of it."

She'd been feeling stronger lately. So much stronger. Like the elements inside her had been dormant, pushed down by something heavy until she could barely reach them. But now? Amalia let that power fill her, just a little, just enough to give her the strength to say what she needed to say.

She only needed to say this once.

"I'm done being a doll," she said. Something crackled in her voice. Fire, she thought. "I'm done letting anyone else control me. I wanted to thank you for trying to break me, Vivian. Because you showed me how strong I really am. And I won't be broken so easily. Not by you. Not by anyone."

Amalia couldn't identify the emotion she saw on Vee's face, but she didn't need to. She found she no longer cared. With a final nod of her head, she turned to leave.

"I wouldn't have done it, you know," Vee called out after her, shifting forward in her cell. Amalia stopped, turning back with a frown.

"Hurt you, I mean," Vee explained. She chewed her lip, as though nervous. "I was bluffing when I told them I would... I wouldn't have actually hurt you if it came down to that. You... you know that, right?"

Amalia's chest tightened.

"Vee," she said in a quiet voice. Vee looked up at her, and Amalia held that beautiful gaze. She believed what she was saying. Believed she wouldn't have taken it any further. Believed, with all her heart, that she would have never done anything to hurt Amalia.

Amalia sighed.

"You *did* hurt me, Vee," she said.

The look of pain that flashed in Vivian's eyes should have meant something.

But it didn't.

This time, when Amalia left, she didn't look back.

CHAPTER 75

FEY

"Gather around, everyone," Fey shouted, waving her arms at the crowd gathered on the Solare lawn and beckoning them closer. Today, at least, the group was smaller than usual. Most of her students with any power over Fire were with Joy and Sana today, learning the careful art of drawing sigils.

Their skills would be invaluable to the realm, in the coming months. They needed to conduct more testing, of course, but Joy's hunch had been right. Whether from centuries of breeding with Witches, or some other hidden similarity between the two Factions, roughly half of all the Shifters they'd tested so far responded to Witch sigils. Not just the Shifters, either. A quarter of the Demons brought in were the same. Suddenly, broken bones and previously deadly diseases that had plagued the Fallen Factions were not only survivable, but easily treatable with the addition of a single healing sigil.

In one single morning, Sana and Joy had uncovered a miracle that could save thousands of lives every year. And they were working tirelessly to train the Witches necessary to ensure every Witch, Demon, and Shifter in the realm were given the opportunity to receive a healing sigil, if they so chose.

But that was their fight, and their legacy.

Fey's legacy was here. With her students.

"Today we'll be working with Air," Fey announced, watching as some of the students preened, eagerly. The Air Witches were always thrilled to show off their skills. "We will be breaking into smaller teams, so—"

Fey stopped.

There was a new face in the crowd this morning, one Fey recognized immediately. She had been waiting for her to show up for a long, long, time now.

Princess Amalia had cut her hair, and now instead of ringlets that reached all the way down her back, her curls were short and wavy, framing her face. The cut was angled longer in the front and abruptly short in the back, cut just below the base of her skull.

The look suited her.

Around her, the students were growing nervous, shifting anxiously, and murmuring amongst themselves as they waited for their instruction to begin. Air, that's what she'd planned today. But Fey couldn't help but think about that pull of Earth from the princess, that roiling under their feet on the rooftop that night. The sheer power of it.

Even Willow would have been proud of an Earth Witch that strong.

"On second thought," Fey announced, staring across the lawn. "Today our focus will be Earth instead."

Years ago, when she had still called herself a Blade, there had been rumors Princess Amalia had so little power that she wasn't a proper heir at all. Rumors she held little more than a fraction of power over Earth.

Fey remembered that roll of power on the roof and smiled. Until that night, even she had believed the rumors.

"I need a volunteer," she said.

There were a few hands raised among the crowd of Witches, but Fey ignored them all.

"Princess," she called across the lawn, gesturing her forward. "Come up here and join me."

Amalia raised her eyes, meeting Fey's gaze without fear.

"It's Amalia," she said, her voice carrying over the lawn, over the whispers. "I'm not a princess anymore, remember?"

Fey's lips twitched. "My mistake," she said, inclining her head. "Come up here, Amalia. Let's see what you've got."

Leandra appeared at Fey's side, her face pinched in anger.

"What are you doing?" she hissed. "Are you going to punish her for finally coming here?"

Fey ignored her. Slowly, Amalia made her way across the grass and up to stand with Fey.

"A strong Earth Witch can move the very ground itself," Fey said, raising her voice to be heard by the crowd. "In the War of the Fallen, our greatest soldiers could bring entire buildings down with their power."

Every Witch watched Amalia as she turned to face them. Fey placed her hands gently on the girl's shoulders. She was trembling, just a little, under the attention of the crowd.

"Breathe in," Fey told her. "Calm yourself. Focus your power."

Amalia took a breath, eyes closed.

When Fey spoke next, she spoke so quietly that no one but Amalia could hear her, choosing to whisper the words right into her ear.

"They think you're weak," she told her. The girl tensed under her hands, but Fey continued. "They see you standing here and think they know who you are. *What* you are. Let it all out. Show them all how wrong they are about you, little sister."

Amalia opened her eyes.

"Do it," Fey said with a smile.

Fey was right. Three hundred years ago, there were Earth Witches powerful enough to take down an entire building. Earth Witches capable of shifting the very stones beneath their feet.

When Amalia unleashed her wave of power, they felt the ripples all the way at the edges of the Eternal City.

CHAPTER 76
CALLUM

This was it?

Callum stood before the building, staring up at the sign, and frowned. *Drink Until the Last Drop*, the sign read, in bright red neon lights. Underneath was an image of a fanged smile, the teeth dripping a cascade of flashing red lights.

It was remarkably gauche.

Shifting from side to side, Callum couldn't help but feel strangely disappointed. He'd expected something... bigger. Grander.

Steeling himself, he made his way toward the door.

A Wolf stood there, barring the entrance, but she moved aside with barely a glance at him, inclining her head as he approached. Her expression shifted, though, as Callum stepped forward to enter. She sniffed the air near him.

An angry growl rose in her chest, and she bared her teeth, moving again to block his path forward.

"You're not the boss," she accused him.

One day, Callum might get used to this constant confusion outside of the Vampire district. He almost laughed.

"I'm afraid not, no. I'm the other one. His brother." He gave the Wolf a friendly smile. "I'm here to see him, though. If he's around?"

The Wolf looked him up and down once again before giving him another sniff.

"Boss should be upstairs, in his office," she said, apparently satisfied with whatever she smelled on him. "Head inside, up the stairs in the back on the right, and follow the hallway. Do you want an escort?"

An escort?

Not sure what sort of escort this place might provide, Callum shook his head quickly.

"No, uh. I'm fine. I'll find him on my own. Cheers, though."

She moved aside, and Callum stepped into the club and entered a brand-new world.

Dear Goddess.

Now this? This was more what he had expected from his brother. The building shook with the force of the music, the lights colorful but dim, the whole dance floor coated in red. Sex. That was the first thing that came to his mind, as he looked around the darkened dance floor, eyes traveling over a world of bare skin glittering with sweat.

Goddess, was this how people danced? Bodies pressed together, grinding against one another? His eyes stopped on a couple near the stairs, two women who were pressed so close there was no chance of even air getting between them. And was her hand really....?

An uncomfortably warm blush rose on Callum's cheeks, and he quickly looked away. Yes. Yes, her hand was really up the other woman's skirt, and *very* busy from the looks of it.

Before he could take another step, a Demon with long pointed horns slid out of the crowd in front of him. He strutted over to where Callum stood, frozen at the entrance and held out a hand, beckoning him forward into the crowd. He licked his lips deliberately.

Callum swallowed, the noise irrationally loud over the club music. Should he...?

A heavy hand landed on his shoulder, and Callum jumped. He turned away from the Demon, staring in surprise at the Wolf who had appeared at his side. The giant, impossibly massive Wolf.

"You the brother?" the Wolf grunted, voice loud over the music.

Relief flooded Callum.

"Yes," he said, trying not to sound too desperate. Trying not to scream *get me out of here, I'm in way over my head.* "That's me, the uh, the brother."

"You still looking for the boss?"

Another grunt from the Wolf when Callum nodded.

"I'm Ferus," the Wolf told him, tapping his own chest. "Follow me. Office is this way."

Ferus escorted him expertly through the crowd and up the stairs, the dancers moving out of their way almost out of instinct. Thank the Goddess for that.

Callum wasn't entirely sure he could say no if another scantily clad Demon tried to ensnare him.

The music got quieter and quieter the further they moved from the dance floor, until finally Ferus took him down a quiet hall, and to a solid wooden door.

The Wolf knocked and waited. Then knocked again.

"You got a visitor, boss," he announced, swinging the door open and ushering Callum inside.

Callum blinked in surprise as they entered, staring around at the room. It looked like their father's study.

"Thank you," Callum told Ferus, shaking off his shock. The Wolf gave a final grunt in response, and left, shutting the door behind him.

Callum's brother sat at an ornate wooden desk, a pen posed above paper, his brow furrowed. In another few centuries, he would be the spitting image of their dad, he realized.

"Callum?" Alastair asked, frowning. "What the fuck are you doing here?"

"You always told me I should visit," Callum said with a slight shrug. His eyes roamed over the room, taking in the shelves upon shelves of books, the expensive wooden furniture. And the Witch, staring at him in surprise. "Hello again, Fey. Always a pleasure."

Fey sat curled in an armchair, a book in her hand. She greeted him with a smile, and it warmed Callum's heart to see her here. He hoped she knew what a positive effect she had on his brother and what a blessing she was in his life. In their lives.

Maybe... maybe now, with the old deSanguine gone... maybe they could be a family once again.

Alastair's soft chuckle brought Callum's attention back to the matter at hand. "Are you saying that's what you're doing here, brother? Visiting my club?" He glanced around the office pointedly. "You're in the wrong spot to enjoy it to its fullest, I'm afraid."

"No, actually," Callum admitted, feeling a little sheepish. He slipped his hands into his pockets. "I'm here on business."

Alastair's eyes narrowed. Gesturing toward the chair in front of his desk, he motioned for Callum to sit.

"And what, pray tell, would the deSanguine want with me and my club?" Alastair asked as Callum sank into the seat.

"Don't do that," Callum said, pulling a face. "Don't use the title, please. You're my brother, aren't you?"

Alastair smiled, the barest twitch of his lips.

"If you're here on business, it seems only proper," he said.

Callum rolled his eyes. "And since when have you ever cared about being proper?"

Alastair opened his mouth to respond, but quickly shut it. His eyes snapped to the door, and his gaze heated. Callum turned.

Goddess...

If the Demon had been tempting, well... he had nothing at all on the Shifter who just strutted into Alastair's office.

"Ferus said you need refreshments." The Wolf at the door smiled. He held a bottle with two empty glasses in one hand, and another glass full of something red and covered in cherries in the other.

Callum couldn't help it. He let his eyes slide over the male, his gaze trailing over every inch of him. The man was stunning. Suddenly, he couldn't recall why he'd put off coming here for so many years. He should be coming here every night.

"Callum, this is Jasper," Alastair introduced. "Jasper this is my brother, Callum."

"A pleasure to meet you," Callum said, in a husky voice. The bartender gave him a lopsided grin, and moved forward, moving with a barely discernable limp. He set the glasses down on the desk and opened the bottle of whiskey to pour a drink for each of them. Still grinning, he set one in front of Alastair.

"Hope you don't mind whiskey," Jasper said to Callum, setting the other glass down on the wood in front of him. "It's all the boss will drink, here."

Callum couldn't take his eyes off him. The muscles, the hard jaw line, the T-shirt stretched a bit too tight over his chest and arms. He was exquisite.

"Pick your jaw up off the floor, brother, he's taken," Alastair snapped. Then, turning to the Wolf, he said, "Aren't you, puppy?"

Puppy? Callum blinked.

"Absolutely, boss," Jasper said with a wink.

"Don't mind him, he's in a mood," Fey said from her chair. Jasper brought the final drink over to her, and she took it from him with a smile. "Thank you, Jasper."

"Anything for you, gorgeous," Jasper said. He leaned down to place a kiss on the top of her hair. "Do you need anything else?"

She shook her head, eyes already back on her book, cuddling deeper into her chair. Jasper's hand remained on her shoulder, trailing his fingers over her skin lovingly.

Oh.

That's new. Callum raised an eyebrow at his brother, a smile curving up his lips.

Alastair just sighed.

"Out with it, Callum. Why are you here?"

Right to the chase. As always.

Callum took a deep breath before he spoke, to steady himself. Somehow this? This was the hardest thing he'd had to do since becoming the new deSanguine.

But it needed to be done.

"I did it. By formal decree, just last night," he told Alastair. "I shut it down, brother. All of it."

Alastair went still. Callum wasn't even sure he was still breathing. From her seat next to the bookshelves, Fey looked up, eyes narrowing.

"I can't guarantee the drug trade in the realm will stop," Callum continued. "But I can guarantee that no one in the Vampire Faction will be providing or selling anything. Not anymore. Not as long as I reign."

Alastair's face was a picture of stunned shock.

"Callum," he whispered, voice heavy with emotion.

Callum held up his hand to stop him.

"It's done. And I didn't do it for you. And I didn't do it for Delilah, either." He took another deep breath. "I did it because it was the right thing to do. I don't want, or need, your thanks for it, brother."

Callum shifted in his seat, looking anywhere but at the other Vampire watching him.

"That's not what I need your help with, though. I want..." He searched for the words, swallowing. "I want to *help*, Alastair. I want to help fix this city. I want *that* to be my legacy."

Fey closed her book, setting it aside.

"Our faction has kept themselves apart from the rest of the realm for too long," he said with a sigh. "It's time we did something. It's time we did something *good* for a change. Helped heal the realm, instead of... instead of just numbing it."

Everyone was so still in the room, watching him. He shifted in his seat, uncomfortable under their attention.

"Our family has money," Callum continued. "More money than I know what to do with, as deSanguine. And I want to invest it in our city, in the communities here, but..." He paused and licked his lips. "I've been sheltered, living in the manse. I don't know where the money would be best invested. I need... I need your help."

He looked up at them, then.

Fey's eyes were bright, a wide smile on her face. Even the Wolf looked stunned.

But Alastair? His eyes were so full of pride, so full of admiration, Callum had to look away.

"I think that's something we can help the deSanguine with," Alastair told him.

EPILOGUE
VEE

Today they hid it in the bread.

That was good. Better than good, even—that was great. Yesterday they'd dosed her water, which had been incredibly annoying. Not only had she gone to bed that night thirsty, but it also had meant she'd had nothing to use for bait.

See, that's the problem with Allium. It has a very distinctive smell, and a very distinctive taste. When Vee's captors realized it didn't work on her the way it worked on other Witches, when it became clear her Faction's metabolism would clear the drug in a few days, they'd had to get creative.

Witches only need one dose of Allium, and snap just like that, their power was gone! Vanished! But not Shifters like her, apparently. They had to keep dosing her, day after day, to keep her power in check.

Her food, her water, every piece of sustenance that came through those cold steel bars in those first few months had been coated in it. It had been hard to eat back then, with that vile taste in the back of her throat with every bite. But that must have been expensive, or at least troublesome, because after a few months they stopped and developed a new system. Now, they dosed only one item of food, each day, seemingly at random.

Today, after smelling each piece of her dinner, one by one, Vee knew it was in the bread.

Fine. She hated the bread they gave her, anyway. It was sweet, like so much of the food that came from the palace. Strange, sweet potato rolls, coated in salted butter.

Vee was perfectly happy not eating the bread. The chicken had been especially delicious tonight.

She held the roll for hours after she'd finished the rest of her meal, staring at it. Memories clashed in her mind—hers and Kallista's, jumbled together, tied in a knot that was difficult to tease apart, even now. Sometimes Vee wasn't sure whose memories were whose. The Demon's thoughts felt like her own, now. Another piece of her.

Witch. Shifter. Demon. Was she a bit of each, now? Vee had no idea. But every now and then, she could see the shadows in her cell move in ways they shouldn't. Sometimes she could feel Kallista, could feel her thoughts and her feelings, out there beyond her cell. And wasn't that just so interesting?

Vee pinched a piece of bread between her fingers and tore it off. She rolled it between her fingers until it formed a ball. Sweet, sweet bread, hiding a toxin meant to keep her weak as a newborn pup. Kallista had memories of enjoying sweet bread like this, from before. Long, long ago, before the bomb, before the wars. Bread with friendly pink frosting. *Conchas*, the word floated up into her head, from memories that weren't her own. Yes, that was what they were called. Conchas. The princess would like something like that, wouldn't she? Something sweet and pink.

Maybe Vee would make them for her, one day.

Pleased with that thought, Vee made her way to the bars of her cage. Pushing her arm through the steel bars, she tossed the piece of bread as far as she could, down the dungeon halls, where it disappeared into the shadows. So far, the guards hadn't noticed the food scraps she'd thrown out there. Maybe it was gone by the morning, taken away by ants, or mice, or even—

Vee froze, arm still pressed uncomfortably far through the bars, at the almost imperceptible sound of tiny claws against stone.

Skit skit skit.

Finally.

Vee moved with slow deliberate care. She took her time, and that was the most important part. A predator knows how to bide their time, waiting for the perfect moment. You can't rush these things.

Pinching off another piece of bread, Vee tossed it into the dark, a little closer this time.

Silence. A long stretch of uninterrupted silence.

Then...

Skit skit skit.

Vee grinned.

The next piece of bread, she threw a little closer. And the next, even closer.

The roll wasn't even half gone when the shadows split, and the rat ventured close enough for her to see.

A scrawny thing, like her. Half starved. Maybe that's why the taste of the Allium didn't bother it. It crept closer to her cell, suspicious, eyes bright and movements quick.

Rats are survivors. Vee could respect that. She was a survivor, too.

Vee gently set the rest of the roll on the ground outside of her cell and pushed it forward as far as her fingertips could reach.

A gift. She hoped the rat understood.

It watched her. Hungry, vicious eyes moved from her to the roll, and back again.

"Go on," Vee whispered. "It's for you."

Cautiously, so very cautiously, he finally moved forward.

He watched her as he ate, suspicious and hesitant, but Vee didn't mind. Her thoughts were focused on other things.

She could hear his quick heartbeat, could finally feel the pull of her power rise in response.

Ba bump.

Ba bump.

Ba bump.

Vee smiled so wide her cheeks hurt.

"You have no idea how glad I am to see you," she told the rat, listening to his pulse.

Her body had cleared the Allium enough that she could reach out, right now, and take control of the creature.

But she didn't. Vee watched her new friend enjoy his meal.

A predator knows how to bide their time and wait for the perfect moment, after all.

THE END

WANT MORE?

Vee and Amalia's story will continue in The Shadow King, The Broken Blade book three

For release announcements, sneak peeks, and bonus content visit our website at evelyn-ward.com and follow us on social media:

ABOUT THE AUTHOR (...S)

Regretfully, Evelyn Ward exists only in our imaginations.

The real authors of this book are M and K, two best friends who share too much, love too hard, and text one another every day.

K is a resident of New York City. She is an incredible editor and plot-hole finder extraordinaire.

M is a resident of Seattle. She is a smut peddler and sometimes scientist (okay, all times scientist).